RHIANNON LASSITER

Ghost OF A Chance

For Steve, with love.

OXFORD

UNIVERSITY PRESS

Great Clarendon Street, Oxford OX2 6DP

Oxford University Press is a department of the University of Oxford.
It furthers the University's objective of excellence in research, scholarship,
and education by publishing worldwide in

Oxford New York

Auckland Cape Town Dar es Salaam Hong Kong Karachi
Kuala Lumpur Madrid Melbourne Mexico City Nairobi
New Delhi Shanghai Taipei Toronto

With offices in

Argentina Austria Brazil Chile Czech Republic France Greece
Guatemala Hungary Italy Japan Poland Portugal Singapore
South Korea Switzerland Thailand Turkey Ukraine Vietnam

Oxford is a registered trade mark of Oxford University Press
in the UK and in certain other countries

British Library Cataloguing in Publication Data

Data available

ISBN: 978-0-19-275562-9
1 3 5 7 9 10 8 6 4 2

Printed in Great Britain
Paper used in the production of this book is a natural,
recyclable product made from wood grown in sustainable forests.
The manufacturing process conforms to the environmental
regulations of the country of origin.

Contents

Prelude

Sixteen years ago

The crying was a small plaintive noise lost beneath the dawn chorus. By the time the early morning mist had faded there was no sound except the water lapping at the shoreline and slopping at the sides of the small rowing boat adrift on the lake.

The first searchers shouted when they saw the boat, raising binoculars and shading their eyes to see if anyone was in it. When someone claimed to have seen a shape slumped in the bow the voices became more urgent. Another half hour passed before someone found the key to the boathouse and a second boat set out across the lake. On the shore the watchers held their breaths as it drew closer to the drifting boat. One of the searchers reached into the bow and lifted out a sopping mass, limp and dripping in his hands. It was clothing, abandoned in the bottom of the leaking boat.

It didn't take long to identify the clothes as belonging to the missing woman. Her family were among the searchers, whose ranks were growing by the hour. The two boats were bailed out and replacement oars found for the drifting one so that the search could continue by water as well as on land.

Boots squelched along the banks as the walkers set off in two separate groups, one walking clockwise, the other anticlockwise around the lakeshore until they found something—or met on the other side. Small twitterings preceded them as their passage through the clumps of reeds disturbed thrushes and sparrows. Out on the water the boats rowed up and down, pausing at intervals while the occupants fished with boat-hooks among the dark clots of weed below the surface. By now they all knew they were looking for a body.

Grey clouds above were reflected in the ruffled water of the lake and the air was damp. In the centre of the lake the island was a tangled clump of bushes and trees, casting dark shadows where they overhung the water. The island shore was unreachable although the boats made more than one attempt. Each time they were driven back by tree branches or by the screams of peafowl.

The peacock feathers glimmered in the bad light, the long extravagant tails hanging like curtains from tree branches where the birds perched. The smaller browner peahens were harder to spot until they whirred out of their nests and launched themselves at the boats, screaming protests.

The searchers pulled back, skirting the island warily, shining torches into the wet leaves and murmuring to each other as the oars rose and fell, carrying the boats sliding across the lake to meet each other halfway.

By then the crying had started again, beginning as a small mew of sound but rising quickly to a wail. The sound drifted out across the water past the floating boats all the way to the shore. It was heard but not noticed. Between the birdcalls and the sounds of wind and water it was a tiny thread of noise, not enough to summon attention.

Among the searchers Keith Stratton scrubbed at his closely

cropped hair, feeling a headache coming on. His wife had given birth to twins last month and broken sleep and squalling babies had made him tired and sluggish at work. Now he was beginning to think he was cracking up because he could still hear those high-pitched cries for attention in the back of his mind.

The boats separated, ploughing back across the water. The searchers were losing faith, suggesting that the lake be dredged or divers called out because they had found nothing. The groups of walkers had met and crossed over, working their way back around the two sides of the lake.

But while one boat kept going the other stopped; in the back Keith was shaking his head and pointing at the island. Slowly, reluctantly, the boat moved into the shadow of the trees. The bushes were not so thick on this side of the island and instead a jumble of rocks rose out of the water; behind them a stony outcrop and a high cave mouth, far out of reach.

The boat rocked as the rescuers debated. A swimmer might be able to reach the rocks and climb up to the cave, but the approach was perilous and choked with plant matter, long blade-like leaves frothing out from slender stems with dense spikes of flowers. At the back of the boat Keith wasn't listening to the others; his head was half-cocked, listening attentively as he studied the shoreline, his eyes roving across the green tangle of plants.

He missed it the first time, thinking the woven wicker strands were a nest, but the crying led him to it and a few strokes of the oars brought the boat alongside so that he could reach out and grasp the basket. It had been lodged between the plant stalks, the water lapping at the dense wicker cocoon. Inside the basket a woollen shawl, still mostly dry, was wrapped around a baby.

As Keith lifted it into the boat the baby's cries intensified, alarmed by the movement and the surprised faces staring down.

3

They had spent the day searching for a missing woman and now none of them knew what to make of their find.

'Like Moses in the bulrushes,' Keith Stratton said eventually. Then, as the baby's mouth opened in another desperate wail, he added: 'I think we better get this chap somewhere warm.'

The baby was a newborn, possibly premature, and weighing only six pounds five ounces. Whisked away into the local hospital it proved to have early symptoms of exposure and malnutrition. In the incubator it began to revive and the rescuers watched it through the glass, Keith shrugging off praise in an abruptly black mood he blamed on a headache.

The mystery of the missing woman and the unexpected arrival of the baby preoccupied the rest of the searchers as they eventually drifted away. Meanwhile the hospital staff had made another discovery. Despite basket and bulrushes, Moses would not be a suitable name. The baby was a girl.

1
April Fool

Tuesday, April 1st

Eva Chance shivered out of sleep to the sound of peacocks screaming outside her bedroom window. The room was cold and her skin felt damp and clammy against the icy sheets.

Huddling under the blankets she curled into a tight ball, huffing her breath into her little cave of space to warm it up. Her whole body was tense and she was shivering so hard her bones ached. She'd dreamt of small dark spaces and lurking shadows and the closeness of the bed seemed suffocating. Throwing back the blankets and drawing the bed curtains she stumbled to the window. The grey light of dawn wasn't enough to banish the heavy feeling of dread she'd carried out of her nightmare.

The Crimson Room was outwardly luxurious. When Eva was ten she'd fallen in love with the four-poster bed and its moth-eaten curtains of blood-red damask. She longed to watch the dawn from the window seat and have as her dressing table the little desk Lady Jane Grey might once have used. But the charms of the room didn't include central heating and it had been a long time since a fire had burned in the marble fireplace.

She forced her frozen feet into three pairs of woollen socks

5

and fumbled herself into a ragbag assortment of clothes—all inherited: a man's cotton shirt with the sleeves rolled up, grey corduroy dungarees, a shapeless mud-coloured knitted jumper with holes in the elbows, and faded green wellington boots. The whole effect, as considered in the full-length silver-framed mirror, was an undersized scarecrow and Eva didn't waste her time on a second glance.

Leaving the Crimson Room, she walked along the first floor passageway; coconut matting lay on top of the faded ancestral carpets, a pale ribbon leading the way to the main staircase, indicating the public route through the House. Eva kept to the matting until halfway down the staircase where she swung herself up on to the banisters and slid the rest of the way down, landing with a flying leap in the front hall.

On the other side of the hall stood a grandfather clock, a massive dark pillar with rings of concentric dials on the front and a glass-fronted case behind which pulleys rose and fell and gears turned, measuring out each ponderous second of the endless days in the House.

The hour hand had nearly reached seven and the minute hand stood at a quarter to the hour; a sweeping second hand tocked around the time dial with little jerks. But it was the next dial out that drew Eva's attention: the calendar dial where two more clock hands marked the day and the month: indicating the first day of April.

Eva stared at the clock. The terrors of the night must have clouded her mind to make her forget what day it was. April Fool's Day. Sixteen years since her mother had died. Sixteen years since Eva had been born.

Eva let herself out through the front door and into the pale grey dawn. She stood in the House's shadow on the ragged half circle of weed-choked gravel that had once been an elegant driveway.

The House looked back at her with five rows of windows, their glassy stare shadowed here and there by shutters or broken into a maze of cracks. Across the golden stonework skeletal strands of Virginia creeper crawled up the ladder of mortar-lines and darker patches seeped slowly down from the sagging heights of the roof. Ivy-wrapped and lichen covered, the House squatted in the ten acres of gardens, landscaped long ago and gone to seed. Mist coiled out of the lake and hung heavy across the gardens and it was hard to imagine there was a world outside. Eva couldn't remember the last time she'd passed the rusting metal gates at the end of the driveway. The boundaries of the House and its gardens were the borders of her world.

Recently the days had blurred into each other until this morning when she'd seen the clock and realized that April had arrived.

'Happy birthday, Evangeline Chance,' she said. 'You might as well spend it breaking mirrors and walking under ladders because there's no way your life could be any more cursed.'

* * *

The House was always referred to with a capital letter. It was very like a capital letter H if you ignored the rambling length of the stables beyond the west court and the dots and commas of summerhouses and colonnades that punctuated the overgrown gardens. It was listed in the books of the stately homes of England alongside an effusive but self-betraying description of the gardens (overgrown and unkempt), the Folly (closed for renovation), the (former) Orangery and the historic furniture and tapestries (minor pieces by unknown craftsmen).

Built in the sixteenth century by grandeur-loving Elizabethans the House had swelled to monstrous proportions, been allowed to fall into decay, and repaired anew by successive generations of Chances.

In the twenty-first century the House was an ageing tyrant. Resenting the loss of its servants the House rebelled with leaking attics, crumbling plasterwork, and a legion of mice and black beetles. The formal gardens had lost their pretence of domestication and ranged wildly across their dividing walls and hedges in fairytale thickets of roses and curtains of ivy. The long lake was choked with weeds and algae formed a thick green carpet across the surface of the water.

The House had been Eva's home for sixteen years and each year she'd watched it decay further, draining her grandfather's savings and every penny of the income it got from grants or tourism, always needing more work and more time spent on it. Eva loved and hated the House by turns. Her grandfather had taught her the waltz in the ballroom and had given her fencing lessons in the long gallery, watched by disapproving portraits of her ancestors. She'd read her way through the library and dusted an endless procession of oddments and ornaments. Every corner of the House held some sort of memory: good or bad.

'Our family fortunes have always been mixed,' her grandfather had told her. 'Chance is a good name for us.'

But it seemed to Eva that all her life things had been getting steadily worse. Grandfather was old now and tired. Since his heart attack last year he'd stopped talking about the future, stopped talking about anything, locked up in the library and scuffling among piles of papers late into the night.

* * *

Eva drifted aimlessly back into the House. The long corridors and empty rooms felt crowded and airless, thronged with a company of shadows. She felt watched by every painting; every mirror, every stuffed owl or carved lion or gnarled knot of woodwork seemed to bore into her with a slow malicious stare.

It didn't help to tell herself she was imagining it. People had been telling her that all her life about anything and everything that seemed real to her. Ever since she was very small Eva had known that Grandfather was the person she could trust to believe her when she told him things—things that were incredible to anyone else.

When she was five she'd made a friend, a slightly older boy with an embarrassed way of hiding his face to disguise the way his mouth was twisted up. He didn't talk much but he'd solemnly joined her when she was playing with an ark of wooden animals, helping her arrange them in pairs. They'd been friends for several weeks before Eva thought to wonder who the boy was and why she only ever saw him in the old nursery on the second floor of the east wing. While her aunts had brushed her off and ignored her questions, Grandfather had actually listened to her story and when she'd finished he'd taken her into the hall where the huge family tree chart hung, listing each branching generation of the family in illuminated letters. Tracing his way up the branches of the tree, he lifted Eva up to see the crabbed writing that spelt a name.

'St John Stanton Chance,' he'd read out. 'Born 1701, died 1707. I think that's your friend. Family histories say he had a harelip, that's the twisted mouth you mentioned. Very easily correctable now, but not at the time he lived, poor chap. Play with him if you want, but I wouldn't mention it to any of your aunts again.'

Since Grandfather had said it was all right to play with 'Sinje' she'd not worried about it when the aunts talked about 'Eva's little imaginary friend'. The friendship had drifted apart anyway when she'd got a bit too old for the toys in the nursery and the last time she'd seen him she'd noticed that Sinje looked awfully small compared to her.

But Eva's imagination wasn't always her friend. She couldn't walk down the grand staircase without every sense she had twanging like a badly tuned violin. The crimson carpet was darker on the last three stairs and there was a smell like a butcher's shop that no amount of cleaning ever seemed to remove. Sometimes Eva had seen that darker patch spread outwards with a lacquered stickiness across the flagstones of the hall. Nowadays she could walk down the other stairs if she had to but she still jumped the last three steps or swung herself over the banisters.

Maybe things would have been different if she hadn't been so alone, she thought, skirting the edge of the stairs and wandering towards the kitchens. But her imagination hadn't helped her make friends either. From school reports she'd learned she was introverted, reclusive, and unwilling to socialize—three ways of saying the same thing. Also that she 'made up stories' which was a polite way of saying she told lies. Ultimately the teachers agreed with the aunts that Eva's imagination was too vivid and Eva had stopped trying in creative writing or art when her best efforts generally earned her an unclassified mark and a visit to the school counsellor. Over the years, her attendance record had slipped lower and lower as she tried to escape the jeering comments of the local schoolchildren who regarded her as their own personal freak show.

The world outside the House felt surprisingly difficult to navigate, as if she had grown up *in* the past, rather than simply surrounded by it. The House didn't have television and the only music she knew was classical recordings on vinyl discs. Conversations about anime or hip-hop or iPods were like listening to an alien language. She only knew what the internet was because of the computers in the school library and there were barely any books in the House that had been published since 1950.

Eva knew she was a freak but she couldn't help it that the past was more real to her than the present day. Sometimes, listening to distant strains of music in the ballroom and hearing the swish of taffeta and lace, she convinced herself she was lucky to have such a gift. Other times, slinking past a priest's hole while ghostly fingers scrabbled at the hidden catch or jolting out of sleep to hear voices whispering in her room, she thought her imagination was an awful curse.

The past few months, Eva had felt nervous every time she opened a shut door or pulled curtains back from a window. Stairs were treacherous and knives seemed sharper; drawers stuck suddenly and then burst free in a hail of unexpected and often unpleasant items. Inexplicable noises came from the water pipes or the floorboards or the windows rattling in their frames. Heavy footsteps followed her along the endless corridors, slowing down or speeding up with her own.

Fresh vegetables wilted when they were brought into the house, linen that had been washed and ironed became crumpled and smirched by a strange tarry residue, small items vanished and larger ones shifted position so that she was continually losing things or walking into furniture. And everywhere there was dust, as if the stuff was coming out of the walls or falling out of the air in an endless gritty rain.

Something was very wrong. Perhaps it was Grandfather approaching the boundary between life and death that made the House feel even more haunted. But if it was Grandfather the ghosts were waiting for—why did she feel eyes following her everywhere she went?

* * *

As the mist shredded to reveal a pale blue sky, Eva left the House by the kitchen door and picked over what was left of the stripped vegetable garden and hauled in a sack of logs from the woodpile. The ancient kitchen range and the wheezing boiler were slowly taking the chill off inside the House but Eva didn't have time to appreciate the warmth. Even though it was her birthday there would be no celebration. Instead she had to prepare for an invasion of aunts.

The aunts always descended on April the first. Perhaps originally it had been to remember Eva's mother or to mark Eva's birthday but over the years their visits had become increasingly focused on the imminent tourist season and they would arrive full of suggestions and plans to squeeze some tiny income from their mouldering inheritance. Eva resented them counting the silverware or running their fingers over the mantelpieces or rearranging small items of furniture. They might have houses of their own but as far as the aunts were concerned this was their home—and they didn't think Eva or her grandfather could be trusted to look after it.

There were sounds in the library of someone moving about. Grandfather was awake and had cloistered himself with his books and papers again. He hadn't even wished her a happy birthday. But then Eva's birthday wasn't exactly a happy occasion for him anyway and Eva would rather he didn't remember it, since the circumstances of her birth brought back such bad memories. She walked quietly past the library on her way to put fresh flowers in the aunts' rooms.

By tradition the family rooms were on the second floor; out of bounds to tourists. The aunts would claim the same rooms they'd had as young women and as Eva bustled about with flowers and vases, she noticed that the rooms seemed to have taken on a certain flavour of each aunt in anticipation of their arrival. There were more Egyptian cat statuettes in Aunt Cora's Rose Room than there had been the last time she'd cleaned it. And she was certain there hadn't been quite so many maps of the British Empire decorating the walls of the Raleigh Room favoured by Aunt Helen. Small objects often seemed to wander about in the House, migrating from room to room with exploratory zeal, and Eva tried to ignore it, putting fresh flowers in the Violet Room for Aunt Joyce beside a set of ceremonial disembowelling knives.

Even then she wasn't done with work and she had no idea what the aunts expected to eat for dinner. They would dine in style, she knew that, and the thought set her running back to the Dining Hall to polish the silver. There might be nothing to eat except watercress and nasturtium leaves but at least the cutlery would shine proudly on the mahogany table.

Aunt Cora was the first of the aunts to arrive. Eva watched the taxi nudging slowly up the drive from the dining room windows. Aunt Cora didn't visit often, preferring her own small cottage with its chintzy armchairs and cabinets bursting with china kittens to the mouldering bulk of the House. She scrambled out of the taxi in a jumble of knitwear, a small dumpy woman with white fluffy hair like a dandelion clock. She fluttered around behind the taxi driver as he unloaded her suitcase. Pointing at the back seat of the car she hovered nervously as the driver brought out her most precious possession—a squalling wicker basket from which a golden brown paw took a hopeful swipe at the taxi driver's nose. He held it at arm's length before putting it down carefully next to the luggage. Aunt Cora carefully counted out the fare and must have added a tip she could barely afford because the driver seemed pleased as he got back into the car;

13

which Eva knew wasn't a normal reaction to travelling with Rameses—Aunt Cora's bad-tempered Abyssinian cat.

As Aunt Cora let herself in the front of the House, Eva retreated up the back stairs. When she was little Eva had been fond of her aunt whose visits were accompanied with gifts of home-baked biscuits and books of Bible stories. It was only as she'd got older that the Bible stories seemed to become more pointed and the biscuits more stale. Aunt Cora had a way of looking at Eva as though she were a half-tamed animal, who might turn and snap, and it made Eva feel twitchy and half-wild.

Taking her furniture polish and feather dusters to the Long Gallery, Eva worked her way along the ranks of her ancestors' portraits and tried to meet their eyes.

'It's not my fault the House is so run down,' she told them. 'You shouldn't have spent all your money on banquets and horses and jewelled shoes.' She eyed a particularly overdressed ancestress whose pouchy neck was collared with ropes of pearls and whose hands were dripping with diamonds. 'It's no good blaming me, Grandfather told me you lost all your jewellery playing cards. And you,' she moved on to another dyspeptic-looking Chance, 'you spent all your money on opium.' She wagged a finger at the rest of the assembled Chances: 'Not one of you bothered to hide any treasure behind the secret doors.'

As she spoke the shadows seemed to lengthen in the room and the atmosphere thickened oppressively. Eva shrugged an apologetic shoulder at the portraits and sidled to the nearest window, opening it wide and taking in a long gulp of the fresh air. As she leant out of the window she saw a silver Bentley rolling confidently up the drive. It drew up exactly in front of the House and a uniformed chauffeur opened the doors for Aunt Helen and her husband.

Aunt Helen had married money, 'old money' people said

sarcastically, since Richard Fairfax was thirty years older than his wife. He had a north country estate, houses in London and France, and multiple investments in the stock market. Eva secretly suspected that he had only rescued Aunt Helen from her single state because he wanted an heir. He and Aunt Helen seemed completely indifferent to each other and competed to lavish rewards on their only son: Felix.

Aunt Helen and Richard Fairfax emerged from the car, turning to look at the façade of the House with critical eyes. Neither of them spotted Eva, raising their gaze higher to look up at the bowing roof. A minute later they were both scurrying out of the way as a red Jaguar came speeding up the drive, spitting gravel chips in all directions. It braked with a squeal and Felix unfolded himself from the low-slung driver's seat.

Felix Fairfax was tall, which helped him to look down on people. He had Aunt Helen's equine and slightly hooked nose, combined with Uncle Richard's calculating look—as if assessing the price of everything. Felix managed to look at people as if he thought they weren't worth much compared to him. Eva ducked back from the window as the Fairfaxes entered the House together, leaving the luggage to the chauffeur to bring inside.

She hadn't prepared a room for Felix, hadn't expected him to show up. But of course Grandfather was ninety now and Felix would be wondering when he could expect to come into his inheritance. Eva spat out of the window and watched with satisfaction as the glob of mucus splattered on the roof of the sports car. As if it wasn't enough that Felix would inherit his father's vast fortune, he was also Grandfather's heir, the solitary male of the next generation and inheritor of the House and grounds.

Eva could easily imagine Felix's portrait hanging in the Long

Gallery. He might not have the Chance name but he had every inch of the haughty arrogance, driven home with a supercilious smile. Watching the Fairfaxes' chauffeur walking back and forth with suitcases, Eva felt sorry for the man. Not only would he have to carry the luggage up two floors, he'd also been stuck with the task of parking both cars. But the Fairfaxes were probably so used to having staff at their beck and call they didn't notice his efforts—any more than they ever thanked Eva for getting their rooms ready. The chauffeur had only just driven off in the red Jaguar when a hooting horn signalled the arrival of the last aunt.

Aunt Joyce's car was a yellow Beetle. Like Aunt Joyce it was loud and garish and pushy. It took up position slap bang in front of the House and Aunt Joyce and her partner got out. Aunt Joyce lived in Chelsea where she owned her own business as a jewellery designer and flitted between fashionable boutiques and popular clubs. She never went anywhere without an escort. Today's man was like the others, tall, dark, and handsome, wearing an Armani suit. Aunt Joyce wore a green and white striped coat over a lushly pink dress with black polka dots. It wasn't until Joyce and her escort had vanished under the portico of the House that Eva worked out what the colours reminded her of—a slice of watermelon, with the male escort buzzing around like a wasp.

Eva could hear people moving around inside the House; the influx of guests was creating a low hum of background noise. Presumably the aunts were taking turns to talk to Grandfather and, all over the House, luggage was being unpacked and rooms inspected. Living people produced a very different atmosphere from the one that usually permeated the House. Eva wasn't fond of her relations but she had to admit that their noisy arrival had caused her haunted feeling to recede—swept aside by her irritation and resentment of the invasion.

Skirting along the shadows of the House, Eva made her way to the library to check on her grandfather. Each time she went to look in on him she felt a touch of dread, fearing that he might have crossed the bar in her absence and she would find him cold and still.

The library door stood half open and through it she heard raised voices from inside the room, an abrupt contrast to the hush that usually pervaded the book-lined walls. Aunt Helen was speaking, her words clipped short with anger, as she laid down the law.

'I simply don't understand how you could have let the House decay like this, Father. It doesn't look as though you've spent a single penny on it since last summer and I told you then the roof was bowing and the attics were riddled with dry rot.'

'Father's not been well and he's had all the worry of Eva . . . ' that was Aunt Cora, her defence as ineffectual as a partridge before Aunt Helen's shotgun approach to debate.

'I always said it was a mistake for him to bring up that girl here. A pleasant home could have been found for her but Father insisted and she's been nothing but trouble,' Helen decreed in a way she'd never have dared if Grandfather had been fit to withstand her. 'Regardless of the situation with the girl, the House needs to be maintained. At this rate Felix will inherit a ruin—and we'll have to spend a fortune to make it habitable.'

'Felix hasn't inherited yet.' That was Aunt Joyce's voice, a husky drawl of disdain. 'Maybe you and Richard should come up with some real cash now instead of lavishing it all on that young oaf of yours.'

'Oh, as opposed to the gigolos you spend yours on?' Aunt Helen shot back.

'Enough argument.' Grandfather's voice was weary. 'If you

want a full account of the finances or to discuss my will, Helen, you'll need to speak to the house agent or my lawyer. I've asked them both to meet me this afternoon. They'll explain, as I've tried to, that money doesn't go very far in a property of this size and Felix will have to take his inheritance as he finds it.'

'I'm familiar with the demands of this House,' Aunt Helen said freezingly. 'I grew up here, after all. And Richard's estate is three times the size. I think I know what sort of work is involved in caring for a country house.'

'Oh please.' Eva didn't need to see her Aunt Joyce to know she was rolling her eyes. 'As if playing lady of the manor in front of a staff of six people is anything like work. I know from my jewellery business how complicated finances can get and how suspicious the inland revenue are of anyone of our class.'

'This is a very difficult House to manage,' Aunt Cora's whispery voice piped up again. 'It has problems one doesn't normally encounter . . . ' Her voice trailed away as Aunt Helen barrelled onwards.

'I suppose this house agent and your lawyer will stay for dinner. I've hired a local firm to do the catering. I anticipated that you wouldn't have arranged anything.'

'That was very thoughtful, Helen,' Grandfather said but outside in the corridor Eva ground her teeth and wished her aunt was a little less thoughtful. If she tried to come to his defence the aunts would simply tell her this was grown-up business and that they were only trying to help. They barely listened to Grandfather and this was his House. Eva's voice counted for nothing at all.

2
Black Sheep

While the aunts lunched on a hamper from Fortnum's, Eva escaped through the side door. Clouds scudded across the sky and a cold wind buffeted the gardens but the landscape was at least devoid of her relations.

Eva knew she couldn't open the House to the public on her own, but she resented the aunts for showing up and taking over. Even the House looked sulky and resentful, the roof sunk into a frown and the stone walls hunched against the wind. It hurt Eva to listen to the family criticizing her grandfather for neglecting the House when it wasn't as if he was going on spending sprees for sports cars or jewellery or cat ornaments. She couldn't remember the last time she'd had a full meal but the idea of eating anything from Helen's hamper of imported delicacies made her stomach roil.

And how dared Aunt Helen imply that Eva was a burden? She did all the work of the House from cooking to cleaning to chopping wood. She'd climbed a forty-foot ladder to clear out dead leaves from the guttering. But it never seemed to make a difference how hard Eva worked, her aunts would always consider her the black sheep of the family. To them she would always be the illegitimate child, the little stray without a proper pedigree, the bad seed of bad blood.

* * *

On the east side of the House was a spreading oak tree. Kicking off her wellingtons, Eva began to climb it, reaching for familiar handholds and pulling herself up through the boughs until she reached a supporting cradle of branches, screened by fresh green leaves. From here she could see two sides of the House: the front drive leading to the door, and over the wall into the kitchen garden and the side door. It was a good place to avoid unwanted callers and keep an eye on when they left. Eva had escaped up here when her teachers came to talk to her grandfather about her missing school and when the vicar had come to ask why she hadn't come to church and when a group of kids from her school had dared each other to come inside the gates and gawk and peer through all the front windows.

Now she watched as a catering van arrived and a stream of people started carrying cool boxes and bags around to the kitchen. Not much later the man in charge of the caterers came out of the side door and smoked three cigarettes while making calls on his mobile phone. She puzzled out the subject of his phone call when a group of teenagers were dropped off by a second catering van, this group wielding mops and buckets and industrial sized bottles of bleach. The kitchen was not exactly in a state to cater for a three course formal dinner. Eva had long ago given up the battle with the ancient kitchen range and concentrated on keeping only a small area clean enough for her and her grandfather to use.

Cradled by the tree, Eva tried not to worry that some of the teenagers looked familiar. It might be the end of term, she thought, trying to remember the school calendar. It had been weeks since she'd made an appearance in even one lesson, or picked up a textbook to revise for the all-important exams.

The arrival of the vicar on his antiquated bicycle gave Eva another pang of conscience. She hadn't known how to tell Father Hargreaves that she'd stopped going to church because the pews were too crowded with the condensed misery of half a dozen sinful and penitent family ghosts. And the graveyard that surrounded the little country church cut a little too close to the bone when she had to walk past her mother's grave with its death date of the first of April. She'd never seen her mother's ghost but each time she passed that simple little gravestone she feared to see Adeline rising out of the earth and pointing an accusing finger.

The arrival of the doctor and his wife had her grimacing at them from behind her screen of leaves. Dr Buxton had last visited a couple of months ago, when he tried to persuade her grandfather to go into a nursing home where he'd be 'properly cared for'. No one seemed to think that Eva was old enough to look after someone or that she might care about the one person who'd always looked after her.

No doubt, like the vicar, the doctor and his wife would be asked to dine that evening. Aunt Helen and Aunt Joyce both loved lording it over the people from the town they'd left behind, vying with each other to tell more glamorous stories of hunt balls in the country and celebrity parties at London clubs.

The last guests to show up were here for business not pleasure. A youngish man in a sober suit arrived in an unassuming green Citroën. He parked the car and tried to smooth down his curly hair while looking in his wing mirror.

As he did so a sleek black Saab slid up the drive and the man turned with an admiring stare as Lisle Langley emerged from the driving seat in a crisp black business suit, carrying a simple black holdall. Eva didn't blame him. The house agent had been working for them for the last couple of years and Eva envied her air of cool competence, which was never shaken by anything. Now Lisle greeted the man with a firm handshake.

'I'm Michael Stevenage.' The man took a briefcase out of his car. 'I'm afraid I'm a little early.'

'Lisle Langley.' Lisle gave him a sphinx-smile. 'The house agent. I'm early as well, I thought I'd take a stroll around the garden and get a bit of fresh air before braving the assembled hordes.'

'It's an amazing old place,' Michael said, looking up at the House and seeming not to notice the dilapidation. 'I've not had any chance to look at it before—my visits have been exclusively on business. I inherited the Chance account from my father this year when he retired; apparently Sir Edward wanted his business to stay in our family. Um . . . speaking of family, a rather home-counties woman phoned me at the office to say I would be expected to stay for dinner, but she rang off before explaining who she was.'

'That would be Mrs Fairfax, she's Sir Edward's second daughter,' Lisle said. 'I had the same phone call myself but I've met her before and I know the form. What she means is that she'll want to grill you about the family finances and she's got a reputation for being a ruthless hostess—the kind who takes no prisoners.'

'I see.' Michael sounded nervous. 'I hardly know anything about the family, I'm afraid. I've not had time to read all the files yet.'

'There are things that you won't find in the files.' Lisle's voice was as cool as ever. 'Come for a walk in the garden and I'll fill you in.'

Michael accepted, following Lisle away from the House like a hopeful dog pantingly eager for a walk. Eva watched as they came closer to her and shifted around on her branch, looking almost directly down on the couple as they entered the kitchen gardens and strolled towards the formal gardens. Once they were out of sight she slid back down the tree, heedless of twigs and tree-sap, and wriggled her feet back into her wellingtons. She wanted to know what Lisle was planning to say.

She waited until the couple were past the kitchen gardens and then followed them through the door, running quickly and lightly across the path to the opposite wall and then into the geometric shrubbery of the parterre.

Eva knew the gardens better than anyone, their secret and private places. If she was right about where Lisle was going she'd be able to circle around and catch up with them.

On the other side of the parterre the Yew Walk began, with irregular hedges that had once been topiary birds and animals. Now they were strange savage creatures looming from the ends of hedges, deformed by extra limbs and protrusions of leafy growths from their original shapes. Eva crept up quietly behind a five-legged topiary animal with a broken trailing wing and saw that she had guessed right. Lisle and the lawyer were standing at the entrance to the maze.

Michael Stevenage was peering doubtfully at the maze's high and tangled hedges and as Eva arrived he wondered aloud if it was safe.

'Oh, it's safe enough,' Lisle Langley said with amusement. 'And a simple enough design. Don't worry, we won't get lost.'

'If you say so.' Michael followed Lisle into the dark green interior and Eva ran lightly down the walk to follow them in. But instead of walking down the leafy corridor and turning left, as they had, she turned immediately right to push aside a springy branch and squirm beneath it into the hedge.

The paths of the maze were predictable, even if the hedges were ragged and overgrown. But those wide hedges concealed other secret paths, not between the great hedges but inside them. Over the years they had grown so wide and so high that it was possible to make your way through the tunnel of branches inside along darker and more convoluted routes, curving and creeping towards the centre. There was no risk of the couple seeing her and as long as she stayed quiet Eva would be able to follow them closely enough to catch their whole conversation.

A few minutes of frustrating small talk about mazes followed as she edged her way after them but eventually the lawyer asked the question she wanted him to.

'What did you mean about details I wouldn't find in the files?' he asked. 'I hope there aren't any skeletons in the cupboards!'

'If there are you'll never find them, they'd be buried under five hundred years worth of miscellanea,' Lisle laughed. 'No, as far as I know there's nothing to fear, but the family can be a little difficult at times.'

'Difficult how?' The lawyer looked thoughtful and Lisle was silent for a moment as if picking her words carefully.

'Sir Edward's elderly,' she said. 'And his health isn't good. He's done pretty well to keep this House as well as he has given that there doesn't seem to be a lot in the bank for renovations. But not everyone sees it that way. I think his daughters remember it as it was when they were young, but back then Sir Edward could afford to employ a staff.' She paused. 'Out of interest, any idea why there's no money now?'

'I couldn't say.' The lawyer sounded cagey. 'But I see I can expect the family to ask.'

'You needn't be quite so close-mouthed,' Lisle said with amusement. 'It's open knowledge that Felix Fairfax will inherit the House. That's misogyny for you. Sir Edward had four daughters but it's the grandson who'll get the property. And how likely is it that a teenager will want to be saddled with a house like this? It'll be a health club or a golf course this time next year.'

'That's a pity, if it's true,' Michael said. 'But did you say four daughters? Will they all be coming to dinner?'

'Three of them will,' Lisle said. 'Cora is the eldest daughter. She's a fluffy white-haired old lady who's a slave to her cat. She'll have brought the cat with her, she always does.'

'I do a good line in listening to cat anecdotes,' the lawyer said mildly. 'My godmother breeds the creatures.'

'Then you'll do just fine,' Lisle laughed at him. 'I bet that polite attentive look has cat ladies eating out of your hand.'

'I don't know about that.' Michael went a bit pink. 'All right, next daughter.'

'The next one is Helen, a huntin', shootin', and fishin' Tory type married to a wealthy and much older man named Richard Fairfax. They're the parents of the golden grandson: Felix.'

'Helen, Richard, Felix Fairfax,' the lawyer nodded. 'Yes, I've heard of Felix.' He didn't add what he'd heard.

'The third daughter is Joyce, who you might mistake for a lady who lunches if she didn't take every opportunity to mention she's a businesswoman. She designs and sells jewellery. Costume pieces with semi-precious stones but very large and . . . distinctive.'

'I expect she'll be wearing the jewellery.' Michael Stevenage laughed. 'I'll remember to admire it particularly. What about family?'

'No husband or children but she'll have a boyfriend in tow,' Lisle said. 'I wouldn't bother learning his name because you'll almost certainly never see him again, she doesn't ever bring the same one twice.'

'I see.' Michael raised his eyebrows slightly. 'Well, I'll take your word for it. What about the fourth daughter?'

'The youngest daughter died,' Lisle said. 'She was something of a local legend around here, the wild child of the family. The Chances are pretty strait-laced but Adeline was a real rebel. She used to run away from home, disappear for months and get picked up by the police halfway across the country. There was always some man involved as well: one was an Irish gypsy, another was a faith-healer—always something weird and psychic with Adeline.'

'Did you know her?' Michael asked and Lisle shook her head.

'Not really. She was a couple of years ahead of me at school, so this is just gossip but she was pretty well known for being a bit out there. I remember one thing about her though: she used to wear a necklace of religious symbols: a cross and a star of David and an ankh and a whole lot more. She used to say she was hedging her bets. If she was, it didn't work.'

'So what happened?'

'Oh, the sorry story ended in a big scandal. She vanished again for a couple of years and then showed up pregnant and strung out on drugs. The family took her in and dried her out and got her acting half sane again. Then one night they take their eyes off her and that's the time she picks to give birth and then commit suicide in the most distressing and dramatic way.'

'Good lord.' Michael looked extremely uncomfortable with the turn the conversation had taken.

Hidden in the hedge, Eva thought to herself that he must have known some of this already from conversations with Grandfather about the will. But Adeline's story wasn't one Grandfather would have told anyone. She was surprised Lisle knew so much about her. The brief personality sketch had brought her mother uncomfortably to life.

'As you can imagine, it's never talked about,' Lisle said, leading Michael around the next corner of the maze. 'That's why I mention it in case you accidentally asked about Adeline or the child—the family are pretty ashamed of their black sheep. The child turned out to be just the same, you see. Another spooky depressive type.'

'Noted,' Michael said. 'It's very kind of you to fill me in like this. I feel like Daniel about to go into the lion's den.'

'Not at all,' Lisle replied pleasantly. 'It'll be easier for me too if I can point you away from any sleeping lions.'

* * *

Eva let their voices grow fainter. Fighting her way out through the side of a hedge, she escaped the maze and broke out into the rose garden, now a thorny thicket of barbed branches whipping out from the flower-beds. Eva dodged the thorns and sprays, trying to fight off her own fears at the same time.

The story of her mother's death and her own birth wasn't new to her even though no one had ever told it to her directly. Over the years she'd pieced it together by listening at doors. Lisle's version was much like the others and hadn't even covered all the dramatic high points. She'd missed out the fact that half the local town had turned out to search for Adeline when she went missing the final time and came back with nothing to show but a tiny blue-white newborn baby, half-frozen and barely breathing and abandoned.

For the first month of her life Eva had struggled for breath in a hospital incubator while her identity was established. Her supposed mother was missing, presumed dead. Her entire life was a question, hedged with half-answers and best guesses.

DNA tests had been needed to confirm that the baby in the hospital was the daughter of Adeline Chance. Adeline's three older sisters had gathered to discuss the matter and the consensus was that the unwanted baby would be better off adopted.

Edward Chance had overruled all of them. Already in his mid seventies, her grandfather was still the autocratic patriarch despite the arthritis that required him to walk with a cane. To everyone's surprise he had said 'nonsense' to the aunts' plans, taken a taxi to the hospital and claimed the baby. He had her christened Evangeline that Sunday and that had been the end of the debate.

But for Eva it meant that none of her aunts had wanted her in the family and when Grandfather died she might very well be cast out into the cold. Turning sixteen meant she was practically an adult and she wondered if the family even expected to support her. With her grades at school she wasn't an obvious candidate for A-levels or university but she didn't have any work experience either and she didn't know anything about supporting herself beyond housework and gardening. The future was looking bleaker and colder every second.

* * *

At the House end of the rose garden, the roses had been trained into a curving arch. As Eva negotiated her way through the thicket of thorns that almost blocked the way out, a scream like a train whistle sounded only metres away. Thorns snagging her hair and her clothes, she fought her way out in time to see a dark shape whirr past her and settle on the broken railing of the south terrace.

It was a peacock. It took a few proud steps along the railing, bobbing its crowned head up and down before losing interest and dropping to the ground, where it pecked in a desultory fashion at the chipped flagstones. The great long gold and green tail swept through the leaf litter like a train, filthy with all the garden grime the bird had picked up. Scattered here and there along the long spread of the terrace other strutting peacocks and their drabber wives came into view.

Eva watched them warily. Peafowl were one of the few things the tourist guides didn't need to lie about. There were still at least fifty of them nesting in the woods and the island although you might not see them near the House for weeks. Peacocks stalked up and down the gardens like exotic potentates of far off lands, bobbing and bowing to each other and posing with tails fanned out for their enraptured wives. Eva was rather less enraptured. Peacocks might sound poetic, but not at 3 a.m. when that eerie scream went off like a rocket outside your window, and that curved beak could deal a vicious peck, enough to leave bruises for days.

Slipping past the birds into the orangery, Eva shut the door carefully behind her. She didn't know why the peacocks were suddenly so attracted to the House but she didn't want to risk them accidentally getting inside. Besides, they were thought to be unlucky and right now Eva saw their arrival as a bad omen for the family council.

But, coming into the main hall, she realized not everyone felt the same way. A vase that had this morning held a desiccated dried flower arrangement was now frothing with golden green feathers, the iridescent blue flares at the centre forming a cluster of watching eyes.

There was something ominous about the display and Eva didn't know whether she blamed her relations, or ghosts, or her own imagination. But the glowing eyes simultaneously drew her and repelled her, the shimmering colours had an oil-slick toxicity and as she moved closer she smelt something putrid and dank. The feathers were wet with foul-smelling mud.

Eva turned her back on the peacock feathers, jumping the bottom steps and escaping up the side of the double staircase, seeking the safety of her room.

* * *

Eva's love affair with the Crimson Room had been bruised by her first experience of inhabiting it during a tourist season. The public rooms weren't kept locked like the family ones on the second floor—instead they were left open for tourists to gawk at. It didn't feel as if you owned your room if you had to leave it pristine so strangers could wander around it and all your personal possessions had to be neatly tidied away so as not to spoil the ambiance. Even her books were banished behind the doors of a cupboard. But despite the regular invasions of the public, Eva still thought of the room as a sanctuary. Like the oak tree overlooking the front drive, it was a place she went to be private.

It came as a shock to open the door and realize she wasn't alone. The room was dim, the window facing the wrong way for the afternoon light, so that everything looked grey. Someone was sitting in the window seat, surrounded by waving layers of grey smoke and a heavy brooding atmosphere. Eva was certain it was a ghost until her eyes adjusted and she recognized her cousin Felix.

He hadn't even noticed her come in, stretched out across her window seat, one hand holding a long thin cigarette. He hadn't even opened the window and he was using an empty beer bottle as an ashtray. His cashmere coat was chucked casually over the end of the bed and three leather suitcases were piled on it, one

30

half open and displaying a rummaged pile of expensive clothes. Of all the rooms in the House, Felix had taken hers.

With a burning sense of outrage and injustice Eva slammed the door shut behind her, and felt a stab of satisfaction as Felix jolted upright, his eyes flaring with surprise. There was a sudden smell of burning wool and she realized he'd dropped the cigarette on his trousers as he brushed at it with a quick panicky motion.

'Get out of my room!' she demanded, her indignation lending her the strength to confront her arrogant cousin. 'How dare you smoke in here?'

Felix's shoulders stiffened and he picked the cigarette up, turning it around in his fingers; then he deliberately lay back in the window seat and fixed her with a cold hard glare. She'd never thought he liked her, in fact he'd always seemed to despise her, but now he looked at her as if she were something he'd just scraped off his shoe.

'You,' he said, not even bothering with her name. 'You've been here all along then, have you? Creeping about and spying on people, I expect, playing some silly childish game.'

'Of course I've been here,' Eva said angrily. 'Where else would I be? I live here. This is my home. And you're in my room.'

'What's the matter? Not getting enough attention?' Felix continued to accuse her, his eyes narrowing. 'Grandfather's sick and you hide away and sulk?'

'I haven't been hiding, I've been slaving away for your lot all day, who do you think runs this place when you're not here? Even though it's my birthday none of you think to wish me many happy returns, all you can do is criticize. And I have been looking after Grandfather, I'm the only one who's here all the time.'

'Wait a minute.' Felix frowned, then dropped the cigarette into the beer bottle and stood up. He was taller than her, almost six foot to her not-quite-five and when he stood he loomed over her in the narrow space of the window alcove.

Eva recoiled, feeling abruptly afraid and claustrophobic at having him so near. From the other side of the room she stared at him.

'Don't touch me!' she said. 'What do you want?'

Felix stared back at her, his expression of contempt shifting to implacable hostility, his eyes hard and his mouth tight.

'You're really not normal, are you?' he said, his voice low and intense. 'You think this is your home? It isn't. You need to face that. This is my House now.'

'It's not your House!' Eva gasped, eyeing him warily from the other side of the bed. 'Not yet. It's not yours as long as Grandfather is alive.'

'But it will be mine,' Felix told her, his voice gaining confidence. 'And then there'll be no place for you in it. You need to move on.'

'Where?' Eva demanded, shaking with rage and frustration. 'This is where I've always lived! I don't *have* anywhere else to go.'

'Not my problem.' Felix shook his head at her. '*You're* not my problem. Once Grandfather's gone there'll be nothing for you here.'

Eva staggered and clung to a bedpost, feeling as if he'd hit her. She hung on to it for support as he walked around and past her, putting the ash-covered bottle down on Lady Jane Grey's desk and opening the door.

'You can have the room for now,' he said, turning to look back at her. 'But when I inherit the House I don't expect to see you here.'

He slammed the door shut behind him and Eva watched him go, left in possession of the room and knowing it was a hollow victory. Even as the door thudded shut, a gong sounded downstairs—a resounding reminder that caterers had been hired to serve a formal dinner. Someone had found the brass gong downstairs and was using it to summon the guests for pre-dinner drinks.

Eva realized she was still wearing her wellingtons and she kicked them off, regarding her mud-stained clothes with sudden alarm. She didn't have time to wash and change. Her hands were scratched and grazed, her hair unwashed, and her dungarees were torn and grubby.

Opening the wardrobe Eva regarded her clothes helplessly. Her uniform blouses and skirts still took up most of the space, depressingly familiar despite the fact she hadn't gone to school for weeks. Next to them hung the gifts of the aunts: Laura Ashley dresses and woollen cardigans from Aunt Cora, silk scarves and a cashmere poncho from Aunt Joyce, and endless pairs of jodhpurs and a hard-hat from Aunt Helen who had obviously confused her with someone else—someone with a horse. The first year Eva had received them she'd been naïve enough to think there *would* be a horse.

Eva sometimes wondered where the girls at school got their clothes from. Whether they were well-off or not somehow they all knew what to wear and how to wear it. Even their school uniform was somehow less stupid than hers and when she saw them on 'own clothes' days or after-school events they looked people with real personalities. Eva didn't want to dress like the girls at school but she wished she had a clue what she *did* want to wear. Too often she looked at herself in the mirror and felt embarrassed. There was nothing she owned she actually liked or thought she looked good in.

Since dinner would be formal she put on her only possible smart dress, the others were all too small or too old or too hopeless. The possible dress was red velvet and she remembered thinking when it arrived that it might not be too bad. In the mirror she saw a stork-thin figure with lank straggles of muddy brown hair in a dress that might have suited an eight-year-old Shirley Temple with its full skirt and puffy sleeves but looked ridiculous on a teenager. Her scratched and muddy legs and the scuffed brown sandals, which were the only shoes that fit, completed the awfulness. Eva took in her reflection and despaired. But when a second gong sounded downstairs in a reminding rumble she had no choice but to go down to dinner.

3
The Thirteenth Guest

Eva had missed the last of the guests arriving but there was a chatter of voices and the chinking of glasses from the Chinese Drawing Room. The adults were gathered there for drinks and when she slipped in no one seemed to notice her. Uniformed waiters circulated with trays and the aunts and their guests sipped their drinks and picked over the snacks, apparently either unaware or uninterested that this was a bit different from the House's usual standards.

Felix was drinking champagne, looking almost celebratory as he stood with one hand on the back of Grandfather's chair, as if he couldn't wait for the old man to vacate it. His gaze swept across the room like a lighthouse beam of arrogance and self-satisfaction, skimming past Eva without acknowledgement.

Eva hung back from the group in a shadowed corner of the room. Usually she would have sheltered by her grandfather's chair but now Felix had claimed that territory for himself.

Aunt Cora had buttonholed the vicar and was dabbing at her eyes with a handkerchief as she spoke to him, casting forlorn looks at Grandfather in between dabs. Aunt Joyce was showing off her latest piece of jewellery to the doctor and his wife: a vast brown and yellow hornet made of gold wire and brass, with zircon-studded eyes. But Aunt Helen was grilling the House agent relentlessly:

'The maintenance seems to have been fearfully slack, my husband and I have been noticing perished plaster and worm-eaten woodwork at every turn. The roof shows serious signs of decay and the state of the gardens is unbelievable. It certainly can't be shown to the public as it is. Did the place make anything at all last year?'

'Unfortunately the running costs of the house swallow all of the visitor income and most of the heritage grant.' Lisle paused for a moment to elegantly sip at her glass of sherry. 'The rest of the grant goes to paying staff wages for the season and after that there's nothing left for development of the property. Most of the stately homes of England have the same problems. A few, like Chessington and Longleat, have branched out successfully into the theme parks and safari markets. But most are suffering the long term effects of estate tax and insurance costs.'

'Are you saying that country houses are doomed?' Felix asked, raising his eyebrows at Lisle.

'Not at all,' she smiled back, her calm unruffled. 'Simply that it's unusual for such a house to be self-supporting.'

Conversation swelled up around the room as everyone began to discuss money. In their various different fields and professions everyone seemed to have something to say about how to make money, or save money, or lose money. Eva thought they didn't need any advice on the last. Every year so far her aunts had tried some new gimmick to impress the tourists and every one had been a disaster: hosting a business conference had almost got them sued; hiring it out as a wedding venue had resulted in three broken engagements; boating on the lake had come within a inch of creating a boat-load of brand new ghosts. Every new venture seemed to be plagued from the very beginning with a snarl of problems.

None of the waiters seemed to have noticed Eva. Several of the boys were the right age to be in her year at school and she'd rather they didn't notice her. One, a big blond guy, looked familiar—but Eva stayed away from boys at school, never knowing the right way to act around them. The other diners lacked her nervousness and Aunt Joyce was on her third cocktail by the time the gong sounded again and the guests set off in a ragged crocodile towards the dining room. Felix was the last to move, helping Grandfather to stand with a solicitous air that Eva didn't trust for a second.

Slipping out of the french windows, she cut across the terrace and into the small salon, entering the dining room by way of a discreet wallpapered door. The long mahogany table gleamed with polish, places laid along both sides, each a perfectly presented island of fine china and cut crystal framed with gleaming silver cutlery and a perfect triangle of a cream linen napkin. White cards with curlicues of black writing were set by each place, clipped into the tail-feathers of a silver peacock place-card holder, and in the middle of the table a vast épergne held an arrangement of ferns and bulrushes. On the far side of the table, beyond the épergne, empty chairs stared each other down across the polished wood.

Eva knew her grandfather would be given the heavy carver chair at the top of the long table and the other guests spread out along its length. Her own place would be at the bottom and she worked her way down one side and then hurried up the other before coming slowly down the first again with the growing realization that there seemed not to be enough places laid.

With Grandfather at the head there were six place settings

along one side and five on the other, each with a person's name printed neatly on a piece of white card. From *Miss Cora Chance* to *Ms Lisle Langley* the names were correct in all respects but one. Eva's name was missing.

She'd heard it was unlucky to have thirteen people for dinner but it was still more unfortunate to be the unwanted thirteenth guest. Whether by carelessness or malice, somehow her name had been left off the list entirely.

Eva wondered if her Aunt Helen had forgotten to mention her to the caterers or if Felix was responsible. Whoever it was Eva squirmed with embarrassment knowing that explaining the mistake would call attention to her in the worst way possible.

Eva heard the burble of voices at the other end of the room as two waiters elegantly opened the doors and ushered in the train of diners. People were shown to their seats, the waiters pulling back chairs for the women, and everyone adjusting the set of jackets or wraps as they seated themselves.

Feeling as if she was in a bad dream, Eva took the empty chair on the other side of Lisle Langley's place setting. Lisle didn't even glance at Eva beside her, her attention absorbed by Aunt Joyce's companion on her other side. He was paying Lisle extravagant compliments, hidden from Joyce's sharp eyes by the vast fronds spouting from the épergne in the centre of the table. On the other side of the table the doctor was dividing his attention between his champagne glass and a meandering story about the Cats Protection League being told by Cora—the champagne was definitely absorbing more of his interest.

Through the forest of gesticulating hands, a group of servers wearing black and white appeared carrying dishes and filling glasses with wine. Eva could hear Helen's and Joyce's voices raised in disagreement about how the House might make some money this season with Helen favouring garden parties, once the gardens had been tidied, and Joyce suggesting reviving the boat rides, if the lake could be made safe.

Meanwhile the wave of waiters were moving quietly down the table, pouring wine and laying plates in front of each diner. The nearest server was a teenage girl in a tight black mini skirt and a tailored white shirt. Her pale blonde hair was shoulder-length and streaked with pink. Eva cringed back into her seat. Of course with the way her luck was going, she shouldn't have been surprised to see Kyra Stratton.

Kyra was the leader of a gang of girls who ruled the school with their clique-inspired confidence. In direct contrast to Eva's own inherited aristocratic poverty, Kyra and her gang never seemed to have any shortage of money and wore the kind of high street fashion that Eva simultaneously envied and despised. With their overloud voices, streaked hair, nose rings, and tongue studs they were the girls that boys tried to impress and were either seen as a giggling laughing group or singly with a shambling lad in tow. Kyra's group had made Eva's school life the kind of experience she'd rather forget. From the very first they'd pegged her as different and from her derided accent to her hopelessly out-of-date clothing, they'd made her the butt of every joke.

She remembered having heard people talking about Kyra doing silver service in London at celebrity events but she'd not made a connection between that and the local catering firms. Her eyes were fixed on the table and her empty place-setting as Kyra came closer. One step, two steps, another plate placed on the table, Kyra moved up behind her, another step—and she was past. Eva watched Kyra's back retreating, her pink-streaked blonde hair swinging over her shoulder as she spun on her heel and headed back up the table. She'd laid a starter plate in front of

Lisle and moved over to place another before the next diner but she'd completely ignored Eva.

Eva stared down at her own empty place and wanted to die. Maybe the empty place wasn't an oversight by her family but a riotous joke cooked up by Kyra and her friends in the kitchen. Maybe the waiters would keep pretending not to see her all evening, until some critically embarrassing moment when she'd be exposed in front of all of them as the leftover thirteenth guest.

Silver grated on china as voices babbled and wine gurgled and Eva felt dizzy and nauseated at the combination of noise and heat and mingled savoury smells and alcohol. Another person passed the end of the table, and Eva felt them pass behind her like a gust of cold air from an open window. She turned to see the servers filing out of the room. Kyra's white shirt and black mini skirt was followed by a magpie figure in an old-fashioned servant's uniform of a black dress and white apron. Unlike Kyra, the magpie girl looked straight at her and her coal-black eyes met Eva's—and one of them flicked a deliberate wink.

Eva jumped with surprise, staring after her as the magpie girl turned to follow the train of caterers. Her black hair was wound into a tight plait, hanging down like a horse's tail under a white mobcap. Kyra was five paces ahead and the door swung shut behind the sway of her hips just before the magpie girl reached it. But the black and white figure didn't even flinch. Instead she walked *through* the door, as if the dark wood wasn't there, her plait the last part of her to vanish with a swinging flick as she walked away.

Even without the antique clothes or the way she'd seen it walk through a solid door, Eva would have known what it was from the cold air it left in its wake. A ghost servant, blending into the group so well no one else had noticed her—no one except Eva.

40

'Ghosts! Now that's a good idea,' someone said loudly and Eva jumped, glancing back along the table to see that Aunt Joyce's companion had unexpectedly entered the debate on how to sell the House. 'Marketing's my game,' he announced. 'I've helped countless businesses reinvigorate failing brands. You just need to play to your strengths.' He took a swig of wine to encourage himself and hurried onwards. 'Aren't houses like this supposed to be full of ghosts? That's the stuff to get people visiting. A ghost walk, that's what they're called. You can't tell me an old place like this hasn't got a couple of local legends you could work up into some kind of attraction.'

'I don't think we want anything like that.' Aunt Helen sounded quelling. 'It all sounds in rather bad taste . . . '

'Nonsense,' Aunt Joyce replied instantly in support of her companion. 'If it'll make some money I'm all for it.' She immediately started to recruit the rest of the table as the debate raged back and forth.

'I'm sure we could manage it,' the marketing expert continued waxing enthusiastic, turning to Lisle beside him. 'And it could be done tastefully, linked to a restoration fund, for example. What do you think?'

'Ghost walks have been a success in other parts of the country,' Lisle agreed thoughtfully. 'But it would be a new departure for the House and would need to be properly managed.'

'But surely under the circumstances . . . ' As people turned to look at Aunt Cora her voice quavered and Eva realized she was on the verge of tears. 'Is it such a good idea to dwell on death?'

Silence fell across the table as the guests looked at each other uncomfortably and for the first time Grandfather's voice came out in a creaking whisper.

'There are more things in heaven and earth,' he said, bringing

41

each word out as if it were a physical effort, 'than are dreamt of in your philosophy.' He took a painful breath and Eva fixed her eyes on him, willing him onwards as he forced the company to listen to him. 'You talk about ghosts—but which of you actually believes in them? Do you believe it's possible to be trapped between life and death and bound to this mortal sphere? Who among you will admit to seeing the ghosts who walk among us? I have seen the ghosts of lost Chances and I say we leave them in peace.'

Eva leant forward, trying to meet her grandfather's eyes across the ocean of crystal and silverware. She wanted him to know that she at least believed him.

'I've seen ghosts,' she said. But her voice hardly seemed to register beyond her own ears and she realized she was whispering.

At the top of the table Felix shook his head and as the noise of everyone suddenly speaking at once swelled up again he stilled it with three ringing chimes of his fork against his wine glass.

'Ghosts aren't real,' he said. 'There's no such thing as a haunted house. It makes a good story, that's all. Personally I don't believe a word of it.' He looked around, making sure he had everyone's attention, and concluded: 'However, I think we should pursue the suggestion of using ghosts as the main attraction for this year's season. Because, quite frankly, it's going to take every penny we can screw out of the tourist trade to even attempt to save the place from collapse.'

'But Grandfather said to leave them in peace!' Eva exclaimed. 'And the ghosts are already stirred up by something. Ghost walks aren't *safe*!'

But no one was listening. Grandfather had sunk back in his seat exhausted and Eva hated to see him like that. Felix's confidence blazed across the table and blotted out his parents' objections along with the last confused protests of Aunt Cora.

As Lisle and Michael began to discuss practicalities, it was clear the battle was already lost—this season's main attraction would be ghost walks.

Eva got up from the table. None of the diners were looking at her, immersed in their conversation, and she made it to the doorway unobserved, felt quietly for the handle and left the room.

* * *

Creeping past the caterers working in the kitchen, Eva left the noise of the dinner party behind her. For the first time since the relations had arrived the House was quiet again, now that everyone was corralled in the same place. But Eva could feel the invisible tension, the watching eyes of history. And so, since her family were determined to stir up trouble, Eva decided to try to head it off at the pass. Maybe the ghosts wouldn't be angry if she explained.

In the twenty-first century people didn't believe in ghosts. They were relics of the past, like the rest of the detritus of bygone ages scattered about the House: something that just didn't feature in the world outside. Eva had never heard any of the aunts admit to seeing the ghosts. Only Grandfather talked about them as if they were really there. As with the spiders and black beetles, the mildew and dry rot, over time the House had acquired the ghosts, like atmosphere. Most visitors never noticed them since the ghosts didn't go about groaning or clanking in chains or carrying their heads under their arms. Their influence was subtle and more insidious.

Whenever the House had been opened to the public Eva's grandfather had always successfully blocked any plans to exploit the ghosts for publicity.

'*No need to disturb things*,' he'd always said and Eva knew what he meant. Ghosts were unnerving—no matter how used to them you were.

Trying to use the ghosts could lead to real trouble. In ignoring their grandfather's wishes, Felix was making a horrible mistake and it wouldn't be him who bore the brunt of it. After the conclave Felix would go back to his father's mansion and it would be Eva and her grandfather who'd have to cope with a legion of angry ghosts, stirred up by tourists poking at them like menagerie beasts.

* * *

In the hall the peacock eyes shimmered in the dimness, keeping a blind watch on the House. Through the glass dome at the top of the stairs moonlight filtered down, giving a dreamy lustre to the staircase, silvering it with diffused light.

Different parts of the House had very different atmospheres. Eva knew the haunted feeling could be easily excused as dust and neglect. In every room furniture was swathed in dustsheets and the windows covered with heavy dark curtains to protect the wallpaper from sunlight. Floorboards let out little *twangs* and *sprungs* of noise and the walls released a patter of crumbling plaster and the fireplaces a rustle of falling soot. But there were other noises too. The stiff swish of a silk dress across the floor, the sputter and flare as of a gas lamp springing to life, a burst of laughter or a tinkle of music from a distant room. The past was never far away in the House. Now Eva felt as if she could reach out and touch it.

Her resolve to try to speak to the ghosts faltered on the brink of the stairs. The magpie servant had winked at her, a gesture that suggested she might be an ally. But here the floor was cold and the moonlight spilling down the staircase fell away from the last stairs into a pool of darkness. Was it her imagination or did that darkness look wet? Could you reason with a phantom stain?

Eva knelt down, her hands reaching flinchingly towards the stain. Her fingertips brushed the carpet and recoiled. Did it feel wet—or just cold? She shivered. Was it only the peacock eyes watching her or was something rising invisibly behind her, ready to pounce?

She stood up quickly, looking around. There was no one there.

But the haunted feeling didn't go away and Eva looked down to see the stain spreading—the blackness dripping down the bottom stair and towards her feet.

With a flying leap she jumped over and past it, clinging to the banisters and turning to look behind her, dreading that the bloodstain would follow. But the shadows were still and the stain lay behind her, quiescent for now.

Laughter slivered through the hall, not coming from the dining room, but higher up. On the galleried landing the light caught the lace edge of a white cap and a pale face staring down into the hall: the magpie girl again.

Eva hurried up the steps but when she reached the gallery the girl was gone. Standing there, undecided what to do, a sound fell softly into the back of her ears, a floorboard creaking under a heavy step. Another footstep followed, heavier than the first: slow, quiet footsteps, coming up the staircase.

Eva took a step, and behind her, down the corridor, something else took another quiet step forward. She stopped moving and the footsteps stilled a second later, echoing her movement. She was being followed.

Eva had wanted to find ghosts and now they had found her. But nothing about those footsteps suggested an ally—or something

45

that could be reasoned with. Every instinct she had screamed with the awareness prey has of the predator. The ghost on her trail wasn't just following her—it was stalking her.

With the depths of the House ahead of her and the footsteps behind, she hesitated; looking up and down the passageway indecisively. And as she hesitated, the footsteps started again, not waiting for her this time, the steps sounding heavier now and more deliberate. Eva strained her eyes to find any sign of movement but there was nothing to see in the dimly lit corridor even though the owner of the footsteps must be getting closer.

Ten feet, five feet, three feet away. Eva's own feet shifted against the floor; her legs began to shake and she couldn't stop them. Her body was taking over, making the decision for her, insisting it was time to move own.

A heavy step fell at the end of the floorboard she stood on and Eva's nerve broke. She turned and started walking briskly, away from the footsteps, onward into the east wing. Behind her, the floorboards creaked as the footsteps followed, keeping pace with her own.

Each step she took was faster than the last and each step behind her came faster still. Before she knew it, she was running, her sandals slapping against the floor in a ragged patter and a scraping slide around a turn in the passageway, thumping down three short steps and clattering onwards. The other footsteps followed: ringing on the wooden floorboards and around the turn, pounding down the stairs and chasing after her.

Running made the sound worse, turned the footsteps from an eerie noise into a horror at her heels. It was closing the gap between them, gaining on her despite her headlong flight. She didn't dare look behind: scared of what she might see—or fail to see. Would the corridor still be empty with the footsteps right on top of hers? Was that a breeze or something breathing chill dank air across the back of her neck?

Her eyes were blurry, blood hammering from her heart in dizzying jolts of pressure, her lungs screaming for more air than she had breath to give them.

'This way!' A flash of black and white appeared suddenly ahead and Eva made for it, her sandals skidding as she hurled herself towards the magpie girl at the end of the corridor.

The footsteps were seconds away, landing in her footprints, as she hurled herself forward. A wiry arm snagged hold of her sleeve and reeled her in, hauling her towards the wall and into a black hole that opened up ahead. Darkness surrounded Eva as she fell hard on to a cold surface, which shook with her impact and—an instant after she hit it—dropped away beneath her with a rattling crash.

After a mad flailing panic, gasping for breath, she realized the hard surface was still underneath her, but descending. She was lying on the floor of a metal cage, dropping down a dark shaft, lit by a single dim lightbulb hanging from the roof of the cage. It was the service lift.

Standing at the side of the lift was the servant girl she'd been following when she first entered the east wing, dressed in her magpie black and white uniform. The magpie girl's face was dirty; there was a smudge of something tar-like near her left cheekbone. She was spinning a metal wheel, cranking the lift down the shaft, and above them the footsteps had faded away to nothing.

'You don't want to let it catch you,' she said, the slight burr of a country accent in her voice. 'It's the Stalker and it'll stay behind you anywhere you can walk or run.'

Eva stood up shakily, the rattling of the cage disguising how unsteady she felt after running herself literally off her own feet. The service lift had been built by Victorians and as far as she knew hadn't been used in fifty years. The stone walls of the House slid by, darkly greasy behind the wrought-iron framework of the lift. As they dropped down between the floors, Eva felt she'd taken a step sideways into another world: one that lay like a shadow at an unexpected angle to her own.

'I know you,' said the servant girl. Her dark eyes were searching as she stared at Eva from across the small space of the metal cage. 'I saw you downstairs, sitting with the family and none of them paying any attention to you.'

'You winked at me,' Eva said and the girl shrugged.

'You saw me,' she said. 'No one else did. I thought you were like me for a second but you're not are you? You're one of them. One of the Chances.'

'I'm Eva,' Eva said slowly, trying to assess the mood of those dark eyes. 'Evangeline Chance.'

'I don't care what your name is.' The magpie girl had a way of jerking her head forward at the end of a sentence, as if she was going to bite. 'Why can you see me when the rest of your family can't?'

'I don't know.' Eva shook her head. 'I've always been able to see things that—things that aren't supposed to exist, like ghosts.'

'Is that what you think I am then?' the girl asked with a quick birdlike glance and Eva winced.

'Yes,' she admitted. 'Sorry. But not in the same way as whatever was chasing me before. You're both ghosts, aren't you? Only you helped me and that thing—'

'The Stalker,' the magpie girl said flatly. 'It would have killed you if it caught you. That's what it does: it follows you and then it chases you and if it catches you, you're dead.'

Eva shivered. She wanted to ask if the Stalker ghost killed real people or preyed on ghosts but she suspected the question wouldn't go down well. However, since there hadn't been a noticeable number of corpses lying around the place or skeletons falling out of cupboards, she guessed that the Stalker mostly attacked other ghosts.

'Why did you help me?' she asked instead.

'That's my business,' the servant girl snapped at her, unexpectedly irritated by the question. She spun the wheel of the lift hard, so the speed of their descent increased, the walls rushing past as they dropped down. 'Maybe I wanted to know why he was chasing you. What makes you so special that the whole House is stirred up around you? You *reek* of trouble.'

'I do not!' Eva felt hurt, thinking that everyone always blamed the messenger. 'It's not me. I'm not the one causing trouble.'

'All the Chances are trouble.' The magpie girl turned to face her as the lift rattled to a stop. 'You're either wicked or you're crazy and the worst ones are both.'

'I can't help that,' Eva blazed back at her. 'It's not my fault what family I was born into or who my relations are. Except for Grandfather, I don't even like them.'

'Oh, whine, whine, whine.' The magpie girl was anything but impressed. 'Try working from sun up to sun down to serve the whims of a cold-hearted monster, a foul-minded sow and a litter of wastrels and scoundrels none of whom are fit to lick your boots.'

Eva shivered again. The air around the ghost girl was chilly, colder than the stone walls that surrounded them. Each time the magpie girl looked agitated the temperature dropped another couple of degrees.

'I'm sorry,' she said. 'I didn't mean to complain.' She had

enough experience of housework to be ashamed of how casually her ancestors had treated their servants. Of course, now her family were about to treat the ghosts equally casually. 'Did you hear what people were saying at dinner?' she asked.

'About visitors hunting for ghosts.' The magpie girl gave her a sly look. 'It's like I told you, they're either wicked or crazy to try it. And there'll be danger when they do.'

'What do you mean? What kind of danger?'

'You should know,' the ghost told her. 'You're right at the centre of it, you're under a curse even if you don't know it. I'm not a troublemaker, never was—despite what was said.' Some centuries-old resentment flared for an instant. 'But I can tell which way the wind is blowing. And all the luck has run out for the Chances, hasn't it?' She gave Eva a long searching look.

'I don't know,' Eva said, thinking of her ailing grandfather and the House about to be inherited by Felix and threatened with being turned into a hotel or a golf club, and the tourists about to gather like vultures feeding from a corpse. 'Maybe the luck has run out. But we're not dead yet.'

'If you say so.' The magpie girl gave her a long look of resentment and Eva flushed.

'I'm sorry,' she said. 'But if my grandfather dies, my cousin Felix will throw me out. And Grandfather won't get better if ghosts are running riot all over the House. If it's going to be dangerous, I have to try and do something to stop it.'

'So you're one of the crazy ones.' The magpie girl showed her teeth in a biting smile. 'Well don't blame me when you wake up dead one morning.' She rattled the door of the cage open and stepped out into the corridor beyond.

'Wait,' Eva said. 'There must be something I can do. I need your help.'

'Oh you do, do you?' The magpie girl jerked her head back at Eva. 'Well, if you insist on meeting trouble head on, you'd best try looking in the cellar.'

And as she finished her last stab of sentence she was gone, between one heartbeat and another, the white of her apron a splash of moonlight on the wall, the darkness of her dress the shadowed angle of the passageway.

4
Invisible Girl

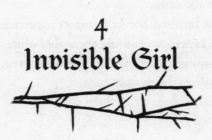

The lift had brought her back to the ground floor and Eva stood in the grey stone passageway wishing she had the courage to walk back into the dining room and demand that everyone listen to her. She knew that the last thing the family should consider was ghost walks but she couldn't imagine what might convince them that the ghosts really existed.

Underneath her feet the stone floor seemed colder than usual and she couldn't help looking down at it and thinking of the cellars. It was ridiculous that she'd never been down there. It was possible there were stocks of food to replenish the empty pantry. The entrance to the cellars was just off the main hall. She must pass it twenty times a day. But her grandfather had always told her to leave the cellars alone. 'There's nothing you need down there,' he said. 'Those cellars are old and unsafe. Forget about them.'

The door was ahead of her now along the passageway, just a few steps would bring her to it. It was ridiculous to feel so nervous of a plain wooden door when she'd escaped one murderous ghost and spent ten minutes in conversation with another. Eva took a few careful steps along the corridor, her eyes searching out the shape of the door ahead of her, expecting the same solid wood surface as always.

It took her a moment to realize the door was gone—no, it was *open*. She could see the stairs leading down, lit by a moving light. She took a slow pace forward, and then another one, trying to look down the stairs without coming too near. All she could see was rough plastered walls and a light already beginning to fade.

There was a rumbling sound and Eva ducked back into the shadows as a teenager came barrelling along the corridor towards her with a trolley laden with dirty plates.

'Oi,' he said when he reached the open cellar door. 'Who's down there?' Footsteps sounded on the stairs and Eva saw the light brighten again as another boy came up the staircase, holding a torch.

'His highness wants some port,' he said, making a face. He was the big blond teenage waiter she'd seen earlier, whose black jacket now had a trail of cobwebs across the back. 'One of the old ladies said there might be some in the cellar so I was sent to look. It's pitch black down there though.'

'Let's have a look,' the one with the trolley said, abandoning it and coming towards the cellar door. 'If they've got no idea what's down there it doesn't matter if we take a bottle or two ourselves.'

'You'll be lucky,' the blond teenager said, as the two of them set off down the stairs together. 'From the look of the kitchen they've got no grub except what we brought this evening.'

'Their sort all eat out, don't they?' the trolley boy's voice grew fainter as he replied. 'But they do their boozing at home.'

Moving up to the edge of the doorframe, Eva looked down. All she could see was a plain wood staircase. The boys were already some way below her and she could see the light of the torch growing fainter again as they moved away from the stairs.

She didn't want to follow them. She didn't know why the magpie girl had suggested she look in the cellar or what the connection was to the ghost's vague references to danger coming. But as the torchlight moved further down she thought this might be her only chance to investigate with other people nearby. It might be horribly embarrassing to shout for help but the two boys had looked able to take care of themselves. Whatever was down there at least she wouldn't be completely alone with it.

As she walked down the first couple of stairs she could feel the noises of the House deadening again. The flight of stairs was steep and the narrow walls of the staircase were made of thick stone under their dusting of plaster. In the light from the corridor she saw spiders' webs overhanging the stairs in long tattered swathes like grey muslin curtains. They were too high to touch her but she kept imagining that they would until her head was crunched down into her neck as she tried to avoid them.

At the end of the flight of stairs was a long large room, all in darkness. Some distance away came the murmur of voices and the yellow glow of the torchlight framed a curved archway. Between Eva and the arch the room was pitch black and she took a deep breath before stepping off the staircase and walking as quickly as she could towards the archway. At each step she put out her hands feeling for hidden obstructions but the path was clear and she reached the arch in time to see the room on the other side.

It was a wine room: along the walls were great wooden racks where the torchlight glinted from dusty old bottles. Huge wooden casks stood in the corners, which might hold anything or nothing. But the boys seemed to have forgotten what they'd come for.

On the other side of the room was another arched doorway and it was here the two boys stood, their backs to Eva so that all she saw was the torch-holder's shock of blond hair and the trolley boy's zig-zagging corn-rows.

'What the hell *is* that?' the blond boy said, the torchlight wavering ahead of them to light the path which Eva still couldn't see. As she moved up along the line of wine racks the corn-rowed boy replied.

'Creeeeepy!' he said, drawing out the word over several syllables, and stepping forward into the darkness ahead. The blond boy followed and after a few heart-hammering seconds she had taken their place at the edge of the doorway, seeing what they had seen.

It was ridiculous to think of it as a dungeon, she told herself. The cellars had been built when the House was first constructed and must have been used over the years as store rooms for household goods and the butler's great barrels and racks of ales and fine wines. But some time over the centuries one of the Chances had begun an unusual collection and had chosen the cellars as the place to house it. It was this unusual collection that altered the feel of the damp dark rooms into something out of a nightmare: a collection of torturer's tools.

Eva had always known the Chances had acquired some gruesome things but it was a subject she preferred not to think about. The House had enough oddments and curios without her needing to take an interest in every item. As long as she didn't look too closely at shrunken heads or mummified cats she could think of them as just part of another cabinet of curiosities. This collection was more menacing and much harder to ignore.

As the cellars extended onwards into a warren of pillars and half walls and side rooms, there was a seemingly endless array of metal chairs and racks and rows of hooks holding instruments crafted to gouge and twist and strain. As she studied them Eva felt a slow horror building but her gaze continued to travel across the expanse, as if compelled to view each item. The boys had vanished into another room but the light of the torch still played across the rusty hooks and frozen wheels. She could hear their voices exclaiming at each new discovery, voices rising and falling in the background.

Eva walked slowly after them, each step increasing her mounting sense of horror. There was a bad atmosphere in the cellar, tenuous and unmistakable like a foul smell, making her gag as she felt it swirling about her. There was something horrible in here; something choking the cellars with its presence like a rotting corpse and the voices of the two boys seemed to dampen into the distance.

Eva tried to avoid touching any of the collection as she followed the light and found herself adrift in the darkness, hearing the boys and seeing the light but not being able to catch up with them. The light seemed to retreat ahead of her and her imagination filled in the shadows with crouching horrors—already she was unsure of the way back.

Light gleamed wetly over the floor, reflected from around a corner, not torchlight but firelight, a molten red glow. One of the braziers was alight, glowing coals inside an iron cage bringing a slow red heat to the corkscrew end of a torturer's iron. Eva stared at the flickering glow, wasting seconds on wondering what had set it burning before she realized she had completely lost sight of the torchlight.

Too late—her realization came as the coals glowed brighter and the red glow reflected across the gleaming sheet of the floor to the wooden scaffold which rose up in the centre of the room. It was a medieval ducking chair with handcuffs and straps, built to hold a prisoner.

There was something sitting on the chair. Its wrists and ankles were swollen with bloodied welts where the skin had been gouged by the iron cuffs, the hands and feet skeletal and blue with cold. The body was twisted and broken, a ragged tatter of cloth and skin and bone. But the head was held up with a rusty brace of iron, the shape of the skull veiled with a century's cobwebs so that it regarded the room from a filthy grey cloak of webbing.

It wasn't real. Eva told herself it wasn't real but the knowledge didn't help. It was as real as pain, as real as anger, as real as hate. It was a dead thing that hadn't died. Ghost was a pale misty word for such a presence.

It was looking right at her. Its presence overcame the rusty malice of the torturer's tools, it filled the room with a swirling furious power, rushing out of the broken body in a tide of contaminating filth.

I see you.

It was a Witch. As it filled her mind with itself she couldn't help knowing what it was any more than she could move or make a sound. It was a Witch and it was turning her mind inside out, scrutinizing the naked feelings it found there and twisting at the ones that hurt the most. The Witch knew all about Eva's most embarrassing experiences, it knew all her secret sadnesses and it fed on her misery. It wanted her scared and in pain. It wanted her to hurt.

Hundreds of years ago a human woman had died on the ducking chair, a woman who had suffered and bled and screamed her anger to an uncaring world. The woman who had died had been a Witch. She'd thought of herself as a Witch because like Eva she saw things that weren't real. She'd used those things to frighten people and to hurt them. The Witch woman had died with enough malice to outlast centuries and now the ghost Witch was more dangerous than the living one had ever been.

I see you—and you're nothing. Last Chance, lost Chance, no more Chances left.

As it took her mind to pieces, Eva knew its thoughts more clearly than her own.

The Witch hated the family; it hated all the living and the Chances most of all. Chances had watched while the Witch died and Chances had displayed the chair in their collection and brought the Witch into the House. She had cursed them as she died—wanting rack and ruin upon them. Now her ghost haunted the House, shadowing the Chances, using her dark powers to blight their lives and bring the family to its knees.

Eva cringed in the deepest corner of her mind, the power of the Witch's thoughts streaming through her. The Witch wanted the ghost walks to happen. It was looking forward to catastrophe, imagining the havoc it could wreak on the ghost hunters. It fed on fear and on superstition and she had brought it the food it liked best. It was anticipating disaster with a bloody broken smile.

'No.' Eva didn't know where she'd managed to find the word but she'd said it. 'No, you can't do that, I won't let you.'

You can't stop it. The Witch wasn't impressed. Its voice was a mocking echo from within her, triumphing in the fact it knew her from the inside out. *I am the rot inside you. I know how weak you are.*

Waves of malice were beating Eva to the ground, forcing her to crouch before the Witch. This was so much stronger than the black anger of the Stalker ghost or the chilly suspicion of the magpie girl; the presence of the Witch was a thick cloud of power and hate, sucking air and light out of the cellars.

'I'll tell the family, I'll convince them to cancel the ghost walks,' Eva insisted and the Witch began to laugh. Waves of unholy glee came rolling from it, surging over Eva and trying to drive her down into despair. The Witch wasn't pretending to find her pathetic, it considered her less than nothing.

They won't listen. They don't hear you. They can't even see you. Unlucky reject child, lost in a dark room, you don't even know what you are.

Eva knew she should ignore the Witch's taunting. It had read her mind and it was playing on her fears, tweaking doubts and insecurities to keep her cringing and low.

'I'm Eva Chance,' she said, clutching for some kind of certainty. 'I don't need to know more than that.'

The Witch's broken body shook like a rag doll, setting the ducking chair creaking and swaying as harsh cracks of sound rang through the room. Eva heard shouts in the distance and the light in the cellars flickered and jumped as the Witch screamed with laughter.

You are nothing. An eye blink, a struck match, a heart beat. A mayfly.

There were running footsteps in the distance and a door slammed, plunging the cellars into darkness. As the noise echoed through the vaults Eva's nerve broke. She could feel the Witch in her head and all around her, the air so choked with it she couldn't breathe. All the ghosts chilled the air around them but the Witch brought a cold so intense it *burned*. Sliding across the wet flagstones she fought her way step by step away from the ducking chair. Far in the distance she saw a shaft of light slanting along a stair-rail and she fled for it.

You're dead, Eva Chance. That's why no one sees you. You died and nobody noticed. You died and nobody cared.

* * *

At the top of the stairs Eva wrenched for the handle and rattled it, shaking the door in its frame. When it finally gave way she burst out into the hallway and tripped over the wheeled-trolley in a

59

scattering crash of breaking plates. She didn't stop to see the result; a cold wind was chasing her as she ran along the corridor, slamming doors and rattling windows all the way to the dining room.

It was empty. The remains of a redcurrant sorbet were melting on the dessert plates, surrounded by abandoned glasses of claret, staining china and glassware red as if the family had been dining on blood.

The conference was over. The family was gone, probably to their separate rooms and the lawyer and the house agent had vanished as well. As the Witch had told her, no one had even noticed her absence.

'I can't be dead.' Eva shivered in the empty room, feeling the cold of the ghost wind swirling around her. 'I'd know if I was a ghost, wouldn't I?' The Witch was gone and she told herself it had been trying to scare her, using her fears against her, saying whatever would make her most afraid.

Along the corridor she heard an adult voice exclaim in annoyance.

'Which of you lot knocked this over? Who's in charge of this trolley? Damon, Kyle?'

There was a pause and then a babble of voices denying responsibility.

'It wasn't us, boss.' She recognized the corn-rowed boy's voice among the caterers. 'We was down the cellar. And most of them plates were chipped anyway. All this stuff is junk.'

'Junk or not I want this lot cleaned up right now. And clear the rest of the dessert plates out of the dining room.'

Marooned at the far end of the room with no way out Eva froze in place as the door opened and the two boys came in.

'Tony had better not take those plates out of our wages,' the corn-rowed boy said irritably, using the trolley to wedge the dining room door open and turning to look back at his friend. 'There was someone in the cellar, wasn't there? Mucking about and making noises. Rattling chains and things like that. They knocked the plates over, coming out ahead of us.'

'No idea.' The blond boy moved into the room and began stacking dishes at the end of the table. 'I wish we'd never gone down there. Let's just get this done and get out of here; this room's freezing.'

Eva waited for them to look in her direction. It felt stupid just standing there, waiting for them to notice her. They'd probably think she was weird for not saying anything. But she didn't know what to say. 'Can you see me standing here?' wouldn't make them think her any less weird.

'Hey, Kyle,' a girl's voice asked from the corridor. 'Is it true you guys found a torture chamber downstairs?'

The blond boy stacked the dishes on the cart, looking over his shoulder as Kyra appeared in the doorway. For the first time Eva saw the resemblance between the two of them. The boy was about six stone heavier and nearly a foot taller than Kyra but both had blond hair and blue eyes. She knew Kyra had a twin brother in another class at school although she hadn't ever seen him. This had to be him.

'I don't know what it was we saw,' Kyle said, waiting for the corn-rowed boy to leave the room with the trolley before adding, 'Don't go looking yourself. There was some messed up stuff down there.'

'Messed up how? You don't look so great. Like you've seen a ghost or something.' Kyra sat herself on the end of the table, her back to Eva. Perhaps she just hadn't noticed Eva on the other side of the room. Perhaps she was still pretending not to see her. Perhaps.

'I told you I don't know what I saw—or heard,' Kyle muttered. 'Laughing—or screaming. I wish it was someone mucking about.' There was a long pause before he added: 'How long before we can get out of here?'

'Maybe fifteen minutes.' Kyra aimed a punch at his arm. 'If we hustle. Let's do that and get gone.'

The boy seemed reassured, reaching out to tousle her hair affectionately and as he did he looked right past her at Eva.

No, not at her, at nothing. His eyes didn't meet hers, they drifted over her, through her, his expression unfocused and blank. Eva stared back at him, willing him to see her—to notice her standing right there in front of him. But his expression didn't change.

'It's a weird sort of place here,' Kyra added, as she slipped down from the table. 'You know that girl I was telling you about, the one in my class. This is where she lived.'

'What girl?' Kyle put a hand on Kyra's arm, steering her out of the room.

'You never remember *anything*,' Kyra said. 'It was only a couple of weeks ago it happened. The loopy girl. The one that disappeared. She lived here.'

'Right yeah, sorry,' Kyle replied. 'There was an assembly about it, wasn't there? She was called Evelyn? Emily? Something like that.'

'Eva,' Kyra corrected him. 'She was in my class. Her name was Eva Chance and she was just this most complete freak you ever met. Everyone thinks she killed herself.'

'And she lived here?' Kyle shook his head as they headed back towards the kitchens. 'Cold bastards she's got for a family. None of them so much as mentioned it at dinner.'

Peacocks screamed on the terrace, beating their wings hard

enough to rattle the windows. Eva hardly heard them. The Witch had been right. She was dead and she was the last to know.

* * *

Eavesdroppers never heard good of themselves. That was an old adage. But she'd never expected to hear that she was dead. Looking down at her dirty fingernails, her cobweb-covered dress, and her feet in their scuffed sandals standing on the floor it seemed impossible. How could she be a ghost?

Wanting more than anything to believe it was just an evil joke, Eva quickly tallied up the people she'd spoken to that day. The missing place at dinner could be a joke on Kyra's part—and all the caterers might be in on it. She'd hidden from the guests and none of her family had seen her. But before dinner she'd found Felix in her room and he'd definitely seen her—Eva staggered with relief. Felix might hate her but he'd seen her and spoken to her.

It was a joke—a cruel horrible joke and the Witch had used it to frighten her senseless. Eva's thoughts shied away from the idea of the Witch and back to Kyra. Kyra had persuaded her brother and the other boy to pretend Eva didn't exist and they'd almost got her to believe them.

Feeling her face sting with embarrassment and rage, Eva found herself walking towards the kitchens, pushing the doors open and looking for Kyra.

There was a group of teenagers in the kitchens. The side door was propped open with a mop and bucket and the boy with the corn-rowed hair was standing at the open door, smoking a cigarette. Kyra, her brother Kyle, and the rest of the catering team were cleaning up the room.

Eva entered just as the peacocks screamed again outside and Kyle spun round to stare outside.

'What the hell is that?' he demanded.

'Relax,' his friend replied from the doorway. 'It's just those big birds we saw earlier, make a hell of a racket.'

'That's a bird?' Kyle looked incredulous. 'Jeezus. It's like a police siren.'

Eva stood in the middle of the room waiting for them to notice her, her flesh gradually chilling as the caterers continued to ignore her.

'It'd give me the willies if I had to listen to that every five minutes,' one of the older women commented when the peacocks finally stopped screaming. 'It sounds like a soul in torment.'

'Maybe it was one of them birds we heard downstairs,' the corn-rowed boy laughed. 'There were these weird noises, like wood creaking and chains rattling and you should have seen Kyle take off, like the devil was after him.'

'You weren't so slow yourself, Damon,' Kyle responded quickly. 'And you were the one slammed the door.'

'Yeah, but it wasn't me smashed them plates,' Damon pointed out. 'So has someone been having a laugh?'

The caterers exchanged glances around the room. Some were suspicious, others amused, considering their co-workers in turn. A couple looked frightened, trying to get the job done as quickly as they could. None of them looked at Eva. She couldn't believe Kyra could coach them well enough to keep up such a concerted pretence. They weren't ignoring her. She was standing in the middle of the room and they just didn't see her.

'It was me,' Eva said out loud. 'I opened the door. I broke the plates.'

'Whoever it was we'd better not have to pay for it,' someone said from the other side of the room. 'Not with all the work we had to do making this place fit to serve food from. Fit for pigs is what I said then and I'll say it again.'

'I hear you.' Damon shook his head. 'Gotta be the worst tourist attraction since the Dome.'

'Tourists?' Kyle looked disbelieving. 'People come to see this old dump?'

'Didn't you listen to what they were talking about at dinner?' Kyra demanded. 'The house and gardens get opened up for the summer and they charge admission. But no one's coming because it's so skanky so they're going to have ghost walks and seances to pull in the punters.'

'I bet people would pay to see that stuff in the cellars,' Damon said slyly. 'It's like a proper dungeon down there. Play some music, get a few waxworks and people'd be crapping themselves. Don't you reckon, Kyle?' Kyle ignored him.

'They spent all evening complaining how broke they were.' Kyra shook her head. 'How can they be broke when this place has got a hundred rooms all filled up with antiques? They're not broke, they're stingy.'

As she spoke she was walking towards Eva and right up into her face. Eva saw Kyra's blue eyes from inches away before she jumped back.

'There's a hell of a draught in here,' Kyra said, moving away from Eva. 'Are we done, or what?'

There seemed to be a consensus among the caterers that they were finished and as the last plates were stacked an older man entered the room and looked around. When he spoke she recognized the voice of authority from the corridor.

'Good job, team. You did well this evening. Don't worry about those plates. Like Damon said, they can't have been worth anything or they wouldn't have been left covered in crap like we found them. Her ladyship's paid up and I reckon we're done for the evening.'

Eva stood in the middle of the kitchen as the group departed. They all seemed to step around her without even noticing they were doing it, shrugging on cardigans and coats and complaining about the cold. Kyra was the last to leave, reaching to turn the lights out. She paused in the open doorway, looking back into the kitchen. She seemed for a moment to be uncertain, her eyes narrowing as she looked towards the place where Eva stood. Then she shook herself, like someone shaking off an unwelcome thought.

'Goose over my grave,' Kyra muttered, turning away.

'Get a move on, Kyra!' a voice called from the courtyard and the blonde girl went out, letting the door bang shut behind her. Outside her footsteps rang across the flagstones, a door slammed and an engine started up.

Alone in the kitchen Eva listened until the van was out of earshot and silence returned. It was a dark heavy silence. In the unlit room she couldn't see her hands or feet or anything beyond her. The House was her territory, she knew each room back to front; she could walk its corridors blindfolded. But this darkness seemed to come from behind her, along the corridor, through the open door to the cellars, up the stairs from the chamber of torturer's tools, from the dark room where the Witch was.

Last Chance, lost Chance, no more Chances left.

5
Magpies and Cuckoos

Wednesday, April 2nd

The mist hung damply over the lake as the dawn light gradually shaded it from black, to grey, to white. The lapping water became slowly visible through the soft haze and the whispering marsh grasses shifted from grey to green.

Eva sat at the water's edge, her velvet dress caked and clammy with mud, her hands and feet raw with chill and her hair a seaweed tangle around her damp face. Stupid with cold, she didn't know how long she'd sat unthinking, watching the night turn to day. She couldn't remember how she'd got here, what had made her come to the edge of the lake; the memories of yesterday seemed to shy away from her, leaving her mind-numb and heart-sick.

Far behind her was the House, even further away was the life she remembered. Birds began to call, the twitterings of wrens and sparrows in the long grasses drowned out by the screams of the peacocks on the island at the centre of the lake.

The Witch had claimed Eva had died and no one had noticed. Kyra's story was that Eva had killed herself; she'd spent her sixteenth birthday being ignored by everyone who'd entered the House. Eva wondered if it even counted as her birthday if she was dead. Was she still fifteen and doomed to be fifteen for ever, watching while the House was sold or demolished and the garden turned into a golf course? Felix had made it clear there was no place for her in the House.

But Felix had *seen* her. Her fogged brain began to clear as she thought about the significance of that. Yesterday she'd hoped it meant she wasn't dead after all. Now that meeting took on a more sinister shape as she recalled how he'd tried to intimidate her and realized that it was possible that his hostility had been an attempt to hide his alarm. Was his strange reaction because he'd just seen his first ghost? Later at dinner he'd told everyone he didn't believe in ghosts and then backed the suggestion of ghost walks. Eva didn't know what her cousin's plan was but she believed he was deadly serious when he'd said the House was his and he wanted her gone.

How had she died? It seemed bizarre that she wouldn't remember. It couldn't be true that she'd killed herself. Eva was sure of it. Despite poverty at home, and bullying at school, and the disregard of her relations, she wasn't suicidal. Why would she be? She'd lived with those things for sixteen years. Maybe if her grandfather had died she might have despaired; she'd felt pretty despairing when she'd heard Lisle and Michael talking in the maze. But even then Eva hadn't given up and slit her wrists.

'I'm not giving up now either,' she said. 'Not until I know what really happened.' She flexed her fingers, trying to force feeling back into them but they remained numb and pale, and tinged with blue under the fingernails.

'If I wasn't dead already I'd probably die from hypothermia,' she said, looking at them, and felt uneasy as if her words had triggered a memory. Like déjà vu, it vanished as she tried to concentrate on it. Instead she forced herself to stand. Her body was cramped with sitting so long and she wondered again how she could be a ghost and yet feel so physically real to herself. She could touch the ground, trickle water through her hands, feel the bite of the cold air. It might not have been so hard to believe she was dead if she hadn't felt so alive.

* * *

The path curved along the side of the lake, past the outlandish white tent of the summerhouse. Eva followed the path automatically. It wasn't as though she had anywhere to go or anything to do. She was dead. Being dead was surely the end of chores. A pity she hadn't realized that yesterday when she'd worked to make the House gleam for her relations.

Out on the lake there was a *splish* of water and Eva turned to look. Was that a boat drifting out on the lake? She frowned at it through the clearing mists and reminded herself that it wasn't her problem.

The boat had its oars, they dragged in the water and bumped at the side of the boat, with a gentle *splish splosh thunk*, repeated hypnotically. The sound carried in the still morning air and Eva continued to watch it, her discomfort growing as she wondered how a boat had managed to drift free of the locked boathouse.

There was a movement in the prow of the boat, a flutter of fabric, a caught tree branch—or an arm reaching out. Eva strained her eyes to see even as her stomach roiled and gurgled with the same motion as the uneasy waters of the lake. Even as a ghost she wasn't immune to feeling haunted and there was something about that boat that wasn't right.

There was a figure in the prow, blurred by the mist, or perhaps not completely there. Eva could see it leaning over the front of the boat, clothed in dark stuff, the face a pale oval in a seaweed tangle of long lank wet hair. Its head turned towards her and Eva felt a chill breeze ruffle past her as the figure stared at her.

It was a woman, a woman with empty watery eyes and a small set mouth. She sat slumped in the boat, staring across the water at Eva, not speaking. It was a face familiar to Eva from paintings, photographs, and her own mirror—the face of the mother she had never met. Adeline.

'Have you come for me?' Eva whispered. The words fell away into the air and yet she felt sure the ghost had heard her even though its expression didn't change. 'Is this the end?'

Perhaps her mother's ghost was death's ferryman, come to take her to the afterlife. Eva took a step forward towards the water's edge. The reeds and irises were thick here, the water stagnant and muddy, a foetid smell rising from their roots.

The ghost raised an arm, pointing at her. Was it beckoning? Eva hesitated and saw the arm motion completed in a raised hand. A warning. She stumbled back from the water as a flight of peacocks came thrumming through the air above the boat in a glimmer of blue and green.

Eva ducked and moved back as they flew over her head. When she looked at the lake again the boat was gone.

It had been a warning, she thought to herself. But a warning of what? She was already dead—what more could happen to her? Other people had mothers who would come and comfort you. Eva had a ghost who had only troubled to appear when the worst had already happened. Some use that was. She was tempted to dive into the lake and find that drifting hopeless figure and give it a piece of her mind.

But Adeline was long gone. She'd abandoned Eva once again, in death as in life. Turning her back on the lake, Eva took the path towards the House.

***

Eva had lost her sandals the night before and her bare feet stumbled over the cold ground. Her progress was awkward and slow as she reached the boundary of the formal gardens and she tripped over the edge of the path. She felt herself falling with the sickening feeling the fall would be bad—and came down hard on the gravel path, her hands and knees scraping through the small flinty stones and all the breath leaving her body in a forced gasp.

It hurt. Her body felt like one giant bruise and her hands and feet stung like fury. She thought it had been hard to move before. Now she couldn't even lift her head. She tasted blood, pieces of gravel pressed into her lips and her teeth throbbed in her mouth.

'Pathetic.' A dark shadow fell across her and feet in black-buttoned boots appeared in Eva's field of view. 'You must have been truly pathetic when you were alive to make such a pitiful ghost.'

It was the magpie servant girl. She squatted down on her heels to look at Eva, with a flash of thin legs in thick black stockings and a torn petticoat. Her hands were black with coal dust and her fingertips raw and red.

'I knew you were dead,' she said. 'I knew it when I saw you at that dinner table, the only one without a place setting and still trying to pretend you were one of them. You must really be stupid if you didn't guess what you were.'

'Go away,' Eva whispered and the magpie girl laughed at her.

'Make me,' the magpie girl said, smiling a hard sharp smile. 'Oh, but you can't, because you don't know the first thing about being a ghost.'

'I know one thing.' A small stab of anger brought Eva's face

71

out of the dirt for long enough to speak. 'I know that there's a Witch in the cellar. The cellar you sent me to.'

'You said you wanted to do something.' The magpie girl shrugged a shoulder but her face was turned away. 'I knew you were the one stirring things up. I knew the Witch was watching you. You don't want the ghost walks, the Witch does. You may as well know from the start what you're up against.'

'Then you did it deliberately?' She brought herself into a little coiled knot on the ground, staring back at her antagonist. 'You knew I was a ghost and you just pointed me right at it. At her. At the *Witch*.' Eva's suspicions had hardened her spine. 'And you've got the nerve to say you're not a trouble-maker.' She spat out blood and gravel on to the ground between them. 'You're scum.'

'And what are you?' The magpie girl spat the words back at her. 'Mud? Pond slime? A maggot on a dead dog.'

You are nothing. An eye blink. A struck match. A heart beat. A mayfly.

A tiny fire burnt inside her in protest. Whatever her family or Kyra's gang or the ghosts thought—she was not just nothing. She had a name and her grandfather had given it to her.

'My name is Evangeline Chance,' she said, and surged upwards, striking the servant girl hard across the face, knuckles hitting hard against skin that wasn't even as cold as her own.

'You hellcat!' the servant girl swore, falling backwards and sitting down hard on the ground. She raised a hand—but not threatening—instead exploring the side of her face where a red mark was already swelling the side of her mouth. 'That stung.' Then she laughed abruptly. 'Perhaps you're not so pathetic after all.'

Eva didn't answer that. She was thinking the same thing. Picking herself up from the ground she checked her own injuries. Chips and flecks of gravel were embedded into her skin in bloody scrapes—but even as she watched the cuts smoothed over, the gravel pattering to the ground to leave her skin still filthy but no longer bleeding. She felt stronger too, no longer so conscious of her bruises or the biting cold. The sudden flare of anger had warmed and strengthened her. Now she was the one looking down at the servant girl.

'What's your name?' she demanded. 'I told you mine. But you never said what yours was. If you even have a name, that is.'

'Of course I have a name, it's Margaret.' The other girl stood up, watching her with a new caution that made Eva feel even stronger. 'They used to call me Maggie.'

'Maggie?' Eva laughed at how close she'd got to guessing it. 'Maggie the magpie girl.'

'I always did like shiny things,' the ghost girl said with a shrug and glanced down at her own black and white costume. 'Not that I got a chance to have any. Call me Magpie if you want—I've been called worse.'

'Me too,' Eva admitted. She hesitated. 'Can we have a truce? You're right about me. I'm not much of a ghost. I didn't even know I *was* a ghost until yesterday. Not until the Witch told me I was.'

'I wasn't sure either,' Maggie admitted. 'I suspected you, but I didn't know for certain. You don't act like one of us.'

'How should I act then?' Eva asked. 'I don't understand how I can have died and still be here.'

'None of us do,' Maggie said sharply. 'Ghost is just a word. It doesn't explain anything.'

'That's true,' Eva admitted. 'But you must know something about it. How did you disappear yesterday? And you went through the dining room door as if it didn't exist—how did you do that?'

'I've picked up a few tricks,' Maggie said, with a shifty sideways look. 'Why should I tell you all my secrets? You might need help but I don't.'

'I thought we had a truce,' Eva said and Maggie laughed.

'Maybe we do—for now. But that doesn't mean I'm going to help you, just that I'm not going to use what I know against you. I had to learn this myself. And before you start whinging about how hard your life is again, try being trapped for almost a hundred years as a servant in a house full of family ghosts.'

'I don't think the family ghosts are going to be much kinder to me,' Eva said, trying not to sound as though she was whining. 'I'm the cuckoo child. No one knows who my father is. To most of the family I don't belong.'

'All the same you'll have to help yourself,' Maggie said. 'I'm not a nursemaid and I have my own concerns.'

'Your own concerns?' Eva frowned. 'What do you mean?' She tried to think of a polite way to ask what personal business a ghost could possibly have. 'Maybe if you tell me about them I could help you.'

'Help me? That's a laugh,' Maggie said. 'You're the last person I'd pick to help me. But I'll tell you for free that every ghost wants something. Why do you think we're stuck here instead of going to heaven—or hell? Because every one of us wants to change things.'

'Change things?' Eva frowned. 'But you can't change what's happened. The past is history.'

'History is what people think happened,' Maggie said sharply. 'It's not the truth. Why don't you think for yourself? You're supposed to be clever, aren't you? I've seen you in the library, always with your nose in a book. This is your House and your problem, so work it out yourself.'

Deliberately turning her back on Eva, she walked away. Her magpie figure walked quickly around the curve of the pathway, vanishing behind the vast swellings of the rhododendrons. Eva watched her go and didn't call after her. Maggie was right. She had to stand on her own two feet—or whatever ghosts had to stand on.

* * *

Eva entered the House through the front door. The door knob turned easily in her hand and the door swung open, giving her pause for thought as she trailed her fingertips over the smooth brass of the fittings and the rougher wood of the door itself.

Her body seemed just as solid as ever as she crossed the hall, solid enough for her to feel shabby and dirty in the tatters of her best dress. And that was another mystery. She'd changed her clothes yesterday—how could a ghost manage something like that. Jumping the bottom stairs and heading up the main staircase, Eva decided to begin her quest for the truth in the Crimson Room. One thing she was going to start doing differently, she thought, trailing a hand up the banister and feeling the wood polished smooth by the hands of a hundred ancestors. Today she wasn't going to slink about in the shadows. She was done with hiding; now she wanted to know who could see her.

But she passed no one on the stairs and reached the door of the Crimson Room unaccosted. Confronted by the closed door she pressed against it lightly, trying to summon whatever it was that allowed her to move straight through. But the power wasn't there and she turned the handle instead and entered—to be greeted by the scene of a massacre.

Peacock feathers were scattered across the carpet, bedraggled and bloodied, their golden green and blue shimmers daubed with clotting crimson. In the centre of the carnage a golden brown cat was crouched on the four-poster bed, tearing at the carcass of a full-grown peacock. The cat was Rameses, Aunt Cora's Abyssinian, and he hissed at her as she entered and then growled, ears flattening back in warning.

'This is my room,' Eva told the cat flatly. 'Get lost.'

To her surprise Rameses skeltered out of the room, tail bushing up like a flag behind him. Eva watched him go and then automatically shut the door before turning to the bloodied heap of feathers with a sigh. It took her a moment to remember the mess was not her biggest problem right now.

Instead she began to search the room, treating it as the crime scene it looked like. If only she'd kept a diary this would be so much easier but she'd never felt the urge. In the window seat were homework books and a revision timetable, Eva flipped through them vaguely. She'd been absent from school a lot this year; since Grandfather's heart attack it just hadn't seemed very important; now she wasn't sure when she'd last actually been to class. There seemed to be an empty space in her memories because she couldn't recall anything unusual happening—let alone *dying*.

The trouble was that days and weeks could pass in the House without anything particularly changing. Kyra had said Eva had vanished two weeks ago and Eva had no choice but to accept that but she had no recollection of the event or of anything else out of the ordinary. Could whatever had happened have been so traumatic she'd wiped it from her mind?

Opening the wardrobe she looked again at the clothes inside. Her hopeless clothes all looked much as she'd remembered them and she tried to think if all of them were here. Aside from the crumpled clothes she'd changed out of yesterday nothing seemed

76

to be missing and she looked around the room and under the bed to see what had become of them. There were plenty of peacock feathers but no sign of the clothes she remembered wearing. Had she just imagined them, then? Was she just imagining the tattered remnants of her red velvet dress, as well? Feeling tired, Eva looked at her reflection in the mirror and frowned. How come she could see herself, looking even more muddy and bedraggled than she'd imagined? Nothing about being a ghost made any sense.

Closing the wardrobe again she searched the rest of the room but there were no clues. No scrawled suicide note, no betraying bottle of pills, nothing to suggest that anyone or anything had met their death here. Other than the peacock, that was.

The dead peacock was hard to ignore. The rusty smell of blood seemed to be growing stronger, as if it was seeping out of the curtains and carpet, the crimson walls closing in around her. The smell wasn't just blood. There was earth and river water mixed in with it and a musty damp undertone that made her think of locked rooms. Eva took a step back as the smell intensified, filling her mouth and nostrils and making her gag. She tasted bile in her mouth and staggered backwards, throwing her hands up before her to ward off the reek.

Darkness closed off her view like a curtain—and was replaced by the pale walls of the corridor and the shut door of her room. Her hands were still held out before her and on each pale wrist there were angry red welts.

Eva stared at the door and her own hands, rubbing at the swollen flesh. She'd been on the edge of panic and now her unexpected escape left her baffled instead. She let her hands fall and stepped away from the door. Whatever had happened it wasn't an experience she was eager to repeat. She wasn't aiming to discover ghostly powers, she was trying to find out how she'd died and not even noticed.

* * *

Exploring the House like a tourist, Eva went into each of the bedrooms in turn. The signs of the aunts' occupancy were scattered around. Aunt Cora's knitting and her crossword puzzles, Aunt Helen's reading glasses and a copy of *Horse and Hound*, Aunt Joyce's pharmacy of rejuvenating creams, make-up, and medicines. But there was no sign of the aunts themselves. The family seemed to have vanished.

Returning to the ground floor Eva looked for them in the dining room, where the smell of burnt toast and ground coffee and the debris of cups and plates showed her they'd breakfasted together. In the drawing room there was the smell of stale smoke and a pile of handwritten papers littering a coffee table. A plant pot had been pressed into service as an ashtray and held a small mountain of cigarette butts and the end of a cigar. Eva paused to leaf through the papers, trying to decipher them. Outside, car tyres crunched on the gravel but she ignored the noise, immersed in the scribbled notes. The phrases *business plan* and *revenue stream* appeared early on and the rest seemed to be calculations of income and tax deductions.

Yesterday she'd thought of the ghost walks as a dangerous idiocy but she'd been mostly concerned about the effect on herself and her grandfather in stirring up the ghosts. Now she was on the other side of the line—one of the ghosts who would be disturbed—and she didn't know what to think about that.

Grandfather. Eva suddenly felt anxious about him. Normally she'd be with him first thing in the morning to bring him his tea and try and persuade him to eat a few mouthfuls of food. Who had looked after him this morning? Come to think of it, who had been looking after him since Eva died? Looking back, the long days of Grandfather's illness seemed blurred, making it impossible to recall individual moments. Worrying about Grandfather had formed the pattern of her days, but at some point the pattern had been broken and Eva didn't know when. She couldn't remember the last time she'd had a proper conversation with Grandfather, or when he'd even simply looked at her, or acknowledged her in any way. She couldn't pin down her last living moment, or even day or week.

There were voices in the library. As Eva hurried in their direction she realized they sounded unnaturally fraught, people complaining and blaming each other, accusations coming thick and fast.

'. . . all your fault, Helen.' That was Aunt Joyce's voice. 'The food last night was far too rich.'

'It wouldn't be if Father hadn't been half-starving himself,' Aunt Helen snapped back. 'There wasn't a scrap of food in the House when we arrived.'

'I tried to tell you how difficult things have been.' Cora's voice lifted pathetically to join in the woe. 'I told you he was worried about Eva. That he hasn't been the same since she disappeared.'

Eva's heart turned to ice. They were talking as if . . . as if Grandfather was dead. Could he have died in the night while Eva was wandering around like a zombie? Could she have missed her last chance to say goodbye? She edged up to the doorway and looked in. The silent sanctum of the library was full of people. The aunts and hangers on were scattered around the room and Felix sat on the arm of a chair, smoking a cigarette and letting the ash drop on the carpet.

On the other side of the library were two strangers wearing

green jackets with the word PARAMEDIC written across the back in yellow fluorescent capital letters. They were rolling a stretcher out of Grandfather's study.

The thin body was shrouded with a thick hospital blanket; a third paramedic moved out behind the stretcher, carrying a medical drip. It took Eva three long heart-freezing seconds to take in the whole scene and then she sagged with relief. Grandfather couldn't be dead if he was on a drip. But then what was wrong with him?

As the whole group moved towards her Eva remained frozen in place. The paramedics pushed the stretcher onwards and the aunts parted like the Red Sea. Only Felix held his ground, ignoring the glare one of the paramedics gave his cigarette.

'I'll want to speak to his doctor,' he said crisply. 'And if I'm not satisfied I intend to call in a specialist from Harley Street.'

'You'll have to call the hospital direct, sir,' the paramedic replied briskly. 'And provide proof of power of attorney for any details of Mr Chance's care.'

'Sir Edward,' Helen objected. 'My father has a title.'

'Yes, ma'am, if you'll excuse us, sir.' The paramedics were having none of the family's airs and graces and Eva was grateful to them. As the stretcher reached her side she fell in beside it, staring down at her grandfather's face. It was grey, the skin papery and the mouth fallen and slumped. But his eyes were open, staring dimly and uncomprehendingly at the ceiling.

'*Grandfather.*' Eva reached under the blanket, feeling for his hand and coiling her own fingers around it tightly. '*Grandfather, it's Eva.*'

Was it her imagination or had his fingers twitched in hers? Eva was moving with the paramedics, the warmth of their bodies around her, the stretcher running heavily over the corridor carpet and then more smoothly when it reached the hall. Everything seemed distant except for her grandfather's hand in hers and his eyes focusing gradually on her face.

'Eva . . . '

'Did he say something?' Someone leaned over, blocking Eva's view and she ground her teeth in anger.

'Did he? Keep listening. Something about this set-up is shifty.' The paramedic lowered his voice as the stretcher was lifted down the front stairs and across the gravel towards a waiting ambulance. 'That woman who called us in said her father had fainted and he's got a bump like a goose-egg on the back of his head right enough. But something about the way he was lying didn't look right to me. More like someone had bashed him over the head.'

The words were just noise to Eva; she was trying to meet her grandfather's eyes again. Hadn't he just said her name?

'Evangeline . . . ' Grey eyes flared with recognition. 'Is that you?'

'Yes, it's me! Grandfather!' Eva lost hold as the stretcher was pushed up into the back of the ambulance, wheels folding away automatically. She scrambled to get in and metal doors clanged shut in her face. The ambulance started up and panic swirled through her mind. This time she wouldn't be left behind.

Throwing herself forward she passed through the metal shell of the ambulance; the air thickened for an instant as the shadow of the metal walls passed through her and she found herself standing in the crowded interior. Grandfather was struggling weakly as an oxygen mask was pressed over his face and Eva felt the paramedics flinch with cold as she pushed past them. She clung to the stretcher as the ambulance began to move, rumbling along the long drive, the House vanishing behind them and the avenue of trees filling in on either side.

'Grandfather, what happened? Did someone hurt you?' she asked, looking at the bloody scalp wound at the back of his head. But her grandfather wasn't thinking about himself or his own injury.

'Eva,' he whispered, so she had to crane to hear him. 'What happened to you? Why didn't you come home?'

The front gate, rusted open, passed behind the ambulance as it crossed the boundary of the grounds and then the darkened interior was replaced by watery sunlight and Eva was standing in the gateway as the word AMBULANCE receded away from her, on the other side of a barrier of thickened air. Gasping for breath she tried to follow it but the boundary resisted with a spongy pliancy. She was not being permitted to leave.

'I hate this!' she yelled, picking up a handful of stones from the drive and throwing them on to the road. They bounced and scattered, unaffected by the force which held her back.

'Why?' she raged at the closed gates. 'Why am I stuck here? I was stuck here when I was alive and now I'm dead I'm trapped here for ever! It's not fair. I don't know how to be a ghost! I didn't even know I was dead.'

She wished she'd tried to show herself to Grandfather yesterday evening instead of pleading with Kyra Stratton to see her. She'd been too panicked to think straight and to remember that Grandfather actually believed in the ghosts. He'd seen her just now. That made two people so far. Grandfather and Felix: a person who loved her and one who despised her. And no one else had seen her at all, not Kyra or the other waiters, not her family, not the paramedics—except the ghosts themselves.

A breeze ruffled the long grass and Eva felt as powerless as a breath of wind. As a ghost she seemed to skim under the surface of the world, barely touching, unable to break through to reality.

Was this going to be the rest of her existence, haunting the House for ever?

Eva turned her back on the road and walked up the driveway towards the House. 'I'm going to fix this,' she promised herself. 'Somehow, I'll find a way. I'm going to find out how I died and if someone killed me I'll pay them back for it. I'm going to haunt my family and everyone else until I've found out the truth.'

She tried to ignore the voice in the back of her head; the influence of the Witch or just her own thoughts.

And then what? Even if you find out what happened, you'll still be just as dead.

6
Corpus Delicti

Saturday, April 5th

Kyra Stratton had been looking for part-time work for months and found almost nothing. All the jobs in shops had been claimed by girls a year older than her; school-leavers who warned her that they were being underpaid. The only work she'd found was the silver service job for Tony's catering firm and she'd had second thoughts about that when it turned out to be at the big creepy house that belonged to the Chance family.

Kyra needed money. Not just for clothes and going out, but serious cash. For the last couple of years she'd been saving every penny she could in expectation of the day she'd be able to leave home and start her real career. Kyra was good with money, everyone said so. She'd been helping with her father's accounts for years. But what she hadn't admitted to anyone was that she was saving for the time when she'd be able to rent a flat and apply to the big London firms, getting her foot on the first rung of the ladder that would end with her as an investment banker. Other girls might dream of being popstars or fashion models. Kyra dreamed of cold hard cash.

The last thing Kyra wanted to do was work for the Chances.

Eva Chance's disappearance made her feel uncomfortable. But it had been the only work going and she'd taken the job. Now, four days later, she was back at the House again. At the rusted iron gates she looked down the avenue of dark trees that marked the driveway and wondered if this was a good idea.

'This is a terrible plan.' Like the sound of her own conscience her brother's voice sounded behind her.

'You don't have to come with me,' Kyra told him, just as she'd told him twice already that morning. 'Seriously, Kyle, I can handle myself.'

'So you keep saying,' Kyle told her, furrowing his brow in true Neanderthal style.

'And it's true,' Kyra shot back, tired of Kyle's completely unreconstructed attitude. 'Look, you can get work with Dad any time you like but he won't let me work on the building sites. Right now this place has the only temp work going.'

'I know all that,' Kyle sighed. 'I still don't like it though.'

'Then go home.' Kyra turned her back on her brother and began walking up the driveway. After only a few metres he came jogging up behind her.

'I can't,' he said. 'I promised Mum I'd keep an eye on you.'

'You promised Mum you'd walk me home from the club last week and you went off and got wasted with your moron mates,' Kyra pointed out. 'You promised Mum you'd revise for the GCSEs and I've yet to see you crack a book open.'

'Yeah, yeah, quit nagging.' Kyle glared at her. 'That's different, all right? This place is . . . ' He shrugged his shoulders. 'It's different.'

'Is this about Damon's ghost story?' Kyra said. 'That thing is played out. Last time he told it he had the two of you facing down some sort of hellbeast with holy water.'

'Damon's an idiot,' Kyle said. 'We didn't see anything. But we did hear something, something weird.' He shook his head. 'Look, you wouldn't walk across the common late at night would you?'

'Too right, I'd run,' Kyra said. 'OK, so what?'

'That's how I feel about this place,' Kyle admitted. 'It messes with my head. The common—that doesn't bother me. This place? I wouldn't want to be here again at night.'

Kyra stopped arguing. For one thing they were almost at the House and its squat bulk dominated the view ahead. For another she was surprised at what Kyle had finally confessed. It wasn't often you heard a bloke admit to being afraid.

Squinting sideways at her brother she thought about how weird it was to have a twin brother. It was like looking at what you might have been like if you were a boy. Kyle was six foot three and muscled with it, a sporty, joking, even-humoured guy whose main interests were beer, football, and console games with his loutish mates. His sandy blond hair was an uncombed mess, his shoulders and neck were burnt red from a day spent shirtless when the sun had suddenly appeared last week. His T-shirt had a ripped collar, his jeans were broken down and even his trainers were torn.

Kyra sometimes wondered how twins could be so unalike. Everything about Kyle was so completely the opposite of her. He was easy going and laid back to the point of horizontality. The shambling lads who slouched up to the house to visit him seemed equally unbothered about everything from homework to personal hygiene.

But although Kyle's loutish loafing world was light years away from her group of groomed gossip girls, she liked having a window into it. Girls who didn't have brothers found boys endlessly fascinating. Kyra had grown up with one and didn't feel quite the same awe.

* * *

Outside the House a group of gardeners with hedge-clippers were working their way along a slowly appearing path through a thicket of bushes with dark waxy leaves. The front door was open and as Kyra approached she could see a notice board had been put up in the main hall. With Kyle following reluctantly she walked up the front steps and into the house.

There was a table to the left of the notice board and a woman wearing a black business suit sat behind it, typing on a sleek black laptop.

'Hi, I'm Kyra Stratton,' Kyra said, approaching the woman. 'I spoke to Mrs Langley on the phone about a part-time job?'

'Ms Langley,' the woman corrected her sharply, in a way that meant she could only be the owner of the name. She rattled the keys of her computer briefly. 'You'll start today on the cleaning rota. If things work out there will be work available on some of the weekends and bank holidays through the spring and summer months. We'll need people who can get the house ready for visitors in advance of each open day and serve tea to the tourists, work in the gift shop and turn their hand to any other work during the open days.'

'I've got exams next month,' Kyra said. 'So I might not be able to work every day at first but after that I'm free and I've got experience on cash registers and as a waiter. I did silver service up here last week with Tony's catering.'

'Very well.' Ms Langley handed her a photocopied form. 'Put your details down on this form including the days you're available to work and hand it in at the end of the day. You'll be paid in cash and you'll need to take responsibility for declaring it.' She looked as if she doubted Kyra would declare it. 'Maps of the house are on the notice board to your right and a register. Make sure to sign in every day so we know who's in the house. Once you've done that please find Miss Cora Chance in the Long Gallery.'

Kyra headed to the right, looking at the notice board while Ms Langley repeated a similar screed of information to Kyle. Not only was it plastered with maps of each floor of the house and different parts of the gardens, there were job lists and work rotas and notes about damage and building work pinned here and there all over the board. The register was on the far side with a felt tip pen hanging from a piece of string and Kyra printed her name carefully before looking to see who else had signed in. Some of her posse had said they might come today but she didn't see any of them listed. Kyle moved up next to her, also holding a photocopied form. Unlike Kyra he hadn't called in advance but it didn't seem to have mattered.

'I've got lifting and carrying, reporting to someone called Mr Fairfax in the Folly,' he said. 'What about you?'

'Cleaning with Miss Cora Chance.' Kyra wrinkled her nose and added in a mutter: 'If the rest of the house is anything like the kitchens it'll be a big job.'

'Sounds like we'll be in different parts of the house.' Her brother scribbled his name on the form. 'Text me every hour, OK?'

'You're turning into a worse nag than Mum.' Kyra rolled her eyes. 'All right if it makes you happy.'

A breeze fluttered the papers on the board and Kyle shivered.

'Brrr,' he said. 'It's colder inside than outside. OK, I'm off to find this Fairfax bloke. Don't forget to text.' He jogged back out through the front door and Kyra turned back to the board, looking for the Long Gallery on the maps. It turned out to be on the first floor and she stepped back from the board and paused.

Something half glimpsed had snagged at her mind and she turned back to the board, to where the register was pinned, the pen lightly swinging on its string in a gust of cold air. No one had come in behind her. Ms Langley was still jabbering away on her phone, now talking about a discount on packing cases. Kyra stared at the list of names, reading the last three over again:

Kyra Stratton

Kyle Stratton

EVA CHANCE

Kyra had always thought it was just an expression about the hair on the back of your neck rising, but standing there in the hall she felt her skin crawling and the hair lifting all by itself. She'd seen that handwriting before: on exercise books and homework assignments, the handwriting of the girl everyone thought was dead.

* * *

When Kyle left his sister in the house he went to find the gardeners who were still hacking at the bushes on the side of the drive.

'All right?' he said, grinning at them. 'Which way to the Folly?'

'Good luck, son,' one of the gardeners said. 'It's on the other side of this lot. Got your machete, have you?'

There was a bitter edge to the laughter as they all regarded the thicket of green leaves ahead and the vague trail of a gravel path somewhere underneath it. The gardeners were wearing work boots and thick gauntlet-type gloves but their clothes were mucky and their expressions were strained.

'Seriously,' one of the older men said, 'you want to watch out for this. It's not how overgrown it is, it's how these bushes take you by surprise.' He showed Kyle a scratch across the side of his face, a millimetre away from his right eye. 'Got that from a holly tree,' he said. 'Branch came out of nowhere and whipped me across the face.' He gestured with his chin at another man, whose right arm was wrapped up in a bloodied bandage. 'Sid got that from a saw that snapped right in half and came flying at him. We're still thanking our stars he wasn't using the chainsaw. You see what I mean?'

'Go carefully,' one of the others added. 'Go slowly, don't disturb anything, don't step on anything and don't mess with anything.'

'OK then.' Kyle was feeling a bit creeped out by their intensity and by the tunnel of darkly glossy leaves that lay ahead. Still, his dad had brought him up to respect what the crew on the job had to say. Whatever the bosses thought, the ground crew were the ones who knew the ins and outs of a site.

Progress through the shrubbery was slow. Kyle couldn't tell one shrub from another but it hardly seemed to matter as the plants themselves weren't exactly separate, they jostled for space across flowerbeds and broke out across paths so that he felt as if he was exploring a jungle and wished he really did have a machete.

Instead he had to settle for pushing stray branches out of the way and peering to discover where the path was going under the bushes. He was almost certain he'd got turned around and was about to give up and go back when he turned a corner and saw a dark tower raised up on a grassy hummock of land. Kyle stared up at it doubtfully.

The tower was round, with three rows of pointy windows

and a roof like a Witch's hat. The walls looked as if they'd been built out of iron, as unlikely as that seemed. Grotesques clustered around the sides of the windows and clung to the lip of the roof, twisted dwarvish figures with cross-eyes and open hooting mouths. The entrance was a metal fretwork door. The whole tower looked as if it had been imported from Gotham city.

Kyle approached it cautiously. The hummock of land was steeper than it had first appeared, just steep enough to make climbing difficult, and by the time he reached the door he was out of breath. It was open, and he shaded his eyes to peer into the dim interior.

'Hello? Mr Fairfax?' There was no reply and he headed inside.

Whatever light made it through the stained-glass windows was filtered through a heavy coating of dust so that the inside of the building was barely visible. He was in a round room with a jumble of wrought-iron chairs piled haphazardly around and a staircase winding up the wall to a higher floor. There was a noise from above and Kyle looked up quickly to see a vast black shadow thrown across the wall as the sound of footsteps began to descend.

'Who's there?' he demanded while, unbidden, his hands took a firm grip on the back of one of the chairs.

'Felix,' a smooth voice answered as a figure appeared on the staircase. 'Felix Fairfax. And who are you? You look familiar.'

Kyle released his grip on the chair. It was the rich kid from the dinner party, the one who'd complained about the wine, the one who owned the red Jaguar in the stables.

'My name's Kyle,' he said. 'The woman in the house told me Mr Fairfax would tell me what work needed doing. That's you, is it?'

'I just said so,' the boy replied crisply, looking Kyle over as

91

though he were a dog or a car he was thinking of buying. 'And what sort of work can you do, Kyle?'

It was irritating being expected to call this prat 'Mister' and Kyle bristled under the cool assessing stare, noting to himself that he would be the taller if they were standing on level ground. The other boy had obviously noticed the same thing since he hadn't come down the last few steps.

'Whatever's needed,' Kyle said squaring his shoulders. 'I've been working for my dad's building firm since I was fourteen. I bench at three hundred if that's what you want to know.' A slight exaggeration, that, but this bloke wouldn't know it.

'Fine.' Felix Fairfax smiled, making it look like an odd and unfriendly expression. 'I have just the job for you, Kyle. You're going to help me find a body.'

Kyle couldn't help laughing, even though it wasn't really funny. But Felix's smile faded and he looked irritated instead.

'I'm quite serious,' he said. 'But if you're not up to the job I'll find someone who is.'

'A body?' Kyle repeated the word. 'You want me to move a body?'

'*Find* a body.' Felix stressed the first word. 'That's right. No one else has been able to find it but it's here somewhere and I don't want the tourists tripping over it. You don't look like the type to be fazed by a dead body.'

Kyle wasn't about to deny that, even though he had a sick feeling in the pit of his stomach. This idiot didn't look as if he was joking.

'Whose body is it?' he asked, although he suspected he already knew.

'A girl's,' Felix said. 'My cousin, if you must know. She was always a weird one, and now it seems she's finally done herself

92

in—just like her mother. Fifteen years old, brown hair, brown eyes, under five foot and skinny. She went missing in the middle of March and I'm sure the body's somewhere in the house or the grounds.'

'Isn't that a job for the police?' Kyle objected and Felix rolled his eyes.

'Naturally,' he said. 'And they claim to have searched but I can't believe they've looked everywhere. They won't be convinced she's dead until we find the body.'

'So you're going to play detective.' Kyle shook his head. 'Look, mate, I signed on for some lifting and carrying, not playing Robin to your Batman.' He glanced around the gothic tower pointedly. 'A fiver an hour isn't enough for me to start hunting corpses for you.' He listened to his own voice, firm and untroubled, pleased he had managed to find an excuse that allowed him to save face.

'So make it fifty.' Felix reached into a pocket of his wool coat and pulled out a wallet, fat with cash. Opening it, he removed a wad of orange-pink notes and peeled off the top six. 'That's three hundred pounds,' he said, fanning the notes out in front of Kyle. 'For six hours' work. Does that make the job more worth your while?'

Only ten minutes ago Kyle had thought of his sister as the cash-obsessed one of them. Money always seemed to dribble through his fingers so that the effort of earning it hardly seemed worth it when he knew it'd all go on rounds at the pub, curry or kebabs. But three hundred quid just for looking about the place suddenly seemed like a good deal, especially when Felix was hardly going to know how hard he was looking.

'I suppose I could have a look,' he said, one hand already reaching out for the money.

Felix counted the notes into his hand and Kyle wondered for

a second if they were real. No one accepted fifties. He'd have to check with Kyra, she was the financial genius in the family. She even kept Dad's books for him since getting her Maths GCSE two years early.

'I want you to start in the House,' Felix said. 'In the Crimson Room, that's a red room with . . . '

'I know what colour crimson is,' Kyle cut him off. 'I'm not thick.'

'If you say so.' Felix smiled again. 'I'll let you find it yourself then, but I want you to look everywhere. There are plenty of ways for me to keep an eye on you so don't think you can just take the money and loaf about.'

'You really are up yourself, aren't you?' Goaded beyond reason, Kyle glared back at the teenage poser in his expensive coat and designer suit. 'I'll do your job for you but don't expect me to lick your boots while I'm at it, *Mister* Fairfax. Or maybe I'll spread the word about how you spend your pocket money.'

The look of alarm on the other boy's face was satisfying and Kyle grinned, raising his hand in an ironic salute before strolling back out of the iron tower. He'd guessed right that no one knew about Felix's plans to play boy detective but as he left the grin faded from his face. If Felix was dodgy for paying someone to do this job—how much more dodgy was it that Kyle had accepted? What kind of idiot took a job looking for corpses?

* * *

Kyra eventually found her way to the Long Gallery, each step helping to bury the memory of Eva's name appearing on the register. She told herself that there would be a perfectly logical explanation for that—she just hadn't worked out what it was yet.

Miss Cora Chance turned out to be an old lady with white

hair, wearing two pairs of glasses, one on top of her hair and another pair around her neck. She was a flustered and fluffy sort of old lady who explained everything three times over and it was a relief when she ushered Kyra to her assigned job and finally left her to it—but not without a muddle of last minute instructions.

'You will make sure to use only the *soft* cloth and a *very little* soapy water on the walls, won't you? And you won't go into any rooms *other* than the ones I showed you? Because my family do rather *cherish* their *privacy.*'

'Right you are,' Kyra said, pretending to enthusiasm to try and get the old bat to go away. 'I'll get the walls sparkling clean, don't you worry.'

Miss Cora looked the opposite of reassured and Kyra waited for the whole rigmarole to begin again with the importance of being careful but just then a horsey looking woman, also in tweeds, appeared at the end of the corridor.

'There you are, Cora,' she said. 'Do you realize there's a Sargent missing from the Gallery. And at least two Constables. I want you to help me look for them. I suppose they could be in storage or being cleaned but that fool of a house agent doesn't seem to know anything about it.'

'Sounds as if she's lost half the police force,' Kyra muttered as Miss Cora hurried off, twittering with possible explanations. From what Kyra could make out it was paintings, not policemen, the horsey woman had lost but the association with the police made her feel edgy.

The police had come to school a couple of weeks ago and spoken to the whole of year eleven about the seriousness of bullying and the importance of letting an adult know if you were unhappy. Kyra had fiddled with a hangnail and tried not to listen. Eva Chance had been described as 'missing' at the assembly that morning but rumours were already circulating that it was 'missing, presumed dead'. Kyra had wondered if someone had found a note claiming Eva had been bullied but as the police constables spoke their piece she had relaxed slightly. They didn't really know anything—only suspected.

Eva hadn't been bullied anyway, not really; there had just been some joking around. And Eva had brought it on herself by always being so weird. At show and tell when they were aged nine she'd brought in a butterfly in a jar. Kyra remembered the rest of the class clutching their Barbies and hand-held games, wide-eyed as Eva demonstrated how butterflies could be killed with a drop of camphor. Even the teacher had been revolted and Eva hadn't seemed to see what was weird about it. 'It's only a cabbage white,' Kyra remembered her saying, as if it made a difference what sort of butterfly you poisoned.

Besides, Eva was always showing off, speaking French in an exaggerated Frenchy accent that sent everyone into whoops or talking about the personal life of Queen Victoria as if she'd been there at the time. More than that, Eva would admit to things publicly that Kyra wouldn't have told her best friend as a deathly secret: like the fact that she had a chamber-pot under her bed and used it when the plumbing wasn't working or that she didn't have a swimming costume because she always swam naked in her own private lake. Sometimes it seemed as if you couldn't get through a day without Eva saying or doing something ridiculous and everyone falling about with laughter. It wasn't a hanging offence to laugh; if it were the whole class would be guilty. So sometimes Kyra and her posse led Eva along a bit, asked questions so she'd say something daft. What was wrong with joking around a bit on a crappy day when you needed a giggle?

It felt weird to be cleaning Eva's house and Kyra wasn't sure if it made it better or worse that the place was so filthy. She was still trying not to think about how Eva's name had appeared on the register. She had enough experience of practical jokes to guess at how that had been done—if only it hadn't happened right in front of her face.

Taking out her phone from her pocket to check the time she was surprised it had been an hour already since she'd arrived and she shifted to the text message function before realizing the phone had no signal. Too many thick stone walls between her and Kyle.

Kyra's wallpaper wiping had already turned the cloth grey and the soapy water was flat and brown in the bucket. Heaving it along to the nearest bathroom she sluiced the water down an antique sink and turned on the taps to refill the bucket; a thin trickle of water came out and she yawned. At this rate she'd be waiting for ages.

Leaning against the door she glanced up and down the hall to see if anyone was about before lighting a cigarette. She had the packet in her hand when a familiar figure slouched around the corner of the corridor.

'Kyra.' Her brother looked first surprised and then annoyed. 'You never texted me.'

'Chill, bro.' Kyra shook her head. 'There's no signal in here, all right? And I'm OK. Except for being bored.'

Kyle didn't look so good himself. He was shifting about instead of standing still, fidgeting with the collar of his T-shirt, rubbing the back of his neck. It was the same look he got when he lied to Mum about where he'd been or how much he'd been drinking. Like Mum, Kyra wasn't fooled by it.

'What've you been doing then?' she asked. 'While I've been slaving away like a skivvy up here.'

'Looking for a red room,' Kyle said, still fidgeting. 'This bloke told me to go and look for something in it and now I can't find the sodding room.'

'There's about a hundred rooms in this place.' Kyra rolled her eyes. 'Did you check the map in the front hall?'

'Course.' Kyle looked defensive and Kyra sighed. That probably meant he'd looked at it for about five seconds and then decided he could find the place without any trouble. 'Come on, I'll help you look for it,' she said. 'I could do with a break anyway.'

On the way down the stairs they passed a girl Kyra didn't recognize, carrying a heavy coal scuttle. She gave them a sharp look, dark eyes boring into them as they passed by. Kyra shrugged, not particularly caring what the stranger's issue was, and led the way back to the map.

The hall was empty. Ms Langley had taken her laptop away and only the table and the notice board remained. There wasn't any red room marked on the map but after a couple of minutes Kyra found a space marked Crimson Room and Kyle said that would be it.

Heading back up the stairs again they continued up to the first floor where they found themselves in a corridor of closed doors.

'My supervisor's one of the family,' Kyra warned, signalling Kyle to speak quietly. 'And she said that a lot of people are staying in the house. This looks like where they're living, since all the other rooms have their doors left open.'

'How will we find the right room then?' Kyle looked frustrated and Kyra rolled her eyes.

'It was the fifth door on the right-hand side,' she said. 'Overlooking the front of the house.' She stopped by the correct door and gestured at it. 'This one,' she said.

Kyle hesitated and then knocked very quietly on the door. There was no reply and with a glance at her he turned the handle and opened it. The room was dark and as the door opened an unpleasant smell wafted out into the corridor: a putrid rotting smell spilling out of the room beyond.

Kyle's eyes widened and he took a couple of steps inside, looking around. Kyra saw him pause and then raise a hand to his mouth, making a gagging sound as if he was about to be sick. Following him in and covering her own mouth against the stench, she looked over his shoulder and glimpsed a dark mass of rotting flesh before Kyle dropped to his knees and was lavishly sick all over the floor, adding fresh vomit to the layers of stench.

Kyra went to the window and pushed the curtains open, fumbling at the unfamiliar catch and finally forcing the lower half of the window to slide upwards, letting a pale light and a gust of cold air into the room.

Turning back to the bed with its gory burden she grimaced. The rotting flesh was crawling with maggots and the bedspread was stiff and shiny with dried blood. Kyle wiped his mouth and looked up, his face greenish with nausea.

'Who is it?' he asked.

'What do you mean?' Kyra frowned. 'It's a dead bird. One of those peacocks that makes all the noise outside.'

'What?' Kyle wiped his mouth with the back of his hand and stood up, looking down at the body. 'Oh God,' he said. 'I really thought we'd found it.'

'Found what?' Kyra couldn't understand what he was getting at. 'What are you on about?'

'Eva Chance,' he said. 'The girl who died. I thought we'd found her body. That's what I was looking for. That's what Felix told me to find.'

***

The four-poster bed had long red velvet hangings and Kyra drew them shut to hide the decomposing body of the peacock while Kyle sat on the window seat and recounted what had happened to him since arriving at the House.

As she listened she drew her own conclusions. She remembered Felix from the dinner party as an attractive charismatic teenager who acted more like an adult, announcing his decisions to the rest of the family in a lordly way. Kyra wouldn't have got away with talking to her parents or her aunties or her grandad like that but she wasn't posh like the Chances. Felix seemed to have been just as bossy with Kyle, ordering him to do something that was dodgy at best.

Kyle hesitated for a bit before admitting that Felix had paid him and taking six folded notes out of his pocket: three hundred quid in fifties. Seeing that much money Kyra could understand why her brother had taken the job but she also revised her estimate of Felix's dodginess upwards. People who offered you large sums of cash up front to do extra work you weren't supposed to admit to made bad employers.

Felix had plainly done a number on Kyle and she wondered if the best way out of it was for Kyle to give the money back and turn the job down. The only problem with that was that if Felix was annoyed enough he could probably have them both fired. Even so, Kyra wouldn't have let that put her off, but the whole situation was weird.

'So Felix sent you to find this body and he told you to look here,' she repeated. 'Do you think he knew about *that*?' She gestured towards the bed.

'I don't know.' Kyle shook his head, still looking a bit green.

'You know, I wouldn't have chundered if I'd known it was just a bird. I honestly thought it was a person.'

'I'm not saying anything.' Kyra thought they had bigger issues than her brother's male ego. 'If it wasn't because of that why would he tell you to look here . . . ' She stood up suddenly and looked around the room, assessing it in a new light. Like all the other rooms she'd seen it was decorated in an old-fashioned way with nothing that looked as if it belonged to a person of today. But there was a big wardrobe and when she opened it she smiled. 'Thought so,' she said. 'Look, this must have been her room. See,' she held open the wardrobe door, 'school uniform—and about the most tragic outfits I've seen outside of a charity shop.'

Kyle got up to look and frowned.

'Looks more like an old person's clothes,' he said and Kyra nodded.

'See,' she said. 'Eva Chance was weird. It wasn't anything we did . . . ' She stopped in mid sentence. She didn't want to get into the whole question of whether Eva had been bullied. Kyle didn't seem to have noticed.

'Looks like the window seat opens too,' he said and lifted it up to reveal a litter of exercise books, folders and other school supplies. 'Kind of a mess,' he added. Kyra was about to ask him how he could judge when his own room was such a pit when he added: 'Like someone's already been looking through here. Everything's sort of stirred about.'

'Yeah.' Kyra looked down at the litter of books. 'Everything else in the room's neat as well. So was it Felix who went through this? Or someone else?'

'If we're not going to find anything, let's get out of here,' Kyle said. 'The smell's not getting any better.'

Opening the window had cleared the worst of it but somehow

closing the bed hanging had made the image of the rotting peacock seem to swell behind it. The room had an unpleasant atmosphere beyond the wafts of putrification and Kyra was willing to leave.

'I hope I'm not the one to get the job of clearing this lot up,' she started to say and then clapped a hand over her mouth to muffle a swearword. '*Fmpf*.'

'What?' Kyle looked alarmed.

'I left the water running!' she told him over her shoulder as she hurried back along the corridor. 'It looked as if it would take ages to fill—but it's probably overflowing by now.' She didn't find it difficult to retrace her footsteps around towards the Long Gallery, Kyle following more slowly behind her.

Kyra's head was full of visions of a flooded bathroom and a tide of water spilling out and washing across the carpet and down the hall. But when she turned around the bend in the corridor there was no sign of a flood. Instead an empty bucket stood against the wall, twenty metres along from the bathroom where Kyra had left it, and the whole stretch of wallpaper showed a bright trellis of colour in contrast to the dim grimy section beyond which was yet to be cleaned. While Kyra had been talking to Kyle, someone had come along and done her work for her.

She touched the wall. It was only very slightly damp and the wallpaper hadn't bubbled or lifted at all as it had slightly in the part she'd done herself. Whoever had cleaned the corridor knew what they were doing and she wondered if one of the people in charge had found the overflowing bucket and given the job to someone more competent.

Footsteps sounded further down the corridor and Ms Langley appeared. Kyra braced herself for a row but the woman didn't look angry with her. Instead she was looking at Kyle.

'You look strong,' she said, with a pleasant smile. 'Can you give me a hand moving some crates?'

'Um . . . sure.' Kyle let himself be led away, shrugging at Kyra.

'I can see you've been working hard,' Ms Langley added, noticing Kyra and nodding at the walls. 'Cora will be pleased.'

'Cheers,' Kyra said absently. As Ms Langley and her brother left she picked up the bucket and went back to the bathroom. On the old-fashioned sink, as she'd expected, the taps were no longer running. But there was a clue to who had turned them off. Next to each tap was a sooty black imprint, the smudged impression of two hands.

Kyra was kept busy for the rest of the day. She only saw Kyle a couple of times: once wheeling a packing case on a metal trolley, the second time from a distance outside in the gardens. When they finally met up again he explained he'd done some work for Ms Langley and then poked about trying to get the lie of the land. He didn't say outright that he was still working on Felix's task but he didn't deny it either. Kyra let the matter rest for the time being. She was still wondering who had covered for her by cleaning the corridor.

7
Footprints in the Snow

Sunday, April 6th

Eva hadn't slept for five days. At first, the corpse of the peacock had put her off returning to the Crimson Room and she hadn't felt tired enough to sleep.

She had set herself the mission of finding out what had happened to her, trailing the family around the House and listening to their conversations. No longer did she have to eavesdrop from behind doors or curtains, now she could stand in the middle of a room and not be noticed. The power that had enabled her to confront Felix in her room and speak to Grandfather in the ambulance seemed erratic at best. Now no one saw her, although occasionally they shivered or frowned when she came close enough. Her finest moment had been writing her name on the registration list in front of Kyra and watching her bully's face freeze with alarm. But if she'd expected Kyra to give anything away, she'd been disappointed. The blonde teenager didn't seem to know anything about Eva vanishing.

Despite her patient detective work, Eva was still no closer to the truth. She had been alert for any mention of her name but whenever the conversation seemed to come near the subject of her own disappearance it skirted the topic instead. Aunt Cora was weepy, Aunt Helen brisk, and Aunt Joyce distracted—and none of them gave anything away. The family seemed to believe that Eva had either run away or killed herself and although she'd never expected much of them, it hurt to realize how little they cared.

In the public rooms Lisle Langley strode about instructing an army of hired staff to clean and wash and beat carpets. All around the House seemed to be coming to life—but to a ghostly unreal life. Ghost world was never silent. The whines and whispers of sound that she'd ignored in her everyday life were louder and more significant here.

The atmosphere shifted from room to room as echoes of ghosts drifted in and out of consciousness, dropping whole floors and wings of the House in and out of time, changing rooms and furnishings as waves of history broke and fell. It was the pretence of the past that attracted the lesser ghosts, Eva decided, as she watched faded rooms glow with vanished glories.

Most of the ghosts didn't even seem to realize they were ghosts. They would appear only to walk down a corridor or sketch a few steps of a dance in the ballroom. They weren't like Maggie, with a sense of what they were or how they came to be, they were more like recordings: music playing in an empty room long after the musician had departed. These misty presences were only strong enough to occasionally squeak a door hinge open or rattle a window, but gathered together they formed a swirling current of prickling energy.

The ghosts with real power were rare. The leaden footsteps of the stalker climbing the stairs were heavy with menace and the lesser ghosts vanished away when the stalker was near. Eva didn't dare to confront the invisible force behind those footsteps.

Like the other ghosts, she fled from it—and then cursed herself for her cowardice.

And behind all the other ghosts was the controlling force of the Witch, the wellspring of the darkest and most powerful energies. The Witch didn't need to rattle windows or squeak hinges but when knives slipped and blood welled and headaches made people snappish—Eva heard mocking laughter in the back of her mind.

The House hummed with emotion. From the angry static of the family arguments to the eerie hauntings of the lesser ghosts, to the seething hate of the Witch in the cellars, influences churned up the atmosphere until the air was thick with the taste of it.

* * *

Sunday morning dawned brightly through the windows of the Long Gallery as Eva paced up and down, trying to think of a solution to her troubles. The windows were small and high up but a glittering quality to the light sent her out on to a balcony to see a world blanketed in whiteness. Snow had fallen during the night and changed the world into an alien and empty landscape.

Trees just beginning to flower with blossom now bore branches heavy with snow. The lawns were carpeted with a heavy blanket of it, walls and hedges and shrubbery vanishing beneath a mysterious moonscape. The sky was a very pale blue and the sun shone dazzlingly in the clear cold air.

Something about snow in April had a magic to it that drew her out of the House into the arctic tundra of the gardens. The peacocks were squawking plaintively about the terrace and ruffled their feathers at Eva as she passed. Out on the croquet lawn she turned to look back at the House and saw the snow behind her lie crisp, white, and unmarked by footprints.

Eva looked down at her feet, bare against the snow. She'd felt cold for days but the snow hadn't made her feel any colder. Her feet appeared to be standing in the snow and she could feel it crunching underneath her—but she left no mark behind her. Only a tracery of bird prints crossed the snow in random dapples and divots.

Bending down, Eva picked up a handful of snow and compacted it into a ball. Throwing it at a bush, she watched the branches shake and a patter of snow fall to the ground. She seemed to be able to affect the world in some ways and not in others. Wandering onwards through the gardens Eva felt released from all the tension that had been building inside the House.

In the muffled silence of the gardens the world seemed to have stopped and it made Eva think of how her own life had come to a full stop.

Maggie had told her that ghosts were stuck in the world because they wanted something. She wondered if that meant that if she discovered what had put an end to her, her half-life would be over and she would go on to heaven or hell. It was an eerie thought and it was a relief when her introspection was halted by a row of footprints across the snow.

They were small and close together, a narrow shoe with a light tread and the line of them came curving along the shore of the lake and towards the slight rise of land where the summerhouse stood. Wondering who else was up so early and walking out through the snow, Eva followed them. The walker seemed to have proceeded slowly, stopping more than once, but Eva almost flew along the track, looking up towards the swooping lines of the structure ahead.

The summerhouse was a white pavilion, an artistic conception of a Moroccan tent. The sides were open to the air and stone chairs and benches were concreted into a semi-circle inside. It was a good vantage point for overlooking the lake back when the family had held regattas. Now the view was occluded by the grove of sturdy young trees that had self-seeded around the rise of land. If the walker had been tired it was the sort of place you might stop for a rest.

The footprints came to an end at the stone floor of the summerhouse and Eva entered hesitantly, shy even though she doubted that whoever was inside could see her. At the doorway she glanced around the elegant white building and her gaze went to the only occupant: a small slumped figure lying on the ground. Kneeling down by the body she saw Aunt Cora's dandelion clock of white hair and a woollen scarf knotted viciously tight around her aunt's neck.

Uncoiling the knots of the scarf, Eva felt quickly for a pulse but her fingers were too cold to feel anything and instead she put her head against her aunt's chest, listening for a heartbeat. She couldn't hear anything through the thick coat and she cursed with frustration, feeling her aunt's hands and chafing them, gently shaking the woman to see if she could get her to revive.

Her aunt made a small sound of protest and Eva gasped with relief, even as she wondered what to do next. Help was all the way back at the House—if she could get anyone to listen to her when she got there.

There was blood in Aunt Cora's hair; Eva saw it as she continued to chafe her aunt's hands and slowed her ministrations wondering if it was safe for her aunt to move. Cora had hit her head and she might be hurt in ways that weren't obvious. Her mind whirled with possibilities and she remembered that Grandfather had a wound on his head as well when he'd been taken to hospital.

Briefly leaving her aunt, she went to the edge of the summerhouse and looked about in different directions, trying to see if any more footprints came and went from the place. But aside from the small prints of Aunt Cora's brogues there were no other marks at all.

Returning to her aunt's body Eva realized she couldn't leave to get help. She would have to stay and hope someone else came. At the very least she could protect the only aunt who'd ever been kind to her from anyone trying to finish her off. Like her own death and her grandfather's injury—despite the absence of other footprints—Eva knew Cora's collapse was no accident. That scarf had been knotted tight enough to leave bruises around her neck. Cora's fall was attempted murder—actual murder if no one came soon.

* * *

As Kyle Stratton followed his sister up the drive to the Chance house, it occurred to him how weird it was to be a twin. It was like seeing what you'd be like if you were born a girl. Kyle couldn't imagine being a girl. Watching Kyra in her silver bomber jacket, denim mini-skirt and Ugg boots trekking along five paces ahead of him, Kyle shook his head. His sister dressed like every other girl he knew. They even borrowed each other's clothes so that there was a clone-like similarity to them. Kyra was popular and sometimes her room seemed to surge with teenage girls in short skirts, flipping their hair and shrieking at each other.

Girls were bitchy and back-stabbing. Kyle was in awe of how easily his sister could blank someone who'd been her friend only a week before. His guy friends didn't have these huge feuds followed by dramatic promises of friendship, just the occasional sulk after having been royally whipped at console games or football.

But when it came to arguments with his sister, Kyra won every time. All the politics and drama of girl world seemed to give her the edge. She was always five steps ahead of him in everything they did, anticipating his objections, over-ruling them and barrelling onwards doing exactly what she wanted. Kyle had done his best to tell her the Chance house gave him a really bad feeling and she'd just gone on as usual.

He was hoping the snow might mean less work but to his surprise the front of the big house was heaving with people, easily three times as many as usual, and even a couple of police officers in luminous jackets.

The twins arrived just as one of the police officers finished announcing something over a loud hailer and the cluster of people broke up into groups, ploughing off determinedly into the snow. Recognizing one of the gardeners, Kyle caught his arm and asked:

'What's going on?'

'Some old biddy's vanished. Didn't show up for breakfast and her coat and hat aren't where she keeps them. We're all supposed to search the gardens until we find her.'

'That'll be Miss Cora,' Kyra said, appearing next to Kyle as the gardener headed off. 'The one who was telling me how to wash the wallpaper. One of the things she wittered on about was how she likes an early morning walk.'

'In the snow?' Kyle had stayed under his duvet until Mum had hauled him out. 'Before breakfast?'

'Not everyone's a layabout like you.' Kyra grinned at him. She was always frighteningly perky in the mornings and did half an hour on the exercise bike before taking a shower and changing for school. Meanwhile Kyle thought he was doing well if he found time to eat breakfast before it was time to leave the house.

'I suppose if everyone's searching we should search too,' Kyle said.

'We may as well,' Kyra said, adding: 'It's what Felix is paying for you for anyway—to look for bodies.'

'Don't say that.' Kyle frowned at her. 'The old lady's not dead.'

'She might be.' Kyra didn't even seem to notice how callous she sounded. 'An old lady in the snow, slips on the icy ground, she could have been out there for hours . . .'

'Shut up.' Kyle turned his back and walked off towards the garden, letting her follow or not as she liked. Kyle had two grandmothers and he didn't like to think of Nan or Granny lying somewhere in the snow. Sometimes his sister just didn't seem to think at all.

It was kind of a relief to walk off on his own, feet crunching into the thick snow, going off to rescue an old lady. Kyle fully intended to rescue her if he could and he reassured himself by thinking of all the non-lethal fixes someone could get themselves into. It wasn't even that cold, he told himself, just brisk.

He wondered if anyone had thought to look for footprints before trekking off every which way. He had no idea if there had been any route described for the search and so he used his own method. Thinking about his grandmothers helped. A middle-aged lady like Miss Cora would keep to paths for her walk. She wouldn't go wandering through woods or in the hedge maze, she'd take some bread and feed the birds in the park . . .

Kyle broke into a run as his thought process reached its natural conclusion—heading for the lake. A lake with its ducks and swans and peacocks would be like a magnet for a middle-aged woman. Kyle was willing to bet she'd had a bag full of bread and bacon scraps when she went for her walk.

He arrived at the lake shore hot and breathless and although he didn't see any ducks or swans a bevy of peacocks were squawking about something not far away. The noise the peacocks were making came from the roof of a tent-shaped building on a little hill of land not far ahead. Heading after the noise, Kyle found the footprints first and hurried onwards after the line of prints, expecting it to end at the building.

What he had not expected was to see a wide-eyed girl in a tatty dress, kneeling beside a humped body. And she clearly hadn't expected him either as she started at his approach and turned to look at him with huge brown eyes full of mute appeal.

'What's happened?' Kyle asked, hurrying towards her. 'Is that the old lady?'

The strange girl looked even more startled when he spoke, even glancing behind her as though she thought he was talking to someone else. Only then did she stammer out a few words.

'She's not breathing well and she's been unconscious for over an hour. Please would you get help?'

Kyle was already grabbing for his mobile phone. He wasted a minute wondering if he should call the House or if there was a special police number before pressing three nines and asking for an ambulance. Diligently repeating the girl's description of Cora's condition he then had to explain about the house and the gardens and this building—'the summerhouse', the girl told him—and the searchers already looking.

The whole business was frantic and somehow Kyle found himself checking Cora's pulse and breathing and giving updates into the phone at the same time. He looked for the girl to ask her to hold the phone and couldn't see her. The dispatcher was giving him instructions and in the flurry of worry about whether or not Cora was really breathing at all Kyle somehow lost track of time until he was gently and firmly pushed aside by someone in a fluorescent jacket and his phone taken from him by someone else, who began to instruct the dispatcher in an authoritative voice.

Falling back from the centre of the action Kyle realized the summerhouse was now crowded with people who had come with the police searchers, and among them was his sister.

'Hey,' she said, grabbing him and giving him a huge grin. 'You found her. You're a hero, bro!'

'Not really.' Kyle looked for the girl with the tangled hair who'd beaten him to the scene and realized she was nowhere around. 'I don't even know if the woman's going to be all right.'

'That's not your responsibility,' Kyra said firmly. 'But you found her. That's the important thing.'

Somehow Kyle didn't feel able to deny it when other people patted him on the back later and congratulated him on the find. If he'd known who the strange girl was he'd have given her credit but something about her disappearance made him feel almost scared to ask if anyone knew who she was. He felt a weird reluctance to hear what answer they might give.

* * *

For the second time Eva watched an ambulance leaving the House and wondered if she'd hear any more about Aunt Cora than she had about Grandfather. All she'd managed to overhear was that he was doing 'as well as could be expected'. Everyone else was trailing back to the House feeling pleased with themselves and Eva followed behind them wishing she could feel relieved.

Kyra Stratton and her brother walked together, people stopping occasionally to chuck his shoulder or slap his back. Each time it happened Kyle looked uncomfortable and Eva could guess why. She had been surprised when he appeared suddenly, and even more surprised when he'd seen her. There'd been no time to worry about that when she was giving him the important information about her aunt's condition. By the time he'd called the ambulance the moment seemed to have passed. Certainly he didn't seem to see her again although she'd watched out through the arrival of the paramedics with stretchers.

Eva wasn't sure how she'd managed to appear. She wondered if it had something to do with the urgency of Aunt Cora's condition and Eva's own need to communicate. But it seemed strange that it had been Kyra's brother of all people who had seen her, especially when she'd tried to show herself to him and to Kyra the evening of the dinner—and that time she'd failed. Did it matter that Kyle had been looking for someone, even if it hadn't happened to be her? Her supernatural abilities weren't easy to predict or explain, her appearances and disappearances were too wrapped up in a complex web of emotional turbulence, leaving her a mystery even to herself.

Now she walked alone among a crowd. The temporary staff chatted to each other and speculated on how Aunt Cora had met with her accident; but no one saw Eva. Although there always seemed to be a space where she was walking, the searchers didn't seem to realize they were leaving it.

Back at the House the staff crowded into the kitchens to claim their rightful reward of hot drinks and Eva saw her family among them. Somewhat to her surprise they all seemed to have stirred themselves to look for the missing woman. Unusually for her Aunt Helen seemed in an almost expansive mood, pressing a steaming cup of tea on Kyle even as Uncle Richard surged forward to shake his hand so that Kyle looked in danger of being scalded with praise.

Felix sidled up once they had gone and produced a money clip with a flourish, pressing it into Kyle's top jacket pocket, but this turned out to be a bad move. Handing the mug on to someone else, Kyle retrieved the notes and gave them back.

'I don't want cash for finding your auntie,' he said with a disgusted expression. Then he moved away quickly and Felix was left holding the notes with a frozen look of embarrassment at his own misstep.

Eva was finding the press of people difficult to take and she followed the overspill out into the dining room where Aunt Joyce was wondering loudly what Aunt Cora had been thinking of to go walking alone without an escort, implying that any one of the family would have jumped at the chance for a brisk morning walk.

That made Eva stop and think. The family weren't early risers as a rule. Aunt Cora always took a morning 'constitutional' walk but Aunt Joyce slept in late and although Aunt Helen rose early she generally spent her time writing letters with Uncle Richard gradually rising and pottering around her in a dressing gown.

If someone had attacked Aunt Cora they would have to have got up early and followed her and accosted her in the summerhouse—all without leaving any footprints. Eva's mind raced with ways you could manage to get to the summerhouse and not leave any mark behind you. Perhaps if someone had been there the night before the snow fell—but then how would they have left without leaving marks? Eva would have seen anyone hiding there. She wondered if the attacker could have been a ghost but she'd never heard of a ghost haunting the summerhouse, although her grandfather had warned her against the cellars and the lake.

Even stranger was the idea of anyone having any reason to attack Aunt Cora. Of all the aunts she was the least offensive, the least likely to have made any enemies; she wasn't even rich. Suddenly Eva wished she'd been less dismissive of Cora. Just because she couldn't think of anything that made her aunt a target didn't mean there wasn't a reason, still less that any reason could excuse what had happened. Cora didn't deserve to be attacked, strangled and left for dead.

Eva was convinced that someone was responsible for this and that same person was behind her own death. She couldn't think of anyone wanting to kill her any more than she could Aunt Cora or Grandfather but she was beginning to resent it on their behalf as much as on her own. Her most loved and most kind relations had been hospitalized and her suspicions were beginning to concentrate on the remaining ones. Was Aunt Helen really relieved that Cora had been found? Was Aunt Joyce a little too loud?

Watching the crowd she noticed Lisle Langley standing with a clipboard, counting people and ticking them off on a register. Looking over her shoulder Eva saw a string of names followed by columns labelled 'departed' and 'returned'. Lisle shivered suddenly and Eva moved away, feeling guilty for the ghostly air of cold she brought with her now.

She felt queasy wondering if that list of names held the name of a murderer: one of the family or one of the temporary staff or searchers. Someone smiling or sipping tea had strangled a middle-aged woman and bludgeoned an old man to the ground and had done . . . had done something to Eva. Did it mean something that they'd picked on the frail and friendless? Who would care if none of them survived the attacks?

Eva blinked, remembering someone who would care very much if Aunt Cora didn't survive. Threading her way through the people in the kitchen she escaped up the servant stairs and headed for the second floor.

Rameses was wailing hopelessly behind Aunt Cora's bedroom door, yowling his frustration to the empty corridors. Eva paused at the doorway, knowing the cat would make a break for it the second she opened the door. Rameses was not the kind of cat to tolerate being shut up for hours without any sign of his mistress and like any cat he found shut doors an abomination.

The last time she'd tried this deliberately it hadn't worked but then she'd managed it accidentally after all so it must be possible. Perhaps trying too hard had been her problem. Eva closed her eyes and moved forward with a slow gliding step, letting her senses drift. There was a brief feeling of constriction and then it was gone and she opened her eyes in time to see the amber blur launching itself at her ankles and thudding with at outraged yowl against the wood of the door.

While Rameses was collecting himself, Eva took a tin of tuna from the ample stack at the side of the room and pulled open the ring pull. A silver spoon lay on the side table and she used it to turn the tuna into the cat's food dish and then replenished his water bowl from the bottle of filtered spring water kept clearly for the purpose. Fortunately his litter tray didn't seem to need attention and Eva sat down on the bed watching while Rameses fell on the tuna and devoured it.

'Aunt Cora's in hospital,' she told the cat as he gorged himself. 'Someone tried to kill her. I know you don't think much of me—especially now. But I'm not doing this for you. I'm doing it for her.'

Rameses finished eating and began to groom his whiskers, regarding her sidelong, his ears flattened and twitching. He knew she was there and he knew something wasn't right about her. He'd known it in the Crimson Room when he'd been frightened enough to turn tail and flee. But Eva had now appeared in a new and more positive role—Bestower of Food—and apparently that was enough to persuade Rameses to politely ignore her peculiarities. He finished his grooming and leapt on to the bed, turned his back on Eva and began to wash himself.

She left him to it. This time moving through the door was easier. She closed her eyes, took a breath, stepped forward, and opened them again on the other side. Stepping through space and trying to think of it as empty gave her a sensation like vertigo, fearing that not just the door but the floor would give way beneath her. The trick seemed to be to be able to concentrate and go vague all at once, summoning the dreamlike feeling of moving freely at will without giving way to the nightmare possibilities of getting stuck or falling.

Eva experimented after leaving her aunt's room, trying to glide up the stairs instead of walking. She hoped none of the other ghosts were watching her stumbling progress. It was embarrassing that you could be a ghost and be so bad at the things ghosts were supposed to be able to do. Eva wished with all her power she could haunt her murderer and bring him to justice. But she still didn't know who was responsible for her death.

She needed help, in more ways than one. She needed answers, and wasn't sure what questions to ask. Only one person had provided a suggestion of either. So she made her way to the top of the House.

At the end of the smallest and meanest staircase in the House were the servants' attics. The attics were a jumble of small sloping rooms, linked by a long corridor. Most of the rooms were full of battered trunks and chests of drawers holding a motley collection of historical debris. The floorboards creaked and groaned beneath Eva's feet as she made her way to the housemaids' room. It was plainly furnished. Two iron bedsteads stood on either side of a small washing stand, a small mirror hung from a nail crudely hammered into the rough plastered wall, and a broken wardrobe leaned against the wall in the dark corners.

She had come up to the attics looking for Maggie, suspecting this might be the most likely place. But although the bare rooms with their unsanded floorboards and rusting iron bedsteads carried an air of antiquity, there was no sign of any activity. Eva had opened a casement window to get some air and noticed two teenagers walking away down the drive, the blond hair identifying them as Kyra and Kyle.

Leaning out of the window she took a deep breath of the April air. It was strange to feel her arms resting on the lip of the window against the roof slates and smell the familiar scent of an afternoon turning to evening and know that none of it was real—or rather, it was real and she was not.

There was a scraping sound nearby and Eva turned to look behind her and saw nothing. The room was as empty as when she'd first entered it but somewhere nearby she felt a pressure in the atmosphere, the shape of a ghost approaching. The scrape was followed by a shuffling sound and she realized with a jolt it had come from outside, looking back through the window just as a hunched figure moved up outside it. For a moment she thought a gargoyle had come to life but the grimy face with its dark suspicious eyes belonged to the magpie girl. She was sitting outside the window, on the slope of the roof.

'What are you doing out there?' Eva asked, relieved that it was only Maggie and not one of the other ghosts and surprised enough to speak as naturally as she would to a living person.

'We used to sit on the roof sometimes when I was alive,' the servant girl replied, not looking at her, but staring down at the long sweep of the avenue towards the entrance. 'Even in your own room you didn't get privacy. The housekeeper might come

119

by on her rounds anytime to make sure you weren't drinking, or doing anything you shouldn't. But out here we could be alone.'

'Weren't you scared?' Eva looked at the slope of the roof angling down to the long drop with a feeling of vertigo.

'Not when I was alone.' Maggie gave her a sideways glance and then shuffled sideways along the roof. 'Why don't you try it?'

Eva hesitated, remembering when Maggie had suggested she visit the cellars, and just the thought of that sent a shudder though her.

'It ain't a trick,' Maggie said, as if she'd read Eva's mind. 'You're a ghost, ain't you? What's going to happen to you if you fall?'

'I don't know.' Eva stood on a tin box and angled her body to sit on the edge of the windowsill, carefully swinging her legs around so she was sitting facing out. 'What would happen?' she asked, trying to get Maggie to meet her eyes.

'That depends.' The servant girl's dark eyes were unreadable. 'On how much control you got.'

Eva looked down at the long drop and swallowed, trying to clear the sudden dryness in her throat. She'd never thought of herself as a coward, except when it came to Kyra Stratton. She'd climbed trees, swum and dived in the lake, risked climbing the mouldering stairs of the folly. But the roof was so much higher than she'd ever been and the tiles were slippery and several slates were loose.

Maggie seemed unconcerned, moving over again to what must have been her original seat in a part of the roof where the last of the afternoon sunshine wasn't blocked by the chimney stacks. She patted the place next to her and Eva took a deep breath and edged out on to the roof.

It wasn't so bad once you were out there. The slope wasn't so steep as it appeared right up at the edge and if you shuffled yourself carefully upwards, still sitting and only looking at the tiles on either side of you, it was possible to move around. Her feet were still bare since she'd lost her sandals and her toes ought to grip the roof more easily than Maggie's black boots. The important thing was not to look beyond the end of her feet to see the tops of trees from *above*.

'You're making too much of it,' Maggie commented. 'You're not going to fall. We never did and we were half starved and tired from working from dawn to dusk.'

Eva shuffled backwards to a place alongside Maggie and shot her a wary glance. But the magpie figure didn't seem hostile, more pensive as she looked out over the gardens. The snow was beginning to melt, stomped down in tracks all across the white landscape and receding to reveal the green of the plants and grass beneath it.

'Did you see my Aunt Cora leave the house this morning?' Eva asked and Maggie flicked a quick look at her.

'You seem to think I've got nothing better to do with myself than watch your family,' she replied sharply. 'All you Chances think your doings are the only ones that matter.'

'I didn't mean it like that,' Eva responded angrily. 'One of my aunts was taken to hospital this morning. Someone attacked her while she was taking a walk—and someone knocked out my grandfather four days ago. I think it's the same person who's responsible for my death too.'

'You think? Don't you know?' Maggie stared at her, surprise one of the few honest expressions Eva had seen on her face. 'Don't you know how you died?'

'No I don't,' Eva admitted. 'That's why I need your help.

121

I know you said you didn't have any reason to help me but can't we work something out? I don't understand anything about being a ghost. I only know I am one because the Witch—' As she spoke she was moving, gesturing expansively and shifting position. As the word 'Witch' escaped her lips a tile shifted and her right foot slipped.

'Watch out!' Maggie said sharply as Eva flailed for a grip on the roof, feeling her whole body slipping.

'I'm *falling*!' There was a lurching sliding moment and then her hands and feet found a purchase and she came to a stop, knees up under her chin in a tight ball of terror, a foot away from the edge.

'You really do need help, don't you?' Maggie's voice sounded sympathetic as she shuffled up alongside Eva. 'You don't even know enough to know what's dangerous.'

'I still feel as if I'm going to fall,' Eva admitted, not looking beyond her own scabbed knees.

'When you're dead,' Maggie began softly, so softly that Eva was distracted from her fright and began to listen at once. 'You start seeing things differently. The shapes of things is what you notice. The feeling of them. What they're made of and how they work. Other things, things you notice when you're alive like how people look and what their names are and what time they'll want their tea—that doesn't matter so much. And time is different too.'

Maggie smiled grimly, her thin hands twisting in her lap.

'All my life I was ruled by clocks,' she continued. 'There was never enough time, time was always after you, catching up, leaping forward so I was always behind with my work. But time's a funny thing. Now when clocks strike it makes me feel like I've got to work and Missus will be ordering me about or the Master is calling us to prayers but the rest of the time it's like I'm drifting and time doesn't even matter. When I'm drifting I'm just here, not even thinking most of the time. Just drifting.'

Her voice even sounded drifty and Eva risked a sideways look across the roof and saw that Maggie's shape was fluttery around the edges, a torn-paper quality that made her look as if she could be whipped away by the wind.

'I felt like that by the lake,' Eva said. 'And a couple of other times, especially when I try to think back to what happened to me. It's as if I could be dragged away to somewhere . . . somewhere bad.'

'You've got to concentrate.' Maggie's voice hardened even as her shape did. 'If you don't want to drift away, you've got to make an effort.'

'But what happens to the ghosts who don't make an effort?' Eva asked. 'Where do they go?'

'Anything can happen if you lose control of yourself,' Maggie said. 'It depends on who you are—or were. What happened to you. The bad things in your life take over, you're trapped in those memories, you live them all over again. Maybe if you're really unlucky you relive the way you died.'

Eva watched her, wanting to ask more and guessing that the one question she really wanted to ask would be unforgivable.

'My work in the morning was to set fires in the family's bedrooms without waking them up,' Maggie continued. 'The Master and the Missus and the rest. Sometimes clocks strike and it's like they're still here.' She shook her head violently, her hair flying free of its plait and falling about her face in greasy black locks. 'I don't think about it.' Glancing at Eva she added: 'And you shouldn't think about the things you're afraid of either. Not if you want to survive.'

'Survive?' Eva forced herself not to look down again and kept

123

her eyes fixed on Maggie, now perched sideways on the roof. 'What more could happen to me?'

'You don't even want to know,' Maggie said warningly. She obviously saw irritation flare in Eva's eyes because it sparked an angry addition: 'If you think I've got all the answers you might as well forget asking. I never had any education besides church school for a couple of years and everything anyone told me about what happens to your spirit when you die turned out to be a lie. How am I supposed to know why when you die it isn't the end?' She paused. 'All I can tell you is that the ghost world isn't a friendly place and right now you exist somehow, don't you? Not every ghost survives.'

'What happens to them?' Eva felt sombre and Maggie looked bleak.

'They fade away,' said Maggie. 'Or they stop being people and become things. Like the Stalker. It doesn't think. It follows you and it'll destroy you if it catches you but it's a thing, a beast, a monster—not a person. There are other ghosts like that but less dangerous: memories, reflections, puppets.'

'Puppets?' Eva repeated slowly.

'Of the more powerful ghosts,' Maggie said. 'Of the most powerful ghosts.' One of her hands was moving deliberately—pointing downwards.

Down was a direction Eva was trying hard not to think about but as she grasped what Maggie was suggesting she felt claustrophobic even out on the roof. Down meant the Witch.

'This House is cursed,' Maggie said softly. 'And your precious family were too mad and too wicked to notice. But now all the luck's bled out of the Chances. And that's your problem. Mine's that I'm stuck in your House with your ghosts and your curse.'

124

8
Seeing is Believing

Wednesday, April 9th

The last week before the House would open to the public had always been exhausting. Each year there seemed to be more and more work. It made a change for Eva to stand still and watch other people rushing about all around her.

The staff were openly nervous ever since Aunt Cora's mysterious accident—and although 'accident' was the word they used you could hear the quotation marks hanging over it. Eva, unseen and unheard by the teams of cleaners and decorators, hovered nearby as they muttered together over their work. Word had got around that two of the Chances were in hospital and a third was missing, presumed dead.

The oddest part of it all was hearing her own name mentioned. It was like attending her own funeral to hear people speak about her in the past tense. It hurt to hear them talking about her so casually, as if her whole life was an open book for people to speculate about, inventing parts of her story and twisting others so that she barely recognized herself in the person being discussed.

'An odd child, touched in the head, one of those special

children, if you know what I mean. One of the teachers at the school told me the Chance girl was failing every subject.'

'I heard she was a virtual prisoner in this place. Old Mr Chance didn't like her to go out—I didn't even know he had a granddaughter.'

'It was only a matter of time before she went crazy, I heard. Her mother was the same way and she killed herself. Stands to reason the girl would be the same.'

But the rumours and misinformation took Eva no nearer to finding out what had happened. As far as anyone knew she'd disappeared in the last couple of weeks of March and the police had been called. But there the story stopped. No one seemed to know anything else. Instead they'd go on to talk about old Mr Chance, in the hospital for a week now; and Cora Chance, taken away in an ambulance three days ago and not seen since.

The remaining family members weren't much better. Aunt Helen had thrown herself into an inventory of the House, which brought out the most critical and the most suspicious aspects of her personality. She insisted that there were things missing all over the House, obsessively counting sets of china and rows of cutlery. But her opinion held less weight when her counting never produced the same number twice.

'People keep moving things!' she could be heard protesting, accusing the staff of having jumbled up her regimented lines of fish-knives and cake-forks or switching furniture about in the empty rooms. And when she wasn't blaming the staff she fingered Aunt Joyce as the culprit. 'I've seen you admiring those Regency snuffboxes!' she'd declare, with a gimlet-eyed stare. 'And now they're nowhere to be found.'

'You're paranoid, Helen,' Aunt Joyce would reply crushingly. 'And you're being ridiculous. You're the one who keeps losing

126

things, perhaps it's your time of life. Any hot flushes recently?'

But Joyce didn't seem much more stable herself. Her relationship with her latest man friend didn't seem to be going so well. She'd supported his original idea of the ghost walks because he was her partner but now she seemed to be having second thoughts—both about the man and about the idea. She looked harried and overwrought, always drinking twice as much as anyone else at mealtimes and staying up late smoking cigarettes on the terrace instead of going to her room. Her man friend, Christopher Knight, the marketing expert, was anything but concerned. Eva had spotted him eyeing up Lisle Langley in the manner of a man who didn't consider himself too attached.

Eva hated to admit it, but Felix seemed to have thrown himself into the work of repairing and reordering the House. Everywhere she went, there he was: watching, instructing, and involving himself with each detail. He wouldn't take no for an answer either. When the original cleaners said that the Solar was covered with too many layers of grime to remove, he fired them and hired more cleaners. When Lisle Langley said there wasn't enough money to have the rushes smothering the lake cut back, he went straight to his father and asked for more money.

Felix's father was still staying in the House although he was less and less in evidence during the rows between his wife and his sister-in-law. Instead he spent his time walking about in the deer park with a gun, taking pot shots at squirrels and generally scaring the life out of the gardening staff. He'd handed over a cheque to Felix with a generosity that made Eva feel angry all over again at how cheaply she and her grandfather had been treated.

But Felix was getting everything he wanted because his parents seemed to expect he'd be inheriting the House soon.

Although they talked a lot about 'doing this for poor Edward while he's so ill', Eva couldn't help but notice they all seemed too busy to actually go to the hospital and she was getting frantic to know how her grandfather was doing. He'd hate it there, away from his books and his things and the House he'd been born in. She couldn't understand why he hadn't insisted on coming back home—unless he was too ill to insist on anything.

Meanwhile, Felix had taken over the library and was using it as his own personal area, locking the doors when he buried himself inside, the smell of cigarette smoke permeating from under the doors the only sign he was still in there. Eva was disgusted that he had taken over her grandfather's space like that but she wasn't surprised—the first thing he'd done on entering the House was to try and claim her bedroom.

But in a weird way Felix was beginning to remind her of her grandfather in the way he closeted himself in there for long hours of the evening, refusing all offers of food or drink as he rustled around in a nest of papers. Maybe he was even looking at the same papers as Grandfather had been and Eva remembered it had been in the library that Grandfather had collapsed. Increasingly she found herself pacing outside the doors while Felix was in there, just as she had while it had been Grandfather at work.

The difference was that Eva didn't respect Felix the way she respected her grandfather. She didn't care about his privacy or his feelings. And she badly wanted to know what he was up to.

* * *

The library in Felix's control didn't look much different from when Grandfather had occupied it. There were the piles of books all around his heavy antique desk, heaps of paper across the brown leather surface and crackling old parchment spread out with books as paperweights. But in the middle of the familiar chaos was a shiny black laptop, and next to that a brass bowl pressed into service as an ashtray and overflowing with stubs.

Felix had gone to inspect the gardens and should be out of the way for at least an hour and Eva didn't feel nervous as she began to inspect the books and papers. Even if Felix came back and found her, what could he do? When he'd seen her before all he'd come up with were threats and Eva wasn't afraid of him throwing her out of the House any more. She had real doubts that he could if he tried, as she hadn't been able to leave the grounds since she'd become a ghost.

She started with the heap of books closest to the desk, all leather-bound tomes full of English history. Felix had bookmarked pages with paperclips at the parts which happened to mention the Chances. Halfway down the pile was a book on Jacobean witch burnings and Eva's hand trembled as she looked at the marked page: a woodcut image of a witch in a ducking chair. Underneath it the words seemed to swim on the page:

' . . . a local land-owner named Chance writes to his wife of a "witch woman drowned for evil and ungodly acts' in an undated letter that appears to be from the same period . . . "

But although Eva forced herself to read down the page there was nothing more about the Chances, just about references to witches in correspondence. She put the book aside quickly, the image of the witch on the scaffold seeming to hang in front of her eyes even once it was closed.

The next pile of books was slimmer, smartly jacketed with the imprints of more modern publishing houses. *Murder on the Orient Express*, Eva read on the first, and then: *The Casebook of Sherlock Holmes* and *The Thirty Nine Steps*. It was a stack of detective stories. Eva looked on down the stack: there must have been

129

about fifteen different murder mysteries. Still wondering, she looked at the next stack and read *The Purcell Papers by Sheridan Lefanu* on the cover of the top book and then *The Woman in White* on the next. These were ghost and mystery stories. As unlikely as it seemed, Felix seemed to have been spending his time in here reading novels.

But why detective and ghost stories? Eva wondered uneasily if he was harvesting them for ideas. But she didn't have time to read them all herself. Instead she turned to the papers on the desk to see if they had any answers. The largest was a copy of the family tree. Eva looked at the bottom of it to see her own name and her birth date in the bottom left corner. There wasn't a death date yet and she wondered what they'd write in if her body was never found. A line from her name led directly to her mother, no mention of her father, and she realized with a dizzying sensation that she was going to be the end of her little tree, like so many dead cut-off branches before her, all the little spurs and twigs she'd wondered over as a child. It made her feel like a ghost in a way that nothing else had so far and she dropped the parchment as if it could drag her in and down on to the page, trapping her there.

Scrabbling for the next paper she saw it was one of Aunt Helen's inventories and clipped to it was another much neater but also hand-written inventory dated 1998. Felix had plainly been comparing the two but both were so long that Eva gave up trying to find out what the discrepancies were after five minutes of trying to decipher Aunt Helen's notes.

Instead she turned to look at Felix's computer. Embarrassingly it took her a couple of minutes to work out how it opened and then the screen came to life with a swirling display of colours. Carefully she touched the lettered part and something else appeared on it: two little boxes labelled 'name' and 'password'.

Eva looked at it despairingly. Name was easy enough but how on earth could she possibly guess what Felix's secret password was. It could be anything at all. Slowly she tapped 'Felix' into the first box and tried Felix's mother's name in the second. The computer made an ugly blurting noise and the words 'password incorrect' appeared in red underneath the second box. It had been a stupid guess anyway, even Felix wouldn't choose something that obvious.

Eva tried 'ghost' and then 'murder' in the password box, each time getting the same warning noise and the red letters. Then she put the computer down and tried to decide what to do next. The computer wasn't helping and she didn't think she could use one well enough to even find where Felix kept his files. The computer classes at school had been the cause of some of her lowest marks ever.

There were still other places to look. She tried the desk drawers and found that Felix didn't seem to have been using them. They were still full of her grandfather's things, his glasses case in the top drawer next to a magnifying glass he used for the tiniest print. There were Eva's own school reports and she flushed to think of Felix seeing them. And there was a letter with the name of the local police force at the top.

It was a very formal letter with an official crime number and three short stark paragraphs underneath which recited the bald facts that there had been no progress in the search for Evangeline Chance, reported missing Monday 17 March, aged 15 years, although searchers had combed the local area and police divers had made two dives in the lake. Nothing had been found and no conclusion had been reached. A victim support number was provided with the news that the investigation was ongoing.

Eva dropped the letter in the drawer and tried not to think about how her grandfather would have felt receiving it.

It was the first hard piece of evidence about when she'd actually disappeared. It was some relief, she supposed, that there had been a search. But since no one had found her body, obviously they hadn't searched hard enough. Then she wondered what Felix had thought. He was the only one of the family who knew she was a ghost. He'd seen her when he'd tried to take over the Crimson Room and although she hadn't known she was a ghost then, Felix must have known she was missing, and the more she replayed that conversation in her mind she thought she could spot the moment when he'd realized she wasn't really there. When he'd told her to get out, he'd been trying to get rid of her ghost. She didn't know if that made her feel better or worse about the way he'd dismissed her.

The desk hadn't helped her much but there was still one place left to look and Eva crossed to the back of the room and carefully unhooked a painting concealing her grandfather's safe. He didn't have much that was valuable but it was for him the natural place to keep important documents. As she slid the false panel of wainscoting aside, Eva wondered if Felix knew about the safe.

A minute after she was sure he did. The combination had been changed. Eva might not know much about passwords on computers but she'd known the combination to the safe because it was 01041992, the day she was born—the day her mother died. But the door no longer opened to that number. Felix had been ahead of her.

But Felix didn't have her advantages, Eva reached out a hand to the metal door of the safe and closed her eyes. There was a wave of cold through her arm and then her hand touched a stack of papers. Taking a firm hold of them, she *pulled* her arm back and opened her eyes to find herself holding a stack of papers, now outside the safe.

Spreading the papers out on the desk she skimmed through them. They were all thick official documents and it was clear from the start that they were all about her grandfather's will.

The papers were full of Latin and legal language, but this was one area when Eva's unconventional upbringing was an asset and it didn't take her long to realize that her grandfather and his lawyer had sent several letters back and forth about certain provisions and codicils in the will. The will itself was on the stiffest paper of all and, after a series of explanations and instructions, it launched into the bequests.

After everything that had happened Eva had been expecting to find something shocking. But just as she'd expected, the House and its surrounding grounds went to Mr Felix Fairfax, sole male heir of the Chance family, in accordance with the provisions of previous wills by earlier Chances. To Felix went the Elizabethan mansion, with one Georgian Wing and Victorian additions. To Felix went the formal gardens, the shrubberies, the sculptures in the classical garden, the carriage house, the summerhouses and pavilions and the peacocks on the island on the lake.

The will dissected her home like a body on an autopsy table, carved open to display its component parts. The cold scalpel of the legal language sliced through the history and mystery and the papers trembled in her hands as her fingers fluttered against the edges. Pulling herself together, she took a firmer hold on the parchment and read on.

To Cora Chance, her mother's Bible; to Helen Chance, her mother's wedding ring; to Joyce Chance, a single string of delicate seed pearls. They seemed small things but Eva could imagine how her grandfather had chosen them individually to be meaningful to each person.

The next name was her own and Eva was almost afraid to read what came next. Anything her grandfather left her would be precious, something to have to remember him after he was gone.

To Miss Evangeline Chance, the will declared, went all the contents of the House. These goods and chattels would be itemized in the attached inventory but included the furnishings and ornaments, the paintings and the tapestries, the books and maps, collections of everything from fine Chinese porcelain to a menagerie of stuffed birds, to time-bronzed Roman coins.

Eva read on in amazement that it was even possible for a will to leave things this way. Felix got the House, the shell of it. But everything not nailed down—and a fair few things which were—went to Eva. Forget that she would have nowhere to keep it, she would inherit several thousand times her own body weight in possessions and Felix would be left with a bare skeleton of what the House had been.

Eva's gaze ran on down the page to the next clause and shivered. It made provision for what would happen if she should die. If she should predecease her grandfather, the will decreed, the contents of the House went to Felix, along with his existing inheritance, and formed one entire estate.

Dropping the will on the desk, Eva glanced at the letters again. This was what her grandfather and his lawyer had argued about in perfect and politely phrased sentences. The lawyer, Michael Stevenage, had argued against dividing the estate. He'd warned that costs and death duties would be vast and the House was no asset without the historic contents. Such a will might not even pass probate and any of the heirs might contest it. Such a will,

Michael had insisted, in increasingly exclamatory italics, was *inadvisable in the extreme.*

Looking at those letters Eva feared the lawyer had been right. The will was a major mistake. And it was a massive motive for Felix. She'd had trouble believing even her most unpleasant of relations could actually want her dead. But finally here was an explanation. If she died Felix got everything, if she lived they had to divide the House and contents. And there could have been a massive battle over the legality of the will, perhaps still might be.

She was still staring down at the lawyer's last letter when the door of the library flew open and Felix walked in.

***

Felix was looking straight at her and his eyes narrowed to slits as he froze in the doorway. Unquestionably he had seen her and Eva remembered the last time they had spoken. She'd been angry with him then. Now she was furious.

'You said this was your House,' she told him, dropping the letters on the desk deliberately. 'But everything in it is mine.'

Felix let the door fall closed behind him and took a step into the room. This time she saw his shoulders stiffen and sensed the wave of fear he was forcing down beneath a fierce possessiveness. That step into the room had been taken to show her he wasn't about to give ground.

'It might have been yours,' he said, 'if you'd lived. But you died.'

'I'm still here.' Eva watched as he took several more slow steps into the room. 'You can see me, can't you?'

'I see it but I don't believe it.' Felix stopped walking towards her and looked her over carefully. For once Eva didn't feel

135

intimidated by that cool stare. What he could see frightened him and she knew it. She forced down the thought that it frightened her as well.

'You don't have much imagination then,' she said. 'Lucky you.' She felt her own face tighten into a sneer as she continued: 'That's what your name means, did you know? You're the fortunate Chance. The lucky one.'

'That's right,' Felix nodded. 'And I intend to stay that way. So, like I told you before, you can clear out now. Whatever you are.'

'I'm a GHOST!' Eva shouted across the library, and up and down the bookcases loose leaves fluttered in an invisible breeze. 'Deny it all you like. I'm dead and someone killed me. And now I'm a ghost and you *CAN'T* get rid of me!'

The towers of books next to the desk toppled over, spilling a ring of books around the desk. Across the room, a loose volume fell from a distant shelf with a muffled thud. Another followed a moment later.

Felix twitched, his eyes jerked to the heap of scattered books for an instant before focusing deliberately back on Eva.

'If you're a ghost, you're not real,' he said. 'So vanish. Begone. Plague this house no more.' His expression was incredulous and Eva felt a surge of fury at the thought that he still wasn't taking her seriously. He thought he could intimidate her with his pathetic arrogance when she'd faced the venom and malice of the Witch.

Books started falling faster all over the room, thumping down on to the carpet like gunshots, even on the upper gallery they were falling, dropping from the high shelves in wider and wider arcs until a book came flying over the railing and arced towards Felix like a missile, missing his head by inches as he ducked.

'Stop that!' Felix's head swung back towards Eva like a snake and her lips spread in a helpless smile as she laughed back at him.

The books rustled like hawks in a mews, stretching their wings.

'Do you believe me NOW?' she demanded, as more books came flying out of the shelves towards Felix. 'Do you hear me NOW?'

He couldn't answer her, diving out of the way of a massive lexicon and rolling just in time to avoid being battered by a whole shelf of histories. Eva could feel the power cresting in the room, a whirlwind with herself as the still cold centre. It was her anger seizing the books and hurling them, her wish to affect him, to have him respect her for a change, a poltergeist power that Eva didn't know she possessed. Like the dark currents that swirled around the Witch, it filled the room and she could sense Felix being forced back by it as much as by the books that continued to hurl themselves at him from every corner of the room. Bookcases were swaying ominously, tilting towards Felix as though drawn by a lodestone.

She had become like the Witch. Eva felt the hair rise on the back of her neck and her thoughts flew unbidden to the darkness of the cellars and saw herself as she had been, quailing under the mocking laughter of the Witch. It gave her pause and as she doubted herself, Felix regained his feet and stumbled towards the door.

'Stop!' The books froze in their path across the room, unlikely birds suspended in the air, pages unfurled like wings. 'Was it you?' Eva asked. 'Were you the one who killed me?'

Felix grabbed the handle of the door and hauled it open, looking back at her from the entrance.

'I'm not a killer,' he said. 'I never laid a finger on you.' He paused as though there were other words still unsaid—and then shook his head and slid through the half open door, slamming it shut behind him.

As the door slammed, the frozen books came crashing to the floor at once and all around the room there were splintering smashes as the tilted bookcases plunged to the floor, spilling volumes in all directions, loose leaves flying open in a blizzard of paper. As the final fragments fluttered to the floor like snow, Eva stood in the middle of the debris, mistress of the field of battle and feeling more afraid than ever.

9
Haunting Season

Friday, April 11th

Eva sat on the stairs and looked down into the front hall. It was a hive of activity. Lisle Langley was updating the notice boards with lists and talking nineteen to the dozen on her mobile phone. Various members of the temporary staff swarmed about with cleaning materials or signs to place around the House. Kyra had passed by with a team of women still working on the Solar, a garden room with glass windows that hadn't been cleaned in years. One of the aunts had had the bright idea to open it up this summer and the cleaning team were finding the accumulated grime of ages tough going.

To the right, along the hallway leading towards the kitchens, Eva could smell a dark and earthy dankness. Twice today already she'd seen the cellar door gaping open, sagging on its hinges. Twice she'd screwed her courage to the sticking point and latched the door shut. But, sitting on the stairs, she could hear a slight creaking on the very edge of audibility and knew it had come open again.

To the left was another hallway leading towards the library where she'd had her confrontation with Felix. She hadn't entered the room again since then but the devastation she had wrought was still fresh in her mind, a shameful testament to her own unbound rage. Ghostly powers were frightening when they could come so unbidden and out of control. And the worst of it was she still didn't know whether to believe Felix or if he'd lied to get rid of her.

There was the sound of laughter outside the front door and two boys entered together. Kyle Stratton, squinting as the sunlight faded into the darkness of the hall, and his friend Damon with the corn-rowed hair who was still laughing as he entered, his dark eyes alight with amusement. Kyle squared his shoulders, trying to ignore his friend as he went to the notice board to sign in.

'Whooo whooo,' Damon laughed again, flapping his arms around behind Kyle. 'I'm a scary tree coming to get you . . . ' He aimed a cuff at Kyle's head. 'You need to chill out, mate. You're jumping at every shadow.'

'Leave it out,' Kyle said brusquely. 'That branch came whipping out of nowhere and it was covered in thorns. You should look where you're walking.'

'You sound like the gardening squad.' Damon rolled his eyes. 'They're doing some serious magic mushrooms, I swear. There's this one dude's convinced the ivy keeps tapping him on the shoulder. Talk about twitchy. And I never even saw your thorny branch thing.'

Kyle looked defensive, his face closing in on itself and Eva thought the House was getting to him. He'd seen her once out near the summerhouse and she remembered how uncomfortable he'd looked afterwards, following the ambulance back. And while Kyra seemed completely unconscious of the family ghosts as she passed through the House, Kyle was different. She'd seen him poking around in the House while doing the lifting and carrying which was his official job. Sometimes when Eva got too close he'd acted spooked, twitching at the slightest breeze and constantly turning to look around him as if he suspected he was being watched. Eva could almost feel Kyle's nervousness: a prickling tension in his neck and shoulders and a wary hesitancy in his mind.

Now he glanced up the stairs and frowned and—just as Eva was wishing that he *could* see her—his eyes widened and he blinked, taking a step forward and then rubbing his eyes and looking again at the patch of staircase where she was sitting.

'Hey!' A newcomer had arrived in the hall and was waving a hand in front of Kyle's face. 'Hello? Can you hear me?'

Kyle jumped and turned to face the man, looking confused.

'Sorry.' He glanced back at Eva but vaguely, no longer focused on where she had come to her feet. 'I thought I saw something.'

'You looked a million miles away!' the man said with a laugh and then turned to gesture towards the pile of boxes and a stack of cardboard tubes. 'I'm Christopher Knight. I'm in charge of the marketing of this place. I've got some posters advertising the ghost walks. Perhaps you boys can help me put them up around the place?'

Kyle didn't look enthusiastic but he moved towards the boxes. Damon got there first and picked up a cardboard tube, shaking out a rolled bundle of paper and uncurling it. Christopher hurried up quickly, looking protective as Damon whistled at the posters.

Eva took a step forward and then froze. The posters showed the house in a photographic negative, white against a black background. But it was the words on the poster that had stopped her in her tracks:

Staring at the gothic writing of the poster, Eva realized Aunt Joyce must be to blame. The only way the marketing expert could have written those things about the east wing and the footsteps and the collection in the cellar was if she'd told him about them. The hauntings were family legends: ones the aunts always pretended were no more than stories. Eva dreaded to think what would happen to innocent visitors paying their money for a tour of the most haunted parts of the House.

'Twenty-five quid to spend a couple of hours looking for ghosts!' Damon exclaimed. 'Has everyone got to pay that much to see this place?'

'Standard admission is ten pounds to tour the gardens, fifteen for a house and garden ticket, less with concessions,' Christopher replied. 'The ghost walks are an optional extra. But one we hope will be lucrative.' He allowed himself a smooth smile as he brandished a stack of pamphlets. 'This brochure recounts the tragic histories of those who have perished in the house and I've spent some time reading up on the history of the Chance family.'

'So you're going to try to creep people out,' Damon said, taking a brochure and flipping through it. 'Telling them ghost stories. I tell some kick ass ghost stories, man. You should have me do one of your tours.'

'I'll bear you in mind,' Christopher said, cutting Damon short. 'But right now what I need is people to put up posters.'

Damon looked annoyed at the brush-off and he shook his head.

'You don't know what you're missing,' he said. 'My story about the torture chamber in the cellars had Kyle here almost pissing himself.'

'Shut up, Damon,' Kyle said but even as he said it Eva had a dropping sensation in the pit of her stomach. The mood in the room was shifting, tension rising from the group clustered at the reception desk.

'I've not seen it myself yet,' Christopher Knight admitted slowly. 'Joyce mentioned that there was a collection of torturer's instruments but she hasn't found the time to show me around yet.'

'Doesn't this place open tomorrow?' Damon pressed his advantage. 'You really should see it before then. Why don't you take a look now? I can do my tour for you as well. Seriously, dude, there's some freaked out stuff down there.'

Eva watched in alarm as Damon led the way towards the cellars and Christopher followed him. Damon opened the door and she heard their footsteps ringing on the wooden stairs, growing fainter as they descended out of sight, leaving the door half open behind them.

Kyle was still standing frozen by the reception desk looking down at the sheaf of unfolded posters when Felix walked into the hall.

Felix glanced around, seeing Kyle first and then glancing at the other side of the hall where Lisle was still on the telephone, paying no attention to anything else. As Felix scanned the room, Eva waited for him to look up and notice her. But this time his expression didn't change. Eva stared down at him, still debating

143

whether she believed his insistence that he hadn't had anything to do with her murder.

Walking casually towards the reception desk, Felix picked up a brochure and began to leaf through it. Only then did he speak to Kyle, his voice low as he asked:

'Have you found anything yet?'

'Not since your auntie last week,' Kyle replied irritably. 'The body you're looking for doesn't seem to exist.'

'The House opens tomorrow. If the tourists see anything . . .'

'It'll make your ghost walks look bad.' Kyle's voice was cold. Facing Felix down, he continued, 'You never said it was your cousin but that's what I'm supposed to be looking for, isn't it? Your cousin Eva's body. Don't your family give a toss about her being dead except for what the tourists think?'

Eva listened with fascination as Kyle revealed what he'd been searching for: her body. She hadn't even considered that herself but of course if she was dead there would be a body somewhere. The fact she was still here meant she hadn't thought about where else she might be and the thought made her shiver, rubbing at the bruises on her wrist that seemed to flare up whenever she thought about how she'd died. Distracted by the idea, she'd missed the rest of Kyle's unexpected defence of her but Felix had heard all of it and he was glowering at Kyle.

'That's none of your concern,' Felix said coldly. 'I didn't hire you to pry into my family's personal affairs.'

'So you didn't. And since I've looked all over this place except for the rooms your family are using, I suppose you'll have to finish the job yourself,' Kyle told him. 'I've done what you asked me to. And you owe me for my time so far.'

'You've looked everywhere?' Felix shook his head. 'In just one week? You weren't even here most of the time. Doing GCSE revision, is what I heard.' He smiled with all the smugness of someone who had passed A-levels and had an assured university place. 'And you've been doing Lisle's lifting and carrying as well. The way I see it you still owe me some hours.'

'You know what you can do with those hours?' Kyle began but before he could finish they were interrupted by the cellar expedition returning. Damon was still chortling to himself and Christopher Knight was flushed with excitement.

'Felix!' he exclaimed, hurrying up to join them. 'Those cellars are amazing. I'm not easily spooked but they really do have a haunted feeling. I think these ghost walks are going to be a real success.'

'Now you got to let me do one of your tours,' Damon added. 'You've got to admit my routine creeps people out a treat.'

'Slow down,' Felix said, looking from Christopher to Damon and Kyle, trying to read their expressions. 'What are you talking about?'

'The cellar,' Christopher repeated impatiently. 'It has a torturer's chamber in it we're using for the ghost walks. And yes,' he looked at Damon, 'I'll see if I can find you some work but that routine will need some editing, I think.'

'Ace,' Damon grinned widely. 'You won't regret it, mate.'

'The cellar.' Felix turned to look at Kyle. 'And have you been down to the cellar yet?'

'I went the first night I worked here,' Kyle said sharply. 'Looking for the wine you asked for.'

'And did you find any?' Felix put an additional level of meaning into that question, staring Kyle down.

'I didn't look everywhere,' Kyle said. 'There's no light down there and we only had a torch.'

'Plus there were all these creepy noises and he started running

145

like someone lit a rocket under his arse,' Damon laughed. 'My boy here thinks the cellar really is haunted, don't you, Kyle?'

'Shut up, Damon,' Kyle snapped. But Felix was already looking at Damon speculatively.

'You seem to know all about this cellar,' he said. 'Why don't you tell me about it? If I like what I hear, I'll make it worth your while.'

'You're on,' Damon said and Felix smiled, unable to resist a mocking glance back at Kyle as he led Damon off to the library.

Kyle had been left alone at the reception desk and as Eva moved closer Kyle shifted awkwardly away from her. He pulled a mobile phone and punched buttons on it before shaking his head.

'No signal,' he muttered and then glanced over at Lisle, now off the phone and talking to Christopher about lighting the cellar tours. 'Her network must have better coverage,' he muttered to himself.

Eva didn't know anything about mobile phones. The House had one single telephone in its own little room just off the kitchens and you called the other person's number by turning a dial to the correct number. Not that Eva had ever had anyone to call.

Watching him, Eva felt an empathy with Kyle's need to make a connection since that was what she wanted herself.

'I suppose you want to talk to your sister,' she said quietly. 'Kyra's in the Solar.'

'Cheers,' Kyle replied absently, looking up with a smile that stilled on his face as he saw Eva.

He really was seeing her now and as his mouth slackened and his eyes rounded with shock she was abruptly conscious of her appearance. She was barefoot and muddy-legged, still wearing the tattered and stained remains of her badly-fitting red velvet dress, her hair a dark matted tangle around her dirty face. She'd

146

seen herself often enough in the mirrors but only in Kyle's horrified stare did she realize how lost and broken she appeared.

'Did you say something?' Kyle's voice was a whisper and she could hear him swallow painfully. 'Who *are* you?'

'I'm Eva Chance,' she said and tried to smile as she added, 'I'm the one whose body you've been looking for.'

'I'm going crazy.' Kyle's face was so white she could see each individual ginger freckle standing out on his skin like a sudden attack of measles. 'Seeing dead people, that's not what I do.'

'Being dead people's new to me too,' Eva said, trying to sound unthreatening and knowing it wasn't working as he flinched with every word she spoke. 'You're only the third person to see me.'

'It's like you're really there.' Kyle lifted a hand and then dropped it again. 'What happened to you?'

'I don't know,' Eva told him. 'I wish I did. I think maybe someone killed me, but I don't know who or even when it happened. I just found myself like this.'

'I can't believe this.' Kyle shook his head but he plainly did believe it. He looked ill with it and Eva hated appearing like this. She hadn't known she could even though she'd wanted to and now for the first time she really felt like a ghost.

'I'm sorry,' she said and Kyle blinked.

'I should be saying that to you,' he said. 'I saw you before, didn't I? With your auntie in the summerhouse. I wasn't sure then but I think I knew there was something strange about you.'

'That's not necessarily because I'm a ghost,' Eva said wryly. 'People did always think I was strange.'

'I'm sorry,' Kyle said again. 'Um . . . is there anything I can do?' He reddened as he asked, clearly aware it was an odd question to ask someone who was dead.

Eva wished she dared ask him for help finding her murderer

147

but that seemed like an incredible demand to make of a virtual stranger. Instead she tried to focus on something he could do for her.

'Could you find out what's happened to my grandfather?' she said. 'He was taken to hospital nearly two weeks ago and I still don't know how he is. My aunt too, I haven't seen her since the ambulance took her away.'

'Of course,' Kyle nodded quickly. 'I can do that for you, no problem.' He looked relieved and she could tell he'd been expecting a Felix-like proposition of corpse seeking. 'How do I get the news to you?'

'I'll be here. I can't leave the grounds of the House.' Eva tried to smile again and wished she hadn't at the distressed look Kyle gave her. 'I do move around a bit but I'll watch out for you.'

'OK then.' Kyle fiddled with his phone awkwardly and Eva remembered he'd been about to find his sister. Her first embarrassment came flooding back, a hot flush of self-consciousness that made her wish she could vanish away.

The room spun, shifting dizzyingly, Kyle's face retreating as though he was being sucked backwards, the floor falling away beneath her. Grasping for something solid, Eva found her hands close over the smooth wooden rail of a banister as her vision stabilized.

She was standing on the first floor landing overlooking the hall, with Kyle only just stiffening in shock where she'd left him.

He put out a hand, hesitantly at first and then slicing it backwards and forwards across the empty air. Revolving in place he looked around the hall and then upwards. Eva watched as his eyes tracked past her position without seeing her. Her moment of wishing herself gone had made her invisible again. Eva wasn't sure if she was relieved by that or not.

Eva was beginning to grasp the way her appearances and disappearances worked. The trouble was that they seemed to be triggered by emotional states instead of rational decisions. It wasn't just that she'd spoken to him that had enabled Kyle to see her. It went deeper than that, bound up with her sudden wish to make a connection and his ongoing quest to find her body and his increasing susceptibility to the supernatural. But when embarrassment had overcome her she'd vanished again and this time he hadn't been able to see her. Perhaps he had also been wishing her away or had accepted that their conversation was over.

She didn't know if Kyle was an ally or not. He was the brother of her worst enemy—but Eva had more dangerous enemies now. Watching as Kyle set off at a jog to find his sister, Eva wished he were anyone other than Kyra Stratton's brother.

* * *

Cleaning the Solar was one of those jobs that just went on and on. Kyra had been at it for hours on Friday with a group of local women and they began again on Saturday with a grim realization that it could take the rest of the day.

The room had huge window panes, and between them the stone walls had been carved into vine shapes and plant forms with a thousand nooks and crannies for dust to gather. Cobwebs had hung in sheets when they first arrived and dirt just seemed to seep out of every crevice. They'd given up all hope of getting the windows clean until the dirt had been removed from the rest of the room but Kyra had lugged buckets of clean water and grey water out until her arms were ready to fall off and her section was still oozing filth.

'Bloody hell.' A woman on the other side of the room threw

her cloth into her bucket, splashing water on to the floor. 'I swear I had that wall clean yesterday and now look at it!' The carvings were choked with a substance both gritty and oily at the same time, made up of cobwebs and insect carcasses. The woman looked halfway to tears as she stormed out. Everyone else exchanged glances.

'She's right.' A girl with a thin sharp face spoke suddenly, appearing from behind Kyra. 'This place is unclean and so it will remain.' The girl spoke sharply, her dark eyes full of intensity.

'Superstitious, much?' All the staff were sharing old wives' tales and funny feelings about the House. Everyone seemed to have a 'gypsy granny' or 'streak of the Irish' that meant they could just sense things weren't right. Kyra didn't believe any of it. Although when she looked at the section of wall she'd been working on she honestly couldn't tell what parts she'd cleaned.

'This house isn't safe,' the stranger insisted. 'There are parts of this house that just can't be made clean. The family know it—they just don't admit it to the staff.'

'You been working here long then?' Kyra asked and the girl laughed with a bitter edge.

'Longer than you'd believe,' she said. 'Long enough to know this isn't a good place to work.'

'Some of us need the money.' Kyra shrugged, wondering why the other girl didn't quit if she was so afraid of the House. From her accent she was local but Kyra didn't recognize her.

'Work's not easy to find.' The other girl had a trick of jabbing her face forward as she spoke, sentences fired out in a rush. 'But if you have to be here don't let them send you down to the cellar.'

'The cellar?' Kyra repeated. 'My brother and his friend went down there. Damon insists it's haunted.'

'Tell your brother to keep out of it!' The girl looked alarmed and Kyra wondered if she fancied Kyle to be so abruptly insisting.

'How come?' she asked. 'More superstitions?'

'People have died down there.' The girl lowered her voice and moved closer to Kyra. There was a cold draught coming from somewhere nearby and Kyra couldn't help shivering. 'There was a butler broke his neck and they said he'd been drinking even though everyone knew he was a temperance man. And a housekeeper drowned in two inches of water—that was an "unfortunate accident". This house is unlucky for lots of people, not just the Chances.'

The girl's intensity was too great for Kyra to write her words off as a joke. And, looking around the room, Kyra imagined she could practically see the Solar getting grimier, grit oozing out of the walls and spider's webs dropping out of the vaulted roof. Through the grimy windows she could see the gardens as a green blur beyond glass that was a smoky tobacco brown. It might be superstitious but she was sure the sharp-faced girl was right when she said the job was hopeless.

She turned back to tell her so and realized the girl was gone. In just a couple of seconds she'd left as quietly and quickly as if the room had swallowed her up—and Kyra had never even asked her name.

* * *

But a new figure had appeared in the open doors to the Solar, peering into the room with a doubtful and confused expression that changed to relief when he spotted her. It was Kyle.

'Hey,' Kyra said coming over to him and aiming a friendly punch at his shoulder. 'Still looking for bodies?'

'Cut it out.' Kyle brushed her hand away and glared at her. 'Look, are you busy? I want to talk to you.'

151

'Not exactly busy,' Kyra said. 'Let's go outside. I could do with some fresh air.'

The Solar led on to a stone terrace and from there they could see out across the formal gardens which were now looking less tangled and overgrown. For the first time for days Kyra could imagine people paying money to visit the House. Still the terrace was covered with dead leaves which had collected in drifts, flashing green and gold where peacock feathers were mixed into the leaf piles.

'What's up?' Kyra asked, sitting on the stone balustrade and looking up at her brother.

'Trouble,' Kyle said darkly. 'The torture chamber's going to be on the ghost tours.'

'Someone was just telling me the cellar was trouble,' Kyra began but Kyle cut her off.

'Let me finish,' he said. 'There's a lot more. Felix was on my case about finding this body and I told him I was finished looking. But he said I still owed him work because I hadn't been spending all my time looking for it. Then he took Damon off to pump him for information about the cellar. I think Felix has got an idea Eva's body's down there.'

'Just keep telling him no,' Kyra said. 'He won't sue you or anything like that.'

Kyle frowned at her.

'You don't understand,' he said. 'I think she might be down there too. I think so because . . .' Frustratingly he stopped at what was obviously the peak of his story and Kyra rolled her eyes, impatient with the cliff-hanger.

'Spit it out then,' she said.

'I think her body's down there because I've just seen her ghost,' he said. 'Twice now, although I didn't realize who she was the first time. But it's Eva Chance. She spoke to me and she told me her name.'

If one of Kyra's girl friends had told her they'd seen a ghost Kyra would have pretended to humour them and then laughed about it later with the others. Ghost stories were for little kids, like ghost trains at funfairs and Halloween. But Kyle was the least imaginative person she knew.

'What did she look like?' she asked carefully. She didn't think Kyle had ever noticed Eva in real life. He wouldn't be able to describe her from memory.

'She looked small and frightened,' Kyle said. 'She wasn't wearing shoes or socks, just a tatty red dress, and her hair was muddy and tangled up. And the air felt cold around her and it smelt odd too, damp and sort of like mildew.' He fisted his hands into his pockets and hunched his shoulders, looking sick again.

Kyra felt cold. Kyle didn't have it in him to make up a story like that.

'She told me she was dead,' Kyle went on. 'She said someone had killed her.' He took a deep breath and went on. 'I asked if there was anything I could do and she asked me to find out how her grandfather was and her aunt. And then she vanished just as quickly as she'd appeared. She was a ghost, Kyra. People don't appear and disappear like that.'

'A ghost.' Kyra shook her head. 'Do you know how ridiculous that sounds?'

'Not nearly ridiculous enough when you've seen her,' Kyle replied. 'I know how it sounds, Kyra. But if you'd seen how scared she was you'd have known she was for real.'

Kyra looked down, over the edge of the terrace into the sea of greenery of the gardens. She didn't need to see it. She'd seen Eva looking scared and lost often enough and the way her brother was sympathizing with the dead girl made Kyra feel uncomfortable. If Eva really was dead and not playing a macabre version of hide and seek . . .

'There's some weird stuff going on,' she said slowly. 'Everyone's freaking out. That room I was in? Someone told me it couldn't be cleaned. She also said the cellars were dangerous and people had died down there.'

'The cellars are haunted,' Kyle said. 'Damon talks about it as if it's a big joke. It's like he just can't see it. That marketing bloke's the same way. He thinks its all a big tourist gimmick. But it felt weird down there. Like something was watching us, something dangerous.'

'I knew this job was too good to last,' Kyra said. 'There goes my last chance at paid work before the exams. "I had to quit because the house was haunted"; that'll look good on my employment history.'

'You can quit,' Kyle said. 'You probably should. But I'm staying on.'

'But why,' Kyra stared at him. 'You never liked it here anyway. Why stay now you're convinced it's dangerous?'

'Because . . . ' Her brother hesitated and then spoke in a rush, 'I want to find out what happened to her. To Eva. She's dead, she's trapped here as a ghost and she's got no one to help her. I think someone killed her and I want to find out who it was. I want to set her free.' He blushed.

'Oh lord.' Kyra felt something click into place as Kyle spoke and realized that for the first time her twin was really seriously interested in someone. As unlikely as it was, something in freakish Eva Chance had got his attention.'I don't expect you to understand,' Kyle said and Kyra kept her face still. She didn't want to embarrass him with how much she understood.

'All right,' she said. 'If that's what you want, I'm with you. But we have to do this sensibly, OK? None of the things people do in horror movies like wandering off into the night because they heard a noise. And you don't go near that cellar until we find out what's down there.'

Kyle didn't seem to know whether to look worried or relieved.

'I'm not asking you to stay,' he said.

'Yeah, I know.' Kyra stood up. 'I'm a big girl, Kyle, I can take care of myself.'

'Against ghosts?' Kyle looked dubious and Kyra stared him down.

'It's not ghosts that worry me,' she said, not admitting she didn't believe in them. 'But you're talking about catching a murderer. If someone killed Eva it was probably someone from around here. Most likely one of the family.'

They both looked over their shoulders automatically and then moved closer together.

'I hadn't thought about it that way,' Kyle admitted.

'And there's Eva's auntie and her grandad as well,' Kyra pointed out. 'If neither of those were accidents, we're looking at a full-on homicidal maniac. Even if they missed the mark a couple of times are you willing to bet they'll go on missing?' She shook her head. 'Are you sure it's worth it, Kyle? To find out what happened to a girl you never even knew to begin with?'

'How can you even ask?' Kyle shook his head. 'It's not just what happened to her, Kyra, it's what's happening right now. She's still here. She's in trouble and she needs help.'

'I never knew you had such a hero complex,' Kyra said, punching her brother on the shoulder. 'Ever since we walked in through the gates you've been trying to protect everyone. Just be careful yourself, OK?'

***

Creeping quietly through the rose garden, Eva could see Kyle and Kyra on the terrace but was too far away to hear their conversation. It was frustrating to hide but she wasn't sure if she wanted Kyra to see her; it had been embarrassing enough appearing to Kyle and he'd been a stranger to her. She wasn't sure how to control who saw her and who didn't. But she did want to know what the twins were saying to each other.

The gardeners had been through this part of the garden, taming it slightly, but roses still ran riot up trellises and across archways, giving Eva enough camouflage to edge slowly closer to the terrace. Coming through a fairytale arch of rose bushes, Eva felt a sharp pinch on her upper arm and thought she'd been snared by thorns until she looked round and saw Maggie's fierce dark eyes glaring at her.

'What are you doing?' Maggie snapped at her. 'That boy's been saying he won't leave until he finds out how you died.'

'Really?' Eva felt a smile grow across her face although she hadn't intended it. It was warming to think that someone had actually cared enough to try and help her.

'You have to tell him not to,' Maggie ordered. 'It's not fair to ask the living to solve your problems for you.'

'But I didn't ask,' Eva said. 'Only about news from the hospital.' She peered through the green leaves at the two figures on the terrace. 'You needn't worry, Kyra won't let him help me.'

'That's where you're wrong.' Maggie still looked fierce. 'She might not care for you but she's loyal to her family.' Her eyes flashed angrily as she added: 'And if you don't tell them not to waste their time, I will.'

'But why?' Eva couldn't understand it. 'You keep saying

156

you don't want to get involved but I don't see why you should begrudge someone else helping me.'

Maggie didn't reply but her lips were pinched tight and her eyes continued to blaze. She seemed to be really anxious for the first time since Eva had encountered her, looking almost frightened.

'Look,' she said suddenly. 'If I help you, you won't involve that boy in your family curse?' She paused and then said quickly: 'I've taught you a couple of tricks but there's much more I could tell you if I wanted to.'

Eva frowned. She distrusted Maggie's sudden offer of assistance but she didn't have much belief that Kyle could help her and the ghost girl did seem to know more than Eva did.

'All right,' she agreed. 'It's a deal.'

10
Notes on a Murder

Saturday, April 12th

Kyle had set an alarm on his phone for the first time ever, and when it shrilled into his ear at seven in the morning he floundered awake and fumbled it off.

He had got to the hospital yesterday just as visiting hours were ending and the hospital staff hadn't been inclined to bend the rules. Feeling a fool he'd left the hospital and run into some mates in town, just going off to the pub. Kyle had fallen in with them and hung out for a while but when they started talking about getting in a curry and going back to someone's house for some console gaming he'd said he had things to do and gone home instead. His mates had looked surprised and Kyle didn't blame them. He felt surprised at himself.

When he'd got home he'd poked about on the internet for a while looking up ghosts and historic houses. But nothing he found really explained what he'd seen. He was sure he'd seen Eva Chance and that she was a ghost. But he wasn't sure he'd convinced his sister about what he'd seen. But Eva had been there—or mostly there—and she'd told him someone had killed her. Kyle had promised to help her and he felt guilty he hadn't done the one small thing she'd asked him to do.

Which was why at half past seven he was on a bus into town, dressed in his least ripped pair of jeans and a clean white shirt lifted from his dad's wardrobe. He'd even cleaned his trainers. Inside the hospital he bought a bunch of daffodils from the gift shop and approached the reception desk.

'We've got two patients named Chance. Chance, Edward and Chance, Cora—both in a private room. Ward Eight, Room A, follow the signs to the second floor and then it'll be straight ahead of you. Morning visiting hours are from eight to ten.'

Ward Eight was a long depressing dormitory full of old people, most of whom looked at death's door. Each frail body was a small hump in the large metal beds, surrounded by hospital machines and trails of plastic tubing. The room smelt as well, of stale piss and fresh antiseptic, a mixture that made Kyle feel queasy.

Kyle looked up and down the room and then blinked as he noticed the door set into the wall just past the nurse's station. The door with a large policeman standing in front of it. The policeman noticed him at the same time and Kyle took a few cautious steps into the room, looking up and down at the signs on the walls. Room 8-A was very definitely the one being blocked by the policeman.

'Can I help you, son?' he asked and Kyle tried to look innocent.

'Um . . . I was looking for Miss Cora Chance,' he said. 'I brought her some flowers,' he showed the daffodils and the policeman nodded.

'I'll see they get to her, sir,' he said. 'I'm afraid no visitors are allowed at present. What was the name?'

'I'm Kyle.' Kyle handed over the flowers. 'What about Mr Chance. Mr . . . um Edward Chance. Could I see him instead?'

'No, sir, he's not seeing people either.' The policeman looked back at Kyle, waiting for him to leave.

'Um . . . how are they?' Kyle asked and the policeman frowned slightly.

'Stable, is what I've heard,' he said. 'They're both stable.'

Stable could mean anything, Kyle thought. He supposed it was better than 'at death's door' or 'circling the drain' but it wasn't exactly positive either. But it was clear he wasn't going to get anything more from the policeman who was looking about as unfriendly as someone holding a bunch of daffodils could look. He'd already begun to move away when the door of room 8-A opened and a man walked out. Not a doctor or a nurse, but a man in a grey suit carrying a briefcase.

'I thought no visitors were allowed,' Kyle said and the policeman glared and the man in the suit frowned. He looked sort of familiar and Kyle tried to remember who had been at that dinner party. He'd been mostly in the kitchen but he thought the man had been one of the guests.

'Very few people have visited at all,' the man said sharply. 'And some seem to have done more harm than good.' He glanced at the daffodils.

Kyle stuffed his fists into the pockets of his jeans, trying to stay cool.

'They're from the hospital gift shop,' he said. 'What, do you think they're poisoned or something? I found that old lady in the snow, you know? My name's Kyle Stratton, I called the ambulance, doesn't that count for anything? I just wanted to see how she was.' As he spoke Kyle felt himself getting angrier and by the end he was ready to walk out but the suited man was too quick for him.

'My apologies,' he said. 'My name's Michael Stevenage and

I admit I've a suspicious mind. I'm a lawyer and it comes with the territory, I'm afraid. And it really is true that the police have left instructions not to let anyone in except for me and Father Hargreaves.'

Kyle hesitated and the lawyer continued:

'Come on,—Kyle, wasn't it? We can't discuss this here. I saw a vending machine somewhere along that way, I'll buy you a Coke and we can talk.'

'I don't need a Coke!' Kyle objected, following the lawyer as he led the way out of the ward. 'I just want to know what's going on . . . I mean, how Cora and Eva's grandfa—how Mr Chance is doing.'

'Cora hasn't recovered consciousness,' Michael said. 'Edward's awake but he's in recovery from his third heart attack this year. Things don't look good, I'm afraid.'

'Oh.' Kyle wished he'd had the sense to leave when the answer was 'stable'. This news was exactly what he'd hoped wasn't true. 'Murdering bastard.'

'Excuse me!' The lawyer's eyebrows had shot right up and Kyle realized he'd spoken aloud.

'I meant whoever tried to strangle Miss Cora and bump off the old man,' Kyle said. 'And probably killed Eva as well. That's why the police are on the door, right? Because it stinks like rotting fish that one person's gone missing, and two have been attacked in less than a fortnight.'

'Yes,' the lawyer said slowly. 'Yes, it does, clearly. But you're the first of the staff to have noticed.'

'Don't you believe it.' Kyle shook his head. 'It's all over town that people are dropping like flies at the big house. The women are going around arm in arm and the blokes aren't much better. Everyone's twitchy.'

161

'And I suppose you've told everyone Cora was strangled?' the lawyer said.

'I didn't need to say anything,' Kyle glared, 'so you can keep your accusations. The paramedics were loud enough talking about ligatures and discolouration and everyone in town watches *Casualty* and *ER*. It's not like we're too thick to understand special doctor talk for "someone's strangled this woman with her scarf".'

'All right, truce,' Michael said. 'Don't take this the wrong way but have the police questioned you yet about finding Cora's body?'

'Only briefly at the summerhouse,' Kyle said. 'I was asked if I'd seen anyone nearby—or any footprints besides mine. I told them I hadn't.'

'Nothing at all?' The lawyer sounded almost wheedling. 'Even just something small would help. The police have Cora's scarf but I don't think they're likely to gain any evidence from that.'

'I can't help you,' Kyle said. 'I'd like to, but nothing I saw could be used as evidence of anything.'

'Then you did see something.' Michael's tone sharpened and he looked closer at Kyle. 'Something that worried you, perhaps? A little detail that preyed on your mind?'

'You could say that,' Kyle half-laughed half-groaned. 'I saw a ghost, OK? I saw someone who's dead.'

'A ghost?' Michael took a step back. 'Are you pulling my leg?'

'Eva Chance,' Kyle sighed. 'I don't care if you believe me or not. It's weird enough that I saw her, I'd just as soon not talk about it. But you asked. That's who I saw in the summerhouse. And Eva Chance is dead.'

'I see.'

Kyle wasn't sure what that was supposed to mean and he hurried on before the lawyer could jump to any conclusions.

'And before you start getting suspicious again, I didn't see any footprints. My sister thinks it's Eva running around pretending that she's dead and playing ghost tricks on people. But I don't believe that. I've seen her and she looks—like a murder victim.'

The lawyer sighed and rubbed the bridge of his nose as if it pained him.

'I'd like to believe this is a prank,' he said. 'But your story is a lot like Sir Edward's. He also insists that Eva is dead and is haunting the house as a ghost—and I'll ask you not to repeat that, young man. But the police have searched, and searched again when Cora went missing, and no one's found any sign of a body. I don't suppose you—'

'Jesus on wheels!' Kyle exploded, slamming his hand into the wall. 'Will people stop asking me to look for the body! I've looked, all right. I've looked everywhere except the cellar and the bottom of the lake. Everyone wants to know where the bloody body is—doesn't one single person care that a girl went missing? If it was my sister my parents would tear the place apart to find her. Not one of that girl's relations seems to give a toss. It's like they think a mouse died under the floorboards and they're worried it might make a stink. Not that a girl is missing, maybe dead, maybe murdered . . . '

'Steady on,' the lawyer said. 'Her grandfather cared very much—it's that which makes me think he won't recover. Losing his granddaughter all but broke his heart, I fear. And the police have looked too. When Eva first went missing they searched everywhere.'

'It stinks,' Kyle repeated. 'And you know it stinks or you wouldn't be here. Do lawyers usually visit their clients in the hospital?'

'All right,' the lawyer admitted. 'It's fishy as hell. Sir Edward's fall was suspicious enough and there seems no doubt Cora was attacked. But the police don't share their thoughts with me and I suspect they don't know what to make of the Chance family. It doesn't help that my client thinks he's being haunted by the ghost of his missing granddaughter. If you do spot any hard evidence of criminal activity, my advice to you is call the police straight away.'

'What about you?' Kyle said after a moment. 'Should I call you too?' He wasn't sure if he wanted the reassurance of authority or a paranoid suspicion that he might need the number of a lawyer if he was going to start tumbling over bodies. He'd found one already, even if it wasn't the one he'd been looking for. A second might start turning the police's attention in his direction.

'You can have my card,' the lawyer said after a long moment had passed. 'And don't hesitate to call if you think of anything that's a bit more concrete than ghost stories.'

'I'm not making up a story about a ghost,' Kyle said, putting the card in his pocket. 'But if you think I'm just some idiot kid and the old man's gaga, you should come and visit the House again. They're opening it to the public tomorrow, you know. Cellars and everything. I don't know if Eva's body will show up, or her ghost, or if the murderer will have another go at someone else. But I think something will happen.'

He didn't say that the tension at the House was so thick it was difficult to breathe or that every time he passed the cellar door he flinched as though a monster might come leaping out of the darkness. He didn't want the lawyer to think he was nuts.

'I hope you're wrong,' Michael said. 'But I'll come to the House tomorrow.'

'Good,' Kyle said. Then as a parting shot, he added, 'Maybe you can look for some evidence yourself.'

* * *

Kyra escaped the cleaning team in the Solar by getting herself assigned to setting up the gift shop. As she stacked up boxes and shelved books, she thought about what Kyle had told her yesterday about seeing Eva's ghost. Despite his insistence, she was still not convinced.

All the staff were suspicious, the stories about bloodied peacock feathers and a maggoty peacock corpse had circulated enough that everyone jumped when they heard that distinctive peacock scream. And bad as cleaning the Solar was, she'd heard enough to know there were worse jobs. The hedge cutting crew looked as though they'd been through a small war every time she spotted them in the garden, their faces grey and drawn and their clothes torn and filthy. Arms, hands, and faces sported bandages or dressings and they set to work with an angry will. Kyra had heard that the foreman had filled out a health and safety complaint form full of four-letter words but the crew battled on.

In the House things weren't much better. People jumped at their own reflections and tripped over shadows.

Bad luck, everyone called it, but they muttered it as though they were worried the bad luck would overhear them. Superstition, Kyra thought. But although she could believe that Eva was planting bloody feathers under everyone's noses she was less keen on the idea of her attacking people. That was seriously unhinged.

Just as her thoughts curved back to the idea of a murderer working his way through the Chances, she heard voices outside and moved to the window as she recognized one of them as Felix's. Any hope she had of catching him doing something illicit faded when she saw he was talking to the vicar.

Father Hargreaves was looking faintly harassed as he spoke, walking back towards his car.

'No, I'm sorry, young man, I can't help you,' he said, shaking his head. 'It's really not at all the sort of thing I can advise you on.'

Kyra flattened herself next to the window and pricked up her ears, wondering what on earth Felix had said to make the vicar look so shocked.

'Come on now.' Felix looked determined not to take no for an answer. 'I've researched the rite but the books are quite clear that it takes a priest to actually perform an exorcism.'

'And I've told you I don't advise dabbling with the supernatural,' the vicar said irritably. 'You'd need a priest experienced in the ministry of deliverance and you're not likely to find one outside the Church of Rome and I don't advise that either. I will pray for your grandfather and for your aunt but I won't be party to any nonsense about ghosts. If you're truly troubled in your own mind about these things I can recommend a good analyst.'

'I assure you I'm not losing my mind,' Felix snapped. 'I don't even believe in ghosts. It's the staff who keep seeing spectres all over the place.'

'If you're that concerned then why make such a feature of the house being haunted?' the vicar asked more mildly, glancing around the stable block. 'I can see a dozen posters from here advertising tours of the haunted torture chamber. I hardly think your grandfather would have approved of such a thing. Nor does it seem entirely consistent if you're worried about superstitious staff. Stop selling beads to the natives and you'll sleep a lot better.'

'I don't need a lecture.' Felix looked furious. 'I wanted some practical help. And I'm not worried about selling tickets to see the horror show in the cellars. If the ghosts don't like it, they can tell me so to my face.'

'My dear boy . . . ' the vicar began but Felix was having none of it.

'Stow it!' Storming past, he hurled himself into the front seat of his sports car and wrestled his keys out of his pocket and into the ignition. The vicar took a step back as the car roared into life.

'Wait!' he demanded. 'Where are you going?'

'To find some real help,' Felix stormed back at him, revving the engine threateningly. 'This is my house. I'm not going to be done out of it by superstition and rumours.' Tyres skidded on the gravel for a couple of seconds before he sped off, spitting chips in all directions.

'Oh dear,' said the vicar to himself, as the car sped away. Kyra was about to move back from the window when she spotted Lisle coming across the square with an enquiring look.

'What was that all about?' she asked incredulously, nodding her head in the direction of the departing car.

'A temper tantrum,' the vicar said, frowning. 'Young men are wild for answers. And I'm afraid the rumours have probably reached him that people are saying Edward's and Cora's accidents weren't accidents at all.'

'Oh dear.' Lisle looked uncomfortable. 'That's news to me as well. I've been working on getting the House ready for the tourists.'

'Then far be it from me to spread idle gossip,' the vicar said. 'I must be off, my dear, please remind the family they are in all our prayers.'

Then he mounted a bicycle as elderly as he was and donned a small round helmet before going wavering off in the direction of the drive. Lisle watched after him for a moment before turning on her heel and heading directly for the door to the gift shop. Kyra hastily busied herself among the piles of fudge and humbugs next in the unpacking heap.

11
Velvet Ropes

Sunday, April 13th

Sunday dawned bright with promise. The ivy clinging to the brickwork walls glowed freshly green as if trying to mask the signs of mould and decay. The weeds that still forced their way through the drive had flowered into daisies and primroses and even the bindweed was blooming in the hedges.

The House basked in the sunshine as if determined to put a good face on things and Eva tried to follow its example. Open days had always made her feel that way. However much she resented the tourists coming, she wanted the House to look its best for them. But this year she wasn't worried about tourists getting lost or locked in a toilet or twisting an ankle. This year the danger was that someone could get seriously hurt.

She'd spent the night pacing up and down the Long Gallery, as she had every night for the last two weeks. Other heavier footsteps had sometimes sounded in the distance and when they had, she'd paused and stilled, wondering if she was writing a ghostly imprint of her own across the floor. By the time the sunshine came sliding in through the high windows she had the beginnings of a plan. With Maggie's help, it might even have a chance of success.

In the bedrooms on the second floor the family were getting ready for the day. They'd divided up the House and gardens between them: everyone assigned an area of responsibility for the day. Aunt Joyce and Aunt Helen would be giving tours of the House. Christopher Knight, Joyce's partner, would be running the evening ghost walk. Richard Fairfax was supervising the ticket sales at the front gate and Felix would be in charge of the gardens.

Eva waited for them to leave, watching as each of them carefully locked their own bedroom door behind them. Showing off the beds, shaving stands and corsets of your ancestors was one thing—but it was quite another to let tourists see your own intimate possessions.

Eva slipped through the locked door to Cora's room, the odd sensation of travelling through solid wood becoming almost commonplace with habit. Rameses was waiting for her with a baleful look in his amber eyes. He was plainly bored with being cooped up in this room without his owner. Eva refilled his bowl and water dish apologetically and then wrinkled her nose at a foetid smell that lingered in the room and changed his litter box too. Rameses watched her and yawned.

'I'm sorry,' she said. 'But if I let you out I'd probably never be able to catch you again and it would break Aunt Cora's heart if you got lost.'

Rameses hunched his shoulders at her, refusing to acknowledge the service she was doing him. Even though she was used to ingratitude from her relations, Eva felt oddly hurt to experience it from a cat.

'Sorry,' she said again, melting back through the door and leaving him alone with his grievances. He'd probably start eating the second she was out of sight.

Downstairs the front hall had been transformed. The notice board had been removed, along with Ms Langley's improvised desk. The flagstones had been brushed and the windows cleaned and the old staircase shone glossily with freshly polished wood. the peacock feathers had been removed and without them the atmosphere seemed lighter. It was a pity to spoil the arrangements but Eva's plan depended on it.

There were metal poles and velvet ropes placed out across half the House, keeping the tourists circling the edges of rooms on pathways of coconut matting, instead of wandering freely wherever they wanted. It only took a few minutes for Eva to collect three poles and a length of rope. Carrying them back to the front hall she placed them in a triangle around the bottom of the stairs and connected them with the rope, cording off a small section of flagstones, discoloured with a rusty brown stain.

As she was tying the rope off, she felt eyes on her and looked up to see Maggie standing on the stairs. 'I've always jumped over the stain,' Eva explained, looking up. 'You saw what happened the one time I touched it. That was when the stalker started following me.'

'You think if you rope the place off the stalker won't rise?' Maggie said. 'How can you be sure?'

'I can't,' Eva admitted. 'Not with everything stirred up like this. But the stain's a trigger, isn't it? Walking over it summons the stalker ghost. And the way I see it the House has lots of places like that, places where the ghosts pay more attention, where they concentrate.'

'Places where we concentrate.' Maggie looked haunted herself, her eyes shadowed by some dark memory. 'Perhaps you're right.'

'It's got to be worth trying,' Eva insisted. 'If we can stop the tourists triggering them, then perhaps the ghosts will stay quiet.

There are ropes like this all over the House and arrows to tell people which direction to walk in. We don't need to move them very much to steer them past the most haunted parts.'

'We?' Maggie said. 'Does that mean I'm supposed to help you with this?'

'You promised,' Eva reminded her. 'And I can't do it all on my own.' She met the magpie girl's eyes with a challenge, showing that this time she wasn't going to back down.

'All right.' Maggie shrugged a shoulder ungraciously. 'I didn't say I wouldn't help. And it's not a bad idea at that. But you talk about a trigger as though it's something that happens by accident. Whenever I've seen someone pull the trigger of a gun it's because they wanted to shoot something.' She glanced at the bloodstain. 'It's not just accidents you need to watch out for.'

They both turned to look towards the passageway that led to the cellar door.

Eva said nothing. She knew the Witch wanted chaos and that by trying to avoid that she was challenging the ancient and malevolent ghost. But what else could she do? She'd promised herself she wouldn't give in—to the Witch's curse or to the unknown murderer. She was determined to thwart any more 'accidents' either unnatural or supernatural.

The next hour was almost fun. She'd never had someone of her own age actually help her with a project before. Being paired up at school meant being left alone while her partner hung around on the edge of another pair. But as she and Maggie skulked through the House, hiding from the hired staff who were beginning to arrive, switching arrows and adjusting the pathways, she was almost enjoying herself. As ghosts they could run rings around the human workers and Maggie winking at her from between the banisters of the floor above, or a hand giving her the thumbs up through the solid wood of a door made Eva start to see it as a game.

Up and down the main stairs, along the winding corridors, Eva tried to find a route for the tourists where nothing would summon even the memory of a ghost. Skip the Solar, festooned once more with ghostly cobwebs as if the room didn't want to be clean. Trace a looping course through the formal rooms to miss out the hidden door of the priest's hole so that no one would hear the death rattle of the troublesome priest in the lightless cell. Block off the minstrels' gallery in the ballroom with its telltale broken banister; too risky that someone might repeat that fatal fall. Move the arrows in the East Wing so that it wouldn't appear on the tour—all the while trying not to breathe the cloying scent that twined through the whole floor. Then on to the Crimson Room to check that no more dead peacocks had appeared in the night.

She wasn't even out of breath when she and Maggie appeared together on the roof at the same instant, to report on their work so far.

'I sent them in a circle round the gun room,' Maggie told her. 'One of your kin blew his brains out in there.'

'I blocked off the priest hole and the minstrels' gallery,' Eva replied. 'But the Crimson Room seems clear.'

'What did you want doing with the nursery?' Maggie asked. 'I don't think he'll hurt anyone, but it might scare them to see him.'

'Him?' Eva thought of the old nursery with its fort of brightly painted soldiers and the musty horsehair smell of the old rocking horse and then realized who Maggie meant. A child with a hare lip, a little boy ghost who had once been her friend. 'You mean Sinje? St John Chance.'

'A ghost with a twisted face,' Maggie said. 'I think he's still there, poor mite. Sometimes I hear him talking to his toys.'

'You don't hate all the Chances then,' Eva said and Maggie flashed her a glare.

'There's few enough of you as innocent as that creature,' Maggie said. 'You might spare him people gawping at him while you're making your mighty plans.' Her tone was sharp and Eva tried to diffuse the tension.

'Of course,' she said. 'Sinje should have his privacy. It's the only room he's got, after all.' She was thinking of having to share her own room with the tourists but the magpie girl was looking less ruffled until Eva's next words: 'Do you know what's the problem with the Solar?'

'That filthy place?' Maggie's eyes darkened dangerously. 'Your kin should know better than to try and clean it. I'll go and attend to the nursery now, my lady.' She vanished on those final bitter words and Eva felt depressed. Their camaraderie seemed to have been an illusion and Maggie was as prickly and difficult as ever. It had been ridiculous to think of trying to be friends with a ghost.

* * *

Kyra had got up early and gone for a jog around the estate. When she got back home her father was outside, working on the extension that had been slowly going up for the past six months when he had time for it around his other work. Builders' families often had to live with work in progress and Kyra made two cups of tea before climbing up to join her dad in the half-finished room above the garage.

'Cheers, pet.' Keith accepted the steaming mug gratefully and made space for her next to him on a stack of two-by-fours. 'What have you got going on today then?'

'Kyle and I are up to the big house again for the open day,' she said, trying to gauge his reaction without looking him straight in the eye. Both her parents had been doubtful about Kyra working in the run up to GCSEs. Only by promising to revise eight hours a day Monday to Friday had she convinced them to let her work weekends. Annoyingly they hadn't raised anything like as much objection to Kyle working—although his predictions had been way lower than hers. A double standard and unfair either way you sliced it.

'Finally got the place looking half decent then, have they?' Her dad didn't seem to be in the mood to argue. 'It was a grand old place back in the day. A lot of us were jealous of the Chances. I used to wish I lived in a house like that.'

'You did?' Kyra had never heard her dad talk like this before. The houses he built were modern ones with wall to wall carpeting, under floor heating and spotlighting: nothing like the Chance house.

'My own dad, your grandad, do you remember him?' Keith asked, nursing the mug of tea in his hands as he looked out over the fields behind the house, his eyes distant.

'Not much,' Kyra admitted. He'd died when she and Kyle were five.

'He was born in that House,' her dad said and Kyra blinked. 'One of the servant girls had got herself in trouble and had the baby in secret in a little attic bedroom. But she didn't live long enough to say who the father was and none of the male servants would admit to it. That was your grandad. He was born just after the First World War. Back then, to be born the bastard of a servant in a rich man's house was like being the lowest of the low. Even though he was a good man and he made the most of his life, he was always bitter about that. The Chances just got rid of him, you see. Gave him to the parish and didn't try and find out if he had family somewhere. It made him feel cut off from things.'

'That's typical.' Kyra felt angry. 'They think they're so grand, those Chances, even though they can't even keep their own house clean and still they treat people like that. Treated Grandad like that.'

'They don't treat their own much better,' her dad said and took a long swig of tea. 'Adeline Chance was the same age as me and she got pregnant the same way your great-grandmother did, not telling anyone until she had the baby and dying before she could say whose it was. She must have been scared to death, poor kid. I'd always thought she was so fearless—but the things that haunt us aren't always so obvious.'

'What was she scared of?' Kyra asked and her dad shook his head.

'They had us all out to drag the lake for Adeline, every man from town. We were searching half the morning before we thought to look on the island and there was the baby floating in the reeds and no sign of Adeline. I think she drowned herself rather than admit to her proud relations she'd made a mistake.'

'You never told me that story before,' Kyra said.

'It's not a story you tell to children,' her dad replied seriously. 'That little baby could have frozen to death out there, and she was in hospital for a month before that old man Chance came to get her. You and Kyle were just babies yourselves but your mother never complained when I went in every day to see that little girl.'

'But why?' Kyra felt uncomfortable. That baby had been Eva Chance and she'd never had any idea her father even knew who Eva was, let alone that he'd helped save her life before she was a day old.

'Because she had no one. Like your grandad. If no one had come to claim her I was thinking of asking your mother if we

175

could cope with a third to raise. But it didn't come to that. Lucky, I thought at the time. But maybe not so lucky for the little girl.'

'I suppose.' Kyra was amazed at the idea that Eva could have been her adopted sister. It was hard to imagine having creepy freaky Eva Chance in your house, having her as a relation even. But if she'd grown up with the Strattons she wouldn't have been Eva Chance, would she? Kyra couldn't bear to ask her father if he'd picked a name for the hospital baby before the Chances claimed it. The whole idea was too disturbing.

Her dad had finished his tea and Kyra only realized her own mug had gone stone cold when he handed her his and picked up his tools again.

'No rest for the wicked,' he said and Kyra winced.

'You're not wicked, Dad,' she said quietly, carrying the mugs out; wishing she had the same confidence in herself. Her father's story made her feel about two inches high. While he was worried about Eva growing up alone, she'd done her level best to make sure that Eva grew up friendless and lonely. She tried to tell herself she didn't care. But it made her feel wormy to imagine what he'd say if he knew how the kids at school had picked on Eva.

* * *

Eva stood in the driveway of the House, steeling herself. With Maggie gone there was still one task remaining—one ghost to be defused. The only problem was that Eva wasn't sure what was the trigger for this last ghost, since she'd only seen her once before. Well, if she was honest with herself that wasn't the only problem. There was also the fact that she was almost as scared of this particular ghost as she was of the witch.

With slow reluctant footsteps, Eva headed out through the gardens and towards the lake.

176

The gardeners had been here before her and had managed to make some impact on the bedraggled irises and reeds around the edge of the water. Their thickets had been depleted and rows of neat stakes marked where the mud became treacherous, lettered signs warning tourists to keep to the path.

The boathouse was still shut and locked. Aunt Helen had been argued out of her planned boat rides when it had been explained to her that the House had only two boats and neither of them was in good condition. The tourists, if they came, were unlikely to relish being rowed around a lake in a leaky boat on an April morning.

But without a boat Eva wasn't sure how to search the lake. She could give up now, there was no reason to assume this particular ghost would manifest to anyone else but her. Still she didn't want to give up. All through the morning she'd been adjusting the velvet ropes to redirect the tourists away from danger. Here the gardeners had already been with their signs and that might be enough.

But Eva couldn't leave it at that. She didn't know what this ghost wanted, hadn't realized until she became a ghost herself that Adeline haunted the lake. She had to know. She'd set herself to search for answers and understanding and this was the great mystery of her birth in front of her: almost as great a mystery as her death.

Reluctantly she waded out into the mud, feeling it slopping and slapping at the sides of her wellington boots. Either the mud or the water had a stink to it, a rotting algae smell that didn't seem to come from anywhere in particular but hung about in her nose unpleasantly.

The water was greenish brown, too cloudy to see the bottom. Eva waded out into it, feeling the cold enveloping her. As soon as she was far enough out to swim she ducked herself beneath the water, feeling the icy shock of it.

Now she was floating, the bowl of the lake all around her, the upturned bowl of the sky above. She'd learnt to swim in this same murky water but never learned to love it, for all that the lake had been one of her mother's favourite places. Or perhaps her dislike of it was because of that fact—or because this was where she'd been found as a baby—the rocking of a boat, the slopping of water, perhaps they were bad memories laid down in her mind from the moment she'd first drawn breath.

Out in the water she felt defenceless. Peacocks rustled the bushes on the dark bulk of the island. Trees shook in a distant breeze. And Eva hung suspended in the water, a strange, slippery, and treacherous element, supported and cradled in the clouded green shade.

'Adeline,' she said, letting her words drift out across the lake. 'I'm here. Do you recognize me? I'm Eva—your daughter.'

There was no answer. Eva continued to float. The water slopped around her. *Splish splosh thunk.*

She didn't see the boat until it was almost on top of her and the drowned face of her mother was staring eye-to-eye with her.

Eva spluttered, inhaled water, coughed it up, spluttered again and found herself sinking, viewing her mother's face through a ripple of water, the wrong way up and receding into green depths.

Water was spilling into Eva as her boots had sunk into the mud, drowning her in a cloud of algae. She was falling into darkness and that darkness was dragging at her, pulling her down, a whirlpool, a black hole, a place of claustrophobic smallness summoning her.

Evangeline.

Was it the voice of the witch in her head calling her? Eva's

178

lungs were gasping and it didn't help to tell herself she didn't have lungs. She did have instincts and right now every pore of her was gasping for air and breath and light.

Evangeline. Something was arrowing down through the murk, a dolphin-swift dark shape in the green depths. As it came she saw its face, the drowned dark eyes, the swirl of black hair. A mermaid mother, a slippery water ghost, it came coiling around and about her.

She wasn't falling any more. The ghost had her, it enveloped her, and she was floating in the coiling swirl of it as it cradled her in the waters of the lake.

Evangeline/messenger/daughter mind-of-my-mind.

It was not the voice of the witch in her head but a new voice, and not just in her head but in her blood and heart and lungs and stomach. It came through her in waves, inside the ghost's thoughts, as the Witch had been inside hers.

Darkness calling you/me/us under Witch/Chance curse.

It was painful hearing the thoughts reverberating from the ghost and into her, more painful still to sense the feelings underlying the wordless words, being part of those feelings.

Maggie had said some Chances were mad, some bad, some dangerous. Adeline had been all three. The mind of the ghost surrounding Eva now wasn't sane. Like the stalker she had been reduced to the bare bones—bare atoms or shreds—of her identity. She was mermaid, dolphin, naiad in these waters. What had been Adeline was now a discarnate shred of personality, barely able to keep one thought in front of another, to express feelings in words. But Adeline was now trying to do just that.

Go back/rise up/escape.

As the mermaid ghost lifted her up through the green waters Eva knew her mother was no threat to her. No threat but no help either. What Adeline had feared and fled from was just what Eva feared now: the influence of the Witch.

Always in my/your head promising/threatening disaster/chaos.

Images came and went in Eva's mind. Adeline as a child, Eva's aunts her older sisters. The same faces, the same criticisms, the same sense of being alone. Grandfather, Adeline's father, a grim despairing presence in the background.

Then came the running away, the escaping, anywhere but the House. Adeline had run to London, to Edinburgh, to Brighton, Paris, Amsterdam. A whirl of clothes, a swirl of hair, and she would be away in instants with no waiting to pack.

This much Eva had known already from the whisperings of the aunts. But in Adeline's mind was the House: not the love-hate relationship Eva herself had with it but a deeper darker antipathy that had no lighter element at all. While Eva had seen some of the family ghosts some of the time, Adeline had seen all of them: a host of supernatural presences with their fears and pains and doubts. Adeline had fled from that and been fetched back and each time she'd been brought back the Witch had laughed at her.

Cursed you/me.

The Witch had been a constant presence in Adeline's mind. The Witch had told her she was mad, had told her she was cursed, had promised that Adeline herself would destroy that which she loved the most.

And so Adeline had come, in labour, rowing a boat out on to the lake. She'd escaped the House in the middle of the night, avoiding her family's influence and that of the ghosts. She'd gone to the place she felt most at home, out across the lake she loved, rowing easily across the twilight waters.

But however far she rowed, however much she tried to escape the grip of the family curse, the Witch had preyed upon her mind.

You are mad, it had told her. *You are weak. You cannot escape your destiny. You will kill your child.*

But Adeline had killed herself instead.

She'd given birth to Eva alone in the dark and then let herself drift in these waters and let the newborn Eva drift too. Adeline had drowned and died. Eva in her Moses basket had floated and lived.

Escape daughter/messenger.

Eva arrived at the surface of the lake, the ripples in front of her eyes resolving into the surface of the water beneath her. She was standing on the shoreline of the lake. Her clothes were dry as though she'd never entered its green and misty depths. She was alone. Adeline had gone.

Eva wasn't sure what she'd expected. Not what she had found. Adeline was no threat to her, nor to anyone else. The mermaid ghost was a swirl of strong emotions adrift in the lake. But Adeline had died rather than serve the Witch and the Witch's curse. She'd refused to believe the Witch's prophecies of disaster. She'd let go and won. She hadn't been afraid to die to avoid the Witch's dark influence.

But Eva couldn't let go and she couldn't die. Whatever message Adeline had brought she couldn't use it. It was too late for Eva to escape.

12
Open House

The House opened at ten o'clock. The massive wrought-iron gates had been shut for the first time for days, just so they could be opened as the first cars turned up, and teenagers in fluorescent tunics were ready to direct the drivers across a field cleared for car parking. Guides at a trestle table on the front drive had tickets to sell, each coming with a rough map of the gardens and a list of what times the house tours ran. There was also a prominent stack of shiny brochures about ghost walks.

The stable block housed a gift shop, full of wooden swords and home-made fudge. The gardens looked inviting, spring flowers splashing colour through the mingled hues of green. Staff and family each had their appointed places to greet or guide the arrivals. Everything was prepared—but would anyone come?

Sitting on the front steps of the House, Eva thought the day seemed hushed and anticipatory, even the wind holding its breath to see if anyone would arrive. Half of Eva hoped the tourists wouldn't come, worried about the danger from the ghosts and the killer who seemed to be preying on the Chances. The other half felt, as she always did, that the vast effort of clearing the House up mustn't be wasted when the House needed money so badly.

She'd made the effort to clean herself up, habit overcoming any sense of futility. Wondering about the metaphysics of it, she washed her face and hands in icy water after the family had used all the hot. Brushing her hair and her teeth seemed bizarre activities for a ghost but she didn't want to look like the bedraggled fright she'd appeared to Kyle. She'd left the tattered velvet dress on despite its rips and tears, since it wasn't as if she had anything better, and she'd slid her bare feet into another battered pair of wellington boots. The incongruity of her appearance had made her laugh at herself. There was no point pretending she was one of the dreadful and awe-inspiring presences of the House, like the Witch or the Stalker. Maggie had more of a sinister air than she did. But Eva had lived all her life in shabby clothes and she didn't see any point in pretending that she was any more impressive now she was dead.

There was no sign of any of the other ghosts; even Maggie had vanished away. The family were all out of sight and the guides at the trestle table didn't even glance in Eva's direction. She was alone, waiting like the House to see what would happen. Her eyes searched the far end of the driveway where it curved, as if she could will people to appear just by looking.

When the first figures rounded the corner she wondered for a moment if she *had* imagined them. But the family of four seemed normal enough. The mother pushed a buggy and the father held the hand of a small child as they made their way towards the trestle table and stopped.

'Two adult tickets for the House and gardens,' the father said, taking out his wallet. 'The kids don't need tickets, do they?'

'Not unless they're over five, sir.' The guides hurried to take his money and hand over tickets and maps. 'Welcome to Chance House.'

Eva could feel the House settling back behind her, preparing to be admired. Already another two families were rounding the bend of the drive, followed by what looked like a tour party of walkers with backpacks. Notes fluttered and coins rattled in the cash box as the guides handed out more tickets and brochures and directed people through the shrubbery towards the gardens.

The first family were already moving past Eva, the buggy wheels crunching on the gravel drive.

'Lovely old place,' the father commented, glancing about him.

'Mmm,' his wife agreed, consulting the map. 'How about looking for this gothic tower—that sounds interesting?'

But the small boy was dragging behind, turning his head to look at the House, eyes growing rounder as they met Eva's.

'Look, Mummy!' he exclaimed. 'A ghost!'

The adults turned their heads to where he was pointing, both looking straight through Eva, before exchanging tolerant glances with each other.

'What kind of ghost, darling?' the mother asked, as the baby in the buggy blinked disinterestedly at Eva.

'A girl,' the child said. 'Her dress is all tore up and she's got wellies on.'

'Smart ghost,' the father smiled. 'I'm beginning to think we should have brought ours, you know how suddenly the day can change.'

'It looks all right now.' The mother squinted up at the sky. 'Come on, Nathan, wave goodbye to the ghost. We're going to see the gardens now.'

'Bye bye, ghost,' the little boy said obediently, waving a chubby hand at Eva.

'Bye bye, Nathan,' she replied softly, waving back.

The last she saw of the family was the child's delighted smile as he looked back at her, waving until he was out of sight.

***

As the stream of tourists entered the House, Eva went to check on Rameses and after a couple of worried moments spotted the golden cat on top of the wardrobe, ears flattened and hackles up. Despite Eva's efforts to neutralize the ghosts, the cat was on high alert. He watched with baleful owl eyes as Eva appeared, the food in his bowl still untouched. He showed no interest when she tapped the bowl encouragingly, refusing to move until she turned back to the door, and then came scrabbling down in a hopeful flurry of paws.

'I can't,' she apologized. 'I've done my best to keep the tourists out of trouble but it's still dangerous out there.'

Rameses stared at the door-handle pointedly and then looked at her, not taking no for an answer.

Eva sighed; they went through this routine every time she fed the cat and each time it got harder to refuse Rameses's imprecations. The room smelt foetid with the much-used cat-litter tray reeking away in the corner. The bedspread was a mess of torn threads and shed fur. Every surface had been swept clear of breakable objects and their remains lay jumbled on the floor.

'I'm sorry,' she said. 'It's safer for you in here.'

Rameses looked back disbelievingly and opened his mouth, uttering a plaintive yowl that tugged at her heart like the screams of the peacocks. Every inch of the furry body was yearning towards the door and Eva felt sick at herself in the role of jailer.

'I know it's been a while,' she said out loud. 'But when this is all over, I promise, I'll let you out. When this is over . . .'

Her stomach squirmed. The smell of used cat litter had got stronger, filling her mouth and nostrils, clinging around her body as through it was seeping into her skin. She rubbed her wrists,

185

trying to soothe the burning wire of pain that suddenly ringed each of them, trying to force back the image of the room as a jail cell and the cat a half-crazed prisoner desperate to escape.

Rameses yowled again. His fur was ruffled up across his shoulders and down the snake-like line of his back, his tail a quivering bottlebrush of exclamatory alarm. Lambent yellow eyes fixed on hers, locked her into place. Eva had read in Kipling that a cat cannot meet the eyes of a human. But it was Eva whose eyes dropped first.

'Fine,' she said. 'I know what it's like to be trapped. And besides, if the Witch wins, who'll come to help you then?'

Rameses seemed to know he'd won and in true aristocratic form he was gracious in victory, striding up to the door with lordly confidence and glancing up expectantly for her to make good on her promise.

'Just stay out of trouble, all right?' Eva said. 'If you see any ghosts, just run.'

Rameses gave her a flat look and Eva rolled her eyes.

'Except me,' she said. 'Obviously. I'm on your side.' And she reached for the door handle.

The cat's confidence didn't extend to allowing her time to hesitate; the second the door was open a crack, the cat was through it, like a streak of lightning. By the time Eva had followed Rameses into the corridor, he was no longer anywhere in sight.

13
Through a Glass, Darkly

Kyra wasn't sure whether to tell Kyle about what their dad had said. But she had the nagging feeling it was important and so she repeated the conversation on the way to the House. Kyle listened thoughtfully to the part about their great-grandmother having been a Chance servant but he was more interested in the part about Eva's mother having drowned herself and Eva as an unclaimed baby in the hospital. Kyra had to smile when Kyle looked uncomfortable at the mention that Eva could have been their adopted sister. But it was also annoying that he cared so much about the rejected rich girl.

'They didn't care about her even then,' he said. 'None of them but her grandfather.'

'She was weird, Kyle,' Kyra said. 'She was odd and creepy and she talked like someone from a history book. No one liked her.' But she felt low as she said it and Kyle didn't even look at her.

'I'm going to try to find her,' he said as they arrived at the gates. 'I'll tell her what I found out at the hospital. Maybe she can think of some evidence that'll convince the lawyer and the police that she was killed.'

As he jogged away Kyra realized that for the first time he hadn't reminded her to be careful.

On her way up the drive to the House, Kyra saw her brother's friend Damon directing the line of parked cars into a field. He grinned at her as she arrived.

'Didya sleep in then?' he asked. 'I was here at eight. I'm keeping the bosses sweet so they'll let me help run the ghost walk tonight.'

'You're a nutter,' Kyra told him. 'Why would you even want to get mixed up with ghosts and that?'

'You're not the only one who likes to earn a bit.' Damon shrugged. 'And it's only a bit of fun, innit? Don't tell me you're like Kyle, you actually believe this place is haunted?' He laughed at her and Kyra rolled her eyes, walking away.

She thought it was probably bravado. Damon had been unnerved by going down into the cellar with Kyle and now he was trying to pretend he'd never lost his cool, practically daring himself to believe the ghosts weren't real.

She was still sorting out what she believed. Her original theory was that Eva had staged her own disappearance for some freaky reason of her own, but that didn't explain the way the old man and Miss Cora had both landed in hospital unless Eva was the one who'd put them there while skulking about the House. Eva as a murderer seemed far-fetched if not quite as implausible as the idea that Eva was now a ghost. So what did that leave? Someone who wasn't Eva who had killed once and tried twice more. Someone very confident or very unhinged. That was what worried Kyra—not ghosts and accidents but a real murderer who was taking more and more risks to achieve some secret aim.

* * *

Kyra's job for the day was to advertise some of the side attractions: the cookery exhibition in the kitchens, the ice-cream stand in the folly, and tea room in the stable-block, as well as the tours of the House and the ghost walks that evening. Collecting a sheaf of flyers, she deliberately shuffled the ghost walk information to the bottom of the stack. Whatever was going on, she thought the fewer people came to hunt ghosts the better.

Unfortunately, she seemed to be alone in thinking that. The guides at the ticket stand told her they'd already sold eight places on the ghost walk and the stables were blazoned with posters showing the torturer's tools from the cellar. As Kyra wandered from group to group of tourists, offering her flyers, she realized how many of them were speculating on whether the House was really haunted. The family parties with children seemed to be treating it as a game, a sort of I-spy for ghosts. But the students and young couples seemed more intrigued and the locals were frankly suspicious.

'A crying shame, that's what it is, hunting for ghosts when that girl's still not been found,' Kyra heard one local woman mutter to her friends. 'It's not decent.'

'Old man Chance would never have let them do it,' a man who looked positively ancient himself was telling his cronies. 'He'd got class, he had. Those daughters of his would sell their own children if there was money in it.'

Despite their rehashing of old scandals, the locals were as keen as the tourists to join in the tours of the House and Kyra tagged herself on to the back of a group. After her dad's story this morning, she'd realized she didn't actually know that much about Eva's family.

The tour group crowded into the front hall where a smartly-dressed woman greeted them with a professional smile that didn't reach her eyes.

'Good morning, everyone,' she said. 'I'm Joyce. Joyce Chance.

189

And I'll be showing you around my family home today. I grew up here, although I live in London now, where I run my own business as a jewellery designer.'

Kyra found her eyes drawn to the woman's outfit. Joyce was dressed in an eye-wateringly bright yellow dress, which showed off the glittering brooch pinned to her shoulder: a scarlet ladybird the size of a giant cockroach, gleaming blood red and spotted with glittering black stones. Kyra thought it was hideous but when a couple of women made polite remarks about it, Joyce whipped out a silver case of business cards and handed them out like party favours. Only then did she start the tour.

They began on the ground floor, following the trail of arrow signs, with Joyce taking the lead and pointing out various objects and features with a possessive air.

'My ancestor, Henry Chance, rebuilt this portion of the house in the eighteenth century after it was damaged by fire. Here you see the panelling has my family's arms carved into it . . . '

Kyra kept to the back of the group, as they trailed after Joyce. She'd seen the rooms before, of course, and she wondered how they looked to the tourists who hadn't had to beat carpets, wash walls, and wipe grime from each curlicue of wood-carving. From the murmurs of appreciation it seemed that the faded fabrics and darkened paintings didn't worry them.

'A grand old place,' one man said as they entered the library, looking up into the vaulted heights where a gallery ran round the top of the room, off limits to tourists since it was only reachable by a spiral staircase. 'They don't build them like this any more.'

'When are we going to see the ghosts?' a little boy dragged on his dad's hand impatiently. 'Is it the ghosts next, Daddy?'

At the front of the group Joyce was talking about how 'her ancestors' had brought many of the objects back with them from the 'Grand Tour', a traditional visit made by 'scions of noble families' to all the capitals of Europe. From the way she spoke about it, it sounded like a cross between a gap-year and an extended shopping spree.

'What's the story about this young aristo that's going to inherit the whole caboodle?' someone murmured at the back of the group, speaking low so Joyce wouldn't overhear. 'Lucky young devil—unless the place really is haunted, I suppose.'

'If I were inheriting a fortune I wouldn't worry too much about ghosts,' a young man from the town commented, to a chorus of laughing agreement from his friends.

As the group moved onwards, still laughing, Kyra realized she wasn't the only person to have been listening to the comments. On the other side of the corridor someone else was standing with a frozen expression on his face. It was Felix Fairfax.

He saw her at the same time she spotted him, and Kyra remembered her brother's warning. But Kyle wasn't here now and she was intrigued to know what Felix was up to. Meeting his glance, she curved her own lips into a slight smile.

'So what do you reckon,' she asked him. 'Is it worth it to you, to live in a haunted house?'

His eyes narrowed, studying her for a long moment before answering with a quirk of his lips.

'It seems to be bringing in the tourists,' he said. 'The ghosts don't trouble me.'

'And you've got to screw every penny out of the tourists, to save the place from collapse,' Kyra said lightly, quoting his own words back to him, and was rewarded by a sharp intensification of that stare.

'The blonde waitress at the dinner party,' he said, suddenly, placing her for the first time. 'You've got a good memory.'

'Better than yours,' Kyra told him. 'But who remembers the staff, right?' There was an edge in her voice that was not pretended. It was one thing to be remembered, another to be defined as a waitress. She didn't like being described so starkly.

Moving away from him she walked on into the next room where the rest of the tour group were looking around rather doubtfully. Even Joyce seemed to find it difficult to know what to say about this stop on the tour. Forgetting Felix, Kyra's own eyes widened as she looked around the room. This was the Solar that she and the rest of the cleaning team had worked on for three days, washing windows, wiping woodwork and mopping the parquet floor. From the look of it now, they might as well have spent their time catching spiders and encouraging them to spin webs. The high ceiling was draped with heavy cobwebs, already dark with dust, the long windows were streaked with a brown greasy fug, as if a thousand smokers had been chaining their way through duty-free packets of cigarettes and not bothering to inhale. The floor was gritty underfoot and slightly sticky, so that even walking into it felt uncomfortable, making her steps wary as a cat picking its way across a muddy path.

'Ah, now you see,' Joyce said. 'The Solar is one of the haunted rooms.' People turned with surprise and her voice gained confidence as she continued. 'My great-grandfather, Thomas Chance, used to lead the family's prayers in this room. He wrote in his diaries that it had a powerful and saintly atmosphere which was conducive to higher thoughts. But one day the family came into the room for morning prayers and it was black with dirt. No matter how the servants tried to clean it, they could never entirely remove the filth. The Chances of the time had to hold prayers in the hall after that. To this day, the mysterious dirt continues to cover the room—even though our staff have used the most modern cleaning methods.'

A few of the tourists continued to look doubtful but the little boy who'd wanted to see ghosts touched a dirty wall with a wondering hand, then looked at his grimy fingers with awe. Kyra bit her lips to avoid laughing and then frowned as Felix moved up next to her.

'I didn't realize we'd asked the staff to clean a haunted room.' He spoke softly. 'Perhaps we should be paying you danger money. Or do the modern cleaning methods include anti-ghost gear?'

'I wouldn't say no to the danger money,' Kyra said lightly. 'But I'm like you, Felix Fairfax. Ghosts don't bother me.'

'Only spoilt young men?' he asked. His tone was self-deprecating and with an added quality Kyra hadn't expected when she'd needled him about his attitude to the staff. His eyes were still studying her and they held a gleam of interest that was anything but aloof.

'You got it,' she said, stepping away and making as if to join the group, who were moving towards the doorway.

'Wait.' He stretched out a hand, curving his fingers around her arm and she realized with a stab of alarm that he was stronger than he looked. But he released her in seconds as she shifted away. 'I can't believe you're interested in seeing the historic kitchens.'

'I'm working,' she said, fluttering the stack of leaflets at him. 'I'm supposed to be handing these out.'

'It can wait,' he said. 'I still don't know what I should call you.'

'Why should you call me anything?' Kyra said sharply. 'I don't give out my name to every bloke I meet.'

'Naturally,' Felix replied smoothly. 'And I don't ask every girl I meet for her name.' He moved a step closer, not dropping his eyes from hers. 'But I'd like to know yours—and your number.' He was the same height as her and he was suddenly up close, in her personal space, only just not touching her. His green eyes were gleaming with intense interest and Kyra's smile spread in return.

'I don't give out my number to just anyone, either,' she said, looking into his eyes. Kyra was keeping her guard up, despite the fact that his sudden interest had roused her own in return. Even aside from the fact he was a toff and her brother thought he was a prat, he might be something even worse than that.

It was strange to look into someone's eyes and wonder at the same time if they fancied you and if they were a killer. Eyes told you a lot about a person: how they looked at you, the air of themselves they projected through their stare. But in the end eyes weren't any better than windows: they could be curtained, or darkened like the windows in this room.

The light from the windows was fading. Kyra glanced up and away from Felix to where the dim shafts of sunshine through the dulled window glass were slowly fading away, deepening the shadows all around them.

'You're sure ghosts don't worry you?' she asked, looking back at Felix and wondering if he had noticed the shift in the light.

'Not enough to distract me from what I want,' he replied, looking straight back at her. 'So, about that number . . .' As he spoke he moved closer, his eyes signalling clearly that he was about to make a pass. Kyra could have moved away but she held her ground, looking straight back into his gleaming green eyes—and saw them flare with sudden alarm as the door of the room slammed shut and all the lights went out.

* * *

Sitting halfway up the grand staircase, Eva felt the House shudder. For a moment her vision greyed out, as if she'd been plunged into darkness. Then the light returned but her stomach

194

lurched with sudden alarm. Something was horribly wrong.

On the first floor a crowd of tourists were murmuring comfortably to each other; down in the hall, sunlight shafted through the open door where a chattering queue were eating ice-creams while they waited for the next tour. Everything was as it should be, but beneath the flagstones a malicious presence was stirring. Something had happened to please the Witch.

Eva rose to her feet, her ghostly senses reaching in all directions, trying to work out where she'd gone wrong. If one ghost had been roused, it might have stirred others; already the dull stain on the hall floor looked wetter and more crimson than five minutes ago. But it wasn't the Stalker who'd been triggered. There was no sound of footsteps; the danger felt further away.

It wasn't coming from the east wing either. Eva was moving almost without realizing it, her footsteps gliding down the stairs and along a corridor, her body sliding like a pin to a magnet towards the source of the disturbance. The priest's hole was still shut up, the ballroom was silent; Eva was racking her brains for a ghost she'd missed. She and Maggie had been so industrious, carefully marking a safe path—

Eva froze. With a dropping sense of horror, she realized there was one ghost she hadn't thought to consider a threat. Her bones seemed to turn to water at the magnitude of her mistake. There was one ghost who remained free. One ghost she had trusted not to cause chaos in the House.

'Maggie,' she said and lunged through the door of the Solar into the darkness beyond.

* * *

Kyle had circled the House once looking for Eva before Lisle had seen him doing nothing and sent him to direct cars in the parking lot. He arrived just as a grinding crash set off a chorus of car alarms as two of the cars being directed by attendants tangled in a sudden and startling collision.

He paused, staring like the people around him at the scene of the accident, as the owners of the two cars burst out and swore at each other furiously, raising threatening fists. Then he shook his head and ran back towards the House. Somehow he was certain the car crash wasn't the thing that had set all his nerves jangling. Something else was happening, something worse than this.

Halfway along the gravel path a circle of people had gathered around a young student, slumped on the ground clutching her ankle.

'I just lost my footing,' she was saying miserably, her eyes watering from the pain. 'I think I've broken it.' She bit her lips hard as she looked down at the ugly angle her foot was twisted at.

Kyle slowed and then, feeling like a bastard for not stopping, jogged on past the group and watched his own feet. The student had plenty of people to help her. Kyle was more worried about someone who didn't.

At the main entrance to the House a sudden gust of wind had whisked all the brochures and leaflets off the ticket table and scattered them about. It was a distraction Kyle didn't even spare a glance for as he shouldered past the queue of tourists and into the House.

As he passed the threshold his skin started to crawl, every single nerve in his body shouting a warning. But as far as he could see, everything looked normal. Kyle's progress slowed as he reached the centre of the hall, and ignoring the curious stares of the tourists he moved carefully towards the cellar door. It was shut.

He'd been expecting to find it open and God-knows-what happening down there and all at once he felt stupid, a victim of nerves and superstition. He'd been so sure something was wrong and even now his heart was thudding as sharp spikes of adrenaline surged through his body. But the door was shut and the flat wooden surface told him nothing. No one was in the cellar; he'd made a mistake.

* * *

A soft white light glowed suddenly in the darkness of the Solar as Felix produced a small torch. He played it across the room, showing the grimy windows through which no sun penetrated and the vaulted walls where the light-fittings hung useless and dead. Across the torch beam sooty flakes fell like snow and Kyra could feel them alighting on her head and shoulders: swathes of cobwebs, insect carcasses, and a dusty grit that made her skin crawl.

The torchlight wavered around the room, Felix's hand not steady enough to hold it straight. They had joked about haunting, testing each other for signs of credulousness, but neither of them was laughing now. Kyra moved closer to Felix and felt his free hand brush against her arm and his fingers intertwine with hers.

Ahead of them Felix's torch beam moved onwards to outline the door which had slammed shut—and the dark figure in front of it, a female form with hate burning in her eyes.

'Eva—' said Felix but his voice fell uncertainly before he'd completed the name. It wasn't Eva. This was a woman in a servant's uniform: her face contorted with rage and her lips drawn back in an animal snarl. 'Who are *you*?'

In answer the creature sprang at him, leaping at him with no care of herself, fingernails flashing in the light as they curved toward his eyes. Kyra felt her arm wrenched hard and lost her grip on Felix's hand as he fell backwards. The torch went

197

skittering across the floor, the beam spinning around and about wildly, illuminating the lurching form of Felix with the ghost ripping and clawing at him.

Kyra scrambled out of the way of the fight and chased after the spinning torch, afraid that the light would go out and she'd have no idea what was happening in the dark room. The torch spun towards the wall and she threw herself headlong after it. She fell hard on to the floor, her chin banging down to the hard tiles, feeling the rest of the impact through her shoulders, hips, and thighs. But her reaching hand grasped the torch barrel and held fast. It was her bad luck that she caught it just as the torch was pointing directly at her and blinding her with too much light.

Kyra tasted blood in her mouth. The fall had knocked breath and energy out of her and she could barely bring her protesting body to twitch the torch out of her eyes. It took endless seconds of panicked blind pain before she could force herself to roll on to her side.

Through streaming eyes she fumbled the torch around and the light wavered across on the struggling pair in the centre of the room. Felix was trying to fight free from the clawing fury of the ghost but losing the battle, already forced down to his knees with his arms wrapped around his head to protect his face.

The servant ghost lifted her head and stared into the light, its dark eyes wild and terrible, the eyes of an insane person.

Her interruption lasted long enough for Felix to wrench himself half-free of the creature but the advantage didn't last as it turned on him again, stabbing at his face with quick flicks of its bony fingers.

'Filth,' the ghost spat. 'Vermin. Everything you touch you defile . . .'

'You're the filth,' Felix declared, fending off blows. 'You're what's poisoning this House, you ghosts are the vermin, like rats in the walls.' As he finished speaking he kicked out hard, forcing the servant ghost back.

'Devil!' the servant ghost screamed. Kyra flinched at the look it gave Felix in return. Felix was making it angrier and kicks and blows weren't slowing it down as they would a human. The ghost was still ripping at him but most of his punches didn't seem to connect. 'I'll show you,' the servant ghost sounded crazed. 'Show you your own twisted soul.'

It had only been minutes since the fight began and the snowfall of debris from the ceiling had continued throughout. Lying on the floor Kyra realized the stuff was falling faster and not just falling, she could feel it beneath her, seeping out of the cracks between the tiles with a squirming unpleasantness. She was standing before she knew she could, just to get away from it.

'Stop it.' Kyra heard herself speak the words and froze in panic as the ghost turned its terrible stare on her. 'Please, don't. Please.' Hearing herself reduced to stammering fear, she felt crippled with the shame of it.

Worse still the servant ghost was still staring at her, those burning eyes impossible to look away from and full of madness. There was no sanity left in that stare, just horror upon horror, brimming over and filling the room.

***

Eva arrived in the Solar to a scene of leaping shadows. Maggie's fingers spiked at Felix and then she whirled and her face leaped out of the shadows, mad eyes staring wildly towards the source of the light.

It took Eva a moment to identify the pleading figure behind the light as Kyra and when she did it made her stomach squirm to recognize the part of her that enjoyed seeing Felix frightened and out of his league and hearing Kyra humbled and begging. It was satisfying to see them get a taste of their own medicine.

It was the same emotion she'd had before in the library and this time she recognized it in time to fight against it. Kyra wasn't her enemy, she told herself. And she had no proof that Felix was either.

Eva was beginning to learn to see with other eyes. The atmosphere of the Solar was completely choked with malice, instead of the grimy discomfort that she was used to. The servant girl's sharp and biting presence was intensified into a thick force of fury. And all around the room filth was spilling out of every crevice, a gritty, oily, filmy writhing of stuff that carried an atmosphere as strong as maggots, faeces, and corrupting flesh. Something very bad had happened here once—no—more than once; something bad enough to leave echoes in the room that would never stay clean. And now it had suddenly burst forth.

Like the room, Maggie was out of control, all the currents in the room swirling about her as her anger in a storm of dark energy. Something had triggered a dangerous side of the servant girl's ghost personality that Eva had only had glimpses of until now. *All the same, I should have guessed*, she told herself. Maggie had begun their friendship with betrayal.

Connected by a cone of light, none of the three had seen her and Eva took a deep breath, trying to work out what was the right thing to say. Ordering Maggie to stop wouldn't work, the ghost girl was done with taking orders from Chances. Appealing to her better nature wasn't going to help either, with Maggie so consumed by hate. As the dark energy built in the room, Eva knew it was feeding the Witch, magnifying the curse that lay over the House and grounds.

'Maggie!' she called out, hearing her voice ring across the room. 'Do you want the Witch to win?' Eva felt the darkness quiver as she named the thing she feared. The Witch was listening, even if Maggie wasn't. 'She's behind this and you're doing what she wants—again. She wants chaos and havoc. You promised to help me so why are you helping her?'

The torchlight swung towards her as she spoke and Eva watched as the beam jumped and jerked as Kyra played it across her, highlighting the ragged frock and wellington boots that were beginning to feel as though she'd worn them for ever.

As the torchlight held her framed, Eva heard a whisper back from the darkness.

'No man is my master,' it hissed. 'I want him dead.'

'Why him?' Eva's mind raced, trying to work out what had happened in here to fire Maggie with bloodlust. 'Is it because of me? Is he the murderer?'

'You Chances.' Maggie's voice dripped with disgust. 'It's all about you. Everything that happens is part of your history, your story, your lies . . . '

Felix interrupted. In the time they had been speaking he had regained control of himself enough to deliver a counter-attack.

'DEPART, TRANSGRESSOR!' he shouted and all eyes turned to him as he produced a small leather-bound book and held it out in front of him like a shield. The torchlight shimmered on the inlaid gilt of the cross emblazoned on the cover. 'Depart!' Felix shouted again and then words began to stream from his mouth, jumbled together in his haste to speak them.

'Depart, transgressor. Depart, seducer, full of lies and cunning, foe of virtue, persecutor of the innocent! Give way . . . abominable monster, give way to God.' Felix had obviously memorized the words and although he stumbled over some of

201

them they continued to come. 'He has stripped you of your powers and laid waste your kingdom, bound you prisoner and plundered your weapons, cast you forth into outer darkness, where everlasting ruin awaits you . . . '

Eva listened, dumbfounded, wondering if this plan stood the slightest hope of succeeding. Somewhere along the line Felix had obtained a Bible and read up how to conduct an exorcism and now he was reciting the part of a priest.

'To what purpose do you insolently resist?' Felix's voice was growing in confidence and purpose with the old-fashioned cadence of the words. 'To what purpose do you brazenly refuse? You are guilty before almighty God, whose laws you have transgressed.'

Eva was impressed at how much he was able to reel out, the confident ring of his voice as he sounded out the ancient syllables of the rite. But as Felix spoke she found herself fighting a growing dread and realized that if the exorcism was working then she was in as much danger as Maggie. The atmosphere in the room seemed darker and darker and even the torchlight seemed to be dimming, as if Felix wasn't helping but extinguishing all hope.

'You are guilty before the whole human race, to whom you offer by your enticements the poisoned cup of death!' Felix thundered like any hellfire preacher. 'I adjure you to depart! Tremble and flee, as we call on the name of the Lord, before whom the denizens of hell cower. I adjure you to be gone! The longer you delay, the heavier your punishment shall be . . . '

Eva was getting dizzy, the room swimming before her eyes, the currents of darkness dragging at her, Felix's words pounding into her aching head and somewhere in the swirling filth the witch relishing the pain and hate and fear webbing this room. Felix hadn't prepared that speech for Maggie, he'd prepared it for

Eva, the words to cast her out for ever from the House—from life and death.

The torchlight faded out, the darkness thickened, the sound of Felix's chant faded away and Eva fell into nowhere world. The walls of her body hadn't been a barrier for weeks as she explored the ghost realm, now the walls of her mind fell open and she was lost somewhere in a whirling empty darkness.

No, not lost, Eva told herself. She was tied to the House. Even as she reminded herself of it she felt the walls of the House ancient and solidly *there*, as real as her bones and her blood. Suspended in that thought she saw things as the House had, visions formed on the stage of her mind like shadow puppets.

She saw the Solar and a man holding a Bible. He was leading prayers in front of rows of black and white uniformed servants. Thomas Chance, her great-great-grandfather, known for his Puritan religious beliefs.

She saw the Solar, the man holding the Bible, a cringing girl with sullen resentful eyes. Maggie, the servant girl, still alive in the vision: alive enough to flinch from the hand that struck at her.

She saw the Solar in shadow. The cold grey light of an early morning. She saw the servants with their bowed heads and cowed minds. She saw the man with the Bible, the shadows gathering around him and a tide of filth welling up from his centre.

She saw Thomas Chance, the puritan aristocrat, beating a servant girl with a leather-bound Bible. She saw him slam the door shut. She saw the blows, saw bruises bloom alongside soot stains on pale undernourished flesh; heard the grunts of effort, fragments of Bible verse, fabric tearing, a voice whispering 'Please don't, please.'

She felt the anger, the powerlessness, the *shame* of it: penetrating deep into the walls. It was an atmosphere that stained the Solar as powerfully as the blood on the floor of the front hall. The shame of the House, of the Chances, of the abused servant girl—no more than a child when this room had seen her brutalized; it was a choking tide of evil memories.

She saw the Solar of the past and a young servant girl with a bruised face and a swollen stomach bending her head at the angry words of her master. She saw the waxy face of the servant girl in death, the boy baby with a tuft of blond hair wailing for a mother it had never known.

She saw the Solar of the House today and Kyra cleaning it, and Maggie appearing to warn her away. Their faces together were both sharp and suspicious, Maggie's black hair and Kyra's blonde like two sides of a coin: death and life.

She saw the Solar and Kyra and Kyle talking outside it, herself and Maggie listening in. Maggie offering to help Eva if she promised not to involve the Strattons.

Again she saw the Solar, Kyra and Felix Fairfax laughing and mocking the ghosts; flirting with the reckless disregard of lovers on the deck of the *Titanic*, the darkness closing in around them.

Eva remembered how Maggie had told her that sometimes ghosts could lose control of themselves and be swept back into the past, dragged back to things that frightened them or to the moment they'd died. The events that played out in the Solar were scenes from Maggie's past, the flirtation between Felix and Kyra the trigger, arousing evil memories because . . .

Eva's eyes snapped open to the dark room and the tide of filth sweeping in, the dark undercurrents, the hopelessness, the hate and the shame. But now she stood apart from all of that, armed with the clue to the mystery.

* * *

Time was running out. Kyle backed away from the cellar door and tried to clear his mind. Ever since he and Kyra were little he'd had flashes of knowing things like when she was hurt, or unhappy. Right now, he was certain she was afraid and that she was somewhere dark and threatening.

Even as he thought that he remembered vividly seeing Eva in the hall when he'd been looking for his sister. 'Kyra's in the Solar,' she'd said and the memory seemed so real that it felt as though Eva was speaking those words again, a cool clear voice projected into the back of his head. *Kyra's in the Solar.*

The Solar was a giant glass conservatory; nowhere could be less likely to be dark, but Kyle found himself moving before he even knew he'd made a plan. Maybe his memory was playing weird tricks on him—or maybe that had been a message.

'The Solar,' he said to himself as he ran down the corridor, 'Kyra, Eva.' The names beating a tattoo along with his pounding feet. He was suddenly sure he'd made the right call when he ran into a cluster of tourists milling around like lost sheep.

'Excuse me.' One of them grabbed his sleeve. 'Our guide seems to have vanished and the arrows seem to say to go into the next room—but the door's locked.'

'The Solar?' Kyle sounded like an idiot even to himself but he didn't care. 'Is it the door to the Solar?'

'I think so . . . ' Kyle didn't wait for the rest of the answer, pushing past the group to tug at the shut door. It was sealed tight; even the handle refused to turn. Kyle broke away from the door, running down the corridor and bursting through the outside door that led to the terrace.

Outside again the sunshine seemed much brighter after the darkness inside the house. Kyle turned round to look at the windows and realized the darkness was more than just

205

a feeling: the windows were black as if the glass had been smoked.

He glanced up and down the terrace, looking for something without quite knowing what, focusing on a stone, a piece of stick and rejecting them before his eye caught on something beside the stone stairs, half hidden under a brown tarpaulin.

**

Kyra's scream came out in a thin pathetic *peep* of noise when her torch found the phantasmal figure of Eva in the room. The light had shaken in her hands as the ghosts had quarrelled and Felix began to speak and the atmosphere got thicker and thicker until she could barely breathe.

In her hands the torchlight had faded, the beam thinning, shrinking, dimming, swallowed finally by the darkness and then Felix's words were drowned out by a banshee scream.

'I go nowhere at your command! You're the seducer, the monster, the guilty one! You're the one who deserves to be PUNISHED!'

The ghost was screaming in the darkness and Kyra frantically pressed and twisted at the dead torch, choking on the gritty smoky air.

'MARGARET STRATTON!' Eva's voice rang from wall to wall. Even the falling grit seemed to freeze in the air. 'It's not Felix you want to kill.' Eva's voice fell softly, gently into the darkness. 'Maggie, listen to me. Someone hurt you, one of the Chances, one of my ancestors. Someone hurt you—but it wasn't Felix. Not all the Chances are the same.'

'The Witch says you're all the same.' The servant girl spat the words out. 'She'll lend us her power to destroy you all.'

'Then what about your child, Maggie?' Eva's voice asked

softly. 'I know you had one, you must have done. A baby sent to the parish to raise.'

'Who told you?' The words were a hoarse whisper. 'I never told. I kept it secret, hid my belly when it grew, bit my lips till they bled when he was being born so I wouldn't cry out. I never said a word. Not when I was dying with the pain of it, not one.'

'The House showed me your past,' Eva said, her voice clear as a bell. 'But you told me too. All the time you were telling me that the family history lied, that ghosts were angry and wanted revenge. But you can't be revenged on the Chances, Maggie, because your son had the same blood and he passed it on to his children and grandchildren. And the Witch doesn't care if the family calls itself Chance, or Fairfax, or Stratton. She's a curse on all of us.'

The room was silent until Eva spoke again.

'You wanted to save Kyra from the darkness, Maggie. You wanted to rescue her. But right now the darkness isn't Felix or the Chance family. Right here and now the darkness is in you.'

* * *

The windows of the Solar were huge diamond-shaped panes, netted together with lead. The wheelbarrow hit the ancient glass with a heart-shattering crash and the whole window buckled around the jagged hole, more panes falling in after the first smashing blow that opened the dark room to the pale gold sunshine of a summer day. Outside the window, Kyle was revealed behind the falling panes.

Still gripping the useless dead torch Kyra watched the light illuminate the broken room. Felix was staring at the falling panes of glass as they crashed into splinters, with complete disregard for the spray of shards that shattered across the tiled floor. The ghostly servant girl had vanished: exorcized or just convinced to leave them alone, Kyra wasn't sure.

One figure remained in the centre of the devastation, unflinching as the air sparkled and glittered around her with airborne flecks of glass. Alone of the people in the room she did not look relieved.

'The ghosts are walking,' Eva said, her eyes very wide and her voice very quiet. 'The curse has come upon us. The Witch has begun her attack.'

14
A Value of X

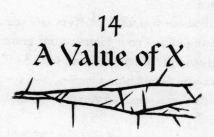

There were shouts from the House and the nearer parts of the gardens. The breaking glass must have been heard everywhere. Kyle had spent his childhood and a fair amount of his teenage years accidentally breaking windows and greenhouses and he spared a thought to wonder how much pocket money twenty square metres of antique glass conservatory would add up to.

Stepping carefully over the shark's-tooth edges of the broken window panes, he entered the Solar. Kyra and Felix faced each other across the room, both of them grimy and gasping for breath. Between them stood a girl in tattered red velvet and wellington boots.

'The Witch has begun her attack,' she said. There was a scream from the terrace and a whirr of feathers as a peacock launched itself into the broken room, landing next to Eva and then screaming again. Eva stared down at it with a worried frown and then turned away. 'I have to go,' she said and vanished.

The vanishing trick didn't get any less strange no matter how many times you saw it, Kyle thought. Felix and Kyra were looking shell-shocked. They recovered their breath a heartbeat after Eva disappeared.

'Apparently, not only do I own a haunted house, the ghosts

are trying to kill me,' Felix said, with a bitter twist to his mouth as he slowly stood up, brushing uselessly at the wreck of his suit. 'That's just great.'

'It really is all about you, isn't it?' Kyra said scathingly, raking him with accusing eyes. 'Your House, your ghosts, your stupid idea. You nearly got me killed just now, you idiot!'

'I didn't hear you complaining earlier,' Felix snapped back at her. 'You were flirting back. And you were going to give me your number.'

'You were what?' Kyle stared at Kyra. 'This bloke? You were flirting with this bloke? You couldn't find a nice friendly mugger to get cosy with instead? I told you not even to speak to him.'

'What business is it of yours if she does?' Felix began and then hesitated, looking at them both more closely. 'Oh, brilliant, absolutely perfect. You're brother and sister, right? I knew she was more than just a waitress.'

'What the hell?' Kyra turned furiously on Felix. 'Now I'm someone because of who my brother is? I should've told my great-granny to go ahead and strangle you, you stuck-up toffee-nosed jerk! Deal with your own damn problems next time.'

Storming off towards the door she wrestled with the handle before it burst open to reveal a crowd of tourists who immediately surged into the room.

'What the hell happened in here?' someone said.

'Looks like a bombsite . . . ' The tourists eyed the filth and broken glass with awed expressions, turning to stare at Felix's grime-encrusted figure as they crowded into the room.

'Ladies and gentlemen,' Felix tried to pull himself together, 'this room is off the tour for the time being—as you can see there's been a slight accident . . . '

'The whole ruddy window's been smashed in with a

wheelbarrow!' someone pointed out loudly and Kyle snickered at Felix's attempts to contain the noise as the peacock started screaming again.

Reluctantly Kyle got a hold on himself, realizing that if he let himself go on laughing he might never stop.

'We need to talk,' he said, looking from Felix to Kyra. 'Seriously. We need to talk about this.'

'Very well.' Felix was still trying to play lord of the manor as he proposed: 'Let's go to the library.'

'Whatever.' Kyra shrugged angrily, following three paces behind as Felix led them through the gawping crowd and back down the corridor into the House. Felix had to unlock the oak-panelled door with a key and Kyle took the opportunity to move closer to his sister.

'What was that about a great-granny?' he asked and Kyra managed to summon a small smile.

'The bad news is she's an insane ghost who's haunting us,' she said, as Felix opened the door. 'The good news is that she doesn't mean to scare people witless—she's trying to protect us from the Chance family.'

'That's the good news?' Kyle would have gone on but by then he had followed Felix and Kyra through the door and saw the library was in no better condition than the Solar. Half of the bookshelves had fallen over and books lay scattered across the room in great drifts. 'What the hell happened in here?'

'Eva Chance happened,' Felix said, shutting and locking the door before crossing to the liquor cabinet and taking out a decanter.

'This isn't a good time to get drunk,' Kyle said warningly.

'Thanks for the advice,' Felix snapped, pouring three short measures of amber liquid into glasses and carrying them back to where the twins stood, handing them one each. 'Feel free to abstain.'

He downed his own glass and Kyra followed suit a second later. Kyle decided to follow their example. The brandy was smooth and slipped down his throat like honey. The kick that followed a second later was anything but gentle.

'OK,' he said roughly, pushing Kyra towards a chair and taking one next to it himself. 'One of you tell me what just happened in there. Great-granny, Eva and all.'

Kyra ignored the chair he'd directed her at and took a different one. Felix slung himself on to the top of a desk. Neither of them said anything for a while but Kyle waited them out. Felix cracked first.

'Like I said, ghosts are trying to kill me. Kyra and I were talking.'

'Flirting,' Kyle said.

'All right, flirting,' Felix shrugged. 'My mistake.'

'Damn right, your mistake.' Kyra glared at him and Kyle sighed.

'It's the part where the ghosts attack I want to know about,' he reminded them.

Gradually the story emerged. Felix kept feeling his neck as he recounted being attacked by the ghost of a servant girl and both of them shuddered and twitched their way through an account of the filthy black rain. But it was the end of the story both found it hardest to tell. It took half an hour to drag it out that Eva had talked the ghost to a standstill and that she had claimed the Strattons were related to the Chances.

'It's the same story Dad told me this morning,' Kyra concluded. 'Eva had the other side of it. Margaret Stratton was abused by Thomas Chance, she had a baby—our grandad—and died. She haunts the Solar because that's where it happened and she was haunting us too and trying to stop Eva involving us. But me and Felix—doing whatever—that was the final straw for her. She attacked him because she thought I was in danger. Eva convinced her to let him go.'

'She told the ghost not to kill Felix,' Kyle concluded and looked at Felix Fairfax thoughtfully. Felix flushed under his stare and Kyle felt surprised at how quickly and easily that aristocratic arrogance had crumbled. 'Why would Eva protect *you*?'

'I'm not the villain here.' Felix tried a haughty look and then sighed, pouring another finger of brandy into his glass. 'I'm not a murderer either, OK? My biggest crime is speeding. It's a new experience for me to have ghosts howling for my blood.' He took a sip of his drink and then added, 'The exorcism was the best idea I had.'

'The exorcism made things worse.' Kyra spoke for the first time in some minutes. She had begun to fingercomb the worst of the dust and cobwebs from her hair. 'There were feelings, images in my mind, flashes like lightning, I can't describe it. But the exorcism was a bad idea.'

'I know it was,' Felix admitted. 'I had some fairly unpleasant scenes going through my head too.' His eyes met Kyra's and they both looked away.

Kyle shifted uncomfortably. This was getting into seriously deep water.

'What did Eva mean about a Witch?'

This time Felix and Kyra looked blank, looked at each other and continued to look blank.

'Eva mentioned the Witch before,' Kyra said slowly. 'She said something to Margaret Stratton's ghost about not helping the Witch and the Witch wanting chaos.'

'She said the Witch was a curse on all of us,' Felix added. 'Chance, Fairfax or Stratton.'

'First ghosts, now a witch.' Kyra shook her head. 'It would be nice if Eva had stuck around to explain instead of going cryptic and vanishing. What was that last part again?'

'The ghosts are walking, the curse is upon us, the Witch has begun her attack,' Felix chanted and the twins watched him uneasily. 'What? I have a good memory. I've no idea what it means but it doesn't sound good, does it?'

'Don't be more of a twit than you can help.' Kyle moved the decanter before Felix's reaching hand could touch it. 'And don't think you can bail on the problem by getting blasted either. Ghosts walking must mean ghost walks. And those are your bright idea.'

'Someone else suggested it.' Felix frowned. 'I just approved it. It was . . . ' he paused. 'I don't know, a challenge, I think that was what I meant.'

'A challenge to the ghosts to come and haunt you?' Kyle wondered if Felix was certifiably insane.

'The House is going to be mine,' Felix said, swigging the last of the contents of his glass mulishly. 'Why shouldn't I run whatever tours I like in it?'

'For the same reason that you shouldn't go poking at an ants' nest,' Kyle said, wondering if Felix really was an idiot.

'Was it a challenge to yourself?' Kyra asked unexpectedly, looking straight at Felix. 'Pretending not to believe in ghosts?'

'But I *don't* believe in ghosts!' Felix exclaimed. 'It's nonsensical.'

'They seem to believe in you though,' Kyle pointed out and Kyra rolled her eyes.

'Felix is right,' she said. 'Ghosts are nonsense. No one believes in them.'

214

'But you've seen ghosts now.' Kyle couldn't understand why the other two seemed to be rejecting the evidence of their eyes. 'You've spoken to Eva.'

'That doesn't make it any easier to completely rewrite everything you know about the world,' Felix said. 'And pinning a label on something and calling it a ghost doesn't make it any more comprehensible.'

'We don't know what a "ghost" is,' Kyra added and Kyle wondered if he should be worried that his sister was back to agreeing with Felix again.

* * *

When Eva vanished from the Solar she found herself automatically returning to the staircase overlooking the entrance hall where she had spent so much time watching the preparations. Here she was a floor and a half above the cellars but she could feel the darkness that filled them thrumming with power.

There were times when the House did feel cursed: when every frayed edge of carpet felt like a potential death-trap that could send you somersaulting down a flight of stairs. There were ways the House could make visitors very unwelcome with its sudden odd angles and unexpected turns. All morning tourists had spilled through the gates and been channelled down the obvious pathways, directed away from danger by arrows in the House. But there had been a delicate balance behind the cheerful summer day out, dark undercurrents that Maggie's wild attack on Felix had brought surging up to the surface. The signs of the Witch's curse were everywhere, if you knew where to look.

In the front hall the triangle of metal poles that Eva had arranged carefully to block off the bloodstain had been moved aside, knocked over perhaps by a passer-by and then helpfully moved out of the way by a staff member. After all, what reason would there be for blocking off that particular patch of floor, aside from a long-faded mottling of the flagstones? Now the reason was all too clear. A scarlet puddle gleamed fresh and wet at the base of the stairs and tourists gave it a wide berth, casting doubtful looks at the nearby signs for the ghost walks as if they suspected shock-advertising tactics. Eva knew better.

Eva's own senses were extended through the House now, ever since she'd reached out to find the source of the trouble that had turned out to be Maggie. The return of the bloodstain was just one of the ways her arrow diversions had failed. From the hidden door of the priest's hole, hands pounded and hammered on the locked door: the pleading voice of a lost tourist unheard behind the solid oak and only the faintest of thuds escaping to puzzle his friends in the room outside. In the minstrels' gallery a pretty young girl smiled down at her male companion from the balcony, leaning forward to quote Juliet's most famous line and resting her weight on the fragile banisters. In the gun-room a group of scientifically minded teenagers were experimentally loading a pair of duelling pistols. By the lake a panicked party of tourists insisted they had seen a weeping woman wearing a nightdress rowing a boat out towards the island.

Everywhere and everything was tinged with danger, with malice and with the sly certainty that somewhere, something was bound to go wrong. Eva couldn't hold the fort on her own, not against every little threat that could be abruptly magnified into danger.

She knew that she had to focus her energies on where they were most needed. The trouble was that at every stage her enemy seemed two steps ahead of her. Had the Witch known how deep Maggie's hatred of the Chances went and deliberately used her as a catalyst for the chain of accidents tripping Eva's sixth sense in every direction across the House? Maggie had vanished into her attic roof-space and all Eva sensed from her was a powerful wish to be left alone. But was there another lurking danger, a trigger about to be pulled somewhere?

She didn't have a choice, she had to try and hold back the flood. But her own small powers seemed very pitiful and weak against the full force of the Witch on the rampage.

* * *

In the debris-strewn library, Kyle was trying to cudgel his brain into action. Felix's and Kyra's technical quibbles about what it meant to be a ghost weren't helping his state of confusion.

'OK,' he said eventually. 'Maybe Felix isn't a murderer.'

'Thank you so much,' Felix drawled and Kyle glared at him.

'BUT . . . ' he continued, 'you were up to something. Hiring me to find a body . . . ' He shook his head. 'That was a strange thing to do. And what happened in this room?' He looked around. 'Why would Eva try and kill you and then protect you from whatever that was in the Solar?'

Felix opened his mouth to reply and then closed it again, actually thinking about what he said this time. When he finally did speak the words came out slowly.

'There's a problem with my grandfather's will,' he said. And then he stopped and looked uncomfortable.

Kyle and Kyra exchanged glances; confirming that neither of them knew where Felix was going with this. Kyle already didn't like the sound of it.

'My grandfather, Edward Chance, changed his will last year without telling the family. I found a copy of it in this room, along with letters from his lawyer.'

'Michael Stevenage,' Kyle said, thinking of the card he still had tucked away in a pocket.

'That's the fellow.' Felix looked vaguely surprised but moved on, evidently not caring how Kyle knew the name. 'Mr Stevenage warned my grandfather that the will in its new form was unlikely to pass probate and would most likely be challenged by members of the family.' Felix took a breath and then said in a different tone of voice, 'He was right about that. I would have challenged it and so would my parents. Maybe the aunts as well. It was a problematic will.'

'Problematic like you wouldn't get the House after all?' Kyra asked sarcastically and Felix winced.

'Almost,' he admitted. 'I'd get the House but nothing inside it. Every scrap of the contents was willed to Eva. Mr Stevenage thought this would be challenged as unreasonable and impractical division of the estate.'

'And you and Eva didn't get on . . . ' Kyle didn't like where this was leading and he wasn't sure what Felix could have to gain by revealing such a motive for himself.

'Eva didn't figure on my radar at all until this year,' Felix said. 'Just listen, all right? You wanted to know what I've been up to. Cards on the table. So listen.'

He took another breath and went on.

'Eva disappeared mid March. But I didn't hear about it at the time and I had the news from my mother. Mother told me that Eva had run away. It wasn't until we arrived here for dinner that I got the impression from Aunt Cora that the reality was more sinister. Cora kept breaking down; she was convinced Eva had killed herself, just like her mother. And then I saw Eva. I thought at first she'd been hiding in the House all along—'

Kyra's eyes flickered at that confirming Kyle's suspicion that she'd been thinking the same.

'I was angry with her and told her so but she didn't seem to understand what I was talking about. Then I started to wonder and I thought if I could touch her I'd prove my own suspicions wrong . . . ' Felix shook his head.

'What happened?' Kyle asked.

'She was across the room in less than half a second. I don't know if she even realized she'd practically teleported. I didn't want to believe it and I didn't tell anyone about it. Then later during the dinner I kept feeling *watched*.' He shifted his shoulders. 'It was uncanny.'

'I've been feeling that too,' Kyra said. 'Except now I know it wasn't always Eva watching me. Great-granny's apparently been watching out for me too. I bet it was her stopped that bucket overflowing.'

'Hush up,' Kyle said, irritably. 'I want to hear the rest of Felix's explanation. He hasn't got to the part about hiring me to find a body yet.'

'Fair enough.' Felix took up the thread again. 'That night at dinner something was pushing me into that ghost walk plan. Maybe more than one something. When I looked back on it later I started wondering if maybe the conversation had been taken that way deliberately, if maybe someone wanted me to feel haunted, wanted the house to seem full of ghosts. Then Grandfather had that accident and was taken to hospital—and that was suspicious too. I wanted to know for sure what had happened to Eva and no one seemed to know. Mother and my aunts all seemed to think it was inevitable, because Eva's mother used to vanish unexpectedly. But as far as I could tell Eva never left the House.'

'So you asked me to look for the body,' Kyle prompted.

'Yes, you didn't look like the kind of person to think he was seeing ghosts. I thought you looked as though you could handle yourself and would take the cash and not ask too many questions.' Felix laughed suddenly. 'Wow,' he said. 'I really couldn't have got you more wrong.'

'I can handle myself,' Kyle said gruffly. 'You were right about that.'

'Yeah,' Kyra chimed in, to his surprise. 'Kyle and his wheelbarrow beats your stupid exorcism plan, no question.'

'Fine, fine,' Felix said. 'We've agreed that was a bad idea. Anyway the next thing was that Eva appeared in the library. I found her reading the will. She spirited it out of a locked safe although she fumbled getting into my laptop. Completely computer illiterate, poor girl. But she could handle herself too. Books were flying at me from all directions when I finally escaped.'

'Eva read the will and attacked you,' Kyle recapped.

'Anyone who reads that will is going to think I had Eva killed,' Felix said. 'It implicates me unequivocally. Forget that it might not have held up in court anyway. The whole situation's a huge mess and I can't help wondering if there's someone who finds it awfully convenient to screw me over.'

'Screw *you* over?' Kyra snorted. 'Felix, you're so vain. You think everything's about you.'

'Even Eva's death,' Kyle agreed. 'That's low, Felix. You meant it about Eva not figuring on your radar, didn't you? All that's in your head is a giant picture of you.'

'That's enough!' Felix snapped. 'I'm giving you all this for free and I've admitted I've made some mistakes but this is how it appears to me—right? This is how I see it. Now do you want the conclusion, or not?' Two hectic spots of colour had appeared on his cheeks and Kyle realized that he wasn't just angry, he was shocked and surprised at their reaction.

'OK,' he said. And then, hating himself that he needed to say it, 'Sorry.' Kyra rolled her eyes.

'The point is,' Felix said eventually. 'That so far the following things have happened: Eva vanished, my grandfather was incapacitated, my aunt Cora was incapacitated, and it's only a matter of time before I'm implicated in these potential crimes because of the will. If all of these things are deliberate actions by someone—a mysterious Mr X—then I can only assume I'm supposed to end up disinherited.'

'You think that's the motive then?' Kyle said doubtfully. 'One murder, two attacks and you think the idea is to frame you?'

'I don't know!' Felix said with an air of exasperation. 'But I'm sure the will has something to do with it. As a motive it makes sense: because wills mean money. Maybe someone or something is stirring up the ghosts as a distraction. But no police force is going to take any mention of ghosts seriously. When they aren't actively coming at me screaming, I'm really not as worried about the ghosts as I am about whoever Mr X is.'

'Seriously?' Kyle glanced at Kyra. 'That was Kyra's worry too. But murderers aren't what worry me. Ghosts do. Ghosts worry me a lot. And I keep thinking about what Eva said about a Witch. I don't like my chances against a Witch.'

'Could the Witch be your Mr X?' Kyra suggested to Felix. 'It could all fit together.'

'Perhaps, if you're prepared to believe a ghost could have killed one person and attacked two more,' Felix said slowly. 'But I think it's more likely the real killer is using the stories of ghosts as cover. If everyone's twitchy with superstition, hearing things and seeing things, it'd be much easier for the real killer to sneak around the place and have everyone write it off to the House being haunted.'

In the gun room a pistol exploded with a sulphurous bang, shrapnel whizzing through the air and people throwing themselves to the ground. A teenager reeled out of the smoke, choking and clutching with burned hands at his chest. Another, eyebrowless, kid gaped at the unexploded twin to the weapon and dropped it as though it were red hot, sending everyone ducking for cover again.

A woman was pulled out of the lake to the cheers of a crowd of onlookers, spluttering her way back into consciousness after resuscitation to object that she herself had only waded into the freezing water in the first place as a Good Samaritan, following the mystery weeping rower who was still yet to be found.

In the gun room Eva dived for the spinning second pistol, catching it and discharging it into the fireplace with another ringing shot and then vanishing into the billowing cloud of smoke and ash. In the Tudor bedroom she felt for the catch of the hidden door of the priest's hole and was gone before it had finished swinging open to deliver a hysterical tourist with a hoarse voice and bruised and bleeding hands into the arms of his friends.

But she arrived too late to stop the souvenir-hunters excavating the stained-glass fragments from the Solar with their bare hands. However fast she moved, however quickly she flew from trouble-spot to trouble-spot at the speed of thought, she couldn't be everywhere at once. But the Witch could.

There was more power in hate than helpfulness, Eva thought bitterly. Maggie had hinted it and then told her outright that hate was what drove most of the ghosts and hate had certainly taken the magpie girl from a sympathetic ally to a sudden threat. Hate had thrown the books in the library and covered the Solar in filth.

Hate was something the witch had in abundance and with it the power to make people doubt themselves enough to slip, trip, and fall. You might write the curse off as just superstition but almost everyone was superstitious in some way and the fears that preyed upon their minds all went to feed the Witch. Every time Eva doubted herself, the Witch gained a little more power.

Each time it was harder to summon the energy, each time she was a little slower, a fraction later. And every time she had to decide to try and help this person or that one, her spirit sank with the weight of the choice. She didn't know how the family and tourists were so oblivious to the ghosts that surrounded them, how they could walk with such confidence into a Haunted House, when every instinct she had was screaming at her to run.

High on the balcony of the ballroom the aspiring Juliet thought she saw the room filled with candles and music and dancers for a second before the banister twisted under her arm and there was an awful wrenching splintering of wood. Shocked arrivals on the balcony leapt to reach her, while others backed hastily away, and Eva flew through the air after the falling girl, reaching her a split and broken second too late.

Juliet had fallen with an ugly wordless cry and lay like an unstrung puppet half a floor below; a hand's-breadth too far for her Romeo to catch her. A dirge of touch-tone beeping began as fingers hit the same key on a cluster of mobile phones.

* * *

The sonorous chimes of the grandfather clock in the front hall resounded through the House, advising all present that it was five o'clock.

It was planned that all the tourists would leave at five, except for those booked on to the evening's ghost walk. But as the afternoon

223

shaded towards evening there were still tourists scattered all over the estate. Eva's switching around the tour arrows had caused problems for those who lost their way in the long corridors of the House and the looping paths of the gardens had overcome walkers who had stopped for a rest and not yet made their way back to the main gate.

The staff at the main gate were gathered near the field still half-full of parked cars, debating who was going to tell the estate manager that not everyone had left and complaining that tourists should have been counted in and out. The series of minor accidents that had plagued the day had left everyone jumpy. When you'd seen five people limp out with twisted ankles you couldn't help wondering if there was someone lying undiscovered with a broken leg.

There were three hours to go before sunset but the day was clouded and the light had a muddy look to it. Out in the gardens the patterns of light and shade shifted in the greenery, the high walls of the maze cast long shadows and from inside them the shrill high voices of confused children interspersed with weary shouts from their parents came with an increasing edge of anxiety.

But to some, the chain of minor accidents acted with strange supernatural force. When the vast thundering crash of the breaking Solar windows had echoed through the House, tourists had flocked to the sound and among those who had stayed to gawk, Christopher Knight had done a roaring trade. The marketing expert had handed out flyers about the ghost walk to everyone present and he'd managed to charm his sometime partner Joyce Chance into repeating her story about the room being haunted. Throughout the afternoon more flyers had changed hands and rumours had floated through the tour groups and the ticket tables on the front drive had been crowded with enquirers. Sceptics and believers argued their cases with equal fervour. Several elderly villagers claimed chairs and benches and held court to younger relatives about things they had heard tell about the big House: stories that had been old even when they were young.

But it was another story that was occupying the interest of the younger visitors, as they queued for the ghost walks; a much more salacious scandal that grew as it was told. For a modern scandal it began with the elements of a historical romance. It was the story of a mysterious orphan girl, an aristocrat, the sole companion of her grandfather, named—improbably and romantically— Evangeline. The mystery girl was only half an aristocrat, the only daughter of an upper-class wild-child who had killed herself in implausibly dramatic circumstances involving a drowning and a baby in the bulrushes. Evangeline, the bulrush baby orphan, had vanished from the House only four weeks ago and still hadn't been found. But a whole series of people had had so-called accidents while looking for her, accidents that flourished in the telling until the listeners might have thought the hospital A&E was overflowing with them. But the Chance family were still pretending everything was fine—and hadn't everyone seen them today doing just that? Even though it was rumoured that the accidents hadn't been accidents at all. No smoke without fire, people said, and paid up for the ghost walk with the fascination of gawkers at a car accident, looking for bodies.

* * *

A siren sounded from the front gate, a whoop of noise building to a wailing cry as disconcerting as any peacock call. The cluster of staff leapt out of the way as an ambulance came screaming through the front gates and juggernauted up the gravel drive.

Shocked and salacious glances were exchanged among the gathered group of ghost walkers, waiting outside the House, as they heard the siren and saw the distinctive white bulk of the ambulance arrive with a screech of brakes. Paramedics immediately unloaded a rolling stretcher and hurried towards the main doors.

'Which way to the ballroom?' the one at the front demanded, throwing the question at a ticket seller by the door. When she was slow to respond he glared. 'Quickly now, lass—there's been an accident.'

'I think it's that way,' the ticket seller pointed and the paramedics disappeared into the House, leaving the hubbub of voices to swell with rumour and speculation. But the voices were silenced when the paramedics re-emerged, two carefully lifting the stretcher down the front steps while a third hastened alongside with an intravenous drip. Lying on the stretcher was the limp form of a young woman, her face chalk white and her limbs oddly twisted. Behind the stretcher a young man came stumbling along, clutching a mobile phone in his hand.

'I tried to catch her,' he was repeating over and over again, his eyes fixed on the woman. 'I tried to catch her. I tried.'

The woman was loaded into the ambulance and two of the paramedics pulled the doors to and started working on the injured woman, while the third led the man aside and made him sit down on a stone bench, telling him that he was in shock.

The waiting tourists were almost equally shocked and some looked dubiously at their eagerly purchased tickets for the ghost walk. The staff had clustered into a tight knot and were wondering what to do. The ticket seller who'd been asked where the ballroom was kept shooting panicked glances towards the ambulance.

'We don't even know what's happened,' she said shakily.

'What if someone else is hurt? What if we're held responsible?'

'Who's in charge here?' the third paramedic left the shocked senseless man and accosted the staff, sending the ticket seller into open panic.

'Ms Langley!' she said. 'Or the family, the Fairfaxes and Joyce Chance. Or Mr Knight. They're in charge, not me. I just work here.'

'And where are these people?' the paramedic demanded. 'Why haven't any of them turned up to explain their reckless attitude to health and safety?'

'I don't know,' the ticket seller wailed. 'I've tried Ms Langley's mobile and I've called the front gate and the gift shop. But mobile phone signals are bad in the House and sometimes in the gardens too . . . '

'Bloody hopeless.' The paramedic shook his head and cast a disgusted glance at the gawking crowd and the signs for the ghost walks. 'Bunch of idiots,' he added for good measure and turned back to the hyperventilating man on the bench.

There was a thud of a slammed door and one of the paramedics emerged from the back of the ambulance and announced:

'She's stable enough to move—come on.' Within seconds his colleague had urged the shell-shocked man into the ambulance and the vehicle ground into motion, moving off with purposeful speed back down the driveway.

Inside the House the grandfather clock jangled the half hour and Christopher Knight, the marketing expert, came jogging around the side of the House, coming to a stop next to the ticket seller and turning to regard the crowd with satisfaction.

'Almost time for the ghost walks!' he said cheerfully. 'Looks like we've managed to get a lot of punters. Good for you.' He slapped the ticket seller on the back and then flinched when she went noisily into hysterics.

15
Ghost Walk

From the windows of the Crimson Room Eva watched the body of the fallen Juliet being carried away. She watched Christopher Knight's arrival and the collapse of the ticket seller without really registering either. Her senses were alert in all directions, waiting for the next alarm. But as the ambulance vanished down the drive the jangled mood of the House quietened in the stillness of waiting and Eva shivered as she thought that the escalation of accidents hadn't sated the appetite of the Witch for chaos and mayhem. In just half an hour the ghost walks were scheduled to begin.

A chill breath of air ghosted up beside her and Eva spun round to confront it. A black and white figure stood there silently, watching her from across the room.

'Margaret Stratton,' Eva said, giving the ghost its proper name. 'What do you want?'

'I never meant to help the witch.' The ghost of the servant girl met her eyes levelly. 'It used me. Used me like he did, your noble ancestor. You were right about that, right about all of it. About the child, about what happened. He never admitted what he'd done, and when I died he sent the baby to the workhouse, his own flesh and blood.'

'Flesh and blood doesn't matter as much as you'd think,' Eva said, thinking of how her aunts had tried to abandon her as a baby.

'It mattered to me,' Maggie said. 'Sometimes I'd see him, my boy, see him like you would in a dream. And then his son and his son's children—the twins, I watched them grow up.'

'You're a family ghost,' Eva said. 'I wondered about that when you said you weren't, what had tied you to the House. Maybe it was because of what happened to you that you became a ghost but I think it's because of your family that you didn't fade away. Because you were watching over them.'

'And the Witch used that,' Maggie said. 'Used me to stir up the memories and now the twins must be as afraid of me as I was of him . . .'

'Like you told me, don't think about that,' Eva said. 'Don't think about the past. Even if it wasn't dangerous, we don't have time. It's the future I'm worried about. The Witch is very strong right now. I've been fighting her for hours.'

'I felt it,' Maggie told her. 'That's why I came. To say that I'll help. Whatever you want, no conditions this time. I'm not even asking you to trust me. But you can use me—if you want.'

'I'll think about it,' Eva said. She wasn't ready to trust the ghost so easily but when Maggie bowed her head, accepting her judgement, Eva felt a stab of conscience. 'I won't have you as a servant to use like a tool,' she said, not meaning to speak out loud but not able to help herself. 'We'll be equal partners or nothing. Now let me think.'

Maggie only nodded, but her posture was less abject than a moment ago, and Eva racked her brains for a plan.

'Where *is* everyone?' she said after a moment, staring out of the window again. 'I've not seen any of my relations for hours.'

'They were all leading tours,' Maggie pointed out. 'Except Felix. He's still with Kyra and Kyle in the library.'

Eva felt uncomfortable for a moment at the thought of an unholy alliance shaping up between Felix and Kyra. But she had other priorities than worrying about people who didn't much like her—compared to someone who had hated her enough to murder her, Felix and Kyra weren't an issue.

'That's Felix accounted for,' she said. 'But where's everyone else?' Reaching out with her mind she tried to locate them with senses she barely understood. Her whirlwind process through the House trying to fend off the attacks of the witch had increased her range. Instead of being bound in space to a particular part of the House she could reach out and feel every presence within it, sifting through the different auras to find the Chance family.

Aunt Helen was irritated about something, irritated but not alarmed. Eva had the impression of a whitewashed room and the smell of antiseptic and gun-smoke and realized her aristocratic aunt was bandaging up the two teenagers who'd been fooling around with duelling pistols. 'Happens all the time,' her aunt's crisp voice played in her head. 'You should see some of the accidents people have on the hunting field. This is nothing.' The two lads seemed half reassured and half frightened by her brisk approach.

Uncle Richard was directing operations on the shore of the lake, ordering people about with military assurance. Eva only had a flash of him and a brief echo of lake water lapping at rocks before the image swam away from her.

Aunt Joyce was excited about something, her mind hummed with glee. Her mind was completely absorbed with whatever she was doing—no chance of her hearing an ambulance. Her mind was full of bright shiny glitter and dazzle, her hands delving deep into a trinket box, holding up a hand to admire the effect of bejewelled bracelets and rings. In her aunt's mind banknotes ruffled.

* * *

Downstairs, in the front hall, the tourists had gathered and Christopher Knight was addressing them from three stairs up the grand staircase.

'Ladies and gentlemen,' he declaimed, 'you've seen the public face of this great House. Tonight I will show you its shadows, its secrets, and the skeletons in the cupboards that have never before been opened to anyone but the family.

'We begin here, in the entrance hall, where four hundred years ago a Chance cousin, known to be a homicidal lunatic, slit his own throat in front of an audience of witnesses who came to bring him to justice for murdering thirteen people. If you look down you can still see the mark of the blood that was spilt that day. Some say his spirit still stalks the House at night.

'Please follow me now to the Solar where we will continue our tour and where just today visitors to the House witnessed shocking scenes.'

He began to walk and the tourists followed him, each one pausing to stare at the bloodstain on the floor as they passed. The stain was still richly, wetly red and even from the next floor Eva could smell the iron of it.

But the tourists hadn't noticed, seeing it but dismissing it like a special effect, and like sheep they followed Christopher Knight along the passageway towards the Solar.

* * *

In the library, Kyra heard the tramp of feet and turned to look at the door. She and Kyle and Felix had been arguing back and

231

forth for the last few hours, none of them reaching a conclusion about what to do. She'd heard the chimes of the clock without registering them but the sound of a tour group beginning to move up the stairs reminded her that time had been slipping away while they were talking.

'The ghost walk,' she said, thumping her brother's arm to get his attention. 'Listen, it's starting.'

The sound of Christopher Knight's voice grew in volume as the man led his party of ghost walkers past the shut library door.

'The room we are about to see was a legend among decades of house servants for its difficulty to clean. I hear that recent employees have had similar problems. We still don't know exactly what happened today but just between you and me, the family are all pretty worried about ghost activity. In fact if there's anyone here with a weak heart or a family history of strokes, I'd advise you not to continue further.'

Kyra sneered at the shut door.

'He's egging them on,' she said. 'How does he know what happened in the Solar anyway?'

'He's dating my aunt Joyce,' Felix said. 'She was leading the tour group that Kyra and I were with, talking up the ghost angle. I suppose he thought it was a pity not to take advantage of the opportunity to use the story. The Solar looks dramatic with the windows caved in.'

'If he thinks it's good publicity that's one thing,' Kyra said thoughtfully. 'But if he believes in the ghosts it's not so innocent. Maybe he wants something bad to happen.'

'Someone wants bad things to happen,' Kyle pointed out. 'It could be Christopher Knight or someone else entirely. But whoever the mysterious X is, we've worked out the ghost walks could be part of their plan. The question is: are you going to let the ghosts walks happen?' He looked at Felix. 'You were the one who allowed them in the first place. You can stop them if you want.'

'Or —' Kyra interrupted, 'we could go and join them and keep an eye out for anything suspicious.'

Felix had looked as though he was about to agree with Kyle's suggestion but when Kyra spoke he flashed a wicked smile.

'Good thought,' he said. 'What if X has been manipulating everyone else, and hiding behind ghosts and witchcraft. If there's a deeper reason for the ghost walks than pulling in tourists, this is our chance to find out what that is.' He jumped to his feet and rummaged in a drawer of the desk, pulling out a small digital camera. 'If I see anything suspicious I'm going to get the evidence.'

'My phone takes photos,' Kyra said. 'But it's hard to take a photo without people noticing.'

'If you go and catch up to the group you can listen to what Christopher Knight is telling them,' Felix said. 'I'll follow and keep out of sight—there are dozens of ways to get around this house without being spotted.'

The two of them were heading towards the door, refining their plans, when Kyra realized Kyle wasn't following.

'Aren't you coming?' she asked and Kyle stood up slowly.

'I'll come with you,' he said. 'But not because I think this is a good idea. If Felix had any sense he'd cancel the ghost walk this second. And if you'd learned anything about ghosts you'd run a mile before you tangled with them. Even if X is using ghosts and witchcraft as a distraction—that doesn't mean the ghosts aren't real. And for all you know you could be walking straight into a trap.'

'Has anyone ever told you that you're really very paranoid?'

Felix said lightly, shaking his head. 'Taking the battle to the enemy is the best strategy. It's in the Art of War or something like that. If X tries anything we'll be prepared. Anyway, X is sneaky but I don't think he's a really dangerous character. Cora and Grandfather are elderly but X's attacks both failed. They may be in the hospital but they're both recovering—nobody's died.'

'Except Eva.'

Felix had the grace to look embarrassed for a second and then he shrugged.

'We still don't know what happened to Eva,' he said. 'But she was probably taken by surprise. I won't be.'

'Like you weren't taken by surprise in the Solar?' Kyle shook his head. 'Fine. Play Sherlock Holmes if you want, I'm not stopping you. But I'm not letting my sister out of my sight.'

*　*　*

Eva drifted behind the ghost walk as it arrived in the Solar. The little family who'd been the first arrivals to the House were still there. The mother and baby were nowhere to be seen but the father was carrying the little boy, Nathan, on his shoulders. The child's eyes were big as the group entered the room. He was the only child there and one of the other men in the group looked up at the little boy with surprise.

'I don't think this tour's for little kids, mate,' he said to the father.

'I'm not little!' Nathan objected. 'I'm five! And I want to see the ghosts.'

'No one said anything about him being too young when I bought the tickets,' his father said, defensively. 'We went home for a rest in the afternoon but Nathan wanted to come back here and see the ghost walk.'

'Seriously.' The other man shook his head. 'You might want to rethink that. Did you see the ambulance outside? This place isn't safe. I'm not worried,' he added hastily. 'But kids?' He shook his head again. 'Well, it's your funeral.'

'I'm sure it'll be fine,' Nathan's father said. But he didn't look as confident as he sounded and he glanced at the door thoughtfully.

As he did, two teenagers slipped through the door. Kyra and Kyle Stratton inserted themselves into the back of the group—neither of them spotted Eva and she didn't try to get their attention. For now she didn't want to be noticed—just to watch. Her quicksilver leaps from problem to problem about the House had increased her confidence and gained some measure of control over her appearances and disappearances. She thought she'd be able to remain unseen—unless some strong emotion shook her willpower or any of the visitors had a strong reason to see her.

It was cold in the Solar. Unsurprisingly, since there was a great gaping hole where the floor to ceiling windows used to be. A row of velvet-roped stands had been placed in front of the broken windows and the lethal shards of glass but the rest of the floor was dusted with a glitter of even smaller glass fragments that crunched underfoot.

'This is the Solar,' Christopher Knight announced. 'As you can see, there was an incident earlier today—almost certainly supernatural in origin.' People looked sceptical but the marketer persevered, repeating Joyce's story of the filth that could not be removed.

Kyra looked pale, her eyes nervously flicking around the room as though she expected a ghost to appear at any moment. Kyle was less obviously concerned but Eva could feel the anxiety radiating from him like heat. He was not the only one to be anxious. Nathan's father was visibly vacillating about whether to continue with the tour, snatching his son up when the little boy took a step towards the heap of broken glass.

'Did the ghosts smash the windows, Daddy?' the little boy asked. And when his father didn't answer he turned to look at Christopher Knight.

'We can't be completely sure what happened,' Christopher said. 'The incident occurred just after a tour had passed through—the only people in the room were a couple of servants and Felix Fairfax—the heir to the House.'

Someone at the back of the group snorted. 'I reckon the ghosts are trying to do him in like he tried to do in his grandad and his auntie and his cousin. Stands to reason, dun' it?'

'Now, now,' Christopher Knight said. 'Let's not get into that sort of speculation.' But he smiled slightly as he spoke and Kyla and Kyra exchanged glances. As Christopher Knight led the tour onwards, Eva moved up next to the two teenagers, close enough to hear their murmured words.

'I get the impression he doesn't really mind people dissing Felix,' Kyra murmured.

'Him and me both,' Kyle muttered back. 'Maybe Felix isn't a murderer but he's still a prat.'

'That's not the point,' Kyra hissed back at him. 'Felix thinks he's being set up. And right now this bloke's not exactly contradicting that impression.'

Eva considered the smooth handsome face of the marketing expert, realizing how little she knew about the man. She'd been concentrating on the members of her family—not on someone she'd never met before the dinner party. Never met at all, since she was dead before Christopher Knight had even entered the House. All she knew about him was that he came from London

236

and had been dating Aunt Joyce. Although the romance seemed to have faded in the last couple of weeks, it was Joyce who had recommended him as an expert in marketing when the subject of ghost walks had first come up. In fact—hadn't Christopher Knight been the one to first suggest the ghost walks?

Eva moved up closer to Christopher as he led the way up a winding set of stairs and towards the next stop on the ghost walk. Tourists crowded around as Christopher revealed the hidden door that led to the priest's hole and looked askance at the scratches of fingernails gouged into the wood.

'Many houses had secret rooms like this during the religious controversies that rocked Britain under the Tudors,' Christopher explained. 'They were called priest's holes because they were used to hide Catholic priests from the threat of martyrdom. But the priest who hid in this House was unfortunate in his choice of hiding place. According to the histories, the family were called away unexpectedly and the person who hid the priest here passed away and the poor fellow was unable to escape from the secret room on his own. He starved to death here.'

The tourists blanched and the Strattons looked uncomfortable but only Eva knew that Christopher Knight was wrong. The troublesome priest had starved in his prison but that wasn't what had killed him.

The ghost was still trapped in the dark cell. It huddled on the narrow shelf of a bed, clutching rosary beads with shaking hands and staring at the open door with blank unseeing eyes, eyes that had been robbed of all sanity. It wasn't starvation that had killed the priest—it was terror. The excruciating pain of a fear that went on and on had driven the priest out of his mind and now his ghost crouched and gibbered, unable to see the open door or even the tourists—lost in the echoing caves of what had once been its mind.

Eva trembled. The small shadowy room tugged at her mind, trying to drag her down into its darkness, into the fear of a helpless trapped creature as its mind was stripped away by voices that came from nowhere, by the insidious whispers of the Witch. *You're trapped. No one will find you. You will die and you still won't escape.*

Eva reeled backwards, dizzily, trying to clear her head of the unwelcome images. Kyle was frowning, peering into the back of the cell. Kyra was looking at her fingernails, torn and cracked from when she'd scrabbled for the torch in the haunted darkness of the Solar.

Nathan's father had had enough. When the little boy hid his face from the priest's hole, the father took a step backwards.

'Time to go now, Nathan,' he said. 'I think that's enough ghosts for you.' He turned an accusatory glare on Christopher Knight as he added: 'This isn't at all what I was led to expect.'

'Sorry, no refunds,' Christopher replied. 'But you're free to leave at any time.' He turned to the others. 'The rest of you, please follow me to the east wing.'

'I don't want to go home!' Nathan suddenly realized what was happening as his father tried to lead him off back the way they'd come. 'I want to see the good ghosts!' His eyes fixed on Eva suddenly and he raised a hand to point. 'I want to see the one with the wellies! I like that one, Daddy! Daddy! I don't want to go hooooooome!' The last word was drawn out in a despairing wail and suddenly the little boy wrenched his hand from his father's, made a lunge towards the group and when he was blocked by another adult spun round and went running off in a third direction—along the dark corridor.

'Oh hell,' his father swore and went pounding after him.

'Ghosts in wellies,' Christopher Knight chuckled, trying to

break the sudden tension in the group. 'That's a new one on me.'

The tourists laughed nervously. But Kyra and Kyle weren't laughing. They alone had followed the little boy's pointing hand and now they were both looking straight at Eva. Twin faces with two pairs of sharp blue eyes: eyes that were becoming accustomed to seeing ghosts.

* * *

For the first few seconds the howling of the little boy made it easy enough for his father to follow where he went. But five paces down the corridor, the thin cries vanished beneath a new louder noise: the siren of a police car.

It had taken Helen Fairfax a good half an hour to patch the teenage boys up to her satisfaction, cleaning out the gunpowder from their cuts in the small scullery just off the gun-room. If she'd considered calling an ambulance at any point, she'd decided against it, either deeming it unnecessary or potentially embarrassing. At the back of the House they hadn't heard the arrival of the ambulance that *had* been called for Juliet.

But it was unfortunate for Helen that just as she was leading the boys out of the front of the House the police car arrived. Her annoyance took the form of hauteur as she regarded the two police officers that emerged from the vehicle.

'Is there a problem, gentlemen?' she asked, to all appearances completely unconscious of the two bandaged teenagers trailing at her heels. 'I am Helen Fairfax, the lady of the House.'

'Good evening, madam,' the first officer said, unable to avoid a trace of irony in her voice. She was a sturdy no-nonsense looking woman with a deliberately expressionless wall of a face. 'Yes, there is a problem. We've had reports of a number of accidents at this venue today. One person is in a critical condition. We've received complaints of negligence from a number of private individuals and from hospital staff and this,' she brandished a piece of paper, 'is a cease and desist order.'

'We're here to shut you down,' her companion added. He was a lean black man with a forbidding stare. Right now that stare was fixed on the two wounded teenagers who cringed underneath the look.

'Nonsense,' Helen Fairfax said crisply. 'A few tourists twist their ankles and you people act as though it's a major event. I've not heard a word of anything worse than sprains or scrapes.'

'Then you must be singularly unobservant, madam,' the female officer said levelly. 'Just half an hour ago a woman was removed from here by ambulance with multiple fractures and contusions and a suspected broken neck. The paramedics who collected her called us as soon as the ambulance reached the hospital. They say that health and safety provision on this property is non-existent and first-aid facilities minimal at best.' She glanced at the two cringing teenagers and added, 'You two had better get yourselves checked over too. I'll have the hospital send someone to pick you up.'

'They're fine,' Helen snapped. 'And they should have known better than to fool around with a loaded gun.'

Both police officers' eyebrows shot up to their hairlines and the woman officer's wall-like countenance cracked as she shot a look of open disbelief at her colleague.

'A gun?' she said. 'There are loaded guns on this property?'

'Amazing,' the man breathed. He shook his head at Helen. 'Lady, you are in so much trouble right now. I can't believe you don't see it.'

'Hey!' one of the teenage boys interrupted as a sudden realization infused him. 'Does that mean we can sue?'

'Don't even think about it, you young lout!' Helen Fairfax's aristocratic air crumbled at that last remark as the situation finally got through to her and the two police officers had to take tight hold of themselves to avoid smiling at her discomfort.

'Let's go inside,' the senior officer said. 'And make sure that all the tourists are off this property.'

'They won't be,' the more talkative of the two wounded teenagers pointed out. 'It's only half past six. There's a whole bunch of people going round the place right now. For the ghost walk.'

'The ghost walk.' The female officer swallowed her surprise and turned to Helen for an explanation.

'Just a bit of fun,' Helen said through dry lips. 'A House tour with some history of our ancestors. Nothing for anyone to worry about.'

As if on cue, a shout erupted from the House and a dishevelled man came running out of the front door. His gaze fixed on the police officers as a drowning man views a lifebelt.

'Thank God!' he stammered as he stumbled to a halt. 'Come quickly! My little boy has vanished. I heard him scream and then he was gone. Please, hurry! He's only five . . .'

'Oh cripes.' The policewoman forgot Helen and turned to her companion. 'Call for back-up,' she ordered. 'And get another ambulance out here. Something tells me we'll be needing it.'

She regretted that hasty remark a second later as the man with the missing child turned to her in horror. But there was no time to be lost in recriminations and she hurried towards the House, trying to ignore the fact that the double doors were wide open like a mouth ready to swallow her.

* * *

Up on the second floor at the entrance to the east wing, the tourists streamed past leaving Eva and the Strattons staring at each other. Through the thick walls the muffled scream of a siren wailed, making all of them jump.

'That's not an ambulance,' Kyra said after a second. 'It's a different noise.'

'Police,' Kyle said. 'It had to happen sooner or later.'

'They're too late,' Eva said, her voice steady although her posture was slumped and weary, the circles under her eyes darker than ever and her skin so pale Kyle could see right through it to the wooden panelling behind her. 'Police might have helped a week ago. But what can they do against ghosts. Against the Witch?'

Kyle heard the word 'Witch' sound with a beat of blood in his brain. Each time he heard it the House seemed darker, the walls closer on either side, the stacks of floors heavy above him. He had to fight off the eerie sensation that this House was alive and a black heart was beating inside it, sending waves of darkness surging through the corridors, swamping the people inside with swirling currents of fear. They were trapped!

'Don't panic,' Kyra said shakily, and it took Kyle a second to realize she was talking to herself. 'There must be something we can do.' She turned to look directly at Eva, speaking to the Chance girl for the first time since she'd seen her as a ghost. 'Can't you do something?'

Eva laughed out loud and in the back of her mind something told her she would never be scared of Kyra again. The blonde girl who had been her bully for as long as she could remember had asked her for help. Unfortunately the joke was on all of them.

'I've been trying to do something ever since I first found out what I was,' Eva said. 'I'm worn to a shred from fending off the Witch. But everything I do is reactive. I'm always two steps behind. And fighting the Witch is like trying to stop the tide from turning, or empty the ocean with a bucket. She's not just a ghost, she's an evil presence, a curse on this House.'

'Then the Witch is responsible for all the little "accidents"?' Kyle asked. 'All the people I saw tripping or stumbling earlier today?'

'Not just little accidents,' Eva said grimly. 'One woman fell ten feet when a banister snapped on the ballroom balcony. An ambulance took her away.'

'No wonder the police have arrived then,' Kyra said and Kyle rolled his eyes.

'I said that five minutes ago,' he said. 'Keep up.'

'I'm thinking,' Kyra snapped back. 'And I don't believe it's a ghost witch that's framing Felix. There's a person behind this and that's what the police are going to think too. Only they're going to blame Felix.'

'My heart bleeds for Felix,' Kyle said and turned to Eva. 'What do you think?' he asked her. 'Was it the Witch who . . . who killed you?'

'I don't know . . . ' Eva shook her head. 'I don't think the Witch kills people directly, she uses other ways, causes "accidents", makes the House dangerous. But she's in all this just the same. She stirred up Maggie, your family ghost. She wanted the ghost walks. She always planned to use them to cause chaos.'

'Felix thinks a person wanted the ghost walks,' Kyra said. 'That someone pushed him into it.' She glanced suddenly over her shoulder and then muttered, 'Where *is* Felix?'

'Christopher Knight suggested the ghost walks.' Eva was looking into the depths of the east wing. 'And now when any sane person would call a halt he's still going ahead with them.'

'And Felix is lurking about somewhere hoping to catch his mysterious Mr X in the act,' Kyle realized. 'Feck. What a disaster this is turning out to be. The next time that idiot suggests a plan I'm going to tie him to a chair or something.'

Kyra gave a strangled cry and her fingers dug hard into Kyle's arm.

'What?' he snapped. 'You really have gone dappy over that bloke, haven't you.'

'Look at Eva!' Kyra snarled back at him. 'Idiot. Look!'

Eva's ghostly form had thinned down to a wraith, her ragged velvet dress shredding into a filthy shroud, her limbs skeletal and blackened with bruises. A breath of foul air came from her body, a smell of blood and faeces and rotting vegetation.

'Eva!' Kyle lunged forward, reaching for the fading ghost. His hands grasped nothing, fingers numbing in the freezing air. But Eva's eyes snapped open, focusing on him, her image slowly reforming as he let his hands drop. 'What happened?' Kyle asked and Eva's voice came thinly from the air he now knew was empty.

'I don't know,' she said. 'But it keeps happening. At first it was only occasionally but now it's happening more and more often. I'm finding it harder and harder to stay focused. It's as though I'm drifting and somewhere . . . ' Her voice fell to a whisper, 'somewhere there's a whirlpool, dragging me down.'

'A whirlpool?' Kyra frowned, rubbing her arms which had come out in gooseflesh at the way Eva's ghostly body had changed in front of her. 'Is that a metaphor? Like those people who see tunnels when they're dying? Maybe you're being sucked off into the afterlife.'

'I don't think so.' Eva's eyes were still weirdly unfocused, staring into an unimaginable distance. 'Maggie told me ghosts could be dragged back into bad memories, into bad places. This feels like a bad place. It smells bad, like blood and filth. It hurts me . . . and I can't focus when the peacocks are screaming!' Her voice had got more and more desperate and the twins exchanged glances. Neither of them could hear peacocks at all.

'If you need to focus, focus on me,' Kyle said firmly. 'I'm right here. Six foot of me, I'm difficult to miss, right? And I'm ready and willing to help you, only you have to tell me what to do, OK? Do I go after your idiot cousin who's ninja-ing about somewhere with a digital camera? Or warn the police that there's ghosts and curses hanging about like wallpaper? Or take down Christopher Knight in case he's the mysterious X who's been taking pot shots at people.'

'I don't know,' Eva admitted. 'It could be Knight. I think it was him who suggested the ghost walks. If he's the murderer, how did he attack Aunt Cora and get away clean? There were no footsteps in the snow by the summerhouse.'

'Maybe Knight's got special snow-shoes or something,' Kyra suggested, casting a glance at Kyle as she spoke, eyes only a little wider than normal. Kyle smiled at his twin. She was playing along, keeping Eva grounded in their speculation. Only he knew from the tightness of her fingers driven like talons into his arm that she was acting a calm she didn't feel.

'The police won't believe you,' Eva said. 'No one will. No one ever believed me that I saw ghosts. No one except my grandfather. And he's not here.' There was a lost quality to her voice, a loneliness that made Kyle ache with sympathy. It was so hard to believe that this girl wasn't real, wasn't alive, wasn't a person any more. A ghost and a corpse rotting somewhere, that's what she'd been reduced to and the surge of anger that went through him then surprised him with its power. Right then and there he would have taken on the Witch with his bare hands.

'I believe you,' he told Eva. 'I don't give a damn if it makes me sound crazy. And now you mention it maybe there's someone else who I can get to believe me too. More than one person.' He pulled out his phone. 'No reception, right. Where's the closest, safest place I can get a signal from here without needing to get outside where the police are?'

'Up.' Eva pointed at a narrow twisting stairway, wooden with bare and splintered boards. 'Up to the attics. But I don't think you should go alone.'

'He won't have to go alone.' A black and white figure appeared on the stairway. 'You can trust me for this, Evangeline Chance. You know I won't hurt my own flesh and blood.'

'You can trust Maggie, Kyle,' Eva said. 'She's your ancestor. And unlike the Chance ghosts she's not bad or mad or dangerous. At least not when it comes to you.'

Kyle tried to find this reassuring and to his surprise he saw the resemblance between the sharp face of the servant girl ghost and his equally sharp-looking twin sister. He found it surprisingly easy to believe she and their great-grandmother were two of a kind.

'OK,' he said. 'Kyra, you're coming too. Don't think for one second I'm letting you go haring off to save Felix from himself. Him and his stupid plan of taking the battle to the enemy.' The servant girl ghost stiffened at his words and Kyra froze for a second before it spoke.

'Come, Great-Granddaughter, Evangeline will save the lucky Chance from his folly. Tell me why you think you would ever be anything more than a servant in the eyes of a Chance and I'll tell you about one Chance that does not think a servant is a tool to be used.'

The Stratton ghost didn't look at Eva but Kyle could almost

feel the force of the emotion that was passing between them, and Kyra had subsided beneath the words, no longer viewing their family ghost with fear.

'Thank you, Magpie.' Eva nodded and turned to go.

'Wait!' Kyle said. 'What are you going to do?'

'I'm going to follow Felix's lead,' Eva said solemnly. 'I'm going to take the battle to the enemy. I'm going to wage war on the Witch.'

16
Cry Havoc!

As the police entered through the front door Christopher Knight was leading his tour group into the shrouded and sheeted rooms of the east wing. Down by the lake, Richard Fairfax had finally mustered the company of searchers and was confident that everyone who had been searching for the weeping woman was now assembled on the shores of the lake.

'Ladies and gentlemen,' he was saying, trying to gain the attention of the crowd. 'This House is reputed to be haunted. The woman you saw in a rowing boat is almost certainly a ghost who died sixteen years ago, drowned in this lake.'

'Ghosts?' The searchers muttered uncomfortably and Richard silenced them with a chopping motion of his right hand.

'I'm not prepared to see good people chasing after phantoms.' He gestured at the woman who had been pulled out of the lake, now wrapped in blankets and being given hot tea that an enterprising member of the ground staff had provided from a thermos.

'There's a ghost walk going on back at the house,' one of the searchers said and then blushed when everyone turned to look at her.

'That's true,' Richard said slowly. 'And maybe some of you are thinking Sir Edward wouldn't have permitted it. But whatever your opinion, none of you people signed up for hunting ghosts, did you? So don't be fooled by what you see on the lake.'

'If you'll forgive me, sir,' a voice spoke out of the crowd. 'There's twenty people here or more that saw the woman in the rowing boat. It's not easy to believe we're seeing ghosts and just let it go.'

'Especially with all the rumours that have been floating about,' someone else murmured from the crowd.

Richard Fairfax felt uncomfortable. Back in his own northern county estates he was comfortable among his grounds staff, sometimes more comfortable than in his own extremely elegant home. He was the kind of man who liked to tramp along the bounds of his estate with a couple of dogs at his heels. And although he kept a formal distance between himself and his employees in his businesses, he was more at ease with his keepers, woodsmen and stable-hands in their conversations about crops and game and farming. He was far from egalitarian in his dealings with his staff but his days in the army made him feel a responsibility for people under his command.

Richard had been drawn into the search when he'd heard the story of the weeping rower and he'd spent long hours sifting fact from fiction. But now he was at a loss to communicate this to well-meaning searchers, muddy and tired from their labours and yet still willing to plough back into the field.

A tow-headed man moved out of the crowd and stepped up next to Richard. The crowd gave him their attention in a way they hadn't to Richard Fairfax even before he'd said a word.

'Listen up, folks,' he said. 'Most of you know me, I'm Keith Stratton. Advanced Building by Stratton and Co in the Yellow Pages. I think we should listen to this chap because this isn't the first time I've been called to search for a woman on this lake. Sixteen years ago Adeline chance disappeared and half the town came out to search for her. Any of you remember that?'

There were mutters of agreement from the back of the group and Keith pressed on.

'Mr Fairfax wasn't here then but he's got the story right. Adeline was pregnant, she left her home in the early hours and rowed a boat out on the lake. She might have been crying, but no one was here to see it. When she was reported missing, police dogs followed her trail to the shores of the lake and there was a boat gone from the boat house. A small wooden rowing boat.'

There were murmurs in the crowd and Keith nodded.

'A boat just like people have told me they saw today. Adeline was very beautiful, you'd have remembered her if you'd seen her. Black hair, green eyes, a way of moving as though she heard music wherever she walked.'

'That's who I saw,' the woman wrapped in blankets exclaimed. 'Black hair, green eyes. That's her.'

'Adeline is dead.' Keith quelled the rumblings from the crowd. 'Her body was washed up a month later. Dying like that, the way she did, if there are such things as ghosts I'd not find it so hard to believe Adeline left an echo of herself here.'

This time when he stopped speaking he didn't try to stop the crowd murmuring. But although there were many curious glances cast at the lake no one was actively moving towards it and Richard Fairfax allowed himself to relax a little.

'That was well said,' he spoke quietly to Keith. 'I'd heard the story but I couldn't have explained it as you did. I never knew Adeline.'

'It's not just Adeline I'm thinking of.' Keith spoke equally quietly but with more haste. 'We never found her when we searched but we did find something. Her little baby, cradled in a basket in the bulrushes, like Moses—except the baby was a girl. It's Evangeline I'm thinking of, sir. The baby that we found. She was lost too, just weeks ago. The only difference is, her body was never found.'

'Evangeline.' Richard Fairfax had a sinking feeling. 'I never really knew her. Then you think it might not be a ghost after all?'

'No, that's not it.' Keith shook his head. 'I meant what I said. It's just that there might be more than one ghost. I didn't know Evangeline either. But what if she took after her mother? In more ways than one?'

* * *

In the east wing the train of tourists following Christopher Knight were finding the corridors unexpectedly long, receding into infinite depths so that a moment's hesitation could leave you isolated from the rest of the group.

Some distance behind them, the police officer and Nathan's father looked at the expanse of the House stretching out in front of them and paused in their headlong pursuit to listen for the crying of a lost child.

In the kitchens, a few remaining members of the hired staff were cleaning up. A teenager with corn-rowed hair checked his watch and then chugged his can of beer, tossing it in a bin as he headed off in the direction of the cellars.

Three floors up, in a bare but not entirely empty room, Lisle Langley's mobile picked up a signal and trilled urgently. The house agent, bleeding and bruised, got to her feet, pulling the ringing phone from her pocket as the words scrolled past on the screen: *You have 23 missed calls and 11 voicemails and 17 text messages*. Thumbing through the text messages, Lisle's nerves

251

twanged with alarm and, ignoring her injuries, she broke into a run.

* * *

Up on the roof Kyle and Kyra and Maggie saw the House and gardens spread out beneath them, beneath the indigo sky. All three Strattons were at ease on the tiles of the roof and in the open air, briefly free from the oppressive atmosphere of the House beneath them.

As Kyle tried to summon a signal on his mobile phone, Maggie and Kyra faced each other across the tiles.

'I never meant to scare you,' Maggie told her great-granddaughter, picking up the thread of their earlier conversation. 'You scared me. Seeing you with that boy. It brought back memories.' Her fingers flicked with anxious tight moments. 'Eva understood. She knew somehow. What had happened. To me.' Her sentences were clipped-off fragments, stutter-stopped signals of things unspoken.

'Felix . . . ' Kyra started speaking, stopped and then started again. 'Look, in the twenty-first century some people think we're past all this class bollocks but there are still toffs and chavs, right? Still the rich and the poor. But we're further on than you think. Things have changed. I'm doing A-level maths and accountancy two years early at school. My teachers are begging me to go to university. My dad thinks I'm going to work for his business, but I've got other plans. I'm going to be a stockbroker or an investment banker in the city, getting million pound bonuses. Money and people and gambling, it's my life. And even if I was interested in Felix Fairfax, maybe a tiny little bit, it's not going to stop me doing what I want and leaving him in the *dust*.' She finished more vehemently than she'd intended, breathing hard at

252

the impact of revealing so much so suddenly in such an out-of-context situation.

'Things have changed.' Margaret Stratton looked away from Kyra into the sky. 'I've watched them changing. Watched you, Kyra. I never realized before that I was watching Eva as well and enjoying the game when you and your friends laughed at her. That was justice, I thought.'

Kyra was silent for a long minute. But how could you lie to a ghost, a ghost that was a great-grandmother who'd lived more horrors than you could imagine, who'd shown more hate and malice than your own worst raging tantrum.

'It wasn't fair,' she said. 'And I knew it too. But I have to be tough. I *have* to be. Things haven't changed enough for that. If you're soft people walk over you, use you: and I don't want that. If I'm a bitch, it's better than being a pushover.' She paused. 'But I never meant to push someone else over the edge.'

Out on the edge of the roof, Kyle sat with his legs swinging over the drop and his mobile phone pressed to his right ear as it trilled a ring tone at him. The ringing went on and just as he was about to give up the ringing stalled and a voice said:

'Michael Stevenage.'

'Um . . . hi,' Kyle replied. 'This is Kyle Stratton. You said I could call if something happened?'

'What's the matter, Kyle?' The lawyer's voice deepened into seriousness. 'Are you at a police station?'

'I'm on the roof of Chance House,' Kyle said. 'I can see a police car in the front drive but I've not seen the police themselves yet.'

'What's happened?'

'I think the police have come because of the number of accidents here today, at least one ambulance was called for someone who fell off a balcony. And when they investigate they're bound to smell something fishy. There've been too many accidents.'

'That's true.' The lawyer sounded cautious. 'So what can I help you with, Kyle?'

'My sister and I have talked to Felix,' Kyle admitted. 'We know about Edward Chance's will. I'm guessing you're suspicious of Felix just like I was. But there's a bunch of stuff you don't know about, Mr Stevenage, that I only found out about today. We think someone's been pushing for the ghost walks and there's one going on right now.'

There was silence from the other end of the phone and Kyle pressed on.

'Even if you don't believe in the ghosts, Mr Stevenage, I know Eva's grandfather does. And I know he would want to know what happened to Eva. That's what I want too. Since I can't help her any other way.'

'Kyle,' the lawyer's voice was more human now, 'what's going on? What made you call me at this point? What are you afraid of?'

'I'm afraid of the curse,' Kyle said. 'Seriously. There's a curse on this House. But if you don't believe that perhaps you'll believe that Felix is playing detective and it's going to get him killed. And Christopher Knight is our top suspect right now so if anyone does get killed you might want to check him out.'

'I'll be there in fifteen minutes,' Michael announced abruptly. 'Don't do anything until I arrive.'

Kyle put the phone back in his pocket and inched over to Kyra and the ghost of their ancestress.

'I called the lawyer,' he said.

'That was your genius plan?' Kyra blinked at him. 'Calling a lawyer?'

'It's the best I could think of,' Kyle said defensively. 'I think he's halfway to believing in ghosts. And he's also halfway to thinking your boyfriend's a murderer, like everyone else in town. The more I think about Felix's plan the more stupid it sounds, he's going to be right on the scene when something really bad kicks off. And it will.'

'Yes,' Maggie nodded jerkily. 'It will. Eva challenged the Witch. And the Witch has been watching Eva all along. It wasn't until Eva died that the ghosts began to walk.'

'What does that mean?' Kyra demanded. 'I can't take much more of this. Every time I think I've got a handle on this crazy place it slips away like jelly. I still can't get over the fact I'm sitting on the roof of a mansion having a conversation with the ghost of my great-grandmother.'

'What happened to Eva was the beginning of this whole thing,' Kyle said, glancing at Maggie for confirmation.

'The ghosts aren't usually so present,' Maggie agreed. 'But something sharpened our attention. I thought it was Eva doing it at first until I found out she didn't even know what she was.'

'Felix said Eva had a reputation for being odd,' Kyle said. 'And Eva said she'd always been able to see ghosts.'

'Some of the Chances can,' Maggie agreed. 'The mad ones usually can.'

'Eva's mother was supposed to be one of the mad ones,' Kyra said and flinched at Kyle's look. 'Dad told me, OK? I didn't know anything about it before. But Dad said that Adeline killed herself and he described her as haunted.'

'If Eva was different, strange or mad or haunted or whatever you call it, maybe that's why . . . ' Kyle paused. 'I don't know, why someone killed her, why the ghosts are so active, why the Witch is so set against her.'

'Yes,' Maggie was nodding along. 'Yes, I think so. It must be

255

why. Eva is different. She burns brightly, like a fire in the cold empty world of ghosts. If you were dead, you'd feel it too.'

'I can feel it without being dead,' Kyle said. 'Not that it does me any good.'

* * *

If Eva was blazing like a beacon in the world of the ghosts, she didn't know about it. What she did see was how much she'd changed. *It wasn't until I died that I knew how much I really wanted to live*, she thought. *I just drifted along, letting things happen to me.* That was about to stop.

Eva walked along the Long Gallery, the painted faces of generations of ancestors looking down on her. Was it her imagination that they looked less stern and disapproving now? Was that a twinkle of amusement from a piratical great-great-great-great-uncle, a glint of a smile from the desiccated countenance of a long-dead countess? Eva nodded to the paintings as she passed by.

At one end of the gallery was a locked tallboy, a cupboard large enough to have dominated a more normal sized room. Eva put her hand to the front of it and felt the tumblers shift in the locked doors, clicking into position smoothly so that the doors swung open soundlessly. The things inside had not been touched for months but no hint of dust marred them. Eva drew them out slowly. A white fencing outfit, with gauntlets, shin-pads and boots. A fencer's mask, the front a featureless black oval of tight mesh. And finally the foil, a slender needle of a sword, the weight perfect for her, the hilt fitting her hand with the familiarity of long years of practice.

As weapons went a fencing foil was useless against both ghosts and witchcraft but it wasn't the physical aspect of the weapon that Eva was looking for. It was that it *was* a weapon and holding it in her hand she felt dangerous. The red velvet dress with its puffed sleeves and full skirt, the wellington boots two sizes too big: those were clothes that made her look foolish, eccentric, and weak. But the white bodystocking covered her entire body, concealing her youth, her strangeness, her weakness, beneath a smooth economy of form: arms, legs, torso. Her hands flexed in the white gloves, her feet fit the white boots. The complications and uncertainties of her identity vanished beneath the figure of the fencer. The mask went over her head, a final metaphor for her experiences in the real world and ghost world alike. She could see out but no one could see in.

Eva picked up the sword again and turned to look at the two rows of her ancestors, facing each other across the room. Raising her chin she looked down the long expanse of the room and stepped into the world of the ghosts.

* * *

Felix had been following the ghost walk at one removed, a spy in his own house as he skulked outside rooms and peered through half open doors. Christopher Knight's marketing patter came in a steady stream of anecdotes and suggestions, light-hearted enough to suggest to the sceptical that the ghost walk was no more than a themed tour, serious enough to keep the more superstitious members of the group twitching at every unexpected sound. The marketing expert had to walk a narrow tightrope between fact and fantasy but he was managing it with consummate skill. Only Felix, watching from the shadows, was keeping a close enough eye on Knight to see that the man was not quite as confident as he appeared. When the tourists weren't watching, Knight fidgeted with his mobile phone, texting or checking for messages. At one

257

point, he hung back as the tourists climbed a narrow staircase and quickly dialled a number.

'It's me again,' he muttered into the sleek silver mobile. 'I'm about half an hour into the ghost walk. I hope this is still what you want. For God's sake call me when you get this message!' He hung up, flipping the phone shut and stuffing it back into his pocket, taking the stairs two at a time to catch up with the ghost walk.

Behind him, Felix crept quietly up the staircase, wondering who Knight had been phoning. The call could have been an innocent one, checking with one of the family or the house agent that they still wanted the ghost walks to go ahead. But Felix was inclined to doubt it. Knight was too on edge—and Felix didn't believe it was a fear of ghosts that concerned the marketing expert.

However, as the ghost walk entered the east wing, it became harder to keep up. Felix had thought he knew the House well enough to follow any tour but the east wing was treacherous. As Knight led the tourists along the corridors, Felix paced them through the interconnected rooms. But the walls were thicker than he'd realized, muffling sounds or distorting them so that at one point he almost opened a door in front of Knight and had to jump back hurriedly and hide behind the open door as the ghost walk came streaming past. Then, five minutes later, what Felix thought was a doorway through to the next room turned out to be a cupboard and he could swear he heard laughter behind him as he cursed his mistake. The laughter wasn't the only sound either. Floorboards creaked and mice skittered inside the walls. Voices murmured or whispered just around the next corner but when Felix came sneaking up there was no one there.

Footsteps seemed to sound from unexpected directions, while

the ghost walk itself had vanished so completely that Felix wondered if they'd departed for another floor. Every minute he spent in the east wing eroded his confidence, little stabs of doubt assailing him, making him wonder if this had been such a good idea after all.

He'd forgotten what a maze this House was and how gloomy the empty rooms could be. It was cold too. Obviously the antique central heating system didn't extend into these abandoned rooms and a damp shivering cold seemed to seep out of the walls themselves, gusting through half open doors or worming up between mismatched floorboards. The few pieces of furniture left in the east wing seemed uncanny in their haphazard randomness. A single chair in the middle of one room, a wardrobe pulled halfway across the doorway to another, so that Felix had to slide sideways through the narrow gap. Sheets were draped over some of the furnishings and their fluttering or billowing fabric was caught by the draughts, making him jump as shrouded forms swum suddenly out of the darkness. They weren't even white sheets, instead patterned with paisley swirls and faded flowers and Felix chided himself for his nervousness. As if a ghost would come clad in Laura Ashley or William Morris print. But it was dark in these echoingly empty rooms. Felix didn't want to betray his presence by turning on the lights but less and less light seemed to make it through the windows, reminding him of how the darkness had closed in like a physical force in the Solar.

It was stupid to have come here alone, Felix realized. He'd had more than enough proof that the ghosts were real but he'd been carried away by the idea of catching a real person in an act of conspiracy. He'd been so certain that the hypothetical X was using the stories of ghosts as a distraction that he'd made the opposite mistake and been distracted in the other direction, looking for physical evidence of a crime.

Felix paused with his hand on the handle of the next door, wondering if he should turn back or if there was a quicker way onwards and out again. He'd lost track of where he was: too many turns taken, too many little sets of steps and half landings to even be certain of which floor he was on. Perhaps he could orient himself by the next window; the view would tell him which side of the House he was on. Opening the door he glanced around looking for a window and spotted long curtains half hiding it from view. The room was dim, a stack of furniture clustered near the middle: an old sofa with the sheet half fallen on to the floor beside it, a dressing table and a stack of packing cases, as mundane an assortment of items as you could imagine.

But as Felix crossed the room towards the windows something about the little collection drew his eye. Was the sofa a strange shape at one end? It seemed somehow humped up—or was that just the way the sheet had fallen? It was strange the way the patterns had faded on those old print sheets, the liquid way the shadows pooled around them. You could almost believe a figure was slumped there at an awkward angle no person would ever choose to sit, half fallen over the edge of the packing case, a sprinkle of dark flowers across the sheet where its head should be.

Felix's footsteps slowed, their echo coming to a stop a second later. He was standing next to the lumpen sheet, his hand reaching reluctantly to touch it, telling himself that it was a trick of the light that made the shrouded shape beneath so human. The sheet was slow to come at his touch, caught on something and then coming suddenly free, revealing the waxen white face beneath it.

Only a mannequin; he caught his breath in relief. Then, shattering seconds later, he was dropping the sheet and staggering back as the identity of that wax-white face registered. It was his aunt Joyce, lying slumped against the side of the sofa, her limbs limp and awkwardly positioned.

On her face a hideous beetle crouched, a ladybird the size of a cockroach, proboscis plunged deep into Joyce's right eye. It was a brooch. It took him a moment to identify it as costume jewellery rather than the insect it resembled, and more lethal than the most poisonous insect. The pin for the brooch had stabbed through to Aunt Joyce's brain.

Felix didn't want to touch her but he forced his shrinking fingers to curl round the woman's wrist. No murmur of a pulse there and he couldn't bear to put his mouth to the bloodied lips of the corpse and try to breathe life back into it. Joyce was dead, the latest victim of the so-called accidents. Had she seen the face of her attacker, did they wrestle together before he tore the brooch loose and plunged the pin into her eye?

Mechanically Felix took out his camera. The flash illuminated the grisly scene as he clicked the button. Once, twice, three times. He no longer knew why he was documenting this. There was a glitter from inside the half open case and instinctively he adjusted the focus, leaning in and taking a fourth picture, the flash lighting up a dragon's hoard of jewels. Felix blinked and looked again, trying to make sense of the image the camera had captured. The contents of the case had been protected with newspaper but eager hands had pulled it back, revealing if not exactly a draconic hoard a very human one. An ornamented jewellery box lay open inside the wrappings, brimming with a shining trove of rings, bracelets, and strings of pearls. Other items lay in the litter inside the case, silver-backed brushes and combs, gilded snuffboxes, ornamented pomanders. Hardly a king's ransom but a very tidy sum was represented here; enough to fetch several thousands of pounds at auction and more wealth than he'd yet seen in the decrepit old House. Were these some of the missing items his mother had mentioned, part of the long lists of inventories he'd been poring over in the library? And, if so, what were they doing here? Joyce Chance and Christopher Knight had been lovers. Was this evidence of a falling out between thieves? The blood was still wet, only just beginning to stiffen the fabric of Joyce's dress. Had there even been time for Knight to have made the attack?

The camera clicked and flashed again, the scene as stark and unlikely as a stage set, Felix's frozen fingers pressing and releasing the button mechanically, recording the details. As unreal as the scene was, it took all his attention. It was moments before he registered that there was a murmur of movement along the corridor, the slow fall of footsteps one after another, coming closer and pausing at the threshold of the door.

* * *

Eva really was in the world of the ghosts now. Stalking down the shadowy corridors with a sword in her hand and a mask over her face, she realized she was now the image of a vengeful spirit, inhuman, impersonal and obsessed with righting the wrong of her death. The thought brought with it a weird sense of calm. All the time she'd been a ghost she'd been slowly becoming more in control of her new self, accepting her new powers and letting go of the past, trying to wrap her mind around the truth of whatever she was now. But when she'd donned the fencing costume she hadn't been conflicted any more. Her ghost self was finally more real to her than her real self had been. The old shy uncertain Eva had been wiped away, erased by the malice of the Witch or the hands of the murderer. Now there was only the ghost.

As a ghost Eva could see things she'd only been able to guess at in life. The force currents of spectral energy swirled down the passages, dark tides of lost memories and vanished desires. Only a few could wrap that energy around themselves enough to make it form a shape: a shadow in a corner, a clutching hand, the sound of a scream or a laugh. Even fewer could hold that shape together for years, around the core of what had once been a personality. The ghosts of Chance House were more haunted than the living had ever been, because the ghosts came from this churning sea of chaos.

As Eva slid smoothly through the currents, keeping hold of her purpose just as she gripped the hilt of her rapier, she had more than one reason not to lose herself in the swirl of psychic energy. All those dark currents led down.

For the majority of ghosts it was as much as they could manage to keep control of themselves in the overlapping layers of history and memory and time, with the gamut of sensations from exultation and despair pulling and tugging at them and the House with its own undeniable personality behind it all. But one ghost had not only managed it, she had wound those dark currents around herself so that she could pull them like the strings of a puppet.

Finally Eva understood the curse on the House was not something separate from the Witch. The curse was the Witch and the way she played the puppeteer with those dark forces, churning up the vortexes of fear and pain and hate.

That's it, the Witch spoke through the currents and Eva could feel the voice in her bones, in her blood, in the veins of the stone walls that surrounded her. *You are finally learning to see as I see. It will be almost a pity to destroy you.* But the Witch had no room in her dead dark mind for pity. She was anticipating ripping Eva's mind open and tearing into the remains with a savage glee that set Eva's hand shaking on the sword.

'No,' she said out loud. 'I don't just see the way you do, I see better. I'm not bound the way you are.'

What do you mean? That the Witch even asked the question betrayed its suspicions and doubt and Eva let it see her own elation at her realization.

'I've got the same power as you have,' she told the Witch. 'I can influence the ghosts and I can do it without having them hate or fear me. I can talk to them. You can only command. You're trapped in your own curse.'

Talk to them, the Witch was laughing again. *That's your weapon? The power you think you have that I do not?* The laughter hurt Eva's head from the inside out. *Talk then, little Chance, talk to the one that comes to you now. Use your power to console.*

The Witch faded out of Eva's mind, withdrawing as another spirit came lurching through the veil of shadows towards her. A ghost she had not encountered before. It came stumbling and staggering, uncertain of how to move in the world it found itself in. And as it raised its terrified eyes to Eva's she recognized the ghost. It had once been her Aunt Joyce.

* * *

The footsteps came to a halt on the other side of the door. Felix watched as the door knob turned across the room. His fingers tightened on the camera, a poor excuse for a weapon but the only one he had. The door swung open, he took a breath—and Christopher Knight appeared in the entrance, a cluster of people appearing behind him in the corridor.

'And here we have . . . ' the words stilled on Knight's lips as he took in the scene in front of him.

264

'Don't come in here!' Felix warned at the same moment but it was too late. There was a gasp from the corridor and then a strangled scream as one person after another saw the dead body.

'Is it real?' someone asked but Christopher Knight answered that question for them.

'Oh my God, it's Joyce,' he said and raised appalled eyes to meet Felix's. Any hope Felix had of proving Knight was the murderer died then. Unless the man was a brilliant actor, he was for real. The shock and horror in his face could not have been feigned. 'What have you done?' Christopher Knight demanded and Felix blanched.

'It wasn't me!' he insisted. 'I just found her here. I was looking for evidence.' He clutched the camera as if it proved anything. 'I didn't even touch her. At least, only to check she was dead . . .'

That went down about as well as you might expect and he caught the muttered words from the back of the group: 'police' and 'murder'.

'I can explain,' Felix tried. But it was already too late. As Christopher knelt beside Joyce's corpse and the crowd stared at the scene with horrified expressions, he could tell he'd already been judged and convicted in their eyes.

17
The Murder Room

In the front hall, the male police constable had just finished taking down rambling and contradictory statements from Helen Fairfax and the two teenage boys who'd been fooling with the duelling pistols when Lisle Langley came rushing down the main staircase. The house agent's usually immaculate black suit was dusty and dishevelled, her hair loosened from its tight pleat and her face and hands scraped and bleeding.

'Good lord, Lisle!' Helen exclaimed, getting to her feet. 'What happened?'

'I'm not sure,' Lisle said and then cast a worried look at the policeman.

'Are you hurt, miss?' The constable managed to retain his poker-face while expressing concern and Helen winced, realizing that Lisle's appearance was going to be added to his copious notes. 'Has something happened to you?' the constable continued.

'I think someone attacked me,' Lisle said. 'Unless it was some kind of joke that went wrong. I was upstairs, just walking around, checking on things, when someone grabbed me from behind. I fought back, of course,' she continued, showing her bruised and bleeding hands. 'But whoever it was, they were much stronger than me. I hit my head, passed out, and the next thing I knew I was lying on the floor.'

'When did this happen?' The policeman had flipped open his notebook and was scribbling again, loops and swirls of shorthand crossing the small pages.

'I'm not sure.' Lisle checked her watch and shook her head. 'I think I might have been out for an hour. Maybe longer. I still feel woozy.'

'You'd better sit down,' Helen said and Lisle nodded, sinking on to a wooden bench and massaging her temples.

'Sorry,' she said. 'I'm not normally like this but I've got a killer headache.'

The policeman nodded and then excused himself, crossing to the other side of the hall and then taking out his radio and muttering into it, still scribbling in the notebook as he spoke.

'While you were out of it things have gone to hell in a hand basket,' Helen said grimly. 'Apparently someone was injured here this afternoon and the police showed up not long ago to investigate our health and safety provisions. Unfortunately these two lummoxes were messing around in the gun room and managed to discharge a pistol—which didn't exactly help our case, despite the fact I patched them up. And just as I was explaining about that some fool man comes up howling that he's lost his five-year-old son on the ghost walk and one of the police goes charging off with him.'

'I see,' Lisle said, her expression betraying that she did indeed see the situation, perhaps more clearly than her employer.

'It's a nightmare.' Helen shook her head. 'And I've been having to explain the situation all on my own. God knows what's happened to my husband, or Felix, or Joyce for that matter. Everyone seems to have vanished into the ether and the hired staff are either idling about the place or having hysterics.'

Lisle had taken out her phone and it beeped gently as she checked her messages, holding it up to one ear as Helen continued her tirade in the other. When Helen had finally wound herself to a halt Lisle tried to fill her in.

'According to my messages there have been quite a few accidents. Your husband had to pull someone out of the lake and there's been a series of minor incidents. My concern is how many tourists are still on site. You said something about the ghost walk, did that go ahead?'

'It seems to have,' Helen shrugged. 'That chap Knight was supposed to be starting it off and I believe Joyce was going to help out. I expect they've reached the east wing by now. Not that there's much to see but according to Joyce it has an "atmosphere".'

'Should we call it off?' Lisle asked. 'Under the circumstances, it might be for the best.'

'I expect the police will see to that.' Helen shot a resentful glance at the note-taking constable as he came back across the hall. 'They seem to be in charge here now. Isn't that so, officer?'

'We're still assessing the situation, madam,' he said woodenly. 'But since there does seem to be some uncertainty about who exactly is present on the scene it would be to everyone's benefit if we could take a register.' He turned to Lisle. 'Miss . . .'

'Ms,' Lisle said automatically. 'I'm Ms Langley, the house agent.'

'Ms Langley,' the constable made a slight correction to his notes. 'What makes you think that the attack on you was a practical joke? You mentioned that as a possibility.'

'Oh, well, it just seems so unlikely that anyone would attack me,' Lisle explained. 'And with the ghost walk going on, perhaps someone got carried away with the fantasy of it.' She glanced at the two teenagers who'd been injured in the gun room. 'People sometimes do silly things.'

'Then you can't think of a reason anyone might want to hurt you?' the policeman pressed on. 'Nothing that might inspire such an attack?'

'No, sorry, I just can't.' Lisle shook her head. 'As I said, I'm not even sure if it was an attack.' She shifted uncomfortably. 'I realize this is going to sound somewhat implausible, but this House is supposedly haunted. I did wonder if I might have accidentally disturbed something—something supernatural.'

'Something supernatural,' the policeman repeated her words flatly as he copied them down. 'Thank you, Ms Langley.' Neither Helen nor Lisle could tell if he was being sarcastic.

* * *

On the third floor, the senior policewoman had managed to halt Nathan's father in his increasingly frantic search for his son.

'I'm sorry, sir,' she was saying, using deliberately calm tones. 'This house is too extensive for the two of us to conduct a proper search. If you'll come back downstairs I'll radio for assistance and we can bring in as many people as we need. Rest assured that we will do everything necessary to find your son and return him to you. But you need to remain calm. Now, shall we go back downstairs?'

'What will my wife say when she finds out I've lost him?' The man was barely listening to her. Abruptly he raised his voice, shouting up into the heights of the staircase above. 'Nathan! Nathan, come back here! Nathaaaan!'

'Please, sir.' The policewoman took his arm. 'Let's go downstairs. I promise you, we'll do everything to find him.'

'But what if you can't?' The man gave her a desperate look. 'Didn't a girl disappear from here almost a month ago and no one's found her either? Oh God, why did I ever bring my little boy to such a cursed place?'

The policewoman opened her mouth to respond but before she could think of what to say she was alerted to the sound of footsteps descending the narrow staircase that led down from what were presumably the attics of the house. A teenage boy and girl, both blond-haired and blue-eyed, were coming down the steps.

'What's going on?' the boy asked, looking from the policewoman to Nathan's father. 'We heard shouting.'

'A child is missing,' the policewoman explained quickly. 'You haven't seen a five-year-old boy have you?'

'Not since the ghost walk when he ran off,' the blonde girl said. 'He's gone missing? I'd have thought you'd have caught up with him in seconds.'

'He got away.' Nathan's father was grey with worry. 'I never should have let him go.'

'We'd better look for him then,' the teenage boy said and the policewoman quickly grabbed his arm.

'No you don't,' she said. 'There'll be no more running off half-cocked. You three had better come downstairs with us.'

'Three of us?' the teenagers exchanged glances and the boy continued: 'You're counting Nathan's dad as the third then?'

'I meant your friend up there on the stairs,' the policewoman said. But when she looked up again she saw clearly that there were only two teenagers. And yet she could swear she'd seen a third person, a thin young woman in a black and white uniform. 'Were the two of you alone up there?'

'Yes, officer.' The boy looked at her guilelessly. 'We were trying to get a mobile phone signal. We'd have noticed if there was anyone else about.'

'All right then.' The policewoman directed them back towards the stairs. 'In that case, we're all going to go back downstairs and do a proper head count of who's here and who's not, OK?'

'OK,' the teenagers agreed and Nathan's father finally consented to be guided back down.

The policewoman glanced back up towards the attics one final time. She could swear she had seen another person on the attic stairs and, come to think of it, she could hear footsteps too, moving about not far away. As she shepherded her little group back down to the main hall she wondered how many lost souls there were in this mouldering barrack of a place and how long it would take to find them all.

* * *

Michael Stevenage the lawyer had to brake suddenly as he arrived at the gates of Chance House. An ambulance and a police van, both with sirens screaming, cut across his intended path and entered through the gates, racing up towards the House. Michael slammed his own foot down on the accelerator and went racing after them.

He arrived at the front drive to a scene of chaos. There was already one police car in situ and the van parked next to it was plainly decanting back-up: a serious looking squad of six uniformed officers. The ambulance crew looked equally grim. As he got out of his car, Michael heard one paramedic say to another:

'Can't believe this bloody place . . . this is the second call-out today. Not to mention the two last week.'

The doors to the front hall were open and people were shouting. A policewoman was standing on the stairs, demanding that everyone shut up and calm down but she was plainly fighting a losing battle. Felix Fairfax was wearing handcuffs, a male officer holding on as if he suspected Felix might do a runner at any moment. A crowd of camera-wielding tourists all seemed to be trying to give their statements at once and the words 'murder', 'blood', and 'stabbing' were repeated like the verses of a round song. Felix himself looked pale and ill, paying no attention to the questions of his mother on one side and a pretty blonde girl on the other. Two men both appeared to be having hysterics. One was the marketing chap Christopher Knight, whose hands were liberally covered in smeary red stains of ominous provenance. The other appeared to be a tourist who had lost a child, since at every moment he repeated this fact to anyone who passed within a foot of him.

The incoming group of police flocked to the senior policewoman for instructions and Michael followed them into the hall, wondering what he should do. Technically he wasn't Felix's lawyer although he did represent the Chance family. Any moment now Helen Fairfax was certain to catch sight of him and demand that he obtain Felix's release. It was a relief to finally catch sight of Kyle Stratton, hovering at the edge of the crowd.

'What's happened?' Michael demanded in a hurried whisper, grabbing Kyle's arm.

'Sheer bloody chaos,' Kyle replied. 'Someone murdered Eva's aunt Joyce and Felix was found right next to the body.'

'When you phoned me, you said something about suspecting Christopher Knight,' Michael murmured and Kyle shrugged.

'I guess I was wrong about that,' he said. 'Since he seems to have a perfect alibi. He was leading the ghost walk when they walked in on Felix and the body. That policewoman keeps trying to do a headcount but she's not having much luck. There's a kid missing too and it's possible someone tried to whack Ms Langley on the head some time this afternoon.'

'My God.' Michael looked around for Lisle. 'Is she all right?'

'Seemed OK to me,' Kyle said. 'But I only just got here.'

Michael was scanning the room as the boy spoke and clocked Lisle Langley sitting on a bench, looking weary. Her dishevelled appearance was a notable contrast to the crisp meticulous aspect she'd had when he first met her and she'd filled him in on the family history. He wondered if she was regretting having taken on the Chances as clients—lord knew he was having some doubts himself.

'What makes you so sure Felix isn't guilty?' he asked Kyle and the boy shrugged.

'He's not the type,' he said. 'I don't like him but I still don't think he did it. Besides, what's in it for him?'

'That's a point,' Michael agreed. 'But probably not one that will weigh much with the police. Felix was on the scene. He had the opportunity. And after the attacks on his grandfather and his other aunt, it doesn't look good.'

'I know,' Kyle said. 'Felix knows too. What I'm trying to work out is who else knows it because Felix said someone was trying to make him the scapegoat—and I think he's right.'

Michael didn't say anything. Felix was young, arrogant, and self-absorbed. Not once had he come to visit his grandfather in hospital. Even if there wasn't an obvious reason for Felix to attack Joyce or Cora the fact that he was his grandfather's heir looked black against him and Eva's disappearance made it more likely that he would inherit everything. Despite Kyle's insistence that Felix wasn't guilty, Michael wasn't convinced. If it came to defending the boy there could well be a conflict of interest— since Edward Chance had been another victim of the attacks. But for now he was the only lawyer there and someone needed to find out what charges the police intended to bring. Slowly,

Michael walked up to the little knot of police surrounding Felix and introduced himself.

* * *

Kyle watched as the lawyer sprang into action, although it was more like sidled reluctantly into action. He wondered if he could have been more convincing in support of Felix—but right now even he was wondering if he might have been wrong. When Kyra came and joined him, he knew she was thinking the same from the way she said:

'The police won't believe Felix was set up!'

'It looks suss, Kyra,' he told her. 'Even I think it looks dodgy. About the only thing Felix has got going for him was that no one can figure out what motive he'd have.'

Kyra screwed her face up but she didn't say anything. Kyle felt bad for her. He knew she liked Felix more than she was prepared to admit. But right now he was feeling pretty grim himself. He'd done nothing to help Eva. Another one of her family had been murdered and he was no nearer to finding out who the killer was. Seeing the professionalism of the police, taking statements and making notes, he felt pretty stupid having even tried to work the problem out with only his sister to help. He leant against the cold stone wall, waiting for the police to get to him.

He and Kyra had been standing there for at least fifteen minutes, not speaking, when a new group of people came trekking into the hall. This group came from the back of the House and their muddy boots left a trail of grime and greenish water behind them. A police constable had found them just as they arrived at the House and led them to join the assembly in the hall. At the front of the group was Richard Fairfax, Felix's father, and his vocal objections froze on his lips when he saw his son in handcuffs. Kyle looked away, it was bad enough that he didn't trust Felix; it was worse seeing the doubt on Felix's father's face. Kyle looked away and as he did he came face to face with another arrival—his own dad.

Keith Stratton didn't seem surprised to see his children there ahead of him. But then he'd known they'd been working there that day. Still, his calm presence was a relief to both of them as he touched Kyle's shoulder and then put an arm around Kyra.

'What's up then, kids?' he asked. 'Looks like trouble.'

'I think Felix is about to be arrested,' Kyle said. 'Someone did in another of the Chance ladies—and the police reckon he's the most likely suspect.'

'I know he didn't do it, Dad,' Kyra broke in to exclaim. 'He didn't.'

'I see,' Keith said and then caught the attention of one of the police. It was the senior woman who noticed him first and came over with a questioning look.

'Is there something you wanted, sir?' she asked politely, although Kyle thought she looked strained.

'These two kids are mine,' Keith said. 'They've been working here all day and from the look of them they're due a rest. Any reason I can't take them home?'

It wasn't what either of them had been expecting and Kyle felt resentful at his dad taking over so suddenly.

'Dad!' Kyra objected. 'I want to stay with Felix.'

'Mr Fairfax is going to be staying at the station tonight,' the policewoman said. 'You can say goodnight to him if you like. Then I think you should all go home.' She turned to add to Keith. 'Leave your names and address with the sergeant over there and we'll contact you all for your statements shortly.'

'Thanks,' Keith nodded. 'Come on, Kyra. We'll go and say goodnight to your friend together.'

Kyle followed them, wondering if Kyra was going to cause a scene. But between her dad and the police she didn't seem to feel able to work herself into the same emotional state she had when the police had put the handcuffs on Felix. Instead she just squeezed his hand.

'This is a mess,' Felix said, meeting Kyle's eyes past Kyra. He rattled the handcuffs and grimaced. 'Thanks for calling the lawyer, that was pretty smart.'

'No problem,' Kyle said. 'Do you think he can get you out?'

'I'm not even sure I want him to,' Felix said. 'Right now a nice safe jail cell sounds a better bet than here.' He laughed carelessly and the police frowned, bystanders looking appalled at Felix's apparent callousness. Kyle wasn't shocked though. He was beginning to guess that Felix acted like even more of a prat when he didn't want people to know how he really felt.

'Good luck,' was all Kyle said and the police watched closely as Kyra hugged Felix. Not as closely as Helen Fairfax though, who watched Kyra through narrowed disapproving eyes.

'Come on, you two,' Keith said, drawing them away. 'I've got my van parked just outside. It's not far.'

As they walked through the dim grey light down the gravel drive, Kyle noticed the gate to the car park field blocked by a couple of scraped and dented cars. His dad had made a lucky call parking outside the grounds. Or perhaps it wasn't luck.

'Dad,' he said, 'you know Grandad was born here? That his mother was a servant girl who died having him?'

'I did,' Keith Stratton said. 'Your grandad told me about it a long time ago. Who told you about it?'

'Well,' Kyle said, thinking about Maggie. 'It's kind of a long story.'

'Then you'd better start at the beginning, hadn't you?' Keith said and Kyle wondered why he'd ever thought his dad was calm. Keith wasn't calm, he was worried. More worried than Kyle had ever seen him.

* * *

As Keith Stratton's van pulled away from the road outside the House it passed a truck: a truck carrying the logo of the county police department. The truck arrived at the House and rolled slowly up the gravel drive, bypassing the front entrance and continuing on towards the stable courtyard. There, beside the gift shop, it parked. The driver got out and, with the aid of a couple of technicians, entered the stable building. Then, on the first floor of the structure, in a long gabled room above the gift shop, the police began setting up a base of operations.

Unbeknown to the remaining members of the family still being processed in the front hall, this turn of events was not exactly a new development. The computers, whiteboards, and tables now being unloaded came from a conference room in the county police department's headquarters: the Murder Room.

A number of people go missing every year in the United Kingdom. Many of those disappearances are only minimally investigated. While the disappearance of a white fifteen-year-old upper-class teenage girl is likely to attract more attention than most, the fact that the teenage girl in question had a known history of mental disturbance, possibly hereditary, and had been taking unscheduled absences from school, meant the case is likely to be considered that of a runaway and active investigation ceases. In the case of Evangeline (also known as Eva) Chance the extent of the search had been for police searchers and dogs to comb the grounds on two occasions. They had found nothing.

There the case had rested for a week, until a note from the local hospital had attracted the attention of the police to Chance House again. This time the girl's grandfather was the victim—of a fall, it was claimed. But the paramedics had disliked something about the house or the family and the A&E doctor had annotated the file with the words 'possible abuse'.

The wheels of administrative systems grind slowly when there's no immediate urgency and the two cases involving Chance House might not have been drawn together at all if on the sixth of the month, less than a week after the grandfather's accident and two weeks from the search for the missing teenager, a full search party hadn't been formed to find a missing middle-aged lady—another apparently accident-prone Chance.

By Saturday April the 12th there was a guard on the hospital room where Edward and Cora Chance lay and a very active, if as yet invisible, investigation was being mounted in the county police headquarters. As yet it was still a missing persons investigation although somehow those involved had come to think of it in another way. But Tilda Abbott, chief investigator in the case, had been rigorous in refusing to call it a Murder Room.

Tilda was the stocky senior officer of the first two police to arrive at the scene that afternoon. Increasingly frantic messages from paramedics and the hospital A&E team had inspired them to show up at Chance House and take in the situation with their own eyes. Within minutes of arriving they had been embroiled in a possible gunshot incident, another missing persons case of a minor, and a potentially criminal disregard for health and safety failings. The junior officer had requested back-up when it appeared there might be another charge of assault and battery to add to that and his call had come in to the station seconds before a chorus of 999 calls about a homicide.

Now, as Tilda relinquished custody of Felix to the officers in the police van and left the processing of the assembled crowd in the hall to the other officers at the scene, she collected her constable with a beckoning look and led him over towards the stables where fat power cables came snaking out of the truck and up the stairs to the new base of the investigation.

While the constable prepared instant coffee at the improvised kettle station at the corner of the gabled room, Tilda stalked over to the largest of the whiteboards standing up against the wall and picked up a black marker pen.

MURDER ROOM, she wrote, in large gravestone capitals. Then as her constable watched she wrote four names underneath it. Edward, Cora, Joyce, Eva. The first two she ringed, adding a note: 'injured'. The third was followed by a word in brackets: 'deceased'. The fourth she followed with a symbol: a big black question mark. Only then did she turn to Peters, the constable:

'It's a murder investigation now,' she said. 'Should have been all along. It's been three weeks since that girl went missing. Is there anyone left that thinks we're going to find her alive now?'

'No bet, ma'am.' Peters brought over the two mugs of coffee, both black. 'You want to call up the search teams again?'

'We're going to have to, with a missing five year old somewhere on scene,' Tilda said, accepting the mug without taking her eyes from the whiteboard. 'And let's hope we find the kid soon. But whether we do or whether we don't, I want a full search of this place at first light tomorrow morning and we won't stop until we find that missing girl.'

'Not in the dark then?'

'In the dark we search the House only and for the missing kid only. The man with the moustache was in the army and you saw what luck his search group had,' Tilda said drily.

'Weren't they looking for ghosts though, ma'am?' Peters suggested and Tilda shrugged.

'Same difference,' she said. 'A body that's been missing for three weeks has got to be buried pretty deep. But we'll find it. And until we do the people living in this House don't move without our knowing about it. In fact, I want them all shipped out of here and put in a hotel. This house is plainly impossible for conducting any form of effective surveillance.'

'Then you don't think it was the lad that done it?' Peters asked and earned himself a frown.

'I don't suppose anything, constable,' Tilda said. 'I collect evidence, I submit that evidence to the crown courts. The evidence will show who is to blame for this.'

'Yes, ma'am,' said Peters but he continued to watch his superior thoughtfully. Something had shaken Inspector Abbott from her habitual calm.

As he watched she took out the marker pen again and wrote, this time in lower-case and somewhat doubtful italics: *'ghosts'*.

'Evidence,' said Tilda, looking at the word she had written. 'That's what we need.' She had left the cap off the pen and was standing with it poised in her hand but she didn't move and together the two police officers stared at the board.

Tricky, thought Peters. No one's going to want to admit to seeing ghosts but you can't help but notice that everyone they'd interviewed today had been almost eager to bring up the topic. 'Ghosts' was the one thing they all had in common. Some of them had been looking for ghosts, some thought they'd seen them and others . . . Well, depending on what you believed someone had become a ghost today. *Creepy,* thought Peters, taking a reassuring gulp of coffee. Something about this place did your head in. Normally he'd never have thought something like that.

Up on the second floor of the House, Eva looked at a very different Murder Room: a room where the word was unnecessary because the brutal fact of it was spelt out in blood where until minutes ago a body had rested, until it was stretchered away after the forensics team had done their job. Black and yellow warning tape crisscrossed the door, sealing off the rest of the room. But there was no sealing off the ghosts.

On whatever plane the ghosts existed the room screamed of murder, of shock and violence, of a guilty thing surprised. The crates of precious items had been taped off too but their sparkle was still visible in both worlds.

Over the case the weak figure slumped, wraithlike fingers scraping at the golden trinkets and misty hands coming away empty, unable to grasp the things they reached for.

'Aunt Joyce,' said Eva. 'Please. Stop.'

The ghost that had been Joyce continued to scrabble at the boxes, muttering and whispering to itself, a chain of thoughts that were barely breath, and Eva felt more than heard the slight substance of their narrative.

'Found something, finally. Helen must have hidden this here. Doesn't trust me. Or someone else—why? Doesn't matter, enough here to pay off the loan, take a holiday as well, maybe in the sun. Get a facial, Botox too, why not? Need to find a new man now Christopher's lost interest—if he ever was interested. Stupid men, fickle. Don't know why I bother sometimes. Maybe I'll find a good one on the holiday.'

'Aunt Joyce,' Eva tried again. Moving forward, she reached out and tried to touch the shoulder of her aunt.

'Someone's coming?' Joyce's eyes widened as she turned and

it took Eva a second to realize it wasn't her that her aunt was seeing, instead she was re-enacting the moment she had seen her killer. 'This is private . . . Wait, no . . . it was you?'

Joyce's body shape churned and rippled, enacting the marks of violence her flesh had suffered. Scratches scraped along her face and arms, bruises bloomed on her cheek and forearms. Then came the tearing of the brooch from her and its return, point first, a ladybird with a deadly sting. The murderer was long gone but the moment of the murder was enacted as though by an invisible man while Eva watched helplessly knowing it wasn't another ghost attacking but a re-enactment that she was powerless to prevent.

Joyce clutched and scrabbled at her face, hands clawing desperately at the obscene carbuncle protruding from her eye. But her other eye was dimming, the stroke had gone home, and her struggles ended mercifully soon.

But even as Joyce's ghost collapsed limp and lifeless on to the sofa, she arose again and reformed into the scrabbling wisp. Her voice was thinner and fainter as she tried to lift the jewels from the case.

'Found something. At last . . .'

Eva groaned. The Witch had struck home with this attack. Eva hadn't liked her Aunt Joyce and had always rather wanted something to happen to humiliate her. Well, she'd got her wish now and in a way that shamed her that she had ever thought of it. To see someone reduced like this wasn't pleasant. And seeing Joyce like this made her realize what those looks from Kyle must have meant, why he'd reached out to try and anchor her. He must pity her just as she pitied this pathetic rag of consciousness.

'Aunt Joyce,' she said, 'please listen. Someone attacked you— you must remember who it was.' Eva remembered Maggie saying the same thing to her, unable to believe you could not know who your killer was. After all, Maggie had been certain of who had ruined her.

Joyce goggled at the box of jewellery, casting a brief sly glance over her shoulder and reaching in again for the gems. This time she didn't seem to notice that she wasn't able to grasp them.

'Helen's suspicious,' she muttered to herself. 'She said the jewellery was lost. Suspected me.'

Eva strained to make any sense of these mutterings. To think she'd prided herself on being able to communicate with Maggie, and talk the servant girl ghost out of her revenge. All her efforts to make Joyce see her had failed; the ghost's mind clouded by the terror and horror of the moment of its death, barely able to see her and panicked by the little bits of her that it did sense. Was this scrabbling fearful thing even Joyce any more? Was this really all that remained of her spirit?

'Aunt Joyce,' she tried again. 'Who was it? Was it Christopher Knight? Aunt Helen? *Felix?*'

'Someone's coming?' Joyce wailed thinly and Eva sighed as she realized the cycle was about to start again.

Then another sound fell softly into the silence, the creak of a floorboard under pressure. Another creak followed, heavier than the first. It was a sound she recognized: the sound of slow, quiet footsteps, coming closer. It was the sound of the ghost triggered by the bloodstain in the front hall, the mad ghost, the killer ghost, the Stalker.

The new-minted ghost heard it too, heard it or sensed it somehow, because she sprang upright, clutching at her face, hands fouled with blood and fumbling at that ladybird brooch.

'Run!' said Eva, trying to pull the ghost out of its own fog of

283

confusion. 'What's coming is dangerous. You have to hide. You have to run!'

This time the ghost saw her. Eva felt it shudder away from her, coiling backwards in a current of fear and guilt and shame. It shrank away as though she was the enemy and still the footsteps came nearer. The door of the room opened on to shadow and then a footstep sounded inside the room.

Using a talent she didn't know she possessed Eva threw her mind away from the room, casting herself out of solidity with the same twist of the mind that she'd used to leap from room to room of the House during the witch's attack.

As she threw herself away the footsteps passed her and the Joyce ghost burst into panicked flight. The dark force of both of them went rushing away, the Stalker giving chase to the ragged remnant of Aunt Joyce.

Without her determination to anchor herself to the room, Eva felt herself being sucked into the dark maelstrom she'd felt before, pulled to a place that stank of blood and filth, a pain like a wire cutting into her wrists, peacocks clamouring for attention.

'NO!' She screamed her own way back into the murder room, forcing herself back into presence, imagining the shape of the white fencer and placing her self inside it. Her right hand clenched hard on the sword and she went racing after the ghosts: her own footsteps ringing hard on the floor as she charged back into physicality.

The chase was on. The whimper of Aunt Joyce's thoughts scurrying down branching corridors and around sudden turns of the stairs. Behind her came hunting the empty malevolence of the Stalker, its heavy footsteps echoing as it followed mercilessly. And after them both came Eva, flying down the passages with her sword gripped tight in her hand. They arrived in the Cheviot

Room, an ominous destination. The walls were carved with hunting scenes and the floor a tiled mosaic of prey animals. Ornamental cases held examples of ancient taxidermy: stuffed birds posed artfully in displays of dried grasses. Pride of place was given to a family of foxes, jaws wired open in an eternal futile snarl. The walls were strung with mounted fish, scales and tails laden with dust. Above them all high on the walls were the decapitated heads of stags, the great antlers casting branching shadows across the moonlit room. From all directions glass eyes stared blindly down into the room.

Joyce's ghost was cornered and the Stalker advanced. It had enough dark power of its own but Eva sensed it was gaining extra force from an unholy ally: the Witch was lending it her power, delighting in tormenting the Chance ghosts. Eva arrived on the threshold of the room just as the Stalker lunged, the footsteps erupting into an almost human shape, a twisted Frankenstein's monster of a man, falling on Aunt Joyce with clublike fists and knotted hands that rent and tore at the last rag of Joyce's spirit.

Against its murderous passion Eva quailed and then cursed her own cowardice as the thing that had been Joyce sobbed and wailed at its ending. Eva hurled herself forward—too late.

The Stalker had already claimed its prey. Joyce's ghost had been shredded; whatever remained of her was nothing but a whisper of a memory, a minor presence in a House already crowded with ghosts. And now the Stalker faced Eva: ready to kill again.

So this was it. Eva had run from this ghost when she'd first found herself in the spirit world of the House. This time she advanced. With a swipe of silver the sword slashed at the monstrous body of the Stalker, leaving a gash of empty air in its black form. The Stalker struck back from nearly twice the height of Eva, trying to club her down beneath its brutal advance. They circled each other, slashing and swiping in turn.

The Stalker had no face. Its head was a doughlike blob on top of its misshapen body. Once it had been a man, one of the mad Chances, but the Witch had got into his mind and he had killed and killed again. Even when he died himself, he'd been filled with enough murderous rage to go on killing. A psychotic ghost, a murderous ghost, an instrument of the witch's curse on the Chances.

Eva sensed its history and the empty evil of its mind struck at her harder than its blows. She was losing ground, falling back before it, pressed against a glass case. She looked left and right for a space to move and saw the hopeless snarl of the fox.

The Stalker raised both arms and brought them down like a hammer—and from behind Eva came an uncanny howl, a metallic screech of sound, as something hurled itself from the top of the case and straight at the Stalker's faceless head. Claws raked and kicked as a golden furry body landed on the Stalker's head, an unlikely hat that savaged the monster beneath it, a live animal that had come leaping out of the shadows of the dead. Rameses: the Abyssinian cat.

It was Eva's chance and she knew it, plunging her needle sword into the heart of the Stalker's chest. Shadows flared like candles in the darkness and something screamed inside her head: the Stalker or the Witch, she wasn't sure. But her stroke was sure and meant to kill, to end the unlife of the thing that had ended that half-life of Joyce. No moral quandary slowed her hand and with every inch of her being she wished ending upon the thing.

The resistance at the end of her rapier gave way and the screaming shadows melted away. The Stalker was no more.

Eva and Rameses together stared at the space where it had

been. Then, with a final hiss, Rameses kicked up a leg and started washing himself as if nothing had happened.

Eva's own legs barely held her and she collapsed gratefully on to the tiled floor. Rameses paused in his washing to headbutt her knee and yowled at her.

'Thank you,' Eva told the cat fervently. 'I think that's the end of it.' Casting out her mind she could sense the bloodstain fading from the foot of the stairs. She had killed the ghost killer. The Stalker had been dispelled, one element of the Witch's curse undone.

So you have learned to kill, the Witch slid the thought slyly into the back of her head. *Savour the taste of it. It will make it all the sweeter when I teach you how to die.*

18
Missing Persons

Monday, April 14th

It had taken longer than the police would have liked to process all the miscellaneous family members, ghost walkers, staff and assorted hangers-on. But eventually they had got them sorted into some sort of order. Ghost walkers were gathered, made to give their names and addresses and to check that no member of their party was missing. Then they were sent home and informed that constables would call on them shortly to take their statements. By and large they got off the lightest, with a tall story to tell and time to tell it.

The people who'd been dragged into the search for the weeping woman on the lake were rather muddier, more tired and embarrassed at having to repeat their story again and again. They had quickly divided into two groups: the pragmatists who insisted they knew what they had seen and they had been trying to be good Samaritans; and the superstitious who were no longer certain what they had seen and inclined to blow it out of all proportion into a ghost story worthy of the West End stage. They too were finally catalogued and packed off back home in the direction of warm baths and anxious housemates with the promise of a visit from the police for their statements in the next couple of days.

The staff were questioned more thoroughly and required to give times for what they'd been doing and when and where on the property. It was past midnight by the time the last of the weary support staff, wishing they'd never signed up for this job, managed to get free of the place—many anxious about a possible health and safety lawsuit.

Only then did the police turn their attention to the remaining people, a forlorn knot clustered in the hall. Michael Stevenage, reluctantly installed as temporary counsel for the accused, had gone with Felix to the police station. Richard and Helen Fairfax, mother and father of the arrested party, were refusing to go to a hotel or leave the spot without an explanation. Christopher Knight, bereaved partner of the murder victim, was talking to Lisle Langley, who still carried the wounds of the attack on her.

Tilda Abbott had returned to the hall from the newly set-up Murder Room and was attempting to persuade the Fairfaxes to go to a hotel, thus far with no success.

'This is ridiculous,' Helen was saying. 'It's completely outrageous you should have arrested Felix. He couldn't have been fonder of Joyce. And he told you he simply found the body. Plainly some thief or vandal took her by surprise. You should be questioning all those people you allowed to leave.'

'And we will question them, madam,' Tilda said patiently. 'However, right now we're still confirming that everyone is out of the building. There is at least one person currently missing.'

'There is?' Richard Fairfax was still catching up with everything that had happened and the grisly murder of his sister-in-law and arrest of his son had rather pushed other concerns out of his head. 'Who? You're not talking about Evangeline are you, because if you are . . . ' He stopped, uncomfortable, and Tilda looked thoughtful.

'I was referring to the lost child, sir,' she said. 'Nathan Plunkett, aged five years old. Now missing for two hours.'

She didn't say that the child had last been seen during the time frame of the murder. Nathan's father had gone home in a police car to break the news to his wife and to collect items of clothing for the police dogs to track. Reluctant as Tilda was to conduct an extensive search in the dark, the preliminary search of the house had achieved nothing more than to make her officers irritable. Police don't like to find themselves jumping at shadows and hearing noises and they were hiding their nerves badly.

'I strongly suggest, sir, that you and your wife remove to a hotel room,' Tilda pressed on. 'This residence is currently classified as an active crime scene and too large to be effectively policed. That means that it will take us hours to search, both for the missing child and for any evidence the attacker may have left behind. You may not be present during this search and it will be better for you to get a night's rest.'

'Rest when my son has been arrested!' Helen snorted. 'How am I supposed to sleep when someone's murdered my sister?'

Shades of Lady Macbeth in that one, Tilda thought to herself, intrigued by how much more concerned Helen was by her son's arrest than her sister's death. Did she suspect her son might be found guilty? All the outrage seemed somehow overdone. She very much wanted to interview both Felix's parents but now wasn't a good time—even if they had had the lawyer present, something they would be certain to demand.

'You cannot stay here, madam,' Tilda said more forcefully. 'You are impeding the police investigation. If I have to officially caution you, I will.'

Helen opened her mouth to object and a hideous scream erupted. Everyone in the hall jumped, including the police. Only Tilda managed to stay calm enough to focus on the source of the sound. It wasn't Helen; impressive though her lungs were, that scream hadn't come from any human throat.

Turning, she faced the front door, left open by the last people to go in or out. On the doorstep was a peacock, its tail fanned out in full display, its crowned head jerking forward as it uttered another devastating scream.

Two more peafowl appeared behind their lord, following the male into the hallway with staccato steps.

'Get those birds out of here,' Tilda snapped at a subordinate, her words unfortunately lost beneath another ear-splitting scream from a second peacock who was at half-cock, tail fanning open and shut as he followed the court into the hall.

Lisle Langley clasped her forehead tight, wincing with pain at the noise, and Christopher touched her hand with concern. Even through the farce of officers trying to shoo indignant birds the size of eagles, Tilda thought his concern interesting from a man who had just tragically lost his partner.

'Have this room cleared,' she told her sergeant. 'Send these people to their homes or to hotels and let me know when the canine unit arrives.' Then she beat a retreat to the stables, dodging as a peacock whirred over her head to perch on the banisters of the great staircase, screaming as it went.

* * *

Inside the House, Eva heard the screams but she didn't jump. It seemed to her she'd been hearing peacock screams all her life and since her death they had sounded almost constantly in the back of her mind, like a siren howling in the distance.

291

But she also sensed the entrance of the police and the object of their search. The small child she had seen arriving only this morning was lost in the haunted depths of the House. One more potential victim for the Witch, one more lost soul needing rescue.

Eva listened, hearing a bevy of tiny noises, the House, its ghosts and the people in the front hall. Filtering out distractions she concentrated with her other senses, reaching out to the source of the noise. *There*.

Rising up through the floors of the House she arrived in a narrow hallway, carpeted with plain jute matting up here on the third floor. The corridor dog-legged around a corner and she followed it round, coming to a large white-painted door with a panel of glass set into the top. Instead of blending through the wood, she put her hand on the handle and opened it. Inside, she looked across the expanse of the long room lit with gas lamps.

Shelves held wooden game boxes stamped with makers' marks centuries old. Rows of carefully painted soldiers of wood and tin were squared into regiments alongside bivouacked nativities of shepherds and kings. On the floor four doll's houses of different architectural periods were gathered in an unlikely village from which animals were escaping two by two on the gangplank of a Noah's ark. Train tracks snaked across the wooden floorboards, steam engines in faded uniforms of their own hauling wagons and carriages past diminutive stations where frozen figures waved an eternal farewell.

Stepping into the nursery was like stepping into the past— her past. Eva's earliest memories were of this room, playing God with the miniature landscapes—commanding armies led by a turbaned Balthazar atop an elephant. Her five-year-old self had craned over the toys, time and place forgotten, making up stories for her first ever friend.

'Hello, Sinje,' she said, taking off her fencing mask and smiling at the boy who stood on the other side of a large wooden toy chest. 'Do you remember me?'

'Hello, Evvy,' the five-year-old ghost said. 'You haven't come to play for a long time.' He wasn't hard to understand, even with the twist distorting his mouth.

'I haven't come to play now, either,' she admitted.

'I know.' Sinje looked at her sword. 'You're hunting the bad ghosts.'

'That's right,' Eva said. 'Have any bad ghosts come in here?'

Sinje shook his head and then put his finger to his lips and pointed at the toy chest, a piratical trunk of bound wood and iron.

'We were hiding,' he said.

Eva realized what he was trying to tell her as Sinje stepped back from the trunk. Bending down she unsnapped the hasps and opened it. Inside a small figure was curled defensively, blinking muzzily up into the light.

'Hello, Nathan,' she said. 'It's safe now—you can come out. It's time for you to go home.'

The little boy climbed sleepily out of the trunk and willingly took her hand. Then, clearly remembering some firmly repeated rules of politeness turned to Sinje and said, 'Thank you for letting me play with your toys and for helping me hide from the scary ghosts.'

Sinje waved, a child as frozen in time as the passengers at the model station. Eva returned his wave. Then she put her mask back on and led Nathan down through the haunted House.

'What happened to your wellies?' Nathan asked curiously, looking Eva up and down.

'I left them behind,' Eva told him. 'What do you think of my sword?'

293

'It's a good sword,' Nathan said. 'It looks sharp. Is that what you use to kill the bad ghosts?'

* * *

There was a small cluster of police vehicles now outside the stable block. Two more vans had arrived, with the search team and four canine units: large Alsatians who strained at the leash. Two a.m. was fast approaching and Tilda Abbott had resigned herself to a sleepless night.

At least her sergeant had been able to report that the Fairfaxes had been persuaded to leave and had announced they would take a room in the town's most expensive hotel. Lisle Langley and Christopher Knight had also been allowed to leave, Lisle to her house and Knight to a more humble hotel in town. Finally Chance House should be empty—of everyone but the ghosts.

Tilda forced back the unprofessional thought and focused instead on showing the search team to the House. Nathan's father went with them, clutching a toy panda and a woolly jumper. At the entrance to the house the dogs started barking and their straining at the leash became more pronounced as they saw the six peafowl who were in possession of the front hall.

'I thought I told you to clear those birds out,' Tilda reminded her sergeant who nodded.

'I'm working on it,' he said. 'The people turned out to be easier in the end. You can't threaten to arrest birds for obstructing an investigation.'

'We can't let the dogs off the lead with them birds flying about,' one of the handlers warned her, as if she didn't know it already. 'It's a safety issue.'

'I'm beginning to think we need a health and safety assessment of this entire site,' Tilda said. 'Fine, keep the dogs back.

Sergeant, let's see about these birds.' She walked purposefully into the house and looked around, hoping to find some area that the peafowl could be herded into. Looking up and around, all she saw was open space and high perches, most of which held peafowl staring superciliously at her.

But there also, coming down the main staircase one step at a time, was a small boy. He was holding a toy soldier clutched in one fist, while the other hand held on to the railings. Tilda's eyes widened.

'Are you Nathan?' she asked, hurrying to meet the child. 'Are you lost?'

'I'm not lost!' the child said indignantly. 'I was hiding from the bad ghosts with Sinje. There were scary footsteps and I hid in a pirate chest. But then Eva found me and said it was safe to come out. Eva's the nice ghost. She lost her wellies but now she's got a sword instead.'

Tilda filed that little speech away for later. She picked the child up easily, her sergeant beside her unsure whether to laugh or groan at how easily they had found the child in the end, and they turned and walked out again.

'Oh my God, Nathan!' The little boy's father fell to his knees because his legs wouldn't support him and the lost child squirmed until Tilda let him go and then went running to hug his father.

'Take him home, Mr Plunkett,' Tilda said. 'He's fine. Apparently he was hiding in a cupboard of some kind. He came out when he wasn't scared.'

'That's not what happened.' The child gave her a disgusted look. 'This is how it happened, Dad . . .'

But Nathan's father was not interested in the story just then. His face had the expression that every parent of a lost child has when it is found, torn between rage and relief and uncertain whether to shake the miscreant to within an inch of his life or squeeze him just as closely.

It was the search team that were Tilda's concern now, wearing deeply ironic expressions at this seeming waste of their time.

'Don't you go yet,' she said. 'Come around to the Murder Room and have some coffee or something, water the dogs. I'm going to get an animal control van to come and get those birds out and then I'm going to want you to search this place from top to bottom.'

'Didn't you just find the lost kid?' one of the search team objected. 'Just what are we searching for, exactly?'

'I'll make a list,' Tilda said. 'But for starters, evidence of three attempted murders, one actual murder, and one missing person who may have been murdered. And any evidence that the murderers themselves might be hiding in the house.'

That shut them up effectively and Tilda turned to stare back at the house and to think about what the little child had said. 'Eva found me and said it was safe to come out.' It was ridiculous to place any stock in a little boy spinning fantasies but the words had chilled her. She thought of that word on the whiteboard, standing alone. What place did ghosts have in a police investigation?

* * *

In the front hall Eva stood at the base of the stairs, watching the peacocks. One of them had perched on the bottom banister, next to where the bloodstain had once stained the stone. Now the stalker was gone the last vestige of its ghostly menace had faded with it. Future generations wouldn't need to step across it for fear of footsteps following them up the stairs. Of course there wouldn't be any future generations living in the House. Perhaps instead there'd be hotel guests checking in at reception and asking directions to the bar.

She felt an odd sense of guilt at having erased part of the House's history: however malevolent and ill-omened that history had been. Then she turned towards the side corridor and the cellar door, and any trace of guilt left her. The ghosts had their own place in the House as long as they didn't cause it harm; those who had cursed it with their malice deserved to be expelled from its walls.

The wooden door was ahead of her. The rest of the House was empty. It was only the ghosts left now. But Eva's senses didn't extend into the cold darkness beneath the House. The cellar was the demesne of the Witch and she filled it with her swirling cloud of hate. The Witch must know that Eva was coming but this time she did not speak inside Eva's thoughts. Instead, the wooden door swung open: an invitation to the blackness inside.

Eva moved slowly down the stairs, sword in hand. Her steps were long and gliding, her free hand sliding along the banister as she moved slowly down. This time she barely noticed the spiders' webs crisscrossing the narrow passage, she'd long passed the point where a mere arachnid could make her squirm.

At the base of the stairs the wine room waited, no longer a mundane storage cellar but the first vestibule of the witch's realm. She crossed it slowly and deliberately, preparing herself for the next room.

Here was the collection of torturer's instruments and Eva wondered what the tourists on the ghost walk would have made of this room. Surely even the least sensitive would have felt the emanations which filled it. It was dark here now and Eva's vision was changed by the darkness. Instead of seeing the artefacts as she had before, twisted metal shapes picked up by the light of the torch, she sensed them. Each implement of torture was crusted with the mental anguish of their victims, layers of pain and shame and fear, smeared together with the memory of the torturers themselves. They had been cold, cruel men, taking perverse pleasure in their distorted surgeon's skills, admiring their handiwork as fingers were wrenched, nails pulled, eyes put out and the most intimate places of the body violated. The vileness of those acts glowed through the ages and Eva's mind swam in the sea of accumulated agony.

She passed by the artefacts, careful not to let the edge of her presence overlap theirs, threading her way through the maze of pain and sending a prayer that the souls of the victims had found rest and were not wandering here, tied to the engines of pain that had tormented them. Like the Witch.

The Witch was waiting. This time there was no light to guide her to the ducking stool but Eva could feel its shape looming out of the darkness ahead. Threading her way between the stone pillars of the cellars, Eva felt the tide of the curse rolling out in great waves from the heart of the cellars, each one filled with sensations that rocked through her with physical force. A stench of blood and faeces mingled with rotting food, a musty dampness to the air, a chill that shivered her skin into gooseflesh, a breath of air that wheezed like an animal in pain, darkness like a rough blindfold across her eyes.

The Witch was watching. The metaphysical darkness that surrounded Eva was no barrier to the dark centre of the haunted House. The witch was watching as Eva came closer, a spider awaiting the looping approach of a fly nearing the centre of its web.

* * *

At the Stratton's house in the estate, lights blazed behind the kitchen blinds. All four Strattons sat around the kitchen table.

Kyra and Kyle slumped in their chairs, heavy-eyed, cold mugs of coffee abandoned on the table in front of them. Their mother perched on the edge of her chair, like the cigarette perched on the edge of the ashtray in front of her: a habit she had given up two years ago and the cigarettes produced from a guilty stash in the back of an old handbag. Keith had finished his coffee and two more, each Irished with a generous slug of whiskey.

'I always felt there was a bond between me and Adeline,' he said into the silence, casting a brief glance at his wife. 'We went out a few times when we were kids. She never invited me to her house—and I wouldn't have gone either. But we walked around the gardens. Addie liked the summerhouse by the lake. She had these curtains, silk and velvet, and she'd hang them all around the place like a great tent. She kept wine there too and sometimes the place would reek of weed. I got the impression she'd had other men there too but we didn't talk about that. Instead she'd talk about how she didn't fit into her family, how she wanted to leave but didn't dare.'

He sighed, not looking at any of them, his eyes seeing that Moroccan tent. His wife said nothing. Ex girlfriends might be touchy subjects for wives; but what was there to say about one dead these last sixteen years?

'I went to look at the summerhouse today,' he said. 'I wanted to remember Adeline—it's the only time I do think about her. I go every year when the House opens. It was this time of year she died.' He shook his head. 'There's an eerie feel about that lake. I remember finding that baby girl floating in the water, lying there in a Moses basket with the peacocks screaming around us. You could hear them screaming today through the mist over the lake, screaming to beat fury. It felt just like that day, all the search parties looking for Adeline and time running out.'

'Do you think her ghost is there, Dad?' Kyle asked. 'Somewhere on the lake?'

'I felt haunted,' Keith said. 'But I always do when I think about her.' He shook off the memory and reached out a hand to his wife, their wedding rings making a small clink of sound as he covered her hand with his. 'I was never in love with Adeline,' he said. 'But I did feel that bond, maybe because she was, what would it be, my half cousin, something like that.'

'First cousin once removed,' his wife replied. The history-keeper of her own family, she was familiar with the landscape of relationships. 'Her great-grandfather was your grandfather.'

'There's a connection between us and the Chances,' Kyle said. 'It's not like family—I wouldn't have Felix as a relation if you paid me. But it's a connection, between us and them.'

'I wish someone had told me before now we might be related to the Chances,' Kyra said. 'Or about how Eva's mother died. Or what the big house was really like. My class, we thought Eva was rolling in it, that she wore old clothes to school because we weren't worth the effort, that she was putting on airs when she never tried to invite anyone round. We thought she ate off gold plates and wore satin when she was at home.'

'Your lot bullied her,' Kyle said. 'If you'd known more about her you'd probably have blamed her family for what happened to Margaret Stratton, being forced to have that man's child and dying from it. You'd have bullied her more, not less.'

Kyra winced. 'Yeah, probably,' she admitted and screwed her face up at the thought.

'I don't like the two of you seeing these ghosts,' their mother broke in. 'I don't like it that this Stratton ghost attacked you. I don't like the ghost of the Chance girl asking for help. The supernatural isn't something you should be meddling with—it's not right. At least you got out of that place with your body and soul intact, but I've half a mind to take you round to the church and get the vicar to douse you with holy water.'

'It might not hurt at that,' Kyle said. 'Because I'm going back to that House, Mum.'

'That you're not.' His mother's eyes were wide with alarm. 'No, you are most definitely not going back there again.'

'Yes, I am,' Kyle told her. 'I have to. I have to see Eva again.' He paused and to his surprise Kyra joined in.

'Me too,' she said. 'I have to talk to her about what happened with Felix. Maybe she saw something that can save him.' She looked pleadingly at her mother as she continued. 'He's in police custody, Mum. For something he didn't do. And when the police get a hold of that will and find out that he's the only person who benefited from Eva's death they'll be sure he's guilty of attacking those other people and killing his aunt. There's a curse on his family and it's going to get him too if we don't stop it.'

'How will trying to talk to Evangeline's ghost help?' Keith asked. 'Didn't you say the ghost didn't know who killed her? Can't you trust the police to find out the facts without the intervention of the spirit world?' He grinned awkwardly but neither of his children smiled back.

'Not when there are ghosts mucking up the investigation,' Kyle said. 'Think about it, Dad. When Felix gives his statement it'll either be the truth and the police won't believe it or it will be full of lies and they'll believe it even less. Kyra's right to be worried.'

'Kyle's right about Eva,' his sister backed him up. 'I did bully her at school but I'm not a monster. I don't actually want her to be trapped in some kind of endless detention, roaming the house as a ghost. Maybe all we can do is persuade the police to find her

301

body but perhaps that might lay her to rest. We could get the vicar to put holy water on her—like Mum suggested.'

'Well, no one's going anywhere tonight,' their mum said firmly. 'It's almost four in the morning. You two need to get some sleep.'

'We'll talk about it in the morning,' Keith promised. 'But your mum's right, get some rest.'

* * *

Eva thought she'd shed the last of the phantom pains from her body but on the threshold of the Witch's realm her stomach roiled with a churning nausea, an involuntary retching at the smell that seemed to choke her throat, mixed with a tearing hunger as though her stomach was trying to devour itself. Her sense of the House surrounding her retreated, leaving her pinioned in the tight dank space in her mind, wrists and ankles burning as though she were the one wired to the ducking chair, not the Witch. Her skin felt hot and cold at once, a feverish spasm followed by a freezing shudder.

In her head the Witch was laughing. *Did you think you were past hurting? Did you think you were free from all pain? This is my chamber of torture, Chance child. This is the rack you are bound to.*

'No.' Eva tried to force her eyes to open against the blackness, to see something, even if it was the dark tunnels of the witch's eyes. Her fingernails stung, a raw scrape of pain against splintery wood. She felt dirty, as though her body were covered with filth. Was that her whimpering, her breath coming in breathless gasps and wheezes? She didn't even know where she was any more, her head was aching, temples throbbing with heavy beats of pain. What was she doing? How had she ever thought she could fight the Witch?

You thought you were free and I was bound, the Witch told her. *But I have sown my curse in every acre of this place and you are the one who is bound. You are lost, Eva Chance. You are trapped. A ghost girl living her last moments. The buried dead.*

Eva struggled to move, to see, to breathe. With every dark thought the walls seemed closer. She was drowning in darkness, invaded by the Witch inside her head. She wasn't the white figure with the sword any more. She was a frightened little girl in pain.

The darkness whirled, the air was thick with the stink of blood and faeces, her body ached with a bitter bone-chilling cold, her wrists stung and burned with a razor sharp pain. Peacocks screamed and the Witch laughed.

Last Chance. Lost Chance. No more chances left.

19
Murder Mystery

Kyle went to bed but he couldn't sleep. Instead he stared into the soft darkness of his room and thought about Eva and the Chances until his head spun. Nagging in the back of his mind was a certainty that time was running out to save Eva and the thought of her ghost alone in the haunted House was agony.

Kyle knew what was up with him. He'd fallen for someone in the most hopeless and impossible way. He felt a weird envy of Kyra, in a similar situation with Felix locked up, but at least she had a chance that everything would work out for her. Kyle had none at all.

Throwing off the duvet Kyle got up and dressed. There was no point just lying here. He had to do something. Quietly he let himself out of his room, carrying his boots so he wouldn't wake his parents as he crept along the carpeted corridor and down the stairs. In the kitchen he put his boots on and, as he bent to do up the laces, he saw a thin sliver of light coming from the door to the garage. Someone else was up.

He knew it was Kyra before he even opened the door and she turned to look at him without surprise, the weary look in her eyes a testament to the fact she'd got no more sleep than he had.

Like most people, they didn't use their garage to keep a car in.

Instead their dad used it as a combined work room and tool store. There were racks of tools along the walls and a battered wooden table took up the middle of the room, scarred with clamp marks and chisel bites from its years as an improvised workbench.

Kyra was standing at the table staring down at it and when Kyle came to join her he saw that she had unrolled an architectural plan: a map of Chance House. Kyle recognized his dad's handwriting noting work to be done. This must be the plan the builders had worked from during the renovations.

Kyra had weighted down one end of it with a box: a colourful box with a picture of a magnifying glass on the lid. Scattered next to it was a heap of cards, two six-sided dice and a straggle of coloured figurines.

'You're playing Cluedo with the House map?' he said out loud.

'You got any better ideas?' Kyra asked. 'Look, Kyle.' She pointed at a yellow figurine, not left by the empty box but placed deliberately on the map in the room marked Library. Next to him lay another game piece: a metal candlestick.

'Colonel Mustard in the library with the candlestick,' Kyle said automatically.

'Or Edward Chance in the library with an unknown blunt instrument,' Kyra corrected him. 'That's where he was found unconscious and the gossip was he had a lump on his head.'

'You're restaging the murder attempts.' Kyle felt slow when he got it. He looked across the map to the gardens and the summerhouse by the lake. There was a white figurine and a piece of rope. 'That's Cora Chance, strangled in the summerhouse.'

'Right.' Kyra pointed to a red figurine in the east wing, lying next to a dagger. 'And this is Joyce Chance, stabbed with a brooch. Cluedo doesn't have a brooch but this seemed the closest.'

'You missed out Eva,' Kyle said and Kyra frowned at him.

305

'No I didn't.' She opened her hand to show him the blue figurine she was holding. 'I just didn't know where to put her.'

Kyle reached out for the little blue token. It was only a representation of a person but it made him feel sad looking down at it.

'Blue is Mrs Peacock,' he said.

'Yeah, that seemed appropriate for Eva,' Kyra replied, still looking down at the map. 'Do you still think her body's in the cellar? This plan doesn't show that.'

'I don't know.' Kyle turned the game piece in his fingers. 'Maybe, probably. How does it help to know where she died?'

'I'm just trying to see it,' Kyra said, still looking at the map. 'Somehow this all must make sense. The police think Felix is the murderer but they're wrong. You know they're wrong, right?'

'Yeah,' Kyle admitted. 'Felix convinced me. But if it's not him who is it? Christopher Knight?'

'Knight suggested the ghost walks,' Kyra said. 'And Felix thought that Mr X was using the ghost walks somehow—that it was an advantage to the murderer for everyone to be thinking about ghosts.'

'But the House is full of ghosts,' Kyle objected. 'So people would have seen them anyway.'

'Not necessarily,' Kyra said. 'You remember the work crews. They had a lot of bad luck which made them superstitious and there was a lot of talk about ghosts but no one actually saw one. If it hadn't been for the ghost walks people would have just written all those accidents off to superstitions or bad luck.'

'You think all those accidents were deliberate?' Kyle asked. 'Eva was sure it was the witch ghost causing them.'

'People thought the old man's fall was an accident at first,' Kyra said. 'And maybe Cora's was supposed to look like one too.

306

Perhaps the murderer was hoping they'd be put down to bad luck.'

'It still doesn't add up,' Kyle said. He was still holding the blue figurine.

'No, it doesn't,' Kyra agreed. 'Look, forget the ghost business for a moment. Let's assume that Mr X, whoever he is, had a reason for the attacks.' She pointed at the figurines in turn.

'Edward Chance in the library—perhaps he was changing his will or he was doing something else particular to the library that was a problem for X. Cora Chance by the lake: perhaps she saw or heard something suspicious—why else attack her? Joyce Chance in the east wing—wasn't she going through some of the Chance valuables? Maybe X was stealing the stuff she found.' Kyra paused and then added, 'Oh, I forgot Ms Langley, she was attacked too, on the back stairs, wasn't it. Give me that blue figure, that can be her since we don't know where to put Eva.'

'Take someone else,' Kyle said, feeling possessive over the blue peacock piece. 'Professor Plum if you like. Maybe it was the ghosts who got Ms Langley, like the girl who fell over the banister and the guy who got shot—that wasn't Mr X.'

Kyra took the Professor Plum piece and put it down on the back stairs, after a moment's thought adding the lead piping next to it.

'We should talk to Lisle Langley,' she said. 'Maybe she saw something too that could be a clue.' She glanced up. 'Oh do stop moping over that blue piece. It's Mrs Peacock, not Eva herself.'

'Do you remember when Eva's ghost starting fading out,' Kyle said, still staring at the blue piece as though it held all the answers. 'Suddenly she was covered with blood and bruises.'

Kyra shivered. 'Creepy as hell,' she said.

'What if that's how her body is now?' Kyle said. 'Broken, bruised and bloody. What if that's the bad place she said she was being dragged back to—the place where her body is?'

'Stop it,' Kyra said. 'You're just making yourself miserable. It doesn't help to think about it.'

'Blood and filth is what she said.' Kyle stared down into his cupped hand. 'Blood and filth and peacocks screaming.'

'Kyle . . .'

Kyra put a hand on his arm but he shook her off, reaching his hand across the map as though drawn by an invisible force, the peacock blue figure hanging from his fingertips.

'Not the cellar,' he said. 'Somewhere with peacocks, somewhere we haven't searched, the place where it all began. Where Eva was born—and died.' Gently he placed the little figure on the island at the centre of the lake. 'That's where she is,' he said. 'Where the peacocks live—that's where Eva's body must be.'

* * *

After more debate than she would have preferred, Tilda Abbott had compromised with the search teams that they would return at dawn. She'd been left with a skeleton team throughout the waning hours of the night, collating the evidence so far and attempting to make sense of the connections. The whiteboard was now covered in scrawled notes and arrows and in some places Blu-Tack or Post-it notes, but one word remained unconnected. No one had touched the word 'ghosts'.

Tilda paced up and down the Murder Room, waiting impatiently for dawn. Whenever a new report arrived she would devour it, avidly. She had sheaves of notes on her desk and was already trying to decide what order to interview people in. Felix Fairfax would be a difficult interviewee, she could tell; perhaps it would be better to begin with taking statements from the other people at the scene?

At 5.30 a.m., half an hour before dawn, the telephone shrilled into sound, making her jump.

'Inspector Abbott,' she said, lifting the receiver. It was the station on the other end of the line and the first words of the desk sergeant banished her boredom.

'There's been a fatality,' he said. 'Dog walker reported a car fire. Officers got to the scene and found a body in the vehicle. Charred, no point in attempting rescue. A proper ID will have to wait for forensics but we've got an ID on the car owner. Joyce Chance, your murder victim. Any idea who could have been driving her car last night?'

'Give me five minutes.' Dropping the phone back on to its cradle she grabbed her coat and headed for the door of the Murder Room. 'A body's been found,' she told her sergeant. 'Another body. Have the search of the House postponed and then come with me.'

* * *

In the garage Kyra and Kyle looked at each other across the map. Kyra felt a pang of empathy with her brother. His obsession with Eva had disturbed her at first but now all she felt was sorry for him. Eva was dead and even if they solved the mystery of how she died, it wouldn't help. But perhaps finding her body would lay her ghost to rest. Maybe it would help Kyle as well to know the girl he cared for was at peace.

But right now her focus was on helping Felix. Find the real murderer and Felix would be free. Perhaps finding Eva's body would yield the final clue to who the murderer was. And yet, looking down at the map still scattered with Cluedo figures,

Kyra felt they were already on the brink of the answer. It was there—if she could only see it.

The theme tune of the *Sopranos* jangled from Kyle's pocket, making them both jump. Kyle pulled the phone out and looked at the display.

'Unknown number,' he said and then pressed the button to answer the call. 'Hello?'

Kyra waited, listening to the one-sided phone call as Kyle was silent for a moment and then spoke again.

'He does? Why me? Right now? Well, OK then. I'll come.' He put the phone down on the table and then looked at Kyra. 'That was Michael Stevenage, the lawyer,' he said. 'He wants me to come and meet him at the hospital. Eva's grandfather has asked to see me.'

'Why you?' Kyra asked and Kyle shrugged.

'The lawyer didn't say. But I went to see him, remember? Eva asked me to. Maybe that's why.' He stuffed his phone back into his pocket. 'Anyway, I said I'd go. I'll try and find out more about the island on the lake. If anyone knows about it, Eva's grandfather must.'

'You're going to go there after the hospital, aren't you?' Kyra said. 'If the police see you, you'll be in trouble. Why not just tell them that's where you think the body is.'

'Yeah, because they'll totally believe me about Eva's ghost hearing peacocks.' Kyle shook his head. 'Besides, Felix hired me to find the body, didn't he? He ought to be pleased if I do— especially if I find something that lets him off the hook.' He walked over to the garage door and opened it. 'Tell Mum and Dad not to worry,' he said and headed out.

Kyra looked at the dim morning light coming in from the open door. If the hospital was allowing visitors maybe the police

310

station would too. At any rate she didn't intend to hang about here waiting for their parents to wake up and forbid her to go.

Letting herself out through the garage door, Kyra closed it quietly behind her and set off at a jog for the town centre.

* * *

Tilda Abbott stood three metres back from the blackened husk of the yellow Volkswagen Beetle, watching the forensics team do their work. The grinning corpse in the driving seat looked nothing like the handsome young man in the designer suit who she'd spoken to only hours ago.

But quick phone calls had established that Knight had never reached his hotel last night, never so much as checked in. Helen and Richard Fairfax had arrived at theirs and made enough of a nuisance of themselves that the desk clerk had remembered them all too well. Another phone call to the contact number Lisle Langley had given had got Tilda the woman herself, sleepy and confused to be woken up so early but definitely alive. It was only Knight who was missing.

Tilda forced herself to look at the wizened flesh that clung to the remains of the skull, the skeletal fingers clutching the steering wheel. At least it had been quick, she thought. The car had skidded off the road and into a grove of trees, hitting one head on. Knight may have never known what hit him. But one thing Tilda was certain of, this was no accident. There had been too many so-called accidents involving the Chance family and their associates for her to believe that. Whether suicide or murder Knight's departure from the world had been a deliberate act.

He'd had an alibi for Joyce's murder so why would he kill himself? He hadn't seemed gripped by despair so much as shock and alarm at the loss of his partner. Tilda found it unlikely that he had been the culprit all along and was now overcome by remorse. Far more likely that Knight had known something, seen something, perhaps the same thing the other victims had seen—and been put permanently beyond telling what they'd seen.

Tilda rubbed her forehead. There was an answer to this somewhere. Somewhere were the connections between the chain of accidents, disappearances and attacks. Like a great snarled knot of twine, or a tangled ball of necklaces, somewhere would be a loose strand that she could pull on to make the whole mess make sense; if she could only find it. Her brows drew together tightly as she racked her brains to make sense of the puzzle.

* * *

It wasn't yet visiting hours and the hospital was quiet in the early hours of the morning, smelling of bleach and antiseptic as the staff took advantage of the opportunity to mop the floors and change stale bedding. No one challenged Kyle as he made his way to the second floor and then to ward eight.

Michael was waiting for him by the nurses' station near to where a solitary police officer continued to guard the door of room 8-A.

'Thank you for coming,' Michael said. 'I didn't get a chance to speak to you last night but thank you for calling me. Unfortunately now the police are on the scene, things don't look good for Felix Fairfax. I told you I was worried about a conflict of interest. Once Felix had been read his rights, I came here to apprise Sir Edward of his grandson's arrest. He was naturally extremely shocked by the news.'

'What's that got to do with me though?' Kyle asked.

'Sir Edward wanted to know what I thought, if there might be any grounds for the police charge,' Michael said uncomfortably.

'I wasn't certain. But in the course of our conversation I explained how you and I had met here at the hospital and some of the things you'd said about, about Eva . . . ' He trailed off and looked hopefully at Kyle. 'Sir Edward wanted to speak to you himself.'

'I see,' Kyle said. He looked at the closed door of room 8-A. 'Um . . . now?'

'If you're willing,' Michael told him. 'He's awake and waiting for you.'

There were two beds inside the private room, each with curtains of hospital green which hung open to reveal the occupants. Miss Cora Chance didn't look capable of conversation. She lay on her back in the first bed, eyes closed. Her head was bandaged and her face was fish-belly white and flaccid. There was a divided tube in her nose, snaking off to some sort of pump arrangement and another tube led out of her arm to a plastic bag fairly obviously full of blood. A third tube snaked out from under the blankets to another plastic bag at the foot of the bed, which Kyle tried to ignore.

In the facing bed, the other occupant of the room was sitting up. Sir Edward Chance was wearing an old-fashioned white nightshirt and his body looked thin and frail inside the worn cotton. His skin looked worn too, creased and crumpled, his thinning white hair a straggle around his head. But his posture was poker straight, his back stiff, his eyes unclouded by any haze and he regarded Kyle with an intensity that brought the teenager hurrying across the room.

'Morning . . . um . . . sir,' Kyle said. 'My name's Kyle. Michael said you wanted to see me.'

'I did,' the old man said. 'And now that I do you interest me greatly, boy. You have a look of the Chances. Something about the jaw-line, and there at your brow. Reminds me of my grandfather. By all accounts he wasn't a pleasant character so it's probably good for you the likeness isn't great. I'm Edward, by the way. Edward Chance, knight of this parish.'

Kyle sank into the chair next to the bed wondering how to explain. Eva's grandfather was much more astute than he had expected.

'It's possible we are related,' he said. 'My great-grandmother was a servant in the House . . .'

'A story so old it should be one of the seven basic plots,' Sir Edward said with a grimace. 'Another black mark against my grandfather's character. Does it make you angry?'

'It would, I think,' Kyle said. 'If I could think clearly about anything. What about you? How are you feeling?' He tried to seize control of the conversation.

'Tired,' Edward Chance said. 'I'm ninety years old. I'm always tired now. I've outlived two daughters and a third is lying over there breathing out her last. It makes me feel like King Lear.'

'We did that at school,' Kyle said. 'He's the one who didn't realize his youngest daughter really loved him. Is that what you're talking about?'

'Education must be better these days than I'd imagined.' The old man looked surprised and Kyle shifted uncomfortably.

'I'm not that great at school work,' he said. 'I probably only remember because we saw the film. It was grim.'

'I'm pretty grim myself nowadays,' Sir Edward said. 'But I don't expect you to sit and listen to my maunderings. It's my grandchildren I wanted to speak to you about. About Felix. And Eva.'

'OK,' Kyle said. He nodded. 'What do you want to know?'

'My lawyer is a young man,' said Edward. 'From where I'm standing he seems almost as young as you. He's careful with his ancient client, he hedges, tries to protect me. He doesn't want to represent my grandson, I can tell. He says he's worried about a conflict of interest. He thinks the boy is guilty or that he is innocent but will be found guilty—I'm not sure which is worse. Tell me, what do you believe?'

'The second,' Kyle said instantly. 'I think Felix looks guilty as sin but I don't believe he's behind the attacks. I don't think he killed your granddaughter. To be honest, I think he hardly noticed Eva was alive—until she wasn't.'

'Thank you.' Edward leaned back against the pillows. 'Strange though it is to be thanking you for such a judgement of the boy. It's . . . uncomfortable to think of your heir as a killer.'

'I'm sure,' Kyle said, remembering the look on Felix's father's face. There was a man who knew a similar discomfort. And, too, Edward had been one of the victims of the attacks. He must have wondered if Felix was trying to put him out of the way so he could inherit.

'Now tell me about my granddaughter,' the old man said. 'My Evangeline.'

'I never met your granddaughter,' Kyle began. He paused but the old man waited patiently until he was able to continue. 'I never met Eva when she was alive but I've seen her ghost in your house.'

'I saw her too,' Sir Edward said, sadness brimming in his tired eyes. 'When I was taken away in the ambulance, I thought I saw her trying to reach me. Then at the gates of the House, she was gone.'

'That's how I saw her too,' Kyle said. 'One moment there, the next—vanished. I'm sorry for your loss, sir. I wish, I wish I had met her when she was alive.'

'So I see.' The old man looked very grieved. 'So I see.' He

315

sighed. 'Do you know about my will?' He nodded when Kyle looked embarrassed. 'Felix was always my choice to inherit the House. He has money of his own from the Fairfax family and he is his father's heir. I hoped he would rise to the occasion when he inherited the House and resist the urge to sell.'

Kyle thought about that. Maybe Felix would have the urge to play Lord of the Manor. He was also perverse enough to keep the House if everyone expected him to get rid of it.

'I wanted to make provision for my Evangeline also,' Edward Chance went on. 'I thought by leaving her the contents of the House she'd be bound to the family. They wouldn't be able to leave her out of decisions. They'd need her to be involved— and to involve themselves with her. Michael warned me against dividing the estate and I didn't listen. If it's that which is behind these attacks I blame myself. It's a dark thought that one grandchild might murder the other for my estate. . . . ' He shook his head. 'I would be Lear indeed to bring my descendants to such a pass. I would blame myself for ever.'

'I don't think it was your fault,' Kyle said. 'Eva said something about a curse.'

'A curse?' The old man's straight-backed posture became even more stiff. 'Has anyone been in the cellar?'

'I have,' Kyle admitted. 'Once.'

'Once is enough,' Edward said. 'Enough for a Chance, even on the distaff side of the family. I would never let Eva into those cellars, never wanted her to see what was down there. The Chances have done some terrible things, young man. That is the burden of knowing your history—to know the shame of it. I should have got rid of that collection long ago but it would have felt as though I was denying our culpability. And where does one draw the line: the House is full of the relics of colonialism, imperialism, and slavery. What item hasn't been paid for in pain? That is the dark side of our pride.' He shook his head. 'If there is a curse it comes from the blood on our own hands. And all the perfumes of Arabia can't wash that away.'

'Eva mentioned a curse too,' Kyle said. 'She said a witch was behind it—a ghost witch.'

'It wants the Chances to suffer,' Edward said. 'And there's no way to rid the House of it. There it lies in the basement, blighting all our lives. My daughter Adeline was obsessed with it—that's why she kept running away. I should have let her run—at least then she'd be somewhere she could come back from.'

'I wanted to ask you about that,' Kyle said. 'When Eva was born and her mother died . . . The baby was found by the island, wasn't she?'

'In the bulrushes,' Edward agreed. 'By . . . well, now I remember, by one of your relations, it must have been. Your father?'

'That's right,' Kyle agreed. 'And her mother, Adeline . . . Sorry, sir, I know it must be hard to think about.'

'We found Adeline a week later tangled in the reeds of the lake.' Edward sighed. 'Those were pearls that were her eyes . . . She drowned herself, I think. To get away from the House and the curse of the Chances. Perhaps Evangeline did the same.'

'No, sir, I don't think she did. I think she was killed. But why did Adeline row out into the lake in the first place?'

'Because it was the furthest away place from the House, I imagine,' Edward said. 'And she always loved the grotto. It must be in a sorry state now—we never opened it up again. But when Adeline was a young girl we often went there on hot summer days. It's cool in the grotto, water bubbling and trickling from the walls. And it's as far as you can get from the House. She'd have felt safe there, I believe.' He paused. 'I don't know why she went by boat. She could have taken the tunnel.'

'The tunnel?' Kyle's eyes widened but Edward was looking tired and didn't seem to notice.

'It starts from the summerhouse,' he said. 'And leads under the lake to the grotto. It was used as an ice house in the days before refrigerators and it was easier to go by tunnel than boat.'

'Thank you,' Kyle said as another piece of the puzzle slotted into place. He now understood how Cora's attacker had escaped without leaving footprints in the snow. And he knew how to get to the island quickly and easily.

'Is there anything I can do for you, sir?' he asked. 'Anything at all?'

Edward Chance closed his eyes and Kyle understood that the old man had meant it when he said he was tired. He truly was tired almost to death and Kyle wished he could think of anything that might revive him from his apathy.

'If you see her again, you might say goodbye to my Evangeline for me,' Edward said softly; a sliver of pale blue showed through his half open eyes. 'Tell her, if there is an afterlife, I'll look for her there.'

'That's all?' Kyle said. 'It's . . . it's not much.'

'It's all I dare hope for,' Sir Edward told him. 'If you were Orpheus, my boy, you could travel to the underworld and bring her out of the realm of Hades. But such things are not possible in our world, if they ever were. Simply tell her goodbye, that will be enough.'

* * *

At the police station there was a bustle of activity, despite the early hour. Deliberately taking her time as she entered, Kyra

318

gathered that a major search of Chance House was being planned and had only been delayed because of a 'recent incident'. She tried to listen harder to find out what else had happened since Felix's arrest but by then she was inside and the desk sergeant had noticed her, so she headed to the reception desk.

'I'd like to see Felix,' she said. 'Felix Fairfax. He was arrested last night.'

Unsurprisingly the police officer was reluctant to let her in. At first he said no although he admitted that Felix hadn't yet been charged with a crime. Kyra kept pressing the matter, asking if there was any legal reason she couldn't see Felix. The officer countered by asking her if she was a family member.

'Of course I am,' Kyra said. 'He's my cousin. My great-grandfather was a Chance.'

The desk sergeant hesitated and just then the phone rang and he answered it, turning his head to muffle the conversation. Kyra stayed as close as she dared and after a couple of minutes caught her own name and then Felix's. But she couldn't make out any more. Eventually the officer put the phone down.

'You can see Mr Fairfax,' he said grudgingly. 'But we'll have to record you both and you have to sign this to say you've agreed to those conditions.'

'Fine,' Kyra said. She signed the form without a quaver. But her mind was working in overdrive to figure out what she could say to Felix without saying anything incriminating.

When she finally got to see Felix it was in the depressing conditions of a police interview room, recording equipment running and a police officer standing at the side of the room. Felix was led into the room in handcuffs wearing a T-shirt and sweatpants a couple of sizes too large. He slumped into the chair opposite Kyra without his usual arrogance but his eyes gleamed greenly from under lowered lashes, wary and thoughtful.

'How are you?' Kyra asked and Felix shrugged.

'Tired,' he said. 'And you?'

'I haven't slept,' Kyra admitted. She looked at the recorder. If she said something cryptic she'd end up catching herself out. She'd have to try and be cleverer than that.

'I know you didn't kill your aunt,' she said. 'Or attack those other people. The police will work it out eventually. Somewhere there must be proof it wasn't you.'

'I hope so,' Felix said. 'They haven't questioned me yet in much detail. But I don't have a proper alibi for any of the attacks.'

'Except the first one,' Kyra said. 'Eva disappeared before you even came to the House, didn't she? Don't you have an alibi for that?'

'Not really,' Felix said. 'I found a police report in the library that said she was reported missing on the seventeenth of March. I was in our flat in London at the time, alone. I can't prove I didn't sneak down here to murder her. And I have a nasty suspicion the police are looking for evidence to tie me to the attacks and the murders—not something that would clear my name. And my grandfather's lawyer was awfully cagey; he hasn't agreed to represent me. My father's calling in his own man but the chap hasn't got here yet—and the cops are going to search the House today.'

Kyra nodded, wondering if Kyle had reached the House yet. They'd moved into dangerous territory now and the look in Felix's eyes told her he knew as well as she did they'd have to be careful with the recorder running.

'You should have hired someone to search the place yourself,' she said. 'Maybe if you had they'd have found something by now. Maybe they'd have worked out what happened to Eva's body.'

Felix was silent for moment and Kyra willed him to work out the message she was trying to send him behind the double-talk.

'Maybe you're right,' he said. 'But if I had hired someone and they did find anything I'd probably be done for disturbing the evidence. I should have thought of that when I found Joyce's body. If I'd screamed for the police when I found her lying there I wouldn't be in this mess.'

'I suppose it depends how clever the police are,' Kyra said, casting a sly glance at the officer watching them. She was wondering what Felix was trying to tell her.

'Yeah, there is that.' Felix laughed wryly. 'I hope they're clever enough to figure out I'm not to blame.'

'That's enough now.' The police officer was looking suspicious, as though he thought they'd got away with something right under his nose. 'I said fifteen minutes and you've had that.'

'Good luck, Felix,' Kyra said, standing up. 'Let me know if there's anything I can do.'

'I can't think of anything,' Felix lied. 'But thanks for coming.'

Kyra left the police station with slumped shoulders, trying to look sad and depressed. She dragged her feet as she wandered away, loitering along the pavement until she had turned a corner. Then she started to run. If she was fast she might catch up with Kyle before he reached the House.

20
A Matter of Life and Death

The twins met at the gates outside Chance House; Kyra came running up just as Kyle was about to enter. Her shout made him jump and when he saw her he hustled her into the bushes at the side of the drive.

'I thought you were the police for a moment,' he said.

'You're not far wrong,' Kyra said. 'I went to the police station. They're about to mount a huge search of the House today. They'll be here soon.'

'So, don't slow me down,' Kyle said. 'Eva's grandfather told me there's a tunnel under the lake that starts in the summerhouse and ends in a grotto on the island. Eva's body's in that grotto. I know it.'

'That explains how whoever attacked Cora could escape,' Kyra realized at once. 'Kyle, you have to tell the police.'

'I'll tell them once I'm certain,' Kyle said. 'If the police find Eva's body they'll take her away. And I promised her grandfather I'd tell her goodbye.'

'But . . .'

'It might be too late for that.'

Both twins jumped as a third voice spoke behind them. Given their fears about the imminent arrival of the police, it was actually a relief to see that the new arrival was a ghost. But it wasn't Eva.

Margaret Stratton, Maggie or Magpie as Eva had called her, was standing next to them. Neither of the twins realized she could move so far from the House. Kyra wondered if it was her imagination or if the ghost looked a little less substantial, as though it was a strain to move so far away from the building. There was a sort of shimmer like heat haze about her that made it hard to focus on her.

'Eva's gone,' the ghost told them. 'She killed the Stalker in the early morning, then she went to confront the Witch. I saw her going down into the cellar, dressed in white and carrying a sword—and she never came out.'

'The cellar,' Kyle said, frowning. 'I thought Eva's body was there but I changed my mind.'

'Her body has nothing to do with it,' Maggie said sharply. 'The Witch is in the cellar. It's where she's most powerful and her power's growing. Every time someone is hurt or afraid it grows, especially when it's a Chance who suffers. Destroying the family is all she wants. Just because Eva's a ghost doesn't mean she can't be hurt—or erased for ever.'

'What are you saying?' Kyle demanded. 'That this Witch has destroyed Eva's ghost? That she's gone for good?'

'Or for bad,' Maggie said ominously.

'Maybe's she's at the lake,' Kyle said. 'If the Witch drove her back to her body . . . she could be there, right?'

'Perhaps,' Maggie admitted. 'If she's anywhere. The Witch is like the Stalker. She can kill other ghosts. Maybe she can kill the living too. That's why I came to the gate to warn you. You mustn't come back to this House. Any curse on the Chances is also a curse on you—I didn't realize that until Eva made it clear to me. If the Witch knew, she'd be after you too. She won't be satisfied until all the Chances are gone and the House is a rotting shell.'

The twins turned to look at the House, silhouetted against the lightening sky.

'No,' said Kyle. 'We can't just give up and run away. We have to do something.'

'Kyle's right,' Kyra agreed. 'Felix is locked in jail. Eva's ghost has vanished. There's only us. If we can't find the murderer maybe we can lift the curse on the Chances. Maybe we can destroy the Witch.'

'NO!' Maggie's hand clutched at Kyra's arm, ice cold claws with ragged nails. Their ancestress laughed hysterically at Kyra's instinctive flinch away from her touch. 'You're still frightened of me,' she said. 'And I'm nothing compared to the powerful ghosts. I was nothing compared to Eva and she fought the Witch and failed.'

'Maybe she didn't,' Kyra said. 'Maybe she's still fighting. Perhaps we could make a difference.'

'The cellar is evil,' Kyle said. 'And we can't fight the ghosts. But perhaps there's a clue on Eva's body. We should go to the lake.'

'I vote the cellar,' Kyra said. 'Or both if we must. But someone has to fight this Witch before she causes another disaster.' She was thinking hard as she spoke and an idea born of desperation burst into her mind. 'And I think I know how.'

'There's nothing in the cellar for us,' Kyle insisted. 'Eva's not there. The cellar belongs to this witch and she's dangerous.'

'Everything's dangerous,' Kyra said, thinking rapidly. 'OK, Kyle, look. Why don't we tell the police what Edward Chance told you—about the tunnel under the lake. It ties up with the attack on Cora. It suggests where Eva's body might be.' She knew as she was speaking that Kyle wouldn't go for it, that he wanted to be the one to find the body. But that was part of her plan.

'We don't know for sure,' Kyle said. 'And if Eva's ghost is under the lake, will the police even be able to see it? They're not Chances, or psychic and they don't know Eva.'

'Fine,' Kyra said. 'Then you go to the lake and I'll tell the police. By the time they've taken my statement you'll have been able to search for Eva. OK?'

'OK,' Kyle said. 'That makes sense.'

But as he set off in the direction of the lake and Kyra turned up the drive, she felt Maggie's dark eyes on her. The ghost servant looked suspicious.

She has the same suspicious mind as me, Kyra thought. *But by the time she guesses I was lying, it'll already be too late.*

* * *

Michael Stevenage left the hospital in a thoughtful frame of mind. Neither Kyle nor Edward had told him what they'd talked about. Kyle hadn't stayed to talk. 'Until you believe that the ghosts are real, there's no point,' he'd said. And Edward had fallen asleep and Michael hadn't the heart to wake him.

He was yawning as he drove through town and he swigged a hasty couple of gulps of warm Coke from a bottle he'd left in the car. He needed a shower and a change of clothes even if he couldn't spare the time to sleep and he headed for home.

On the B-road there was a diversion, around the scene of what looked at first like a car accident. But slowing down to obey the directions of some temporary signs Michael recognized the burnt-out Volkswagen and pulled over instead.

'No stopping,' a police officer told him when Michael wound down the window.

'But I know that car,' Michael insisted. 'It belongs to one of the Chance family. I'm their lawyer.' He automatically fumbled a card out of his card case and then took a new tack when he recognized a familiar figure at the scene. 'That's Inspector Abbott over there. She knows me.'

Luckily the detective recognized him from the night before and although she didn't seem pleased to have him showing up so unexpectedly, she was courteous enough to fill him in on the most recent incident.

'It's Knight,' she admitted. 'The car belonged to Miss Joyce Chance but he was a registered driver.' She paused and excused herself as one of her team waved her over to the car. Michael waited impatiently for her to return. When she did it was with a steely look in her eyes.

'The brake cable was frayed,' she told him shortly. 'But the abrasions look deliberate. And there was a canister of petrol loose in the car that exploded. This wasn't an accident. Someone wanted this man dead.'

'Then it wasn't Felix, since he's been in jail since last night,' Michael began but the detective cut him off.

'Don't get ahead of yourself, Mr Stevenage. That cable could have been cut at any time. Now, if you're not doing anything right now, I suggest you accompany me back to Chance House so we can interview you. I strongly suggest it.'

Michael felt a sinking feeling in his stomach. He wondered if arriving so coincidentally he had shifted suspicion away from Felix and on to himself

'I was heading home actually,' he said. 'I live along this road.'

'Very convenient,' Tilda Abbott replied drily. 'Nonetheless, I think it would be best if you accompanied me now. Leave your car, you don't look awake enough to drive safely.'

She glanced at the blackened husk of the Beetle to underline the point. Michael knew when he was beaten and followed her back to her own vehicle.

* * *

Kyra found what she was looking for in the scullery. She'd remembered seeing it there when they'd been cleaning. A heavy silver cannister, leaning in a dusty corner. As she heaved it into a canvas sack and dragged it towards the door, Maggie clutched at her, begging her to stop.

But Kyra had got used to those icy hands by now and she knew Maggie wouldn't hurt her.

'This will work,' she insisted. 'Come on, Great-Granny, stop getting in the way and help me. This weighs a tonne.'

'Don't go in the cellar,' the ghost pleaded. 'You don't know how dangerous ghosts can be.'

'Yes, I do,' Kyra said. 'You showed me, remember? You were trying to destroy the Chances yourself. Now's your chance to make it up to the family. Help me!'

'You promised Kyle you wouldn't, you said you'd tell the police about the tunnel while he went to look for Eva,' Maggie tried again.

'I know,' said Kyra. 'I lied.'

She felt bad about that. But it had made sense to split up and even though Kyle had been adamant that the cellar was too dangerous Kyra was determined to do something to end the curse on the Chance family—for Felix's sake more than her own. She'd lied to Kyle so he'd go to find Eva. But she'd never intended to give up her plan.

'The Witch is evil, Kyra. She's ancient and cruel and wicked,' Maggie sobbed. 'Please don't.'

'Look, Maggie,' Kyra swung on her. 'I owe Eva this. I owe her for bullying her since junior school. I owe her for every time I wrote her off as weird and pathetic. My brother's in love with her. He thinks if he finds her body he can save her somehow. Hell, maybe he thinks he can kiss her sleeping body and bring her alive again—and he's going to find a rotting corpse lying in some forgotten corner of this stupid grotto. She's dead and her ghost is gone. But this is something we can do for her.'

'Liar,' Maggie spat, dragging at Kyra's arm as she lugged the heavy sack along the passageway. 'It's not for Eva you do this. It's not Kyle who's lost his heart to a Chance. You're doing this for Felix. For that seducer . . . '

'Yes I am,' Kyra said defiantly. 'If I can lift the curse maybe the truth will come out. Maybe the police will start looking for evidence that Felix isn't the murderer.' She dumped the sack on the flagstones and turned to face her ancestress's ghost. 'And I'm doing it for me too. And for you, Great-Granny. You want to live for ever as a ghost in thrall to this Witch? I'm doing it for all of us. For our family, for Eva's family, for everyone bound up with this haunted House.'

'She'll kill you,' Maggie whispered, her eyes brimming with phantom tears.

'I don't think so,' Kyra said. 'But if she does—well, I'll come back and we can haunt her together. But wouldn't it be easier just to help me now?'

She reached for the handle and opened the cellar door.

* * *

As the glittering sheet of water of the lake appeared before him, Kyle set his sights on the summerhouse and kept running. He had a horrible feeling that he was being stupid about all this. He had no logical reason for any of his guesses or feelings: only a theory that Eva's body was in the grotto and a pale hope Eva's ghost might be there too. He knew Kyra had thought it was hopeless but at least he'd convinced her that the witch was too dangerous.

Kyle's footsteps slowed as he arrived at the summerhouse and he had a sick feeling as he remembered that he'd never been able to convince his sister of anything before. He hoped it was just paranoia he was feeling—not a premonition that his twin was about to do something very stupid and dangerous.

'I'm one to complain,' he said out loud as he came into the summerhouse. 'This is pretty stupid too.' There was no sign of a secret tunnel. The small white building had no walls, only graceful columns, and the only furnishings were a circle of benches concreted into the stone floor. Kyle felt all around the benches and the floor, feeling for secret switches and trying to keep off an increasing sense that time was running out.

He stood back from the stone-tent shape of the summerhouse and tried to look at the building logically. His dad was a builder after all and builders didn't design things with fiendish cunning— they put them in the most obvious place. And servants coming to collect a bag of ice wouldn't want to have to haul up flagstones every time. There would be some sort of lever system.

Kyle went back to the circle of benches and began to push and prod at them, not forcing them but trying to come at them from odd angles. It was like taking the back off a mobile phone, he thought to himself. You could push and yank and work a screwdriver into the side but in the end, if you found the right way of pushing, the bloody thing would come free as sweetly and easily as if you hadn't just spent three hours messing with it. And there, just as he completed his thought the bench gave beneath his hands. Apparently, you had to take hold of a side piece of marble and pull and lift like opening up a sofa bed. Then the whole bench slid aside and a dark hole opened in the floor, steps leading down into the darkness.

Stupid, Kyle thought at once. He hadn't brought a torch.

* * *

The cellar stairs were narrow and cobwebby but Kyra told herself that so were the stairs down to any basement. Their shed at home was full of spiders. She bumped the sack down after her, trying to keep a grip on the rough canvas with one hand as she wielded an arclight torch with the other. She'd collected it from the scullery remembering it was likely to be dark.

It was dark. Dark and quiet and almost mundane. She followed the tunnel of light down into the darkness and arrived at the wine cellar. She paused for a breath and to prepare herself for what came next, and heard a light patter of feet hurrying down the stairs behind. It was Maggie of course, but a Maggie now prepared to help. She was holding a sack of her own, as lumpy and heavy looking as Kyra's, slung over her shoulder with a practised air.

'This should help,' she said. 'I had to do this every morning in the old days. Of course that was going up the stairs, not down.'

The ghost had gained more than courage, Kyra could tell. The heat hazey vagueness had gone and her black and white figure was crisply and coldly defined against the grey stone of the cellar. There was a forcefulness about her and Kyra smiled to herself. She'd bullied the ghost into helping but now she had one ally at her side. They went on through the next vaulted archway into the rooms of the collection of instruments of torture. The tools glittered in the torchlight as Kyra and Maggie threaded their way through.

It was cold down here, the chill seeping out of the walls and the floor. There was a brooding stillness to the cavernous cellar. Even the arclight seemed to be dimming and Kyra shook it a bit to encourage it—remembering how terrifying the Solar had been in the dark.

'Which way?' Kyra whispered.

'Over yonder,' Maggie muttered, jutting her chin ahead. Her voice fell softer still as she added in a low murmur, 'She knows we are coming. She finds us pitiful. A servant and the great-granddaughter of a servant. We're no threat to her. She wants us to come.' The arclight fell on the ducking stool, a stark black shape, greasy black wood bound with iron bands. The chair was empty as far as Kyra could tell but the darkness seemed thicker around it, the cold more intense and the atmosphere heavy like thunder.

Kyra moved towards the ducking stool, not allowing herself to even think about her plan in case the Witch could read it from her mind. But after one step she faltered. The darkness around the ducking stool was coiling together, snaking into a shadow of a shape. It sat in the chair like a propped-up puppet, its arms lay along the black wooden arms of the chair, its legs were strapped to the heavy struts of the chair legs. Its hips and shoulders looked dislocated, twisted at agonizing angles, its wrists and ankles were bound in iron cuffs and an iron band held its neck to the back of the chair.

It was as thin as a skeleton, only a mummified layer of skin keeping the collection of bones together. The skull trailed a veil of cobwebs and as Kyra watched the thing appear a spider came crawling out of the empty eyesockets.

'The Witch,' Maggie moaned, the sack she held sliding from her nerveless grip.

I see you. The words came not from the shrouded figure but from inside Kyra's head. *I see you and I know what you fear.*

And with a final despairing flicker, the torch light went out.

* * *

The first few metres had been all right. Enough light seeped in through the entrance for Kyle to find his way down the narrow stairs and along the beginning of the tunnel. But after that the light dimmed with every pace he took until he was walking in complete darkness.

It was cold down here and damp. His right hand on the wall of the tunnel brushed against rough stone and slimy yielding stuff that might have been moss or mould. His feet stumbled on bits of stone that had crumbled away and sometimes he found himself splashing through a stagnant puddle of water.

In his left hand Kyle held his mobile phone, tapping at it every couple of minutes to keep the display on. It was a dim and unsatisfying light, only penetrating a few centimetres into the darkness. He found himself shuffling his feet, in case the floor ahead abruptly gave way into a sinkhole or he found himself falling over a body. Eva's body.

He remembered Eva's grandfather talking about finding Adeline's body. *Those were pearls that were her eyes*, he'd said. In the hospital room that had sounded poetic. Now in the tunnel it sounded horrendous.

'I'm such an idiot,' he told himself bitterly. Why had he insisted on exploring the tunnel. As he'd come down the stairs he'd had a weird moment of déjà vu, an impression of Kyra also descending a stairway into darkness. He'd felt a grim certainty that his sister had lied to him and was doing exactly what he'd ordered her not to do.

332

'Of course she is,' he muttered to himself. 'When did she ever do what she was told?'

Go forward or go back? With each step he was more and more certain that Kyra was in danger. But with each step he felt equally certain he was coming closer to the heart of the mystery, to finding Eva—dead and undead.

He wasn't sure how far along the tunnel he'd got—he'd forgotten to count his shuffling footsteps. But he was just hoping that he'd got perhaps halfway when a scraping grinding sound came echoing along the narrow passageway—the sound of the bench moving.

Kyra must have called the police after all, he thought with a gush of relief. Then a second later came the question: why would they need to move the bench when the passage was already open? The answer was a low boom that thundered down the tunnel: the sound of the passage closing.

The police wouldn't have closed that opening and neither would Kyra. Someone else was coming. Someone who knew about the secret passage. Someone who wanted it kept hidden. Someone who knew that Kyle was there ahead of them.

Kyle stopped scuffing his feet and splashed his way hurriedly through the next puddle. He was alone in the dark with the murderer following him. He had to reach the other end of the tunnel before they caught up.

* * *

Kyra froze. It wasn't the darkness—it was the sudden sense of the presence of the Witch. Maggie had tried to warn her; Kyle had tried to warn her. Even Eva's disappearance had been a warning but Kyra hadn't listened.

The part of her brain that insisted ghosts weren't rational had convinced her that people's fear of the Witch was superstition. The other part of her brain that feared the ghosts had triggered a false bravado. She remembered Felix saying he'd agreed to the ghost walks as a challenge to himself and to the supernatural. She'd done the same thing, and now there was a Witch in her head.

Pathetic. The Witch's voice was like your own worst thoughts about yourself. *It's hardly worth revenging myself on such a halfbreed watered down Chance. Evangeline was a challenge. You're barely amusing. A peasant with dreams of a city paved in gold. You realize none of your dreams will come true? You'll have a string of children by a local clod and clean the houses of the wealthy for a pittance.*

It was a dreary and hopeless future and the thought of it dragged Kyra down. She felt tired and stupid and small.

All you know is how to make people do what you want. Small petty people like yourself. You have no power where it counts. Like your ancestress, you're a servant. A servant and the offspring of servants. A pretty nothing for men to amuse themselves with until your looks are gone and leave you a faded nothing of no use to anyone.

The atmosphere was stultifying now, heavy and close so that it was an effort to keep standing upright. The useless torch hung heavy in her hand and Kyra felt it slipping and let go.

Ice cold fingers closed around her hand, keeping it in place around the barrel of the torch. It was Maggie's hand. The servant ghost didn't speak but she was doing something. Kyra felt a surge of energy running from that cold grip into hers. The torch felt it too because Maggie's touch conjured a dim light in the dark room. There was the ducking stool again and the shadowy form of the Witch caged within it.

Kyra couldn't meet those empty eye sockets and she didn't try. The Witch could say anything, think anything, and have her believe it. She was the voice of all the doubts you'd ever had, echoed back and magnified with malice.

'And what are you?' Kyra muttered. 'A hunk of junk in an old cellar.'

She reached down for the two sacks and found Maggie ahead of her.

'Mine first,' her great-grandmother's ghost said, and upended her sack at the foot of the ducking stool. Sticks of wood scattered in a spray across the floor, larger logs rolling to a halt at the chair's foot, a litter of smaller twigs pattering after. 'I had to lay fires for the family and their guests,' Maggie said. 'Now it's your turn.'

Kyra wasn't sure if Maggie was talking to her or to the witch but either way there was no time to waste. She pulled open her own sack more carefully and wrenched open the top of the silver canister. A new smell filled the close space, eye-wateringly chemical.

'Paraffin,' Kyra said and sluiced the ducking stool with it up and down—and threw the canister after it. 'I thought of exorcism but this way seemed better. You haunt that chair, don't you? What will you do when there's nothing left to haunt?'

She reached into her pocket and pulled out a silver Zippo lighter, flicking it open so the flame burned merrily in her hand. The witch was silent in her head and Kyra smiled wickedly.

'Is this what you're afraid of?' she asked and threw the lighter at the ducking stool.

* * *

Kyle could hear splashes behind him as he ran. And worse, the darkness was lightening. Whoever had followed him into the tunnel had the foresight to bring a torch and the stream of light was catching up to him.

Kyle had run cross country for the school team but a slimy slippery stone tunnel was not the ideal surface for running and it seemed the faster he went the less in control he was, stumbling through puddles, stubbing his feet on loose rocks, arms scraping against the walls where the tunnel narrowed. Banging his hand against a wall he bruised his knuckles and dropped his mobile phone. It fell with a sharp crack followed by a rippling splosh and he cursed and kept running. But still the light came along the tunnel behind him.

His headlong flight came to a sudden end when he ran into a wall. A rough splintering barrier noticeably different from the solid blocks of stone of the tunnel walls: a wooden door. Kyle wrenched at the doorknob and felt it turn uselessly. The door was locked.

Behind him the light grew brighter. He had come to a dead end and the murderer was advancing on him.

* * *

The flame of the lighter blazed in the heart of the woodpile. It extended a long tongue and licked at the logs. Little flickers of fire leapt up across the sticks and the twigs crackled. A ripple of fire crossed the pool of paraffin beneath the ducking stool. The fire was taking hold.

The fire went climbing up the legs of the ducking stool, rising like vines up the rivulets of paraffin, blooming new flames in red, yellow, blue and green. The fire was conquering the darkness at the heart of the chair. Was the Witch melting or retreating? Black smoke belched out from the pile and Kyra took a step back and then another.

The fire roared and spouted new tongues of flame, rising up from the wood pile and wreathing the ducking stool in flames.

The paraffin burned fast and furious and at the heart of the inferno was the Witch.

It came rushing out of the blaze, a boiling cloud of smoke and ash, a formless thing that twisted and writhed in the air above them. The Witch was screaming in their heads, screaming as perhaps she had screamed long ago when she died. Kyra and Maggie turned to flee from the burning screaming thing at the heart of the darkness.

The smoke went with them, acrid and choking, roiling out of the blazing chair, and the swooping screams of the Witch came with it. And in that boiling blackness Kyra realized something and the horror of it went through her like a knife.

The Witch wasn't screaming, she was laughing, laughter that rang with triumph.

You haven't killed me—you've freed me. That chair was a cage. Now I have found a better vessel. One better suited to house my spirit.

Then the malevolent presence was past them and free while the fire blazed on, consuming the ducking chair—but not the Witch.

* * *

A sound came bubbling along the corridor, a rising swooping howl. It chilled Kyle even before he realized that the sound was crazed inhuman laughter.

A dark figure was approaching along the tunnel, indistinct behind the blinding beam of the lantern light. Kyle squinted into the light, trying to size up the approaching person. They looked thin and spindly behind the torch, more a shadow than a substantial presence. He clenched his fists, prepared to attack: and then he saw the gun.

It was black and solid in the figure's right hand and it held him pinned in the beam of the lantern. At this range it would be impossible to miss.

The laughter cracked like a whip, ringing off the walls. The light swung crazily for an instant and then a metal object spun toward's him and fell to the floor with a dull chink. The light steadied and Kyle looked down to see a key lying on the shiny wet floor.

'Take it,' a voice rasped from behind the lantern. 'And unlock the door. You've come this far. Now see what's on the other side.'

* * *

Kyra fled from the burning cellar, smoke boiling out of the cellar door. Her eyes were streaming and each gasping breath burned in her throat and lungs. Maggie came after her, pale and tremulous, her dark eyes full of horrors.

'She didn't burn,' she said. 'She didn't die!'

'I know, I know.' Kyra looked around wildly. Where was it? She spotted the red box on the other side of the hall and stumbled towards it. She smacked it with the butt of the torch and heard the glass crack sharply across one second before a siren began to wail.

'Where did she go?' Maggie followed Kyra out of the front door.

'You're the one with supernatural powers, you tell me,' Kyra snapped.

Maggie frowned and seemed to concentrate. But Kyra's own words had triggered a feeling of danger, somewhere deep within her, a psychic sense of her own.

Ghost and girl stared at each other.

'Kyle,' they said together. Then they started to run.

21
Mouldering in the Grave

The darkness covered Eva like a blanket—or a shroud. This was the dream she'd had on the morning of her sixteenth birthday. The claustrophobia, the bone chilling cold, pain cramping her body, a rotting foetid smell that clung around her.

She was trapped. She was alone. But inside her mind was the voice of the Witch. *You have always been here. Wherever you thought you were, whatever you thought you did. You have always been here in the dark. You are the buried dead.* The Witch was right. Eva knew it the way you know things in dreams. She knew it and she feared it. Every muscle, every sinew, every nerve she possessed strained to be somewhere else—if only in her imagination.

A distant trickle of water conjured a memory, a grey and faded memory in which she drifted cloudily.

The sound of oars dipping in the water, the liquid gurgle and splash, a smooth sliding of green waters beneath the rocking of a rowing boat brought to mind a misty March morning. Hadn't she been here before? Water lapped against the tree roots, the rowing boat rounded the side of the island, moving up close to the underbrush, frightening the peacocks from their nests as it nudged into an almost invisible channel, a path through the overhanging trees.

Then ahead a slab of porous lichen-draped rock, an awkward jetty with a rusting iron hoop driven into the rock. She remembered her own hands weaving the boat rope into a knot, the feel of the rust flaking beneath her fingers, a dreamy unconsciousness as she stepped out of the boat and saw the sculpted entrance to the grotto.

Eva didn't want to enter that dark tunnel. It spoke silently of dark spaces within, of stalactited ceilings, pools of stagnant water, and dank dark tunnels with no escape. She didn't want to go on but the gaping mouth was open and its cavernous depths called to her and she was compelled.

There was no way to escape. The choices she had made that March morning were already history. Her memory summoned her onwards and between the laughter of the Witch and the screams of the peacocks she entered the open mouth of the cave.

* * *

Kyra's heart pounded as she ran, Maggie floating beside her like a supernatural sat-nav. Interspersed with directions that weren't much more complex than 'left', 'right', and 'through the trees' the ghost provided a narrative of what she sensed.

'Kyle is under the island. Someone is following him in the dark. Their mind is a shell for the Witch to live in. The Witch is laughing at Kyle, the Witch is inside the killer's head. The witch is laughing, she's laughing . . . '

'Stop it,' Kyra panted. She was moving up the hill, checking her phone as she got on higher ground and heading towards the white pavilion of the summerhouse. 'Someone's following Kyle? Who is it?'

'I don't know.' Maggie was shimmering with the effort of extending herself so far from the House. 'I can't reach him.'

'Then I'll have to try,' Kyra said as they arrived at the summerhouse.

The next five minutes passed like a hundred million years as Kyra searched the floor for the entrance to the tunnel Kyle had guessed must be there.

'It must be here,' she said. 'Kyle used it, didn't he?' She wrenched at one of the stone benches and then the other. 'Come on, move, you bastards! Move!'

Maggie fell to her knees beside her, a rush of cold air as she threw her own force against the bench. There was a shift and shudder in the stone, a grinding rumble abruptly cut short.

'It's jammed,' Kyra swore. She jumped up, clenching and unclenching her fists, trying to think of what to do.

* * *

Kyle fumbled the key into the keyhole, his flesh creeping as he turned his back on the sinister presence with the gun.

It was still chuckling to itself; psychotic for sure, he thought— but not too insane to pull a trigger. He would have to hope for a moment of inattention in which he could seize an opportunity to break free.

The key turned in the lock with ease; the lock felt oiled and the hinges of the door were whisper quiet as it opened under his hands.

On the other side of the door the tunnel gave into a wide space. It wasn't completely dark. Light came rippling in upside down reflections across a rocky ceiling. Water trickled and gurgled and swirled somewhere nearby.

'Keep walking,' said the voice behind him. 'Not far to go now.'

'Why are you doing this?' Kyle said, trying to tempt whoever it was into talking some more. He had thought he recognized the voice that time. When it wasn't laughing it sounded more familiar, more human.

'All in good time.' A sinister chuckle and a painful jab of something hard into his back. Kyle flinched and walked forward letting the figure prod him onwards into the heart of the grotto.

* * *

Outside the summerhouse Kyra fumbled her mobile phone out of her pocket. She had no signal.

She swore at it savagely and almost threw it into the lake before realizing how stupid an idea that was, just in time. This was ridiculous. She looked at the useless mobile again, punching in the numbers 999 just in case by some miracle you could still call in an emergency with no bars of signal. The laws of physics defeated her, which was just unfair since she was standing next to a ghost.

'Can you get help?' she demanded, turning to Maggie and the ghost lifted its hands helplessly.

'There's few that can see me,' she said. 'Only a few have the sight to see ghosts. I can try but what shall I say? Even if they see me, who'll stay to hear the words of the dead?'

Kyra tried to imagine the reaction of a policeman to a ghost appearing in front of him and shook her head, trying to think of an alternative.

'You can warn Dad. He knows about you, Kyle and I told him last night. Go and find him and tell him what's happened. He'll think of something. He has to.'

'If he's not within the grounds of the House I'll not be able to reach him,' Maggie warned.

'Try anyway,' Kyra insisted. 'You can't go any further so you have to go back.'

The ghost eyed her doubtfully and then reluctantly vanished and Kyra dropped her phone as it suddenly began to ring. She dropped to her knees and scrambled for it. Only one bar of signal but it was dialling.

'You're through to the emergency services,' said a voice on the other end of the line. 'Please state the service you require.'

'Police! Quickly, please,' Kyra said and a second later she was stumbling out a story into the ear of the dispatcher. 'This is Kyra Stratton, I'm at Chance House by the lake, my phone's got almost no signal. My brother's trapped on the island with someone, I think it's the same person who killed Joyce Chance yesterday. There's a murder investigation going on right now. Felix Fairfax was arrested but he's not the murderer. The murderer's on the island right now.'

Even as the great burble of information poured out of her Kyra was kicking herself for how improbable it sounded, like something out of an Enid Blyton book. She was babbling almost as badly as the ghost had in her effort to get out all the details before her phone cut out.

'Is your brother in physical danger?' the person on the other end of the phone asked and Kyra's voice rose as she yelled her reply, trying to force conviction into her words.

'He's trapped in the grotto with someone who's killed at least two people and hospitalized another two. How do you rate his chances?'

Her only answer was a flat dead tone before the phone went silent, no more signal. Kyra tried to breathe.

Kyle would be OK, she told herself. Maggie would find Dad and the emergency dispatcher would believe her. Maybe already Dad was running for his car and a squad of police and an ambulance team were scrambling towards their vehicles. Maybe they had a boat or a helicopter they could bring quickly enough to make a difference.

But Kyle's life was riding on a maybe and Kyra didn't think that was enough.

She looked around the shore of the lake towards the sagging shape of the boathouse and crossed her fingers that there'd be at least one boat fit to be used.

* * *

There was a damp chill to the air in the grotto. The stagnant water in the pools mingled with the stench of rotting vegetation. The atmosphere was chokingly close, a foul smell leaking up through the tunnels. Light rippled oddly up and down the walls, pale shafts of sunlight leaking through the limestone just enough to make the deeper tunnels look blacker still. Water gurgled and lapped like chuckling laughter in the distance.

Eva's mind drifted onwards into a familiar darkness. This place was the source of the darkness inside her head, the darkness that had dragged at her from the beginning, even the stench of it was the same: blood and faeces and rotting food.

The memory played on, a recording of the past, every instant scripted, the pages turning one by one bringing her closer to an inevitable and grisly conclusion. These were the last minutes of her life sliding slowly past her eyes.

In her memory, Eva found herself passing by a stack of crates, plain wood, each about a foot square, just like the packing crates scattered throughout the house while it was being refurbished. Like Joyce she'd lifted the lid and seen the glitter of precious metal within. The crates were evidence of a deliberate theft. She had crouched here in the dank darkness, stunned by her discovery, wondering who had hidden them here and then there had been the sound of footsteps arriving.

Those footsteps echoed in her head as her dream self moved onwards and the grotto widened out into a central cave. The memory *hurt*, it pulled and tugged at her, there was a sudden flaring pain in her head and her vision blurred. Her hands scraped and scrabbled on rock as another explosion went off inside her head. Like Joyce, again, she had been set on from behind. She'd shut her eyes against the dizzy swirling images of rock and stone. Something drew tight around her wrists and ankles, something lifted and bound her.

And then there was nothing but darkness and the mocking laughter of the Witch in her mind.

So now you know it all, Chance child. You tried to flee from these memories, to escape the pain of your body and use the powers of your mind. But I am the only witch in this House and so I have brought you back to where you belong.

It wasn't a memory any more. This was the dark place the witch had sent her. The Witch had sent her mind plummeting back to where her body was buried.

I have one more surprise for you, the Witch whispered. *And for him.*

* * *

'I have a surprise for you,' said the figure in the darkness. 'It's only fair that you should see it before you die.'

Kyle's stomach turned over and he found himself thinking of his sister. All this time he'd been worried about Kyra doing something dangerous and now he was going to get himself stupidly killed. But thinking of Kyra didn't produce the same sinister sense of her somewhere in the cellar. Instead he had a feeling she was very close, that she knew he was in trouble and was rushing to save him. He needed to play for time.

'What kind of surprise?' he said, trying to keep his voice light. 'I've already found a secret tunnel. It's got to be something big to beat that. You used that after you strangled Miss Cora, didn't you?'

'Oh, it's much better than that.' The chuckle was back in the voice of the murderer. 'I've been saving this up for a long time.'

* * *

Eva was suspended in the darkness, past and present seemed to blur and blend together, tied together by the watching malice of the Witch.

Open your eyes, the witch whispered. *See where your body lies.*

Eva's eyelids felt heavy. All her ghostly powers seemed to have left her. The smell of blood and faeces was strong here; it rose out of the rock pool and Eva gagged at the stench. Light flickered in the dark room and the Witch crouched in the back of Eva's mind, eager with anticipation.

There was a lump of rock at the centre of the room, a broken stalagmite at the centre of the rock pool. Seated on the rock, bound with wire at wrist and ankles, gagged head thrown back under the drip of the stalactite above, was a body. It wore a faded print dress and its head was surrounded with a tangled mass of brown hair and its arms and legs were bare. It was wasted and drawn into itself, the cheeks hollow, limbs twig-like, wrists and ankles bloodied and raw, thighs caked with faecal matter.

It was Eva's body, and as she stared at it across the room, it opened its eyes—and she slammed back into its feeble shell, bound once again to the world of flesh.

* * *

The torch pierced the darkness and shone like a spotlight on the figure bound to a broken stone column in the centre of the room. It was the sight he had dreaded, a wasted corpse of a girl he'd last seen as a ghost.

Eva opened her eyes. Kyle had one second to look into that horror-stricken face, to see her eyes flare in the lantern light, to see them look past him and widen further. The barrel of the gun came down hard on his head and he saw nothing more.

22
Death of a Ghost

The figure in black placed the dark lantern at the side of the rock and considered the girl's body. The rag that bound the girl's mouth was wet with water from the stalactite above, a thin trickle of life bleeding down from above. Amazing really, that anyone could survive so long in the cold dark room with nothing more than that to sustain them. And yet the girl's eyes were tracking the movement of the dark lantern.

'Little lost Chance,' the killer said, the words echoing in the dank cave. 'You should never have come here. Everything was going so well until you found my collection. But I was merciful, wasn't I? I could have killed you then but instead I let you live. Are you grateful?'

The girl made a sound, not a word, not even a moan, just a small sound: a tiny mew of noise.

'You had to go wandering about the grounds,' the person in black frowned at the helpless girl. 'When you stumbled across my secret I had to shut you up. But you were just the start of the trouble, weren't you?

'Your grandfather had left you everything he could, a hundred thousand objects that would need to be inventoried, including all the ones I'd taken. Sooner or later he'd have stopped blaming the ghosts, when he noticed how conveniently all the items that vanished were the most valuable ones. I had to stop him. But still I didn't kill him, just a hard enough blow to keep him out of the way. You should be grateful. It would have been easy enough to finish the job and smash his head in while he lay there helpless.'

The attacker turned to look at the unconscious heap of Kyle's body, lying half in, half out of a rock pool.

'It was all easy. No one suspected me. Even when I came out of the tunnel under the summerhouse, Cora was surprised to see me; she'd forgotten the tunnel under the lake. But I couldn't let the old fool tell anyone about my secret route, could I? Or they'd have found my collection and the game would have been up. I had to put her out of the way and that time I thought I had. Luckily for her that it snowed that morning and I had to go back down the passage and make my way out across the lake. I thought she'd be sure to die of hypothermia but instead that stupid boy found her still alive.'

The black-clad figure shook its head at the inconvenience of having their plans upset again.

'Joyce was almost too easy. I found her prying into my trove, the one last crate I hadn't had the chance to move. She would have stolen it herself if she had the chance, always prying into drawers, looking for anything that was valuable. I hoped I could blame the theft on her but instead she came blundering along before I was ready and then she'd seen too much. It was merciful really—the old bat was getting more pathetic each time she visited, always with a new man in tow.

'And Christopher,' the killer's voice dripped with contempt, 'he was hopeless. So easily led. It only took a few words about ghosts in the drawing room and he was suggesting it as though it was his own idea at dinner. The ghost walks were the perfect red herring, everyone scared of their own shadows, too pre-occupied to notice what was really going on. I had different staff members pack the crates and move them from place to place. It was all too easy to change the labels around, move a few out towards the gardens, then I could take them down the tunnel when no one was watching.

'If only Christopher hadn't been leading those tourists by the nose he'd have made the perfect scapegoat too. And Felix would have done just as well. But Christopher got suspicious when Joyce died, he wanted me to cut him in on a slice of the action or he'd go to the police. Some loyalty he had to his lover, spineless cringing maggot of a man. I can't really be blamed for arranging his death, surely? Especially when it got the police so conveniently out of the way. It was trivial to arrange his car accident. A frayed cable, a can of petrol, and a slow burning fuse.

'And this boy wasn't much of a challenge.' The killer spurned Kyle's body with a contemptuous foot. 'These country bumpkins are so slow. Whatever he thought he was doing, he should have kept his wits about him. Well, he'll be company for you at least.

'You see, my dear,' the killer approached the broken stalagmite again, 'I'm just going to have to kill you now. Originally I thought I could set you free, but somewhere along the line things have taken on a will of their own, and now you're just a loose end for me to tie up. It's strange the way things have worked out. As though it was meant to end this way.

'So let's say goodbye, Eva. I like to think we always got on and in other circumstances we might even have been friends.'

The killer raised an eyebrow at the dying girl fastened to the stalagmite. Were those dull eyes still tracking? The girl hadn't attempted to struggle free after the first week of her confinement.

'Eva? Do you have anything to say?'

And approaching the stalagmite, the killer adjusted the black scarf, pushing back the crown of the wool hat to reveal glossy chestnut hair. Lisle Langley had always looked good in black.

* * *

Eva looked into the face of her killer and knew she was dying. These last weeks had only been the rehearsal after all, not the main event. Now her life would end as the Witch's had, tied to a torturer's chair while her killer gloated over her.

No wonder she had heard peacocks screaming in the back of her head. They were screaming now. With dream-like certainty she realized that it was the House that had called them, sending them as warnings and reminders, baleful eyes, bad luck and triggers of her own fears. The peacocks had been the key, the X on the map, the puzzle she'd never completed.

Moistening her lips, tasting lime on her tongue, she tried to find a word.

'Witch,' she whispered.

Slowly a malevolent smile grew across Lisle's face. It was not a human expression. It was the smile of something that had been dead these past five hundred years. It was the smile of the spider that rode inside the killer's head.

Yes, said the Witch. *I lied to you, Chance child. You're weren't quite dead after all. But I didn't lie when I said no one cared. I didn't lie when I said no one saw you. You've been drifting in my ghost world. But now you're back where you started and there are no more Chances left.*

And as the Witch whispered in the back of Eva's mind, Lisle raised the gun and moved forward, still wearing the Witch's smile on the human mask of her face.

351

* * *

'Stop it,' a small voice sounded from the other side of the cave. 'Put the gun down.'

It was Kyra Stratton. Eva's eyes widened as she looked past the possessed Lisle Langley to where her childhood tormentor stood at the edge of the rockpool.

'It's over,' Kyra said. 'The police are on their way, and my dad's coming too. They'll all be here any moment. There's no way you can kill Eva and Kyle and escape with all the things you've stolen. Just give up. Maybe if you plead insanity your sentence won't be too bad.'

'How did you get down here?' Lisle was back in control of her own face as she turned to confront Kyra.

'You jammed the tunnel entrance,' Kyra said. 'But it doesn't take any special skill to row a boat.'

'Clever girl.' Lisle took a harder grip on the gun. 'Too clever for your own good. I sent the police on a wild goose chase across town, they won't be back here in time to stop me leaving. It's a pity I've got to leave most of my haul but I know when to cut my losses.' She reached out for the handle of a small suitcase, an innocuous black travel bag incongruous amongst the stack of packing cases. 'And I don't need time to deal with these two—they're both out of action and neither of them has any strength left. I just need time to deal with you.'

Then, coolly and deliberately, she shut her lantern.

There was a splashing sound and a curse, a gasp and a scuffle and then a thread of mocking laughter.

'You can't win, girl,' Lisle said and this time her voice was the voice of the Witch.

I've grown stronger as you lay dying, the Witch added in Eva's

352

mind. *Now I will live again and you will be the ghost. Perhaps in five hundred years your hate will be as powerful as mine.*

There was another scuffle, an ugly scrape of metal on rock. Lisle had the advantage of knowing her way around the grotto and the witch riding in her mind gave her an uncanny knowledge of where she was in the dark. Kyra had no such advantages. Her only plan had been to cause a distraction long enough to keep Lisle from shooting her prisoners. Eva didn't know if Kyra's bold words about the police had been a bluff but she feared that Lisle was right and any help would arrive too late.

Eva tried to move and almost passed out as a wave of pain greyed her thoughts, the wires sunk into her wrists and ankles held her bound and her body was a battered shell. Her mind was only loosely tied to it, a balloon anchored to a fleshy shell. One more wave of pain and the cord would be cut and the balloon would finally float free.

But her mind had been floating free these past two weeks. She'd been haunting the House as a ghost, her mind drifting while her body lay rotting in this cave. And as she'd lived in the world of the ghosts she'd found her own strength, she'd glided through doors, she'd moved arrows and signs, she'd released unlucky tourists from traps and tricks and prisons of their own.

Eva let go. She let go of her body and all its earthly pain. A farewell to flesh, she thought as she walked out of her body. One final carnival.

She walked in spirit across the cave, sidestepping the blunderings of the possessed woman in the dark. Kneeling beside Kyle, she untied the rope from his hands and wrists and paused to brush her cold lips across his forehead.

'Wake up,' she whispered in his ear. 'Save yourself and your sister.'

And then like a moth in the dark she brushed past the Lisle-Witch.

You're not free, she thought at the thing. You're trapped more tightly than ever. To be free you have to let go. There was an explosion of sound, a gunshot echoing in the cavern. Kyra screamed and Kyle erupted out of the water in the middle of the fight. He wrestled with Lisle, arms twisting painfully, and then the gun flew away and landed with a heavy splosh in the water.

It was followed by a splashing scuffle and Kyra exclaimed:

'She's getting away!'

'Stop her!' Kyle fumbled for the lantern and opened its shutters in time to see Lisle's shadow vanishing around an arch of the grotto.

Kyra ran to the archway and swore; turned back despairingly.

'She's taking the boat.'

The grotto had more than one opening and Kyra had entered from a curving jetty within the grotto itself. Now Lisle had claimed the boat and was rowing herself away, her suitcase stowed in the stern.

Kyle poised himself to jump and then stepped back from the brink. He thought of the brush of a cold mouth against his skin, a benediction, a farewell.

'Lisle doesn't matter,' he said, turning away from the jetty. Then he staggered out of the water and towards the stalagmite in the centre of the cave. The girl's eyes were closed as he unsnarled the biting wires that bound her body to the rock and lifted her in his arms.

'Kyle?' Kyra's voice was shaky. 'What are you doing?'

'I'm not saying goodbye,' he said.

With a smooth scudding of the oars Lisle moved the boat out on to the lake. The witch rode with her, sending waves of malice back across the lake. This vessel was feeble: a sarcophagus of bone and blood. Already it had failed her and the tattered remnant of Lisle's mind cringed inside the overshadowing of the Witch.

Lisle's shoulders burned as she heaved at the oars, the witch lending her a supernatural strength. Ghost and murderer together, their minds were blended in the need to escape. They had failed to destroy their enemies but their hatred of the Chances was strong enough to try again.

The oars stilled in the water. Lisle wrenched at them and the waves calmed around the boat. On the shore a convoy of police cars came racing along the lake path.

The water swirled and from the depths of the lake a spectral presence rose up from the weedy depths. Pale hands took hold of the oars and drew them away from Lisle, sinking below her clutching hands into the waters of the lake. A pallid figure drifted mermaid-like beneath the prow of the rowing boat.

Witch, it whispered. *You tried to take my daughter. But she defeated you.*

Adeline. The Lisle-Witch stared into the waters of the lake. *You're dead.*

But not forgotten, the Mermaid Ghost whispered. *I've guarded my daughter from your darkness. And now it is your turn to be lost and forgotten.*

The waters rose, lapping at the sides of the rowing boat. Soon the bag of jewellery was awash in green water, springing and seeping through the sudden gaps in the wooden planks. Lisle scooped out the water with her hands frantically as the troop of police came running round the shore of the lake, all watching her adrift and sinking.

Bound! Tricked! Cursed! The Witch screamed as the waters closed over Lisle's head.

23
The Cruellest Month

Wednesday, April 30th

Amid the soothing pastel shades of a private hospital room an old man sat beside the solitary patient's bed. The girl in the bed looked like a war veteran. Thick white bandages ringed her wrists and ankles, a host of tubes snaked in and out of her body, replacing vital fluids and feeding her intravenously. The chart at the end of the bed ran to several pages of ailments from the life-threatening (pneumonia and bronchitis), to the embarrassing (nappy rash and piles). Bruises, scrapes, and sores still hadn't faded from the chilled and waxen skin and from her skeletal fingers to her frost-bitten toes the girl was painfully thin, the victim of a month's starvation.

But she was alive. Asleep perhaps, in just such a coma as her aunt had never wakened from—Cora had slipped out of life even as Eva was returning from the dead—but while there was life people hoped.

The door opened and the twins came in. Kyra was carrying an oversize novelty card and a florist's cone of paper in the other hand.

'The flowers are Dad's idea,' she explained, tipping the cone to show them the contents. 'They're bulrushes. Symbolism, I guess. The card's from my class at school. It's not exactly a get well card; more of a "we're sorry we've all been such jerks to you" card.' She grimaced at it. 'I don't know if she'll want it.'

'Put it next to the others,' Eva's grandfather said. 'She can decide about it when she wakes up.' He turned to nod gravely at the blond boy beside Kyra. His hair had been shaved to a light fuzz that exposed the messy scar above his right ear, stitches still holding the torn flesh together. 'Hello again, Orpheus,' he said.

'It's Kyle,' Kyra pointed out and Kyle punched her arm lightly.

'Mr Chance knows that,' he said. 'Orpheus brought his girlfriend out of hell. Or he almost did.' He tried to smile but failed. 'There's been no change, sir?'

'No change.' Sir Edward shook his head.

The twins sat down, Kyra by the window, Kyle in his accustomed chair on the other side of Eva's bed. Like Edward, he hadn't left the hospital in the last two weeks. First he'd needed surgery on his own head wound and then when he'd woken up he'd discovered Eva lay just down the hall, her condition officially still critical—but alive.

Kyra had got off more lightly except that she'd had to explain things to their parents. Keith and Sally Stratton had shown up at the same time as the police just in time to see a battered and bleeding Kyle carrying Eva out of the tunnel, followed by Kyra with a bagful of diamonds and sapphires.

'It's evidence,' she said, offering it to the senior detective who was staring at them as though she was the last piece in a very tricky jigsaw. 'And there's more evidence in the grotto. Packing cases full of stuff Lisle was planning to steal.'

It hadn't been a very eloquent speech but it was head and shoulders above the last words of that strange day. The team of police had to call for back-up when they dragged Lisle out of the lake. After the paramedics had revived her, she'd come back to life with a vengeance, spluttered and sworn and fought the police officers, claiming supernatural powers and that Eva and the Chances were under a curse she had laid centuries ago.

Local woman claims to be possessed by ghosts of haunted house, ran the newspaper headline, followed by the shocking story how *Lisle Langley (aged 36) had used her position as house agent to steal from a ninety-year-old man and imprison his teenage granddaughter in an improvised jail in a secret cave. Her killing spree left three people dead: strangled, stabbed and set on fire!* The newspaper report followed with an impressive account of Lisle's crimes. *Twin teenage heroes faced the monster in her lair and rescued their innocent schoolgirl pal*.

The twins had taken to skulking in the hospital, each of them appalled at being called heroes. Kyle was still crossing his fingers into knots that Eva would wake up, Kyra felt ill whenever anyone praised her for saving Eva's life, aware it wasn't Eva she'd tried to save. *Aristocrat framed for the killer's crimes—now cleared to begin a degree at Oxford.*

Kyle and Felix had reached a grudging rapport. Kyle agreed to accept that Felix was dating his sister as long as Felix attempted to behave like a human being with genuine emotions. So far he'd been doing pretty well: half the flowers in Eva's hospital room carried his card and—more to the point—he was paying out of his own inheritance to begin repairing the worst dilapidations of the House—including the fire-damaged cellars. That particular incident had been attributed to Lisle and Kyra hadn't felt any urge to correct the record.

The Fairfaxes, Helen and Richard, overwhelmed with relief that their darling offspring wasn't a murderer after all, hadn't even raised the vexed issue of the will and limited their efforts to arranging the sober funerals of Cora and Joyce. Christopher Knight's body was still unclaimed in the hospital morgue but it seemed likely that family guilt would see him interred at their expense.

Felix wasn't the only one trying to make amends. Kyra had shown up with a box of finance textbooks and was poring over them with Edward Chance. These past two weeks Kyra had alternated studying for her GCSEs with forensic accountancy of Lisle Langley's bookkeeping. Not only had the house agent been forming her own collection of the most valuable artefacts from the House, she'd also been siphoning off the House repairs fund and cooking the books to disguise the theft.

'It's amazing,' Kyra was saying. 'Lisle could have been caught at any time. But no one even suspected her. Everything she did was either put down to ghosts or accidents or not noticed at all.'

'She was very efficient,' Sir Edward said grimly. 'I admired her competence. I can see her coolly planning the theft. But the violence of the attacks, that's not Lisle.'

That had been Lisle's excuse as well. She'd been pulled out of the lake and resuscitated by the paramedics but what had regained consciousness had not been anyone Lisle's friends and colleagues would recognize: a screaming banshee who had to be kept sedated and even so needed six prison guards in riot gear to move her from her cell. Her case might take a year to come to court with Michael Stevenage's dogged insistence on collecting every last scrap of evidence to assure a civil conviction for theft along with the criminal charges of murder. But already it looked as though she would be serving her time in a mental hospital instead of a prison.

Kyra was suspicious of this ploy, thinking this was Lisle's

last trick, the plan she'd proposed herself to distract the killer from her prey. Kyle wasn't so certain. He'd been followed by Lisle through the tunnel and he could easily believe the need for the prison guards in riot gear. That hadn't been a normal woman laughing in the darkness at his heels. It had been a thing possessed. And if Kyra had been successful in driving the witch from the ducking stool, the closest suitable home had been in the dark caves of Lisle's mind. He dreamed about it every night: a ghost presence revived, a person possessed, two dark minds orbiting each other, souls drawn together in cruelty.

'Your thoughts look very dark, my boy,' Edward Chance said, looking up from the accountancy books to meet Kyle's eyes.

'April's almost over,' Kyle answered him. 'It's been weeks since we found Eva. Why won't she wake up, sir?'

'Perhaps because she has been wandering for a long time in the valley of the shadow of death. Perhaps it's taking her longer to find her way home,' the old man said gently. 'But she's there. The doctors say she could wake up any minute. And when she does she'll have to learn to be alive again.'

'She thought she was dying,' Kyle said, looking at the girl lying in the bed. He had seen her as a gleaming vision, her kiss brushed against his face, her voice whispering a farewell in his ear. He'd never known her alive and even now it was still difficult to think of her as truly real.

Kyra's mobile phone trilled and she snatched it eagerly out of her pocket, pressing it to her ear.

'Felix!' she grinned, already heading towards the french windows, slipping outside into the pretty garden the hospital provided for private patients. Kyle and Edward watched her wander off to sit under a tree, all her attention fixed on the phone in her hand.

'They're good for each other,' Edward commented. 'But I hope your ancestress isn't spinning in her grave.'

'I think she accepted it in the end,' Kyle said. 'And Dad said he found her grave in the churchyard once he knew what to look for. There wasn't an inscription but according to the church records Margaret Stratton was buried in a pauper's grave. Dad's going to have a new inscription cut which says something like "she returned good for evil". I think he's going to do everything he can to make sure she's laid to rest. Having a ghost appear when you're in the shower will do that to you.' He tried to laugh. 'Telling you to call the police or else a witch will kill your children. Dad can't go in the bathroom without his mobile and a big concealing towel.'

'Tell your father I would like to contribute to that inscription,' Sir Edward said. 'If he will permit me.'

'I'll ask,' Kyle said. 'But I don't think Dad will object. I suppose it's only fair really.'

'As do I.' Edward Chance reached for his stick and tottered upright. 'No, don't trouble yourself, my boy. I think I can make it to the lavatory unaided. You stay with my granddaughter. I don't want her to be left alone.'

Kyle sat back down in his seat and turned to look at the still figure in the hospital bed, watching the faint pulse beating in her neck.

'Eva,' he said. 'Evangeline.' His hand reached to touch hers, lying curled beside him. Slowly he stroked the thin fingers, avoiding the bandaged nails where she'd scraped her fingertips raw on the rock of the grotto. Starved, abused, tortured, she was still his gleaming girl. Bending his head, he touched his mouth to her cold forehead. 'Eva,' he said. 'Wake up.'

He drew back slowly and found himself looking down into

361

clear brown eyes, watching him quietly from the bed. Her fingers moved in his hand and words whispered from dry lips into the quiet room.

'I feel as though I've been asleep for a hundred years,' said Eva Chance.

Acknowledgements

I am supported by a network of friends and colleagues who provide encouragement and criticism in equal measure. There are far too many to name here but some honourable mentions should go to the following.

I owe an incalculable debt to my mother, Mary Hoffman, a literary maven in whose footsteps I follow. My agent, Pat White, and her assistant, Claire Wilson, are always available to navigate my craft through the shifting shoals of publishing. My editor, Jasmine Richards, and her assistant Michelle Harrison, have worked hard to help me make this book the best it could be. As always with my OUP titles I am indebted to copyeditor Kate Williams for her meticulous attention to detail and thoughtful suggestions. Any mistakes that remain are, of course, my own.

For the last few years I've had the wit, wisdom and wine of Writers Square to rely on. Thanks to Frances Hardinge, Ralph Lovegrove and Deirdre Ruane for critiques of more different drafts of this narrative than anyone should have to remember.

And thank you to all the friends and fans who follow me through my website, Facebook, Twitter, Library Thing and other sites and social networks across the web.

About the author

Rhiannon Lassiter was born in 1977 and has been making things up ever since. Her first novel, *Hex*, was accepted for publication when she was nineteen years old. *Ghost of a Chance* is Rhiannon's tenth published novel.

Rhiannon is also a fictional character. Events from her family life have been fictionalized in books by her mother, the award-winning children's author Mary Hoffman, most prominently in *Specially Sarah* and *Special Powers*.

She has written a non-fiction book about the supernatural and says she's open-minded about the paranormal: 'I believe there are more things in heaven and earth than are dreamt of in our philosophy.' Rhiannon adds she's never seen a ghost but she's felt haunted in places like the British Museum's Egyptian collection.

In addition to writing Rhiannon has worked in marketing and communications. For ten years she was the designer and web editor of children's review publication *Armadillo*. From 2008 to 2009 she was a judge for the Arthur C. Clarke science fiction award. Her ambition is to be the first writer-in-residence on the Moon.

Rhiannon's official website can be found at: www.rhiannonlassiter.com

If you enjoyed *Ghost of a Chance*, don't miss:

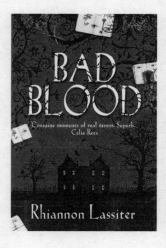

Turn the page for a spine-chilling extract . . .

Catriona always woke up early. Back home she had a television in her room and she'd watch MTV before breakfast and while she got dressed for school, letting the beat of her music thump through the house.

The window of the bedroom she'd chosen had pale pink curtains and by seven in the morning the room was as bright as if she'd turned on the light. Getting out of bed Catriona picked her MP3 player up off the bedside table and looked at her suitcase, lying open on the floor. Somewhere in there were her travelling speakers but she didn't really feel like getting them out. Going over to the window she had to reach past the doll's house to open the curtains and she smirked at it, remembering how she'd got the room the day before.

It was weird thinking that this could be Katherine and John's mother's room. She hadn't thought of that when she picked it. Opening the top drawer of the chest of drawers she wondered if there'd be anything there, but it was empty. Putting her make-up bag and her jewellery box away in the top drawer, she unpacked her underwear and some tops into the other drawers and looked about for somewhere to put the rest of her clothes. The only other storage place was the thing like a built-in wardrobe on the other side of the room and she opened it up.

It wasn't a wardrobe but a cupboard, with six shelves inside, all of them covered with junk. She frowned, wondering how she was supposed to hang up her clothes, before actually looking at what all of this stuff was. The top two rows had boxes, too high for her to reach. The next row had a boxy-looking camera and several thick bundles of photographs with rubber bands wound round them. On each the top photograph was bleached and faded so that the images were ghostly white blurs. Curious, Catriona took down one of the bundles and tried to unwind the rubber band. It slithered loose when she picked at it, like the dead skin of a snake, and the bundle sprang apart at one side, the other gummed together by the remains of the rubber band.

Picking off the bits of rubber with her long nails Catriona got the other photos unstuck and began to sift through them. The first group were of three girls sitting in a garden that Catriona recognized as the one at the front of this house. On the back someone had scrawled names: 'Anne', 'Emily', and 'Charlotte' on different photos, depending on who appeared. They were taking it in turns to take pictures of each other because only two of them appeared in each one, right up until the last of that group where they must have found someone else prepared to hold the camera for them. Looking at the three of them Catriona tried to solve the puzzle of the names to guess which one might be John and Katherine's mother.

Emily turned out to be a girl with curling ringlets of blonde hair wearing a blue velvet dress with sleeves that trailed to the ground. She had the figure for it, Catriona thought jealously, looking down at her own almost flat chest. Charlotte was a girl with black hair and dark eyes, dressed in black leggings, pirate style boots, and an almost knee-length white shirt. Anne was easily the dullest one, Catriona decided. Her hair was the same light brown as her children's and she was wearing a patchwork dress and a long white lace shawl.

The next thirty or so photographs in the bundle had been taken in really bad light, making the shadows too dark or the girls look washed out, and in most of them Catriona couldn't make out much more than some trees and sometimes the shape of a building. Flipping on to the end of the stack she didn't see anything interesting and put them back on the shelf next to the other bundles. She might tell John about them later. That way she'd get the credit for doing something nice and she wouldn't have to tell Katherine.

Catriona ignored the next shelf, which was full of little china ornaments of animals, and squatted down to look at the bottom one. This was piled up with shoeboxes. 'CLOTHES' was written on the first one and she opened it up to see doll's clothes, tiny scraps of velvet and silk and even fur, sewn with almost invisible stitches. Catriona took out each item carefully, admiring the work that had gone into it. The next one was labelled 'JEWELLERY' and she opened it expecting something made out of beads or plastic. But instead there was a jumble of bracelets, rings, and necklaces, gleaming silver and gold, or with spots of colour that Catriona thought might actually be small precious stones, or at least semi-precious. She sifted through the box for a while, wondering if it could possibly be real. If so it must be worth hundreds of pounds and she was amazed it hadn't been stolen. She felt a pang as she shut the box but she wasn't a thief.

The third box wasn't labelled and it felt heavy when Catriona dragged it forward on the shelf and she wondered if there might be more jewellery. Inside there was a gleam from metal objects; it wasn't jewellery, but steel blades, poking out of what must have been about thirty pairs of nail scissors all rusted and blunt. Catriona put the lid back quickly, wondering if Anne Stone had been a little crazy. What could anyone need that many pairs of scissors for and what had blunted them like that?

The last cardboard box was the largest and it was the only one that had been tied up with string. Whoever had tied it had used what seemed to be a mile of the stuff, wrapped round and around the box, and tied it up in the most tortuous knot. Catriona had to prise at it for ages, using her nails to tease the knot open; ironically there didn't seem to be a single usable pair of scissors in the room. 'DELILAH and her DRONES' was written on the box and when Catriona finally got it open she caught her breath in shock.

Naked, faceless, hairless dolls lay jumbled up together like bodies in a mass grave. All of those on the top layer had faces rubbed smooth and featureless, except for the gaping holes where their eyes should be, savagely gouged out by something with a small sharp blade.

Catriona dropped the box and it fell on its side, spilling dolls on to the floor. And as the naked, eyeless dolls slid out, something else came with them, something that could only be Delilah.

She was a small girl doll in a white dress. Her blue eyes stared blankly forward and a small smile curved her red lips; her long ankle-length hair was tangled around the arms and legs of the drones and Cat saw that it was more than one colour: blonde, black, and brown.

She could only be home-made, at least Catriona was sure the hair had been, and at first she didn't like to touch any of the dolls. But it was the only way to get them back in the box and when she picked up Delilah she realized the little doll's joints were articulated, so she could move not only her arms and legs but her wrists and each individual finger. Delilah was serious weirdness but she was also a work of art, like a creepy sort of mascot.

It had looked as if her hair was in even worse knots than the string around the box but when Catriona tried to release her the long silken strands came easily, sliding out of its tangles in the same way that Catriona's own hair did. She smoothed out the last few tangled edges of Delilah's hair, and stroked it back into place. It felt soft and sleek under her fingers, and she felt reluctant to put Delilah back in her box after all that work. It was then she remembered Katherine asking about the dolls and, with a feeling of malice, she slipped Delilah and three drones into the pockets of her dressing gown.

* * *

It wasn't until they were all sitting around the breakfast table that Catriona revealed her find, standing Delilah up on the table with one small hand resting lightly on the glass of the milk bottle. Across the table Katherine looked at the doll and bit her lips.

'Where did you find her?' she asked.

'In the cupboard in my room,' Catriona said. 'Someone's customized her; I think that's human hair. I bet if I took the head off you could see how they'd done it.'

'Bizarre,' Roley said, through a mouthful of cornflakes, eyeing the doll doubtfully. From her other pocket Catriona took out three of the eyeless, faceless dolls and stood them up next to the girl doll.

'Meet Delilah and her drones,' she said, waiting for their reaction.

'Did you make that up?' Roley asked, picking up one of the drones.

'It was written on the box I found them in,' Catriona told him, adjusting the doll again so that her hand rested lightly on the shoulder of a drone.

'I don't like them much,' John said, looking towards his father.

'Someone made a real house of horrors, didn't they?' Peter said. He picked up the girl doll and looked closely at her hair. 'Delilah, I wonder if you came by that hair honestly?'

'You mean like Samson and Delilah in the Bible?' Katherine asked. 'She cut his hair off, didn't she?'

'How could a doll steal someone's hair?' Catriona said, watching the doll dangling helplessly in Peter's hands.

'Oh, put that horrible thing down,' Harriet said, pouring herself a second cup of coffee. 'I agree with John. Those dolls are extremely unpleasant. It takes a sick mind to make something like that.'

'Why did you bring them down?' John asked, his eyes fixed on Delilah as Peter set her down on the table.

'Your sister was asking about them,' Catriona said, shrugging casually. 'I thought she'd like to see them. You know, someone went to a lot of effort. There are at least thirty drones in the box. All with their eyes cut out like that.' As she spoke she adjusted Delilah's position again, sitting her on the edge of a cereal bowl and stroking her hair back into position.

'Creepy,' Roley commented. 'Sounds like voodoo or something.'

'Voodoo like black magic?' Catriona asked. Her eyes met Katherine's across the table as she added: 'Your mum lived here, didn't she? Do you think she was the one with the sick mind?'

Crockery clattered and glasses jangled as Katherine stood up sharply from the table and Peter had to lunge to stop the milk bottle falling over.

'You're the one who's sick!' Katherine shouted across the

table. 'I hate you!' Her voice rose in a scream as she ran out of the room. Replacing the milk bottle, Peter got up and went after her.

'You deliberately provoked that, Cat,' Harriet snapped angrily. 'That was a cruel thing to say.'

'I didn't mean it,' Catriona said defensively. 'You were the one that said it was someone with a sick mind that made them. I just suddenly remembered that her mother lived here. I didn't mean it the way she took it.' She put a plaintive note into her voice and opened her eyes wide, looking innocent.

Roley made a face at her across the table as Harriet started to talk in her 'understanding' voice now, reminding them that Katherine was sensitive about having lost her mother. Catriona ignored her brother and nodded along to Harriet's talk. It was Katherine's fault if she was going to be so sensitive, she thought. Besides, probably it was her mother that had made the dolls, it only made sense.

Suddenly remembering that John was still there, Harriet stopped mid-speech and began to talk brightly about plans for meals. But John hadn't been listening anyway, he was looking at the three drone dolls. They had fallen over when Katherine shook the table and now one lay on its face, the other two on their backs, staring with empty eyes up at the ceiling. Sitting comfortably on the edge of the cereal bowl, Delilah smiled her small hard smile as if the chaos of the breakfast table had pleased her.